Aria

Aria Appassionata

JULIET HASTINGS

Black Lace novels are sexual fantasies.
In real life, make sure you practise safe sex.

First published in 1996 by
Black Lace
332 Ladbroke Grove
London
W10 5AH

Reprinted 1996

Copyright © Juliet Hastings 1996

Typeset by CentraCet Limited, Cambridge
Printed and bound in Great Britain by
Mackays of Chatham PLC, Chatham, Kent

ISBN 0 352 33056 2

The Story of the Opera

*C*armen, a beautiful gypsy girl, is arrested for causing an affray. She taunts her guard, the young corporal Don José, into a dangerous infatuation so that he fights his commander over her. For Carmen, José is prepared to desert the army, abandon his childhood sweetheart, the virginal Micaela, and take refuge in the mountains with Carmen and her smuggler companions.

Carmen is becoming bored with José's jealous possessiveness. She plays at fortune telling with her friends Mercedes and Frasquita: the cards foretell nothing but death for her. Escamillo, a famous entertainer, arrives looking for Carmen. José, in a jealous fury, challenges him to fight and she intervenes to save Escamillo's life. Micaela arrives to call José away to his mother, who is dying.

When José returns Carmen refuses to accept his love and declares her passion for Escamillo. Mad with jealousy, José kills her.

Aria Appassionata

Cast of characters

TESS CHALLONER	*Carmen, Mezzo soprano*
DAN ASHBOURNE	*An actor*
JAMES JONES	*Director*
ANTONIO VARGUEZ	*Don José, Tenor*
EMMA RIDLEY	*Micaela, Soprano*
LEO HEDLEY-WHITE	*Escamillo, Baritone*
CATHERINE GIBBS	*Frasquita, Soprano*
JEANNETTE BALDWIN	*Mercedes, Soprano*
RICHARD SHAEFFER	*Escamillo #2, Baritone*
JULIAN FARQUHAR	*Répétiteur*
ADAM SOMERVILLE	*Assistant Director*
BOB	
STEFAN	*Stage hands*
CHARLIE	
SARAH CARTER	*A Tarot reader*
DEAN	*A waiter*
BENEDETTO CORIAL	*Conductor*
MICHAEL HANSON	*Tess's agent*
CHORUS, ORCHESTRA, BACK STAGE AND FRONT OF HOUSE STAFF	

Overture

Hampstead, June

*B*irdsong and traffic noise competed to wake Tess up. She opened her eyes and looked up at the high ceiling. A bar of sunlight had pierced the curtains and glowed across the white plaster.

She lay breathing deeply, savouring the knowledge that Dan was lying asleep beside her. She could smell his warm skin and a faint trace of his expensive fragrance. How long could she make herself wait before she rolled over and looked at him?

The bed smelled wonderfully of sex, a salty, hot smell that caught at the corners of Tess's nose. She shut her eyes and swallowed. Between her legs the muscles of her sex clenched, squeezing together, signalling resurgence of desire.

Unable to resist a moment longer, she rolled onto her stomach and looked at Dan. He was fast asleep, sprawled bonelessly beneath the blue and white duvet, taking up more than his fair share of the space as usual. Tess folded her arms over her pillow and rested her chin on them and gazed.

Dan was miraculously handsome. Tess had always thought so, and since the TV drama in which he starred began to play to massive audiences every Sunday night,

1

she knew that practically every woman in the country agreed with her. The reviews in the papers called him 'The new Cary Grant' and he had that look of the forties film star, that perfection of bone and skin, that sleek polished air, even when he was fast asleep with his soft hair tumbling over his forehead and his chin darkened with stubble. Seeing him lying beside her, Tess couldn't believe her luck. Every Englishwoman's fantasy was in her bed.

She had sung the title music for the TV series and had met him when visiting the set. He had just broken up with his previous girlfriend, an actress, and seemed interested in Tess and in her singing. He didn't seem quite so interested any more, but he was still the best-looking man Tess had ever seen. Quite a catch, considering he was only her second lover ever. They had been together now for three months, and the tabloids were beginning to lurk outside Tess's Hampstead flat to get pictures of *new heart throb Dan Ashbourne and his gorgeous girlfriend, aspiring diva Tess Challoner*. In three months nothing had changed for Tess. Every time she set eyes on him it was the same: she wanted him.

But he was so fast asleep. She frowned, then reached out gently and touched her fingertips to the smooth, biscuit-brown skin of his tanned shoulder. He was warm and sleek as a coiled cat. He took a deep breath when she touched him and rolled away from her, heaving the covers up and muttering. Tess very, very softly drew the duvet down again so that she could admire the perfection of his back. He had broad, strong shoulders, and the hair on the back of his neck was kept very short, almost shorn, absurdly boyish. She leant forward and drew in a deep breath. His nape always smelled wonderful, concentrated *eau de Dan*, as if two square inches of skin produced enough pheromones to fill a concert hall. Beneath the delicate, vulnerable skin of his neck his spine curved away in a fluid groove, inviting her to run her fingers down between his shoulder blades, down

2

behind his ribs and his taut flanks, down to where the arches of his muscular buttocks lifted the duvet with their unexpected softness.

She sniffed his neck again. He murmured complainingly and fumbled for the duvet. Tess drew back a little and crossed her arms, lifting her full breasts. Her nipples were tight and erect, signalling the desire that Dan's body awoke in her. But to wake him up ... She sighed and pushed back the covers on her side of the bed and got up.

It was warm in the room. Tess stood naked before the window, letting the bar of June sunlight trickle over her pale skin. She linked her hands and stretched them high above her head, closing her eyes and breathing deeply. The muscles of her rib cage obeyed her, stretching outwards to draw in air, the singer's raw material. She let out the air slowly, playing the breath steadily through the column of her throat.

The tall mirror in the corner of the big room reflected her figure. She was a little above middle height and profoundly feminine in shape. Her breasts were splendid, high and full and lush, and her shoulders and arms deserved a Victorian evening gown to show them off. Her waist was narrow when her lungs were not full of air. Below the tuck of her waist her buttocks and thighs were rounder than was convenient. It was always hard for her to look convincing in a boy's part, which singers in her mezzo soprano range often needed to do. She had shapely calves and ankles and big, businesslike feet and hands. Catching sight of herself in the mirror, she leant over a little so that the bar of sunlight fell on her face. It illuminated a heavy dark mane of shoulder-length, tousled hair, falling in unruly waves rather than curls and sparking in the sunlight with a fiery auburn glow. Her skin was very white. She had a true redhead's porcelain skin, and sunlight brought her out into golden freckles, never a tan. She shook back the rough tendrils of fringe that hung over her high forehead and stepped a little closer to the mirror, examining her face. Striking, rather than beautiful: good in stage make-up or photographed in black and white. Unforgettable, according to her agent's blurb. She had high, sharp cheekbones, arched dark brows over heavy-lidded green eyes, a strong, narrow nose and a wide, generous, full-lipped mouth. Normally the corners of her lips were curved upwards in a faint unconscious smile. Now she tugged forward her hair to shade her face and pouted at the mirror, trying to command a sensual, smouldering look. It didn't really work, and she laughed at herself.

In the bed Dan moved, rolling over and flinging out one arm. Tess looked at him with a surge of sensual yearning and caught her breath, longing to go over and kiss him and wake him like a prince in a fairy tale. But somehow she didn't dare. Instead she stooped and picked up her silk overshirt from the floor and slipped it on as she went towards the kitchen.

Not many young singers can afford a flat next to Hampstead Heath. Nor could Tess. She had inherited the flat from her grandmother, who had also been a singer, though in music hall, not in opera. It was the top floor of a grand Victorian house. Tess's bedroom had once been the nursery and her big, high sitting room had been the children's playroom. She had a big old rocking-horse in the corner of the room, to recall its previous existence and because she liked rocking-horses. The kitchen, which looked out over the Heath, had once been the nurse's own bedroom. It was bright with sunshine, and green with the reflected light from the trees outside.

Tess pottered about in the kitchen for a few moments, making a pot of tea: Darjeeling, which Dan preferred. Left to himself he might well have started the day with a glass of wine, but Tess tried to keep his alcohol intake fairly low on the grounds that actors need to take as much care of their voices as singers do. As she filled the pot, she heard footsteps in the flat and the sound of water running in the bathroom. Dan must have surfaced.

4

She worked faster, pouring the tea deftly into brightly coloured mugs. With a mug in each hand, she went back through the living room and into the glowing dimness of the bedroom.

Dan was back in bed, his eyes shut. She came towards him a little hesitantly, one step at a time, wondering if he had gone back to sleep. When she was within touching distance of him he opened his eyes and raised his perfect brows at her.

'You woke me up,' he accused her. 'What are you, a bloodhound, sniffing at my neck?'

'Sorry,' Tess said guiltily, offering the tea by way of recompense. Dan looked supercilious, but accepted the mug, sniffed the fragrant steam and took a tentative sip. Tess pulled back the duvet and got into bed beside him. His body was perfectly proportioned, smooth and glossy as an ancient Greek statue. She drank a little of her own tea and put the mug down on the bedside table. Her fingers itched to stroke Dan's close-grained, silky, tanned skin. But she was shy of initiating lovemaking, uncertain where to start, unsure of herself as much as of him.

There was silence. Tess raised her eyes from the ridges of muscle on Dan's flat belly and saw that he was looking at her quizzically. He said archly, 'See anything you like?'

'You know I do,' Tess managed to say. She wanted him so much that she was beginning to tremble.

Dan quirked the corner of his mouth in a half smile and set down his mug of tea. He pushed the duvet off him, down to the end of the bed, revealing the long lean length of his muscular body. Tess's throat went dry and she swallowed convulsively. His prick was already hard, lying flat against his belly, gleaming in the glow of sunlight through the open curtains. Dan stretched out on the bed, lifting his hands above his head, and closed his eyes. He said lazily, 'You know what I like.'

A word of permission was all that Tess needed. With a little moan of suppressed excitement she leant forward and laid her cheek on the taut plane of his abdomen, staring open-mouthed at the wonderful smooth column of his cock. His masculine, subtle smell filled her nostrils. Shivers of desire crawled between her shoulder blades and made her nipples ache. Her lips felt the softness of his belly, moved a little so that her tongue could explore the shadowed hollow of his navel, then began their journey down the almost invisible seam of fine brown hairs that guided her way towards his groin. She avoided touching his penis with her lips, letting its heat strike through the skin of her cheek as she moved on to the hollow of his loins. His balls were tight and firm in their lifted pouch of skin. She brushed her nose against them and he gave a little gasp, then purred and stretched, lifting his cock towards her lips. 'Suck it,' he said. 'Tess, suck it.' His hands lifted from the sheet and found her shoulders, pulling her forward over him. She would have liked to tease herself a little longer with the anticipation of delight, but she opened her mouth obediently and allowed the hot, smooth head of his cock to slide between her full, wet lips. For a moment she sucked him as she would a stick of rock, letting her lips slide up and down the length of his shaft and shivering with pleasure. It was wonderful to hear his breathing deepen and feel his body tense and stiffen.

'Ah,' Dan murmured, 'ah, that's good, Tess.' He put one hand into her thick hair and held her head still, lifting his hips towards her face so that his cock thrust more deeply into her mouth. Tess's fingers tightened on his narrow flanks, digging into the taut tanned skin. Her bottom was lifted high into the air as she leant forward to suck him, and between her parted thighs the lips of her sex were moist and swollen with lust. For a moment she imagined herself moving, lifting herself over his body, lowering the glistening flower of her vulva towards his face for him to use his strong tongue on her. He would lap and probe at her most sensitive parts, drawing her quickly to a shuddering climax as she

6

sucked him. But she could not move while he held her head, and besides, it was daylight. She was shy, and the thought of straddling his face so that he looked up directly into the delicate, intimate folds of her sex made her shudder with a frisson of apprehension. She couldn't, she couldn't. She tried to concentrate on the wonderful sensation of his cock moving in her mouth and the delicious friction of her engorged nipples against the fine dark hairs on his long thighs.

Between her working lips his cock was twitching and beginning to throb as he approached his climax. His breathing became hoarse and determined, harsh gasps in rhythm with the thrusts of his thick phallus in her mouth. His hand knotted in her hair. Suddenly she sensed that he was not going to stop, that he meant to come in her mouth. She wouldn't have minded, but she was desperate for release herself. Fighting against his restraining hand, she pulled back, panting.

'What's the matter?' said Dan sharply.

'Nothing.' She felt guilty and selfish. 'I just, I wanted . . .'

'Wanted to be fucked,' Dan finished brutally. 'No problem. Come here.' He fumbled in the little box on the bedside table where the condoms lived and quickly covered his eager cock in its second skin. Then he reached down and caught hold of her by the shoulders, pulling her up towards him. His lips descended onto hers and she shuddered and submitted to him, lying between his hands as limp as a rag. Her open eyes feasted on the sight of his beautiful face as he kissed her. He laid her down on the bed and pushed her thighs apart with his knee. The muscles of his arms and shoulders flexed as he took his weight. Tess sighed with delight as she felt him between her open legs. She ran her hands up his arms, shivering open-mouthed as her hungry eyes took in all the perfection of his body. His cock nudged its way between the lips of her sex, easing slowly inside her. She was wet, ready, eager. As he filled

7

her, she drew in one deep breath after another, relishing the heat and thickness of his cock as he slid it up into the heart of her. He looked down into her eyes, frowning almost as if he was angry, and then he began to move.

Nothing special, no banquet of Eastern delights, no athletic or dramatic expertise, just the most simple, basic sex, his rigid cock sliding strongly in and out of her vagina, his body rubbing against her pulsing clitoris. But the shaft of sunlight through the curtains fell over his back and shoulders and lit his soft hair with tendrils of gold, and the sight of him transported her. He took her to orgasm with his beauty, not with his body, as if a young god had come down from Olympus and taken some humble mortal to be his bride. She cried his name, clutching him with her hands, her mouth and eyes wide open as her climax jerked through her. His eyes were closed and as he came he snarled like a beast, his body arching and twisting as his cock pulsed deep within her.

She reached up to draw him down on top of her, longing to feel the wonderful weight of him. But he shook free of her hands and rolled onto his back, breathing fast, his eyes still shut. Tess lifted herself on one elbow, suddenly anxious. Dan was usually at his most affectionate after they had made love. She wanted to ask him what the matter was, but the words would not come. Robbed of the contemplation of her pleasure, she snuggled down beside him and pressed her face to his golden arm.

The telephone rang. She would have ignored it, but as soon as he heard it Dan gave a heavy, angry sigh and rolled over away from her. She sat up and lifted the receiver and said huskily, 'Hello?'

'Tess!' said a well-known voice. 'Tess, darling, your dreams are coming true. You've got *Carmen*. Congratulations, duck. Crack open the bubbly.'

'Oh,' Tess said, hardly able to speak for surprise and amazement and delight. 'Oh, Michael, really? When did you hear?'

Nothing is as happy as an agent who has just earned himself a fat fee. Michael's voice positively dripped satisfaction. 'James just rang me. It's yours, darling. Rehearsals start in two weeks. Can you come over? They're faxing the offer through.'

'Yes,' she managed to say. 'Yes, of course, as soon as I'm up. Michael, did he tell you who else is in the cast? The other main parts?'

'Sure.' There was a rustle of paper. Tess just registered that Dan had heaved himself to his feet and stalked off towards the bathroom, but she was too excited to watch him go. 'Let's see,' said her agent's voice. 'They managed to get Antonio Varguez for Don José, how about that? This will be a classy production. For once they'll have a José who looks as good as his Carmen. Emma Ridley got Micaela, nearly big a break for her as it is for you, duck. Frasquita, Catherine Gibbs: Mercedes, Jeannette Baldwin.'

'Oh, Jeannette!' exclaimed Tess, after a moment's hesitation. 'This will be fun. We worked on a student production of Cosi once, she's great.'

'Isn't she black?' asked Michael. He went on without waiting for an answer, which was typical of him. 'Anyway, who else is there. Oh yes, Escamillo, Leo Hedley-White. Don't you know him, too, Tess?'

'Leo?' Tess repeated, her voice almost inaudible. 'Er, yes, I do know him. Quite well.' This was the understatement of the decade. Leo was the man who had taken Tess's virginity, four years ago when she was a struggling 23-year-old singer and convinced that she was the last virgin in London. 'Gosh,' she said, suddenly eager to see Leo again.

'Look, duck, I'm up to my neck,' said Michael. 'Come round when you can, will you? I'll be there. You're a peach, you'll be a wonderful Carmen. Love you.' The phone clicked and buzzed at her. She looked at the receiver wonderingly.

'Good news?' said Dan's voice behind her.

She turned and saw him standing in the half-light of the sun through the closed curtains, glowing like a fallen angel. His face was shadowed and unreadable. 'Yes,' she said, breathless with excitement. 'Yes! I got *Carmen*, Dan. I got it.' She jumped to her feet, opening her arms as if she expected a hug. 'I've got a bottle of fizz in the fridge,' she said eagerly. 'Let's get it out and have a drink before I go over to see Michael. This is it, Dan, this is the big break. It's fame for me from now on.'

Dan looked puzzled and, she could have sworn, discontented. She wanted him to understand how important this success was to her. 'Dan,' she explained, 'I did tell you about it, didn't I? Opera in the Park? It's the biggest open-air opera festival in London – in England. People have made their names from being in it. And *Carmen* – well, it's the big show of the festival! And they've got Antonio Varguez, Dan. Women will come miles to see him. There were hundreds of women auditioning for the part. Hundreds! Women with much more experience than me.'

'Congratulations.' His voice sounded thin and acid. 'Mind you, I should think they didn't have many others at audition with tits like yours.'

Tess stared at him, astonished and hurt. Dan had touched a very raw nerve. Even at audition she had been anxious about quite how explicit the director might want this production to be. She forgot the champagne in the fridge. Unconsciously she reached out for her shirt and held it in front of her, shielding herself from his sudden hostility. She said, feeling crushed, 'I think it might have had something to do with my voice.'

She still could not see his face. He said coldly, 'I suppose this means you'll be busy for some time.'

'Rehearsals start in a couple of weeks,' she said, 'and the performance is at the beginning of July. There's never enough time to rehearse, whatever it is, you know that, Dan. I'm sorry if – '

'Don't be,' he interrupted her. He came a little closer

and pushed back his heavy hair with one hand. 'Tess, this is a good time to tell you something. I, ah, I won't be seeing you again.'

She took a step back and sat down on the bed, clutching her shirt across her so tightly that its buttons bruised her breasts. Her throat hurt. She didn't know what to say.

'You'll be cut up about it, I suppose,' Dan said callously. 'But it had to happen. I started seeing Philippa a couple of weeks ago and she's told me to finish with you now. You just can't keep my interest, Tess, darling. I'm afraid you're insipid.'

It was bad enough to be dropped, but to be dropped and criticised in one fell swoop was almost more than Tess could take. She clenched her fists, trying to regulate her breathing so that she could reply. After a moment she said in a husky, choked voice, 'Do you mean you've been seeing Philippa *at the same time* as me?' Philippa was Dan's co-star from the TV series, a very glamorous cookie indeed.

Dan nodded and shrugged. 'Can you blame me?' he asked coolly. 'Let's face it, Tess, our sex life hasn't exactly been overpowering, has it? And Pippa's an animal in bed, an absolute animal. I – '

'You've been sleeping with her?' Tess could feel tears burning behind her eyes. Her lower lip was starting to tremble. All she could think about was that she had to get him away from her, get rid of him, so that she didn't have to look at him and be reminded of how beautiful he was and how cruel. 'I think,' she managed to say, desperately trying to sound calm, 'that you'd better leave now, Dan.' She got to her feet and pulled on her shirt and went through to the sitting room. She climbed onto the rocking horse and began to rock to and fro, staring in front of her and trying to ignore the sounds of Dan moving around in the bedroom, picking up his things. What a bastard. To tell her now, just when she was

11

feeling good about herself and successful. To have sex with her and then to tell her. What a bastard!

After a few moments Dan came into the sitting room and looked across at Tess. She set her jaw tightly and said nothing. He raised his eyebrows and went to the door. She heard his feet on the stairs and then the distant sound of the front door slamming, followed by a little jabber as of journalists converging.

Oh God, Tess thought. *Ashbourne drops singer for sexy co star.* Her failure would be in every gossip column in every tabloid for the next week. She would have to go to ground, hole herself up with her singing teacher and a score of *Carmen* and hope that nobody came after her. She should have been celebrating the biggest break of her career, the part that every mezzo dreams of playing, the part that was going to make her an international opera star: but all her pleasure and pride was gone. She felt six inches high. She leant forward until her forehead rested on the rocking-horse's silky mane and began to cry.

Act One, Scene One

Covent Garden, one week later

The rehearsal room was in the back streets of Covent Garden, one of the little quiet streets where nobody has bothered to spend any money and nothing seems to happen. No bars, no shops, just grimy brick buildings and nondescript doors with flaking paint.

Tess stood on the doorstep for a moment, breathing hard. One hand was clutching the strap of her canvas satchel, containing her score – the music to the opera – and a large bottle of mineral water. The other was unconsciously gripping at the front of her blouse, crumpling it beyond repair. She had agonised over what to wear. Michael had told her the production was to be modern, contemporary, but even so, what does Carmen look like? She had settled for a plain white linen blouse and a full denim skirt. A battered knitted jacket hung on her shoulders in case the rehearsal room proved to be an icebox. She had bought herself a new pair of shoes as a reward for getting the part, smart, flat tan loafers, and now she was shaking in them.

'Idiot,' she told herself. 'Why be nervous? You're the star! Come on. Just because Dan dropped you – '

Because Dan dropped you your self-confidence has

evaporated. She shook her head and went through the door and up the stairs.

'Tess!' screamed a shrill, raucous voice. Tess looked up and ran the rest of the way, holding out her hands. The woman who had spoken was tall, athletic-looking and black, with long hair in a myriad of tiny plaits, each tipped with a brilliant bead. She seized Tess and embraced her and kissed her sloppily on both cheeks. 'My God!' she exclaimed. 'It must be six years, is it six years? And we promised never to lose touch!' Her speaking voice sounded like a circular saw cutting through hardwood.

'Jeannette, it's wonderful to see you.' Tess squeezed the strong elegant back and drew away, smiling into Jeannette's fabulous eyes, huge and almond-shaped with smoky blue-tinged whites and dark, dark irises. 'I, I meant to keep in touch, but – ' *But the last time I saw you you tried to seduce me.*

Jeannette was being a little disingenuous. Tess vividly remembered visiting her at her awful student flat after their show was finished. They had sung through their duets, exchanging parts for a laugh, and talked into the night about men. Tess had confessed that she was still a virgin and Jeannette had first refused to believe it and then become fascinated by it. They were sitting side by side on the battered futon and Jeannette leant forward and kissed Tess on the lips. Tess could still feel the shiver of mingled horror and delight that had filled her. She hadn't known what to do. She was frightened, aroused, uncertain. Jeannette put her long hands on Tess's breasts and touched her nipples and the sensation flew through her like an electric shock. She had heard her voice moaning as if it were someone else's. Perhaps, if Jeannette had been a little more gentle, things might have gone on. But as it was Tess had fought down the feeling of spiralling excitement and jumped to her feet and fled, mumbling some ridiculous excuse, out into the cold, hostile London streets and straight into an extortionately expensive taxi.

'I'm looking forward to this so much,' said Jeannette, kissing Tess again. 'Honestly, Tess, you've deserved this break. It's marvellous. You'll be fab.'

Tess wished she felt as confident as Jeannette sounded. She was going to say something modest and unassuming. Then she saw Leo coming towards her, mousy and tousled and friendly, smiling his familiar, warm, lopsided smile, and she glanced at Jeannette apologetically and abandoned her and turned to hug him.

'Hello, darling,' Leo said, putting his arms round her. He felt the same, he smelt the same. Actually he felt a little broader than he had three years ago, but that just made him more comforting to hold. She lifted her face to his and he rubbed noses with her. 'How are you?' he asked.

When Leo asked her a question he really wanted to know the answer. 'Scared,' Tess confessed, and felt better at once.

'No need,' Leo whispered. 'You'll knock them dead.' He smiled into her eyes, then stepped back a little. 'Now,' he said, 'let me introduce some people. Tess, Emma Ridley, our Micaela.'

'Tess!' exclaimed a little blonde vision. 'I've been looking forward to meeting you *so* much. Won't this be fun?'

Tess leant down to exchange kisses with the air on either side of Emma's cheeks. Emma was a tiny thing, like a porcelain doll, pink and white and crowned with a mass of tumbling curls of light-brown hair, just shading towards gold. Her body was delicate and rounded, slight but unmistakably feminine, and her voice, unlike Jeannette's, was as sweet in speech as it was in singing. Huge blue eyes looked up with an expression so relentlessly gentle and innocent that it set Tess's teeth on edge. She detested overdone theatrical luvviness. 'I'm very pleased to meet you, Emma,' she said.

15

'And this is Catherine Gibbs,' said Leo. Something about the tone of his voice caught Tess's ear and she gave him a quick, acute glance. Although he was introducing Catherine, he was looking at Emma with an expression that no one could mistake, an expression of eager, hopeful desire. Tess turned to meet Catherine and said something polite without even noticing what she looked like. It was absurd to be jealous, she hadn't seen Leo for three years, but the way he looked at Emma made her insides crawl with possessive fury.

Catherine Gibbs was saying something. Tess shook herself back to the present and made herself pay attention. She saw a woman who was short, opulently built, fleshy and strong, with a handsome face and a pair of fine dark eyes under a mass of heavy brown hair. Big breasts thrust aggressively against the fabric of a cheese-cloth shirt which did nothing to hide the darkness of the areolae beneath it. 'I'm sorry,' Tess said, 'I missed that.'

'I was just saying', said Catherine, 'that you'll make a great Carmen. I always imagined her with red hair. You'll look just right.'

'Do you know what the director has in mind?' asked Tess at once, interested despite herself.

'Not really. But I heard – ' Catherine launched into some operatic gossip that had recently come her way about the eccentric, exotic productions favoured by their director, James Jones. 'Both the sopranos topless,' she exclaimed, 'and covered in glitter!'

Tess listened for a while, then felt herself becoming more and more nervous. She had known when she auditioned for the part that James tended to the extreme, but the more she heard, the worse it felt. Why had she got herself involved? Why not stick to nice, safe, ordinary productions? 'I'm just, er, just going to find the loo,' she said, sidling away from the company.

'Me too,' said Jeannette quickly. 'It's out here, Tess darling.' She took Tess by the elbow and guided her out

16

of the big, light rehearsal room into one of the cold, cruddy service corridors and down it towards the loo.

When they were inside and the door was shut Jeannette turned at once and caught hold of Tess's arms. 'Right,' she said. 'Come on, Tess, out with it. What's the matter with you?'

'It's nothing,' Tess said, shaking her head. 'It's just . . .' She felt weak and stupid. After a moment she lifted her head and looked up into Jeannette's liquid eyes and said, 'It's quite simple, really, Jeannette. Did you hear about – about me and Dan?'

'Dan Ashbourne? I heard he dumped you. Stupid bastard. Actors are all the same. Brains in their bollocks.'

'Well, it gave me a bit of a shock,' Tess admitted. 'And I – I knew Leo quite well, a few years ago, and I had hoped, and – but he – '

'All he's interested in', said Jeannette succinctly, 'is the contents of Emma Ridley's knickers. Right?'

Tess nodded hopelessly. 'So frankly, Jeannette, I'm feeling a bit – disappointed.'

'How do you come to know Leo, then?' asked Jeannette. She hitched her tight bottom onto one of the cracked basins and folded her long elegant arms, looking curious. 'You must have met him after you left college.'

'Oh yes. We were in a production together, just little parts. It was *Figaro*. I had second bridesmaid and he was gardener.'

'And?'

'And I really liked him, and after the after-show party he took me home.'

The taxi pulled up outside the big Hampstead house and the interior light came on. Leo scrambled for the door and paid the driver. 'Hang on a moment while I get her out,' he had said with a grin.

The driver leant through his window and laughed as Leo clambered back inside. 'Tess, come on,' he said. 'Come on, you're home. Up the little wooden hill.'

Tess had been more than half asleep, fuzzy with lateness and unaccustomed booze. She lifted her head with difficulty. Leo's face swam before her. She realised dizzily that Leo hardly seemed to be drunk at all. He helped her out of the taxi, put his arm tightly around her waist and half-carried her to the door.

'Keys,' he murmured. She fumbled in her bag, found the keys and promptly dropped them. Leo laughed at her, caught the keys on his toe and tossed them up to within reach of his hand. He wrestled with the door, got it open and turned on the light.

'Leo,' Tess slurred as they staggered up the stairs, 'oh Leo, I think I've had too much to drink.'

'You certainly have,' Leo agreed as he unlocked the door at the top of the stairs. 'Let's get some water down you, or you'll have a prize hangover tomorrow.'

In the kitchen Tess stood by the sink and obediently drank glass after glass of cool mineral water. Gradually the waves of muzzy drunkenness receded and she felt rather better. She looked up at Leo and managed a fairly composed smile and said, 'Leo, you are kind. However are you going to get home? It's so late. Do you want to sleep on the sofa?'

Leo's pale eyes were suddenly very intent. He came and stood in front of Tess and said softly, 'Tess, I brought you back here because I want to make love to you. If you don't want me to, you'd better say so right now, and I'll go.'

'What?' Tess swayed with shock. The thought hadn't crossed her mind. One reason she had stayed a virgin so long was that she was quite dense when it came to spotting the signals of male attraction.

'I want you,' Leo whispered. 'I've wanted you right through rehearsals.' He reached out and put his hands on her face and looked into her eyes. He had a round, cheerful, boyish face, but now it was tight with anticipation. 'You're beautiful,' he said. 'I want you so much,

Tess.' He held her face more tightly and leant forward to kiss her.

Tess stood frozen, unable to react. Alcohol still coursed through her blood and her brain. She liked Leo very much, but she didn't know if . . .

And then his lips were on hers and he was kissing her, first gently and then with suddenly increasing passion. She gasped with surprise and pleasure and let him pull her into his arms, pressing their bodies together. His warm tongue explored her mouth and his hands were strong and tight on her shoulders and buttocks. Tess's nipples were aching and she tore her lips free of Leo's and flung back her head, protesting, 'Oh God, Leo, I . . .'

Leo's warm mouth fastened tightly to the hollow of her neck. 'Tess,' he whispered into her skin, 'Tess, I want you so much. Please, please, let me.' He guided her out of the kitchen towards the big, battered, comfortable sofa in the gloom of the living room. She came unprotesting, not knowing what she wanted, but unable to resist his quick decisive movements. He lowered her onto the sofa and laid his big body on hers. For a moment the sensation was terrifying. He was heavy and hot and he pinned her down like a trapped animal. Then his lips found hers again and suddenly the fear was gone and the feel of his weight was deliriously exciting and even her helplessness was erotic. His hands moved, sliding up under her loose T-shirt, pushing it up and up until her breasts were exposed. Leo made a noise halfway between a growl and a grunt and pushed his fingers inside her bra, seeking out her nipple and squeezing it as his tongue lashed the inside of her mouth.

Tess cried out. He was pinching her nipple hard and she could not prevent her body's eager reaction. Her back arched tightly upwards, offering her breasts to his searching hands. He squeezed again. It hurt her, but the pain was delicious. She said his name and caught hold of him by his curling hair, pulling his mouth back to hers.

His penis was bulging through his trousers, hard as a piece of bone. It felt wonderful and frightening. What would they do? She didn't have any condoms, of course she didn't, why should she have any? Would Leo have one? How in God's name did you put one on? She wished she'd practised with a cucumber, or whatever it was you were supposed to use. She wanted to touch his penis, but she was afraid to.

Leo was not afraid to touch her. His other hand reached down, found the rucked hem of her skirt, moved up underneath it. Tess moaned in protest as his fingers touched the inside of her thigh, stroked the soft skin, ascended. She thought, Oh Christ, elderly M & S knickers. I wasn't ready for this!

His fingers found the edge of her panties. She stiffened, expecting him to put his hand inside, but instead he very gently stroked the taut fabric that covered her sex with his fingernail. The movement sent a shudder of pleasure through her and she cried out in shock and delight. She clung to Leo and her hips began to move in involuntary arching ripples as he put his tongue in her mouth and squeezed her breast and stroked and stroked the swelling bud of her clitoris through the damp fabric of her panties. Waves of sensation made her whimper and writhe. It was like the pleasure she could give herself when she masturbated, but with an astonishing additional dimension. She did not know what would happen next. Leo set the pace, the rhythm, like the conductor leading the orchestra, drawing her onward quickly or slowly according to his whim. She lay in his arms quite helpless, responding to his slightest movement, to his lightest touch.

Then his hand left her sex and moved to the waistband of her panties and found its way inside. He murmured, 'Tess, I want you. I want you so much. Let me have you, Tess, let me make love to you.'

Suddenly Tess was afraid again. She stiffened and tensed as his fingers wormed their way downwards, burrowing gently through the soft curls of her pubic hair, reaching for the delicate folds of her labia. Tess closed her eyes tightly. In a moment, in a moment he would know she was a virgin. He would laugh at her. She couldn't bear it. Suddenly she pushed him away and dragged herself up, saying, 'No, Leo, no.'

He clawed himself upright, gasping. 'Tess,' he protested, 'what's wrong?'

She shook her head. 'Too much to drink,' she muttered, 'I need – ' and she staggered through the bedroom and slammed the bathroom door shut behind her.

It was true that her bladder was full, though she was so tense that for long moments she couldn't empty it. When she wiped herself the paper came away gleaming with her juices. She washed herself thoroughly and splashed her face. Her heart was pounding. She looked at herself in the mirror and her green eyes looked unsteadily back.

'I want him,' she murmured to herself very quietly. 'I do, I want him. But I'm afraid.'

'Tess.' It was Leo's voice outside the door. 'Tess, are you all right?' He sounded anxious, apprehensive. 'Are you angry with me?'

Tess looked down at her hands. She couldn't stay there all night, shut in the bathroom. It was absurd. She took a deep breath and went to the door and opened it. Leo blinked at the sudden light and smiled at her. Behind him the bed loomed in the shadows.

She swallowed hard. 'Leo,' she whispered, 'Leo, I'm a virgin.'

He did not laugh. His face eased into the kindest, gentlest smile imaginable. 'Tess, darling,' he said, 'I had guessed.'

It was so late that it was almost early. The first birds were beginning to sing outside the window and the dark sky was streaked with grey. Leo led her over to the bed and turned on the bedside lamp. Tess turned it off again.

21

He said, 'No, I want to see you,' and switched the light on.

Then he began to take her clothes off. She was ashamed of the battered old bra and the comfortable knickers, and more ashamed of her nakedness beneath them, but Leo breathed deeply in wonder when he revealed her breasts and her white flanks. He stooped to draw one nipple into his mouth and Tess almost sobbed with the sharpness of the pleasure. Gently he pushed her onto the bed and with one hand stroked down the length of her body. He said, 'You're beautiful.'

Tess lay very still, watching as Leo removed his clothes. Her head was spinning. It was really going to happen, it would be now. She put her hand to her mouth as Leo pulled off his boxers and stood by the bed quite naked. The bedside light glowed on him. His skin was very pale, pink and white, and his legs and his chest were covered with golden fur. His cock was strongly erect, thrusting eagerly forward from the soft nest of his tight balls. Tess's mouth went dry as she looked at it. She found herself wondering whether it was big or small, thin or fat. Then he knelt beside her on the bed and kissed her and she didn't care.

He lay down beside her and pulled her gently into his arms. She came willingly, but she was still afraid. 'Leo,' she whispered, 'will it hurt?'

He shook his head. 'Sometimes it hurts, sometimes it doesn't. Tess, darling, don't be afraid.'

'You know what you're doing,' she said, with a little, nervous half laugh. He was only about a year older than her. How could he be so calm when she was so anxious?

'Yes. Hush.' He kissed her again and took hold of her hand and put it on his penis. It was hot, silky and dry, and so hard that it startled her. It felt lovely. She lifted her head cautiously and looked down. Her white hand was wrapped around the dark shaft. Its shining, glossy head thrust towards her, the tip dewed with transparent moisture. She very gently moved her hand and Leo

22

smiled and murmured and closed his eyes. 'That's nice,' he said. He let her touch him for a moment. Then he put his hands on her shoulders and pushed her back to lie flat on the covers. He kissed her and arched his body over her.

No, she thought, not yet, I'm not ready. But she need not have feared. Leo kissed her mouth, her throat, her breasts. His hands rested on the insides of her thighs, pushing her legs apart. He slid down her white body, brushing his lips against her ribs, her belly, the edge of her hipbone. Tess realised what he was going to do and opened her eyes wide, breathing fast in anticipation. She was afraid, but everyone had always told her that it was . . .

Bliss, ecstasy. Leo's face was pressed close between her spread thighs and his warm hard tongue was probing gently, gently into the damp whorls of her secret flesh. Tess cried out and her body twisted. Suddenly she realised how close the tension of fear was to the tension of sexual arousal. Leo's hands moved up to her breasts and his nails scratched against her taut nipples as he licked and licked at the trembling stem of her clitoris. Tess cried out again. 'Oh God, oh God, I don't believe it. Leo, Leo.'

Leo did not cease his gentle caresses. He scarcely seemed to touch her, and yet the delicate quivering tip of his expert tongue made her writhe and moan. She sobbed with pleasure and lifted her hips towards his face. His hands clasped her buttocks and opened her to the darting thrust of his tongue and the quick nibbling of his lips. She heaved and cried out as her orgasm swelled and burst inside her like a ripe fruit, filling her with aching, shuddering pleasure.

For long moments she hardly knew where she was. Then she felt Leo's lips on hers and she kissed him eagerly. He tasted of her and she shivered with a sense of delicious lewdness. 'Leo,' she murmured.

'Has a man ever made you come before?' he asked

softly. She shook her head and saw his eyes brighten. 'Good,' he whispered. 'I'm glad. Was it good, Tess?'

'Oh – ' She pulled him close and ran her hand down his body, reaching for his cock. It seemed to have swelled even further, as if his caressing of her body had actually aroused him. It moved Tess deeply to know that Leo found it erotic to give her pleasure. She wanted to repay him somehow. She licked her lips and said shyly, 'Leo, shall I – would you like it if . . .'

He smiled at her. 'I'd love it. Just for a little, Tess, or I'll be over-excited.'

Tess couldn't have explained what she had expected him to taste like, but somehow she was surprised. Things she had read had suggested that taking a man in your mouth was more of a chore than a delight. But when she flicked her tongue experimentally over the swollen head of Leo's cock it tasted – odd, pleasant, slightly salty, warm and satisfying. And when she opened her lips and allowed the thick hot shaft to slide up between them the urgent immediacy of the sensation made her moan. This was something she would like to do for herself, not just because it was good for Leo. She timidly touched his balls with her hand and he gasped with pleasure. But then, just as she felt she was beginning to understand the rhythm of his suppressed movements, he put his hand in her hair and gently drew her head away.

'No more,' he said, when she began to protest. 'Not now. I want you, Tess.'

'Oh,' Tess whimpered, feeling helpless and stupid, 'Leo, I don't have – I'm not on the pill, and I don't – '

'Hush. I've got one.' He spirited the little packet out of the air and smiled at her. 'Know what to do with one of these?'

She shook her head, wondering why Leo's face glowed so with delight. 'I'll show you,' he said. 'Tear it open, come on.' She obeyed him. Her fingers were clumsy with alcohol, inexperience and anxiety. He showed her patiently how to find out which way out it was, how to

24

position it over his eager penis and roll it down. 'There,' he said, when she had managed it. 'Full metal jacket.'

Tess drew back her hands and looked up into Leo's eyes. 'Leo,' she admitted miserably, 'I'm frightened.'

'Don't be,' he said softly. 'Tess, sweetheart, pretty Tess. Don't be scared. You'll love it. Trust me.'

He kissed her and laid her down on the bedcover. She closed her eyes, trying to calm herself. Leo stooped over her and kissed her lips, then parted her thighs with his hand. She expected that he would enter her at once, but although he was trembling with urgent desire he did not. He knelt between her spread legs and put his hands on her hips, drawing her closer towards him. He lifted her buttocks onto his strong thighs and put his hand gently between her legs, stimulating her sex with his fingers.

A shaft of intense pleasure pierced Tess, making her gasp. She opened her eyes and looked down the length of her body. Leo was kneeling upright, watching her with brilliant eyes. With one hand he caressed and teased her clitoris and with the other he held his penis and rubbed it against her labia, over and over again. It felt hot and smooth and slippery with her juices. The sensation was so delicious that her fear began to leave her. She flung back her arms and arched her back, moaning with delight.

Leo did not stop. With his fingers and the swollen head of his eager penis he rubbed at her moist tender flesh until she was moaning rhythmically, lifting her hips towards him, intensely aroused. He did not stop until Tess's cries and movements showed that she was almost at the point of climax. Then, smoothly and without hesitation, he put his hands under her thighs and lifted them and as he did so the stiff shaft of his cock slid between the lips of Tess's vagina and began to penetrate her.

'Oh, God,' Tess cried out as a sudden pain made her flinch. But Leo leant forward over her, her legs hooked over his arms, and thrust firmly until the whole length of his penis was sheathed inside her.

'There,' he whispered. He leant forward to kiss her, tilting up her hips towards him. Tess gave a desperate, aching cry. The feeling of his hot, hard cock filling her was like nothing she had imagined. She felt utterly helpless, utterly possessed, taken, ravished, powerless.

'Leo,' she whimpered. She didn't know what to do. She couldn't move. Every breath pressed her body against his and filled her with a sort of shivering heat. 'Leo, don't, don't.'

'Too late,' Leo murmured. 'Too late, Tess. And now I'm going to fuck you.'

She clung to him and he began to move, easing his eager cock even further into the clinging tightness of her virgin flesh. Then he withdrew and thrust. Tess's eyes opened very wide and she gasped as she felt the wonderful sensation of him sliding within her. She wrapped her ankles around his hips and moaned with delight. He thrust again, rhythmically, deeper and deeper within her spasming tunnel, and with his hands he caressed the stiff tips of her breasts. Tess closed her eyes tightly and gave herself up to the sensation of being taken. Fear was gone, replaced by surging delicious pleasure. She heard her own voice making strange animal sounds, moans, whimpers, cries, as Leo's strong, thick cock moved urgently in and out of her. He grunted and clutched at her breasts and his thrusts became more sudden, fast and deep. Tess opened her eyes and looked up at his face, tense and concentrated, his eyes tight shut, his lips drawn back from his teeth like a snarling dog's. Her body was doing that to him, was turning him from a kind gentle man into a rutting animal. His hands spasmed, gripping at her nipples, and suddenly sensation sparked in her breasts and her sex, and she flung back her head and gasped as another orgasm rushed through her.

'Yes,' Leo grunted as he felt her clutching him with

the urgency of her climax. 'Yes, yes, yes,' and with a last lunge he flung himself down on her, panting as his cock shuddered inside her. She wrapped her arms and legs around him and held him tightly. Her head was spinning and outside the window the sun was rising.

'Wow,' said Jeannette enviously, 'I wish my first time had been like that.'

Tess smiled rather ruefully. 'The trouble is, Jeannette, that's what Leo really likes doing.'

Jeannette frowned. 'What, virgins? Where does he find them?'

'He found me. We stayed together a few months, but then he – lost interest, I suppose. He likes teaching, that's what it is. It's not that he was nasty to me, he wasn't, he was always really kind. I'm very fond of him. But it was stupid to think that he might be interested in an action replay.'

'He sounds like Prince Calaf in *Turandot*,' said Jeannette with a grin. 'Making ice cold virgins tremble at his touch. But honestly, Tess, don't you think it was a good start? For you, I mean?'

Tess looked down. 'He was wonderful. But – '

'But what?'

She shook her head. 'I don't know. Jeannette, I don't know. He always knew what I wanted, he always gave me everything. I don't know how to ask, I don't know how to – ' She shrugged helplessly. 'I still feel as stupid as I did then. And then, with Dan just dropping me for that – actress – '

She was just about to confess what Dan had said, that he thought she was boring in bed: *insipid*, that was the deathly word. But then Jeannette glanced at her watch. 'Oh, Christ,' she said, 'we've been in here half an hour, Tess. What will people think? They'll have started without us.' She caught hold of Tess's hand. 'Look, tell me more about it another time, yes? They've got us a flat to share, me and Catherine and Emma. It's amazing, it's

27

just behind Piccadilly, one of the sponsors has lent it to the company. Come round and stay one night. You can tell me all about it then.'

'You're sharing with Catherine and Emma?' Tess repeated cautiously.

'Yeah, but that's all right. I know Catherine quite well, she's great. And Emma – well, I'll just have to put up with her.'

'Why put up with her?'

'Oh, she's a little bitch. Butter wouldn't melt in her mouth, but just you try crossing her.'

'She's very pretty,' said Tess mournfully.

'Handsome is as handsome does. She's the biggest prick-teaser in the business, believe me.'

'Leo must think she's worth a try.'

'I wish him luck.' Jeannette curled her lip scornfully. The haughty expression made her look like the Queen of the Nile. 'He won't be the first man to try, but our little innocent Emma is waiting for Mr Right.' Jeannette shook her head, making her plaits bob and swirl. 'God, Tess, will you keep me talking? What will James think if we're late? Come *on*!' And she caught Tess by the wrist and pulled her back to the rehearsal room.

The room was full of people now, the whole of the cast and nearly all of the chorus. There must have been two dozen singers there. Nearly everyone was young and physically attractive. Tess saw a number of people she knew from college and from other productions and she waved at them, but there was no chance to talk. The director, James, had just arrived. He was a good-looking man in his fifties, with carefully cut receding iron-grey hair and a face that was dominated by a big, sharp, well-shaped nose. He was deep in conversation with a younger man, whose long dark hair was tied back from his pale face in a neat ponytail.

'Know who that is?' whispered Jeannette in Tess's ear.

'Adam Somerville,' Tess supplied. 'Assistant director.

I worked with him last year. He's good, but he's never done a big show like this before. He's younger than me.'

'He still seems to be quite friendly with James,' commented Jeannette archly, watching as the grey and the dark head bent together in eager discussion.

'They're – ' Tess leant close to Jeannette's ear to whisper. 'They're, well, boyfriends. And what do you mean, he *still* seems to be friendly with James?'

Jeannette smiled knowingly. Then Tess forgot her question and stared, amazed, as from behind James another man appeared. 'Oh,' she whispered, 'oh Jeannette, look: it's Antonio Varguez. Isn't he *gorgeous*?'

'Whatever turns you on,' muttered Jeannette. But Tess had not heard her. She was gazing in amazement at the smooth, olive-skinned, aquiline face of the best young tenor in Europe, the one they called the new Placido Domingo. She'd seen him before, of course, in productions here and there, but she'd never worked with him or been so close to him. He was fabulous. Not too tall, broad-shouldered and athletic, with hot, dark eyes and raven-black hair that fell in waves over his high brow. His lips were perfect, well cut with a cruel twist to them that made her feel helpless.

Unbelievably, he was coming towards her, and he was smiling. 'You must be Tess Challoner,' he said, holding out his hand. His voice was limpid as a clear stream, warm and caressing and only slightly accented. 'Antonio Varguez. Call me Tony.'

Tess took his hand and managed to say, 'I'm really pleased to meet you.'

'You look wonderful,' he said, holding her hand up and turning her around like a dancer. 'Stunning. A red-headed Carmen. What a production this will be, eh?'

'Ah hah,' said the crisp, authoritative voice of James Jones. 'I see our principals have met. Well, you look good, both of you. Let's hope you sound as impressive.'

Tony smiled as if he didn't think this would be a problem. Tess felt herself blushing. James looked at her for a moment, his eyes narrowed thoughtfully. Then he said, 'All right, gather round, everyone. Let me tell you what this production will be all about.'

Cast and chorus gathered around. 'All right,' James said. 'I'm sorry the designer couldn't be with us today, but he's provided me with all his drawings. We've been working on this for some time. Now, you all know that for an Opera in the Park production this one is going to get a lot of attention. That's primarily because we've got Tony in the cast.' He extended his hand to Tony, who smiled and inclined his head gracefully, accepting the compliment. 'But I want this to be the hottest production of Carmen that anyone has ever seen. It's going to be dripping with sex, dripping, like a workout in a steam room. If any of you feel like doing it live on stage, go ahead.'

The room filled with nervous giggles. Tess glanced apprehensively at Tony and saw to her relief that he was smiling as if this was no concern to him. He said below his breath, 'I'm game if you are, Tess, darling.'

Another blush fired Tess's cheeks. She didn't know what to say, and instead looked quickly back at James.

'Here's the setting,' said James, and Adam unrolled the first of a big clutch of drawings and held it up. 'Tacky, eh? The thing is to make it like Cuba. A crumbling, corrupt régime, coming apart at the seams, everyone out for what they can get. The soldiers are all bastards and the women in the factory are all exploited tarts. No wonder Carmen can't wait to get away.'

'What about Escamillo?' asked Leo curiously. 'Do they have bullfighters in Cuba?'

'We'll do better than that,' said James. 'He's a TV star, a big star, the star of some show like *Gladiators*.' He passed his eyes up and down Leo's thickset body. 'Better start doing your sit-ups at night, Leo.'

Leo grinned, not the least concerned. 'Costumes can do miracles,' he said.

It was an exciting concept. The cast pressed closer

around James and Adam to look at the designs, exclaiming at the overtly sexy styling of the costumes and the deliberate tawdriness of the simple sets. James took them through the main structure of the opera, explaining what he had in mind for each scene and how the rehearsals would work.

'Adam's in charge of chorus movement,' he said. 'He'll be coaching you all in how to look as if you're shagging like rabbits and carry right on singing.'

Adam grinned at James. 'Come to the expert,' he said, grasping the air and thrusting with his hips. 'You'll all be expert by the time I've finished with you.'

'All right,' said James. 'Let's do some work getting to know each other. Actor's exercises. Adam, darling, you take over.'

They didn't sing a note all afternoon, just worked on exercises to build trust and understanding of each other's physical styles. They built bridges out of each other, mimed, fell and caught each other, leant forward and back. Tess was flattered to notice that whenever they had to work in pairs Tony hurried over to claim her as his partner. His body was strong and flexible beneath his loose shirt and faded jeans. She began to think that perhaps the production wouldn't be a dead loss as far as men were concerned, after all.

Adam identified two of the chorus, a man and a woman, as guinea pigs for his live-sex-on-stage simulation. He had a good eye, because the couple he had chosen didn't seem to mind at all. He formed the remainder of the cast into a rough circle and then choreographed his chosen pair into a variety of positions chosen for maximum erotic effect.

'The thing you have to convey', he said, 'is immediacy. If I ask you to hold a position, hold one that looks as though something incredible has just happened to you. Look, Tom, on top of Gina. As if you've just entered her. Yes, that's it, that's great. See his face? See the tension? And Gina, how would you feel? Yes, fabulous. Look

31

how her back arches, look how her breasts stick out. It's that first moment. Perfect.' He slapped the man, Tom, on the rump. 'Lovely, the pair of you. I'll have you front stage centre if you're happy with it.'

Tom and Gina got up and grinned at each other. They didn't seem the least bit embarrassed. Tess could only imagine that they had known each other before, that perhaps they had already been lovers, that Adam had known and turned the knowledge to his advantage. She hoped that was the case. The idea of simulating sex with a total stranger before an interested audience was enough to make her cringe with mortification. And yet Tom was hitching at his jeans as if they were uncomfortably tight at the crotch and Gina's nipples were pressing tautly through the fabric of her baggy T-shirt. They had actually been aroused by what Adam had asked them to do.

They had finished what James had wanted them to do and now people began to drift away. Tess stayed for some time, discussing the rehearsal schedule, and then went to the stairs. She looked around for Jeannette, but her friend was already gone.

'Tess,' said a warm voice behind her. She jumped and turned round. It was Tony, smiling at her. 'I wondered', he said, 'if you fancied going out for something to drink? Or a meal, maybe?'

Tess was taken aback. 'Oh,' she managed, 'well, thanks, Tony, but – but I really have to get home. Things to do, you know.'

He smiled. 'Fine. No problems. Another time, maybe.'

'Yes,' she stammered, 'I'd like that.'

Tony smiled at her again, then gave a little Mediterranean bow and turned to go. Tess watched him, her lip caught between her teeth, wondering why she had refused. Timid, so timid.

Suddenly she realised that she'd left her canvas bag upstairs. It had her score in it, and like many singers she was ridiculously superstitious about her score. She hur-

32

ried back up the stairs for the bag, found it, drank a gulp of mineral water and thought about Tony.

Certainly one of the best-looking men she had ever met. And so smooth! His attention to her was very flattering. Still thinking about him, she went through the door at the side of the rehearsal room to find her way to the loo.

She stopped in the shadows, staring. There in the corridor, illuminated by the glow of light through a slanting loft window, stood Tom and Gina, kissing deeply. Tess began to recoil, meaning to dart back into the main room. Then she saw with a frisson of excitement that Tom's jeans were open and Gina had her hand inside them. Tess pressed her hands against the cold, hard door and stared open-mouthed. Gina drew out Tom's cock, smiling and laughing throatily as she rubbed her hand up and down its stiff scarlet length.

'Come on,' Tom hissed. He pressed Gina against the wall and lifted her skirt. She was wearing delicate lace knickers and Tom shoved his hand inside them and pulled them out of his way. He spread her legs and put the head of his cock against her body and thrust.

Gina cried out and lifted her thigh to hook it over Tom's thrusting hips. Tess gasped, because now she could see everything. She could see Tom's hot, eager penis drive deep between the soft, swollen lips of Gina's sex, lie for an infinite second deeply embedded in her, and then withdraw, glistening with her juices, to thrust again. Gina moaned and put her hands on Tom's buttocks to pull him into her harder and Tom pushed his hands up inside her T-shirt and began to pinch and pull at the distended nipples of her pouting breasts. Their mouths joined, parted, joined again, their tongues darting and thrusting as Tom's erect cock darted and thrust into Gina's willing body.

Suddenly Tess couldn't bear any more. Not caring if they heard her she jerked the door open and rushed through it, slamming it behind her. James and Adam turned from the production designs to look at her in surprise and concern, but she ignored them. She ran for the stairs and tumbled down them, gasping as she felt the cool air of the street on her hot cheeks.

'Dear God,' she whispered, covering her face with her hands. 'A baptism of fire.'

Act One, Scene Two

The rehearsal studio, three days later

'*L*ook, Tess.' James's strong voice sounded suddenly impatient. 'How many times do I have to tell you? It's no use just singing. You have to act too.'

'I am,' Tess protested, bristling. 'I am acting.'

'Who are you being, then? If it's Carmen it's nothing like the Carmen I've got in my mind. You're too bloody nice.'

'Nice?' Tess's voice lifted in disbelief. 'Nice!'

'Nice. You look as if Tony's doing you a favour by looking at you. Listen, Tess, darling, Carmen thinks she's the sexiest thing on legs. Of course Don José wants her! Every man wants her! She can take him or leave him alone. The only thing that surprises her is that he doesn't fall for her straight away. Tess, I don't see any of this in what you're doing. You look more like Micaela than Carmen, and I'm sorry, dear, but you can't reach Micaela's notes.' He swung away from Tess, throwing up one hand in an irritated gesture. Tess stood looking at the ground, wishing that the planks of the rehearsal room would open and swallow her up. She glanced up at Tony. He raised his arched, dark brows at her sympathetically.

'Now,' said James, 'let's try it again from the top. And

remember, Tess, you want to screw him. You just set eyes on him, and you want to screw him. I want to see it in your face.' He tossed Tess a little plastic rose.

Tess caught the flower and held it against her breast, breathing hard. She remembered how she had looked into her mirror and tried to smoulder at it, tried to look sexy. She had failed then, in the safety of her own bedroom, with her lover lying asleep in the bed. How could she smoulder at Tony now, with James watching her with cool appraising eyes?

'Off you go,' said James, and Tony began industriously to polish an invisible weapon.

Tess took a deep breath and lifted her head. *'Hey, soldier. What are you doing there?'*

Tony glanced at her and then away again. *'Polishing my rifle.'*

'Can't you think of something better to rub, soldier?'

'No!' James shouted. 'Tess, listen to me. When he looks up at you I want your eyes to lock with an audible sound. Do you hear me? I want his face to change as he looks at you. I want the sight of you to go straight to his cock, I want him to get a hard on the moment he sets eyes on you. Do you understand me? And your face has to show it, darling, it's got to be there in your eyes. All I see at the moment is a timid English girl trying to look like a stripper.'

Tess fought tears. She couldn't bear the thought of crying in front of James and Tony, no matter how bad she felt. 'Look,' she said earnestly, 'James, I'm doing my best. I just can't do it, can I? James, give me some help. Tell me how to do it.'

'Listen, darling, I'm not a woman. What do I know about it? I want you to find out how to do it. I want you to be amoral, self-centred, just going after kicks. Get out and screw someone, darling, and find out what it feels like. There's only room for one virgin in *Carmen*, and Emma's got that part.'

There was a long silence. Then James said, 'Well,

enough for today. I've got others to work with, Emma's waiting. Tess, don't take it to heart, darling, but I think you'd better get some research under your belt. Get my drift?'

'I can't do this,' Tess whispered as James left. 'I can't do it.'

'Hey, of course you can.' Tony looked anxious and concerned. 'Come on, Tess, you'll be fine.'

If he had been callous she would have been able to cope, but his sympathy was more than she could bear. She burst into a storm of tears. 'What does James know?' she demanded, snuffling hopelessly. 'He's gay, for God's sake. What does he know about women?'

'Tess,' said Tony, putting his hand on her arm, 'you need some tea. Come on back to my place, it's just around the corner. Couldn't you do with a cup of tea?'

Tess dashed her hand over her eyes and looked up into his face. She wasn't fooled for a moment, but his eagerness was flattering. She said, 'All right, Tony,' and picked up her bag.

She had heard that Tony's flat was a gem, and it was. Right in the middle of Covent Garden, but quietly situated. It was on the top floor of an old commercial building and it glowed with light. 'Gosh,' Tess said. By comparison her cosy little place in Hampstead looked old-fashioned and suburban. Everything in Tony's apartment was modern and chosen by someone with strong and distinct taste. The floor was bare boards, polished to a waxy gleam. There was little furniture, and what there was, was made of metal, bare wood and natural linen. It looked like the design section of a glossy magazine. The walls were hung with handsome Bokhara rugs, their warm dyes of scarlet and rose and saffron providing a welcome touch of colour. The last rays of the June sun filtered through the high windows, illuminating the whole flat with a light like liquid gold.

'Nice place, isn't it?' said Tony. 'It came like this.

Belongs to some interior designer. My agent found it for me. Right in the middle of everything, too.'

'Oh.' Tess was faintly disappointed. She had hoped that the flat reflected Tony's own taste. She wandered into the big living room, reaching out to run her fingers across the silky pile of one of the rugs. There was a big black grand piano in one corner and she went over to it and pressed down a few of the keys. She picked out the theme of Carmen's first aria, made a face and turned away.

'Now then,' said Tony, 'would you like a drink? There's some wine, if you like. Spanish, of course.'

'I shouldn't,' Tess said. Like many singers, she firmly believed that alcohol was anathema to the voice. 'I'd love some tea, if that's all right.'

'Tea. Sure, tea. I may take a little while, Tess. I don't seem to have got the kitchen quite sorted out yet.'

Tess followed him across to the long galley kitchen in one corner. Everything suited the style of the flat, elegant and minimalist. The cupboards were made of a wood so pale that it was almost the colour of milk and the work surfaces were solid granite, dark grey faintly flecked with white and shining like glass. The utensils were gleaming chrome and the kettle looked like an object from the Tate Gallery. Tony stopped by the sink and looked around. 'What's the problem?' Tess asked hesitantly.

'Oh,' said Tony, 'I just haven't really found out where everything is . . .' He stood looking helpless, and Tess smiled and began to open the cupboard doors. She soon found a packet of Earl Grey tea and a teapot, an extraordinary utensil more or less triangular in shape and glazed in very brilliant colours. She made the tea and found a couple of mugs for it.

'Thanks,' said Tony, accepting the mug she handed him. He smiled at her. 'Just a plain old hopeless man, eh? Can't even make my own tea.' He put his hand familiarly on her shoulder. 'Come through and sit down,' he said. 'Let's talk about the part. James is certainly giving you a hard time.'

There was only one place to sit in the whole of the huge living room, and that was a massive sofa, big enough for half a dozen people. Tess sat down cautiously at one end of it, cupping her mug of tea in her hands. Tony went over to the sound system and chose some discs. After a second the room filled with intense, threatening chords.

'Oh,' said Tess at once, '*Tosca*. I saw you in this, Tony. I thought you were a wonderful Caravadossi. They should have made a recording.'

Tony was clearly very pleased. 'Thank you,' he said, gracefully enough. 'It's a great role. Though if I'm honest I didn't really think that my Tosca was up to it. That's a really hard part for a woman. Top class sopranos only, and in that particular production I wasn't sure – ' he stopped talking, took a deep breath and came across to the sofa. He sat down next to Tess, closer to her than felt entirely comfortable. She would have moved away, but the big padded arm of the sofa prevented it.

'Listen, Tess,' said Tony softly. 'Don't worry about what James says. You're the best-looking woman in the cast. Things will be fine.'

Tess frowned at him a little. 'Tony,' she said hesitantly, 'there seems to be a bit more to it than what I look like.' She tried to smile in a careless, cheerful way. 'You know, some acting? And singing?'

'Oh, you'll be fine,' Tony repeated, leaning a little closer. 'Listen, I know you sound great. I heard you with Julian the other day.' Julian was their répétiteur, their rehearsal pianist, note teacher and unofficial vocal coach, a callow young man fresh out of Oxford. 'You sounded wonderful. You've got a world class voice. Combine that with your other assets, and the critics are bound to love you.' He grinned admiringly at Tess's breasts.

Compliments on her physical appearance were not really what Tess was seeking, but when they accompanied compliments on her voice she didn't feel able to reject them. Tony was obviously doing what he could to make her feel better. She said sadly, 'Thanks, Tony,' and hid her face in her mug of tea.

Tony drank a little of his own tea, then set down the mug. He looked at Tess narrowly for a few moments, as if he were trying to think of something to say. Then he shook his head, leant forward and took her mug from her hand.

'Tony – ' Tess said, drawing back a little. But he just leant forward and put his hand behind her head and held her still so that he could kiss her. For a moment she pulled away from him, resisting. Then she thought, Oh, what the hell, and opened her mouth and succumbed.

He kissed beautifully. His lips were sensitive, his tongue strong and searching and delicate. It felt wonderful to be kissed by someone new, someone exciting and handsome and unusual. In recent weeks, before they split up, Tess and Dan had hardly kissed at all. Tony moved very close to her and wrapped his arms around her, pressing her close against his hard, muscular body, and she revelled in the novelty of it. She closed her eyes and let her hands see for her. They touched his face, his neck, his hair. Dan's hair had been very fine and soft, like a child's; Tony's was strong and glossy and springing, crackling with life. She dug her fingers into the silky harshness and breathed in deep shuddering gasps as he kissed and kissed her.

He wasn't in a hurry. It was wonderful, as if there was all the time in the world. They sat on the sofa enmeshed, mouths meeting and parting, tongues entwined, and as the sun set outside the high windows the tea grew cold. Music surrounded them, swirling and expansive, Caravadossi and Tosca singing passionately of their shared ecstasy of love. Tess felt herself melting, dribbling away into helplessness, everything within her warmed and liquified by the gentle glowing flame of Tony's expert lips.

Then suddenly he changed, as if the sunset had freed the beast in him. He set his lips to her throat and sucked and strained her to him. One hand released her back and cupped her breast, stroking, fondling, every movement revealing a sudden intense urgency. His touch sent an icy chill of arousal shooting from her nipple to her loins. She responded helplessly, throwing back her head to invite his lips to travel down her throat to where her pulse hammered below the delicate skin. With a sudden shock she realised that this wasn't just a snog, that Tony meant to go all the way. She didn't want to. It would look cheap. She caught hold of his hand and pushed it away and said, 'Tony, please.'

'Please?' Tony whispered. He smiled at her. His eyes narrowed into dark glittering slits and the twist of his cruel mouth made her bowels turn to water. 'Please, Tess? Please what?'

She swallowed. 'I don't – we shouldn't . . .'

Tony smiled again. 'Oh, come on,' he murmured. 'Remember what James said to you? Screw someone, darling, and find out what it feels like?' He took hold of her hand and put it on the front of his jeans. She breathed faster as beneath her fingers she felt the hot pulse of his erect cock. 'Ready to help, Tess,' Tony whispered.

Tess couldn't take her hand away. The warmth, the contained energy of his erection held her fingers as a magnet holds iron. She swallowed again, hard, looking into Tony's shadowed face. It had taken Leo eight weeks of rehearsals to bed her, and then she had been surprised. It had taken even Dan Ashbourne, the handsomest man in England, four expensive dinners and two carefully-administered bottles of champagne. How could she succumb to Antonio Varguez the first time he asked her?

Because he was gorgeous. Because he was what she so wanted to be, a happy, successful opera star. Because nothing seemed to worry him. Because she admired him. Because the wry twist of his beautiful lips made her

41

stomach lurch. Because she knew his phenomenal reputation as a lover.

On the Puccini recording the deep menacing voice of the villain Baron Scarpia sang as he waited alone in his study for Tosca to be brought before him: *God made different wines and different women, and I will try them all.* Tess half heard the music and shivered. She couldn't say *yes.* She couldn't say *no* either. She couldn't say anything. She just sat with her hand quivering on Tony's fly and looked into his face and waited for him to make the decision for her.

Tony stroked her hand and smiled into her eyes. Then he put his fingers to the buttons on her blouse and began to unfasten them. Tess sat very still, watching as the crisp crumpled white linen parted to reveal the white skin beneath it. She was wearing a pretty bra today made of stretch lace and Tony nodded in gentle, deliberate approval at the sight of her dark, taut nipples protruding through the fabric. He muttered something incomprehensible in Spanish, then put his hands very deliberately over the swell of Tess's breasts. He leant forward to kiss her and as he did so his fingers coaxed down the tight fabric of the bra, revealing her erect nipples. He began to flicker and scratch his beautifully manicured nails across them.

'Oh,' Tess moaned into his open mouth. Her breasts felt very cold, as if his fingers were icicles. The feel of him teasing and scratching at her nipples was so intense that it was almost unbearable. She jolted helplessly as if she would pull away, but she was trapped between him and the arm of the sofa. Tony smiled and thrust his tongue deep into her mouth and began to pinch the swollen pink buds, squeezing them tightly between finger and thumb in a remorseless, driving rhythm that made her body jerk and writhe.

'Wonderful breasts,' he whispered, never ceasing to squeeze and torment her engorged nipples. 'Beautiful.' With one hand he began to push off her shirt. He reached

42

behind her back, found the fastening of her bra and deftly unhooked it. Bra followed shirt to the floor and Tess found herself naked from the waist up, feeling desperately vulnerable. The skin of her neck was flushed and her breasts were swollen and tender. Her heart was thumping.

'I bet I look like one of the sopranos in James's last production,' she joked, trying to defuse the tension that she felt. 'All I need is to have myself covered in glitter.'

Tony met her eyes. His face was quite still and burning with ferocious eagerness. 'You don't need covering in anything,' he said softly. 'You need uncovering.' And he reached out for the buttons that closed her skirt.

'Oh no,' she moaned. She didn't know why she was resisting him. She simply couldn't let him strip her, reveal her nakedness to him before he had unfastened so much as one button of his shirt. It made her feel like an object, a possession. She caught hold of his hands as he began to unbutton the skirt and jerked at them, looking pleadingly into his face. 'Tony, please.'

'Tess!' He twisted quickly in her grip so that suddenly instead of her holding his wrists he was holding hers. 'Tess, don't worry. I know what you need. Let me.'

It wasn't right, but she didn't know how to say no. How could she argue with his confidence, with his experience? She gave a little half sob of acquiescence and slumped back against the sofa and let him continue unbuttoning her skirt. At last the denim fell open and Tony sighed with pleasure and leant forward to place a kiss on the soft curve of her stomach, just above the top of her panties. As he did so he slipped one finger elegantly below the fabric and before she could move or react he was stroking delicately at the damp folds of flesh between her legs.

'Oh,' Tess moaned, taken aback by the suddenness of it. 'Oh God.'

'You're wet,' Tony hissed. He knelt over her and leant forward to explore her panting mouth again with his

43

tongue. With his left hand he stroked and caressed her breast and with his right he squeezed her sex, all his fingers working as if he squeezed an orange. Tess moaned again and arched her back and as she did so he thrust two fingers deep inside her, twisting and coiling them within her so that she cried out sharply into his mouth. Her body tensed and clamped around his probing fingers as if it wanted to draw them into her further.

'Feel that,' he whispered. His words stirred against her lips, mingling with her moans. 'Feel that. Just my fingers fucking you, and feel how good it is. And that's just the overture, Tess.' His fingers withdrew and then lunged into her again and her hips jerked unconsciously upwards, wanting more. For a moment Tony obliged, pushing his fingers hard into her aching, slippery wetness. Then he pulled his hand away and caught at her, turning her round. She whimpered in protest but he ignored her. His black arched brows were drawn down in a tight frown of concentration. 'Like this,' he hissed, 'like this.'

He arranged her on the sofa, lying face up with her buttocks raised up on the low, soft arm, her naked body sprawled lengthways, her legs dangling helplessly. The position felt very exposed, very vulnerable, and for a moment Tess wanted to resist, to ask him to love her a little more or at least to let her touch him. But he moved with such assurance, such determination that she did not dare.

Tony got to his feet and looked down at her. His eyes shone with pleasure and anticipation as they moved up and down the length of her naked body. She lay very still, looking up at him, feeling his gaze on her skin almost like a physical touch. He had made her assume such a lewd position, the soft mound of her sex lifted and thrust towards him, that she did not know how to react. As she lay there in the twilight, breathing fast, she realised that she was almost unbearably aroused. She

44

wanted to seize him, strip his clothes from him, lick and suck his cock and balls, grapple with his tight buttocks and make him take her. But she said nothing.

Very slowly Tony began to unbutton his fly. He moved around to stand between her legs. Taking one ankle in each hand, he lifted them to rest on his shoulders and looked down with a faint smile into the open wetness of her sex. Tess closed her eyes, shuddering with mingled shame and excitement. For a moment nothing happened. Then the head of his cock nudged between her labia and she took a long, shivering breath.

The hot smoothness spread her a little way, then stopped. She opened her eyes and whimpered in puzzlement. Tony looked down at her and smiled, so callously that she could almost have wept.

'Put your hands on your nipples,' he said. 'Pinch them. I want to see you do it.'

Tess never thought of disobeying him. Obediently she slid her hands over her breasts, found the swollen peaks, began to tease them into even greater hardness. The lips of her vagina twitched and spasmed around the head of Tony's cock and she moaned.

'Now,' Tony hissed, 'now tell me what you want me to do to you.'

She stared up at him, disbelieving. He ran one hand down her leg, down her smooth calf and the silken inside of her thigh, and with one finger flicked at the engorged aching bud of her clitoris. She cried out helplessly. 'Tell me,' he repeated.

'I can't,' Tess gasped, and she truly could not make her lips say the words.

'Tell me,' Tony insisted. 'I can wait all night. Say, Tony, please fuck me. Please put your cock up me and fuck me until I come. Say it.'

She was almost in tears. She had never uttered the word in a sexual context in her life. It was a swear word, it was rude, it was an expletive, not something that she might want to be done to her. She couldn't ask. 'I can't. I can't. Please, Tony, don't.'

He touched her clitoris again. The sensation racked her. She tried to lift her hips towards him, tried to draw his penis inside her, but he laughed and held her down. 'Say it.'

'Oh, God!' She was desperate. How could he make her suffer so? 'Please, Tony, please, please do it to me.'

'Do what? What?'

'Oh!' Her voice was almost a scream now, a scream of frustration and shame. Her body's desire at last overcame her modest reluctance and the words made themselves heard. 'Please, please fuck me. Please, please, Tony, fuck me, fuck me.'

And Tony leant forward and thrust and his wonderful, hot phallus entered her. She flung back her head and actually screamed with the pleasure of feeling him inside her at last. It seemed to take forever for him to penetrate her and she opened her eyes wide as she felt herself filled to the very neck of her womb. She cried out to him, shouting encouragement, and he held her legs close against his chest and drove himself into her again and again. She writhed like an animal impaled on a spear, forgetting her modesty, forgetting that she was naked and he was clothed, forgetting everything except the sensation of his iron-hard cock plunging into her and her hands on her breasts and his fingers flickering teasingly over her clitoris, dragging her up and up to a plateau of pleasure and holding her there and then thrusting into her with such violence that she came screaming, beating her head up and down on the cushions of the sofa and fighting against his restraining hands. In the rush of her orgasm she didn't even notice whether he had come, only that he withdrew from her as soon as her spasms stopped.

After a few moments she lifted her head and said huskily, 'Tony?'

He leant over her, smiling. 'You'll ruin your voice, shouting like that.'

'What did you do to me?' she asked. She was almost afraid. Neither Leo nor Dan had drawn her into violent pleasures. She began to realise what the phrase *an animal in bed* might really mean.

'Just gave you what you wanted,' Tony said, still smiling. 'Let's have a shower. The shower's great. I'd like a shower. Come on.'

She would have liked to pull him into her arms and hold him close, but he caught hold of her hand and tugged her up from the sofa. She came obediently, though her legs were shaking, and followed him to the bathroom.

Even then, even in the bathroom, he did not let her undress him. When she reached for the buttons on his shirt he smiled at her and drew her hands away and said, 'No, Tess, darling, that's a man's job.'

Tess stepped back, rebuked, and watched as he unbuttoned his shirt. It was warm and bright in the big marble-tiled bathroom, and she stood with her arms wrapped around her, conscious of her nakedness. Tony unfastened the shirt and shrugged it off. His skin was an even olive-brown, so smooth and glossy that he looked as if he had been polished like a wooden carving, and the muscles of his chest and abdomen were perfectly defined.

It felt odd to be seeing his naked body now, when she had already felt his powerful cock ravaging her. Nervously Tess said, 'Well, Tony, if ever the voice goes, you could get a job as a Chippendale.'

He smiled at her, not the least disconcerted. Nothing remotely approaching a compliment was unpleasant to him. 'I can't bear the stereotype fat tenor,' he said, flexing the muscles of one arm for her to admire. 'I go to the gym every day when I'm not in a production. And I like other sorts of exercise, too.' His mouth twisted into a smile and he came over to her and drew her hands away from her body. 'Don't hide yourself. Let me look at you.'

Something told Tess that this assured possessiveness was less flattering than it felt. But despite her uncertainty, she felt herself stirring again into arousal as he positioned her naked before him so that he could look at her as he pushed off his jeans. I'm a sex object, she thought as his hot eyes moved up and down her body. He's treating me like a sex object. She didn't know whether it was the sexiest thing that had ever happened to her, or the most degrading.

Tony straightened, kicking his jeans aside. He was as smooth and satiny from the waist down as he was above, except for a dark, glossy triangle of curls at his crotch. His penis was not fully erect, but thick and limp between his legs. He stood before Tess for a moment, letting her look at him, then reached for her hand. 'Shower,' he said firmly.

The shower was huge, easily big enough for two, and the water sparkled around them like champagne. The tiled walls were icy cold and Tess flinched when Tony pushed her against them, but then he began to stroke her between her legs and she forgot about her goosepimples.

He brought her to another orgasm there, leaning against the wall of the shower, whimpering and shaking and almost falling as his clever fingers caressed her and the tingling water poured over her naked breasts. Then he turned off the water and yanked open the door of the cubicle, flung a towel onto the floor and pushed Tess down onto it. He dropped on top of her, his wet body sliding against hers, and she reached out eagerly for him, wanting to touch him, to explore the silkiness of his skin. But this was not what Tony had in mind. He crawled up over her, straddling her throat with his strong thighs, and with his hand guided his now swollen cock towards her lips.

Tess opened her mouth eagerly to take him in. He gave a sharp, wordless cry as her lips framed themselves into a tight O and caressed the thick wet stem of his glistening penis. She lifted her hands to stroke the taut arches of his buttocks and he growled and pushed his hips forward, driving his hot shaft so deeply into her mouth that she almost choked. She had no choice, his weight was above her, pinning her down, forcing her to accept him as he thrust himself deeper and deeper, working his cock to and fro between her lips as if he was fucking her mouth. The sensation was frightening and yet oddly liberating. Even Dan, who loved more than anything else to have her suck his cock, even Dan had never sat over her face and forced her to take him in this way. She tried to make a sound and could not. Tony's penis was gagging her, and her helpless silence aroused her. When he suddenly withdrew from her mouth and flowed over her and kicked her ankles apart she knew she was ready for him and she reached up to clasp his shoulders and pull him down towards her.

'Not so shy now,' Tony hissed. 'Not so shy, Tess? Ready for me?'

'Yes,' Tess gasped, wanting him. 'Yes. Yes, Tony.'

'I'll show you,' Tony breathed through his teeth. He caught her hands from his shoulders and pulled her wrists down to the floor, holding them firmly above her head. She struggled, trying to pull free, but he laughed and leant his weight on her and pinned her down. 'Mine,' he whispered as he entered her. 'Mine, mine.'

And she was. His, all his, his possession, his slave, the captive of his body. If he had asked her to call him lord, master, she would have obeyed. He was strong and fierce and his body filled her with a furious pulsation of lust such as she had never known. Leo's gentleness, Dan's selfishness paled into insignificance beside the direct determined energy of Tony's thrusts. She could no more have resisted him than she could have lifted a cathedral. She did not climax again, but pressed her body tightly against his and tried to reach up with her teeth to bite his smooth brown shoulder as he snarled and plunged inside her. She was powerless beneath him, and yet as he growled and her hips bucked up to meet his thrusts she felt power, tremendous power, as if he were the prisoner and she the captor. When he cried out and she felt his cock pulsing inside her as he came she writhed and lifted her ankles to wrap them around his quivering buttocks.

Then he hung over her for a moment, sweat trickling from his cheeks to the bridge of his aquiline nose. He pulled out of her with a little grunt and smiled into her eyes, a smile of satisfaction, not of affection. 'Time for bed,' he said.

Tess frowned anxiously. Jeannette and Catherine were coming to her flat tomorrow morning, taking advantage of a small gap in the schedule to practise one of their trios in private. It would be awful if she wasn't there. But she didn't want to get up and leave, she wanted to lie all night in bed with Tony, feeling his wonderful hard smooth body and smelling the odd complex scent of his hair. She said, feeling rather strange, 'I, I'll need to get up early.'

'Fine,' he said. 'Me too. I'll go to the gym.'

But he didn't set the alarm. Tess woke because her natural clock told her it was morning. She was lying in Tony's arms, as they had fallen asleep, her cheek resting on his shoulder, her body pressed against his, thighs entwined, close and safe. His skin was unbelievably smooth. She looked up and saw him fast asleep, his chin shaded blue with stubble, his cruel lips firmly closed.

Dan had never held her all night. It felt so secure, so protected. She took a deep breath and let it out in a long shiver of satisfaction. Yesterday she had been uncertain of the wisdom of letting Tony make love to her. Today, waking in his bed and in his embrace, it seemed like the best decision she had ever made.

The clock by the bed said quarter past eight, and Jeannette and Catherine were coming to the flat at ten. Tess reluctantly began to detach herself from Tony. He murmured and smiled as she disentangled herself, but did not wake.

Never in her life had Tess stayed overnight at a man's house without meaning to. She had no clean knickers and only yesterday's blouse. She stood by the bed for a few moments wondering what she should do about it. It felt hideously embarrassing. In the end she picked up Tony's dressing gown, a handsome affair of striped silk, and went off to find the bathroom.

Washed and feeling a little more composed, she moved through to the kitchen and put the kettle on. Morning was not morning to Tess without a cup of tea. She was a tea addict. The teapot was still on the cold, glossy work surface, full of dregs, and she busied herself washing it up, then found the mugs and washed those up too.

The kettle had just boiled when Tony appeared in the doorway, stark naked and pushing his hand through his hair. He saw her standing by the kettle and smiled. 'Tess,' he said, coming closer, 'you're wonderful. It's such a change to find a woman who doesn't mind going into the kitchen.'

Tess glanced at him and then quickly away again. He had a morning erection, hard and eager. The smooth column of his cock was dark, like the rest of his skin, glossy and inviting. She wanted to touch it, but she had a rehearsal to go to. 'Do you like tea in the morning?' she asked brightly.

'Tea second,' Tony said. He came up behind her and caught hold of the sleeves of the dressing gown, pulling them down so that Tess's breasts were bared and her arms were tugged behind her back. 'Sex first.'

'Oh,' Tess whimpered, wriggling in his strong grip, 'Tony, I don't have the time.'

But he ignored her. He pulled the dressing gown further down her arms, wrapping it around and around until she could not easily free herself. Then he reached round her and took her breasts in his hands and fastened his lips to her neck. His body was pressed up against

51

her, tight against her buttocks. The heat of his erection seared her through the thin silk of the dressing gown. So demanding, so eager. So unlike Dan. She realised now quite how much Dan had lost interest in her. Tony was muttering as he scourged her neck with kisses and his hands roamed all up and down the length of her, exploring her, touching her in places she had not dreamed could be erotic: the sides of her ribs, her collar bone, her flanks. He wanted her, and knowing that he wanted her made her feel so womanly and desirable that she stopped caring about whether he would make her late for rehearsal. She let her head fall back and sought his lips and kissed him. He smiled and with one hand he felt between her legs and began to tease the warm flesh there into willing moistness. Tess's body undulated around him, fixed at two points only, by his probing fingers and his consuming lips. Her breathing deepened.

Tony's rigid penis was trapped between the cheeks of her buttocks. He pushed himself against her like a cat wanting to be stroked. 'Hey,' he whispered in her ear, 'have you ever seen *Last Tango in Paris?*'

The question startled Tess out of her erotic haze. 'What?' she asked apprehensively.

'I've got some butter somewhere,' said Tony, smiling. 'Bend over.'

Tess hadn't actually seen the film, but she had heard of the infamous butter scene. She pulled away from Tony, wrestling her arms free of the dressing gown and trying to cover herself. She couldn't tell from his face whether he was joking or not. 'No,' she said anxiously, 'Tony, I – '

'Just joking,' he said with a smile, coming forward to grab her arms. His smile changed a little, becoming wicked. 'But I do want you to bend over. Bend over, Tess.'

He tried to make her turn around. She resisted him. 'Tony, no, I don't want to.'

'Bend over!' He had raised his voice and suddenly he spun her around and with unexpected strength forced her face down over the granite work surface. Her breasts flattened against its cold hardness. He pulled her arms above her head and held both her wrists in one hand, then leant forward until she could feel his hot breath on her ear. 'Do as I tell you,' he whispered.

She was afraid. She tried to move, but his weight prevented her. His body was warm and hard and his stiff cock was trapped between her thighs. 'Tony –'

'Just be a good girl,' he whispered. 'Do as I tell you. Just do what I say, Tess, and you'll have a good time. I promise. Now, don't struggle.' His other hand passed quickly between her spread legs, testing her wetness. 'Good,' he hissed. His hand withdrew and was replaced by the head of his cock, hot and smooth, thick and hard as stone, driving up inside her with such suddenness, such completeness, that she could do nothing but gasp. He penetrated her completely and then lay within her for a moment, quite still. Tess moaned and with a tremendous effort lifted herself a little way towards him so that his tight balls rubbed against her tender, swollen clitoris.

'Don't move,' he hissed in her ear. 'Do as I say. Lie still. I'm in charge.' Tess whimpered and tried to move and suddenly Tony's weight above her increased and he slapped her with the flat of his hand on her naked flank, hard enough to make her cry out. He repeated sternly, 'I'm in charge!'

His thick shaft was filling her, tormenting her. She wanted to writhe on it, heave her body up towards him, squirm as that smooth, hard cock slid inexorably to and fro within her eager flesh. But he was so strong, so dominant. She did not dare to disobey him. She made herself lie very still, eyes tightly shut, taut nipples chafing against the coldness of the stone, not moving a muscle. A sense of delicious freedom began to fill her. With Dan she had always felt responsible, as if failure to orgasm would be her fault, her problem. Now Tony had taken that responsibility from her. She laid the weight of her pleasure between his strong hands, passive and unprotesting, shuddering as she waited for him to serve her.

'You have a beautiful arse,' Tony whispered. His weight lightened slightly and he arched his hips, slowly withdrawing the thick length of his rigid cock from her moist willing flesh. 'I want to fuck your arse, Tess. I will soon, I promise.' He was still holding her wrists against the cold stone, and now with his free hand he felt between the cheeks of her bottom. His fingers dipped into the damp flesh that clung to his penis and then slid back. Tess gave a little whimper of protest as she felt him pressing at the tightly-closed flower of her arsehole. She would have tried to wriggle away, but the head of his cock was still lodged between the lips of her sex and if she moved she might lose it. She could not bear to lose it, and so she lay still and breathed faster as his finger pressed, pressed again and at last slid into the virgin tautness of her anus.

'Oh,' she said, astonished by the extraordinary sensation, the dark fullness of pleasure. 'Oh, God.'

'I told you,' Tony hissed. He began to move his finger in and out, thrusting it into her arsehole as if it were a penis. Tess rolled her head from side to side, desperately fighting against the urge to move. Pleasure pooled around Tony's probing finger and between her legs where his thick cock lay at her entrance, parting the soft labia and just fixed within her tunnel. Her breasts ached and burned against the icy granite. Tony moved slightly behind her and the movement made his cock rub against the front of her sex, just barely touching her clitoris, and hot bright flashes of sensation like forked lightning leapt from her engorged flesh and made her jerk and cry out.

'Feel,' whispered Tony. 'Feel it.' A second finger joined the first, sliding deep into her anus and then withdrawing. Tess jerked again and he snarled behind her ear and tugged at her wrists. 'Keep still!'

'Oh God, oh God,' Tess moaned helplessly. In a moment she thought she would have to pull away, to escape from the remorseless, deliberate thrusts of his penetrating fingers. She could not bear the hybrid of pleasure and pain any longer. But just as she thought she must struggle, he withdrew his fingers and thrust into her again with his hot cock, spreading the tender lips and driving himself deep within her. His hand encircled her flank and began to rub at her pleasure bud and, as if he had set light to a pool of oil, Tess felt ecstasy like liquid fire flooding through her. She opened her mouth and cried out, possessed by the blazing spasms of orgasm.

Tony stopped touching her. He reached up and took hold of one wrist in each hand and dragged them up behind her back so that she was bent like a prisoner over the cold stone, crying out as he plunged his stiff cock into her with ferocious strength, deeper on every stroke. He went on and on, tireless, beating his body against the soft cushion of her buttocks. His breath hissed over her back. Then he said through his teeth, 'Ask me for mercy.'

Tess hardly heard him, didn't understand him. He tugged at her arms, hurting her. 'Ask for mercy!' he repeated, jerking painfully at her wrists.

The frantic lunges of his ravenous cock were drawing her into an abyss of post-orgasmic pleasure. She heard his order and could barely speak to obey him, but at last she managed to moan, 'Oh, please, mercy. Mercy.' It didn't feel foolish to beg him, to plead with him. It felt wonderful.

'No mercy,' Tony snarled. 'No mercy – ah – ' and as if her words had touched a fuse within him he gave one final frantic thrust and shuddered as he exploded into orgasm.

Tess lay very still as his spasms subsided. Her head ached and she was cold, but she had never felt so delectably wanton, so fabulously shameless, in all her life. She would have liked to free her arms, but she could not move until he permitted it.

After a few minutes Tony withdrew and let her go. He patted her on the rump and said, 'There you are, Tess darling. Get screwed, James said. Happy to oblige.'

Tess straightened, stretching her aching limbs. Tony smiled at her and went on, 'Don't worry about anything, Tess. I'll look after you. It'll be fine. Just do what I say and everything will be fine.'

A tiny voice within Tess told her that this was not what James had had in mind, and that Tony's suggestion was flawed. Had he sounded somehow deprecating? But it was such a relief to feel looked after. With Tony there to reassure her, she wouldn't have to worry, she wouldn't have to take responsibility for anything. She hesitated for a moment, but then she smiled. 'Thanks, Tony,' she said. She reached up impulsively to kiss him and he laughed with pleasure as her arms went around his neck.

Act Two, Scene One

Later the same day

'Dammmit, dammit, dammit,' Tess muttered as she bounced irritably up and down on the platform. Why was the Northern line always so bloody slow? At this rate she was going to be late.

At last the train came and she sat in a half-empty carriage, thinking about Tony as she jolted and rattled towards Hampstead. Mentally she ticked a variety of boxes. Handsome, yes indeed. Sexy, certainly. A good lover? Well, he had certainly given her several orgasms, which had not been Dan's strong point. And he was so refreshingly open about what he wanted, he didn't just lie there and expect her to service him. A bit demanding, perhaps, a bit dominant, but wasn't that a very erotic thing to be?

She was so wrapped in her day-dreams that she almost missed the station. She leapt from the carriage as the doors closed. They shut on her bag and she swore, wrestled it free and hared along the platform towards the lift.

It was a bright, warm summer day in Hampstead. The poseurs were already sitting sipping the first cocktail of the morning in Café Dôme and people were wandering up and down the high street languidly peering into the shop windows. Tess swerved her way between them and ran up Flask Walk towards the Heath and her house.

At the first junction she saw Jeannette and Catherine on the other side of the road, walking towards her wrapped in conversation. She called out to them, waved and dodged over the road between two taxis. 'Sorry,' she panted as she hurried up to them.

'Whatever are you wearing?' asked Catherine, her eyebrows meeting her hairline. 'That looks like – '

'One of Tony's shirts!' shouted Jeannette in her buzz-saw voice.

'Oh,' Tess said, terribly flustered. Blood rushed to her cheeks. 'Oh, it, er – '

'We already know you went back with him last night,' said Catherine. 'Don't bother to try thinking of excuses. Emma told us.'

'Emma told you?'

'She was working with James after you, remember?' Jeannette took hold of Tess's elbow and began to steer her along the street. 'When she came back to the flat last night she was only too eager to tell us that Tony had spirited you off for tea and sympathy.'

'Said she thought you were in a hurry to get a grip on him,' added Catherine, looking arch.

'Me in a hurry! The little – !' Tess broke off and walked on for a moment fast, scowling down at the pavement.

'I told you she was a prize bitch,' said Jeannette from behind her.

At this point they arrived at Tess's house and she was occupied with finding the keys, letting them in and showing them the way upstairs. Then it was time for Jeannette and Catherine to exclaim over her lovely flat. Tess explained modestly that she hadn't actually *earned* it, and she made them all a cup of tea.

They took their mugs out onto the little terrace carved from a small section of flat roof and sat in the sun, admiring the view over the Heath and the panorama of

London laid out below. 'Wow, this is the life,' said Catherine. 'What a place.'

'Tony's flat is lovely,' Tess said, and immediately wished she hadn't opened her mouth.

'Oh, Tess,' groaned Jeannette. 'What is it about him? Honestly, Tess, don't you think his ego is big enough already? You've fallen into his arms after less than a week of rehearsal! He's going to be so swollen-headed it's untrue!'

'And he's such a sexist,' said Catherine, scowling. 'I worked with him on a production last year, and – '

'Don't,' Tess said unhappily. 'Don't go on about him. He was nice to me after James said – ' She broke off abruptly and changed the subject. 'We have to practice,' she said firmly. 'I've only got till just after lunch. I have to see Julian at three for word-bashing.'

'Oh yes, Julian,' said Jeannette under her breath as she and Catherine followed Tess from the terrace. 'Now there's one it would be fun to go after.'

Tess only half heard this remark, and she didn't reply. She led the way into the living room. Julian had recorded a piano accompaniment to their trios on a cassette and she put it on now. 'Time to work,' she said.

They did work, hard, until hunger stopped them a little while after noon. Tess didn't have enough food in the fridge to feed all three of them, so they wandered out of the house to find a baguette somewhere in Hampstead.

A little coffee shop provided filled ciabatta rolls and cappucino. There was a free table on the pavement and they sat down to enjoy the sunshine. Jeannette and Catherine both looked at each other and then at Tess, who closed her eyes, knowing that more questions were on their way.

'Tess, don't get defensive,' began Jeannette. 'I just want to know what James said that upset you so much. Christ, it might be me and Catherine he decides to have a go at next. I know he can be a filthy-tempered git when the mood takes him, but what was it in particular?'

Tess took a long breath and let it out in a heavy sigh. 'Oh,' she said, 'it's just that he's absolutely obsessed with sex. That's all he thinks about.' It was harder than she expected to admit what James had said. The old sensation of fear, of inadequacy, came rushing back. 'And he was saying that I looked – that I was too nice to look sexy. That I looked like a typical English girl.'

Catherine looked equivocal. 'I wouldn't say you looked typically English,' she commented, 'but I know what he means.'

'He told me – ' tears were hovering on the edge of Tess's words. She fought them, swallowing hard. 'He told me to – to go out and screw someone. To understand Carmen better, you see? He wanted me just to find someone I fancied and do it.'

'So you went straight off and let Tony screw you,' said Jeannette callously. 'Is that really what James meant?'

'I didn't,' Tess protested, but as she spoke she knew that Jeannette was right.

Jeannette knew, too. 'Who took the initiative?' she demanded. 'Who started it?'

'Tony,' Tess admitted miserably.

'There you are, then,' said Jeannette, sitting back and folding her arms with a satisfied air.

'But – ' Tess began. Then she stopped and put her face in her hands. Had that fabulous sexual experience with Tony been for nothing? Had she learnt nothing?

'Tess,' Catherine said, quite gently, 'I know what James meant. Jeannette was right. He sees Carmen as sexually very aggressive. That's why you needed to take the initiative. Just letting a man have you might be fun, but it's not, ah, aggressive.'

'But,' Tess said, looking up with a hopeless air, 'what am I supposed to do? Go out and seduce someone?'

'Why not?' asked Jeannette bluntly.

Tess stared. 'I don't know how,' she said after a

60

moment. 'Or who! I mean, who on earth is around for me to seduce? Am I supposed to hang around outside a boys' school or something, like a dirty old woman?'

'Don't be daft,' said Catherine with a grin. 'There's an obvious candidate in the company.'

Jeannette laughed to herself, but Tess looked amazed. 'Who?' she asked suspiciously, after a moment's puzzled thought.

'Julian,' said Catherine simply.

Tess gasped with sudden understanding. She sat back in her chair, hugging her knees to her chest. Julian! He was young, not yet 22, and very handsome in a blond, floppy-haired, Brideshead sort of way. And he seemed very reserved, shy even, certainly not the sort to take advantage.

She would never in a million years have thought for herself of making a play for Julian. In particular she would not have dreamed of seducing one man the day after she had first made love with another. But the idea had a sort of mad appeal. Julian was so young, so callow, like a half-trained puppy. Irresistible!

She had been silent for a long time. Catherine glanced at Jeannette and smiled, then said softly, 'Like the idea, Tess?'

'Oh,' Tess shook herself back to the present. 'Well, I mean, perhaps this afternoon I could ask him round to the flat for a drink, and – '

'Hey, no, that's not what I had in mind,' Catherine interjected quickly. 'I don't mean have an affair with him, Tess. I mean fuck him. This afternoon, at rehearsal. No complications, no strings.'

'Fuck him?' Tess echoed, though her voice was barely audible. 'This afternoon? At rehearsal?' She shook her head slowly, drawing back into her chair. 'Oh no, Catherine. I couldn't. I couldn't.'

'Why not?' demanded Jeannette. 'He's cute enough. Wish I'd thought of it. I'll have him when you're finished, Tess.'

Tess still couldn't believe it. 'You mean just say to him, what about it? Then and there? In the rehearsal room?' She sounded hesitant, reluctant. And yet as she thought about it she felt a strange, warm tingling beginning in the pit of her stomach. There would be just the two of them, alone in the rehearsal room, nobody interrupting them, all the time in the world. It was like something out of a film, something that would happen to a real star. What would Julian do? How would he react? If she said, 'I want you to make love to me,' how would his face change?

Suddenly reality intruded on the fantasy. 'But,' she said, 'he probably doesn't even fancy me! He's never suggested he has.'

'He's too shy to speak a word to you,' laughed Jeannette. 'Listen, Tess, if you're prepared to give it a go, I guarantee we'll turn you into the most irresistible vamp that poor little preppie has ever seen.'

'He'll eat you up with a spoon,' added Catherine.

'Really?' Tess looked from one to the other. Excitement tingled between her shoulder blades and made the hairs on her arms stand up. She had never seduced anyone in her life. The idea frightened her and aroused her at the same time. 'Really?' she asked again, leaning forward a little.

'Really,' said Catherine. She lifted her cup and drained it. 'Come on,' she said. 'Let's get back to your place and get you ready.'

'I don't want to look like a tart,' Tess said anxiously. She was standing in her bedroom and Jeannette and Catherine were rooting through drawers and wardrobes, exclaiming over things, flinging them onto the bed or the floor for future reference.

'You won't,' Jeannette reassured her. 'Sexy, yes. A tart, no. Honestly, Tess, I don't think you possess a single garment that could be described as tarty.'

'I think we ought to start with this, don't you?' said Jeannette, holding up a black Wonderbra.

'Definitely,' said Jeannette. 'OK, Tess, strip off. Let's get started.'

Tess hesitated and pursed her lips. Then she began to unbutton Tony's shirt. It smelt of his body and hers. It was as if she was taking off her experience with him, freeing herself for something new.

'God,' Catherine said admiringly, 'you've got gorgeous tits, Tess. They'll knock poor little Julian for six.' She brought the Wonderbra over to where Tess stood naked and held it out to her. 'Gorgeous,' she said again, and with one hand reached out and touched Tess's right nipple, just fleetingly touched it. The little rose-coloured peak stiffened at once. Tess flinched and drew back, but Catherine just smiled at her, an innocent open smile, and turned away.

Jeannette and Catherine thought that ease of access was important. After the Wonderbra they handed Tess a pair of high-cut, flimsy black lace panties. It was too hot for stockings, so her legs stayed bare. Jeannette brought over a bottle of perfumed body lotion, Dune, and said, 'Rub your legs with this. Make them all silky and delicious.'

Tess obeyed. The lotion felt smooth and cool and it left the skin of her legs tingling slightly. She looked down at herself in the low-cut bra and skimpy panties and took a deep breath. She was dressing for sex, dressing for seduction, and that in itself was enough to turn her on.

'You don't want to look overdone,' said Catherine. 'How about this?' She held out a little fitted low-cut top made of cotton jersey in simple white. It fastened down the front with dozens of tiny, horn buttons. Tess took it and began to fasten the buttons from the top down.

'No,' suggested Jeannette, 'leave the top couple undone. So it looks as if more might follow?'

'But that almost shows the bra,' Tess said.

'Exactly,' said Jeannette. 'Look at that cleavage. He'll be helpless.'

'Got any short skirts?' asked Catherine.

Tess shook her head. 'I don't like them. Don't think my legs are up to them, if you want the truth.'

'This is the thing,' said Jeannette. It was a long, flared skirt in jade-green sandwashed silk, buttoned at the front and with slits in the side seams. 'This is fabulous, Tess. When did you get it?'

'Dan wanted me to buy it,' Tess admitted. 'I – I haven't actually worn it very often.'

'Wear it now,' said Jeannette, and Tess made a little face but put the skirt on. 'Perfect,' Jeannette said. 'He can see your legs, and you can unbutton the skirt to let him look at you.'

You can unbutton the skirt. She was going to offer herself to Julian. She imagined herself standing in the rehearsal room, leaning over slightly to unfasten button after button, slowly revealing her legs to the knee, to the thigh, dipping so that her full breasts were dangling before him, almost totally exposed. What would he do? Would he stare and blush and gasp? Run away? Seize her?

For a moment she closed her eyes. The flesh between her legs felt wet and warm. She imagined Julian gaping open-mouthed at her breasts, then imagined his eyes travelling down, down to the open front of her skirt, to where the negligible scrap of the panties encircled and caressed her tender mound of love. For a moment her brain just imagined that she would slip her hand down her body and gently draw aside the crotch of the panties, revealing the dark-red glossy fur and the pink folded flesh beneath them. Then she shook her head in protest at her own imagination and opened her eyes.

'Still with us?' asked Catherine, smiling. Tess's self-absorption was not lost on her. 'Good. What about these for shoes?'

Sandals, fairly high heeled, pretty but practical.

Nothing out of the way. Tess nodded gratefully and put them on.

'Make-up,' said Jeannette.

'Make-up?' Tess frowned unhappily. 'Jeannette, I don't wear make-up when I can avoid it. It's so bad for the skin, and I have to wear it on stage, and – '

'Oh, come on!' exclaimed Jeannette, whose own enormous eyes were ringed with dark kohl. 'Make an effort! Just a bit, come on.'

They frogmarched her to the bathroom and stood one at each shoulder while she put a little, dark-olive shadow on her heavy lids and thickened her bristly dark lashes with mascara. She resisted eyeliner and accepted a little neutral lipstick. Her pale skin was flushed, as if she had been running. She looked excited and eager.

'That's better,' said Catherine, looking at her face in the mirror. 'He won't have seen you dolled up before. Bound to have an effect.'

Tess's nerve was failing her. 'I can't do this,' she said. 'I don't know what to do.'

'Hush,' said Jeannette, putting her arm around Tess's shoulders. 'You'll cope. Imitate Lauren Bacall, or something. You know; *if you want me, just whistle*. Vamp him. And remember how it feels, and then Carmen will be able to do it too.'

'I tell you what,' said Catherine. 'Jeannette and I will wait for you here. Then when you get back you can tell us all about it.'

Tess went to find her bag with the score and the inevitable bottle of mineral water. When she had it over her shoulder and was ready at the door, Jeannette grinned and fished in her handbag and held out a couple of condoms. 'Here,' she said. 'You may need these!'

'Two?' squeaked Tess.

Jeannette shrugged. 'Maybe you'll get lucky.'

'We want a full report,' said Catherine. 'We'll be waiting.'

* * *

65

Tess emerged from the bowels of Covent Garden station, blinked at the sun and felt in her bag for her sunglasses. As always the station was surrounded by people waiting to meet their companions. She stood for a little while watching faces, wondering which of the girls were waiting to meet girlfriends, which were waiting for men, which of the men were gay. Turning her head, she saw herself reflected in the plate glass window of a fashion shop, and she narrowed her eyes thoughtfully.

I look attractive, she thought. Sexy. Somehow, as she watched her reflection, she did not feel that urge to smile. She lifted her head and put back her shoulders, watching her full breasts, thrust upwards by the Wonderbra, rising and falling with her breathing. Would Julian want to touch them? Or would he just ignore them?

That one negative thought was enough to eliminate all the impetus that had carried her through a half hour tube journey. She wrapped her arms around herself and shook her head feverishly. Seduce Julian? Forget it! She would just go and rehearse her notes and words, like a serious professional singer. She hitched her bag further up onto her shoulder and stalked away from the station and towards the rehearsal room.

Then, as she walked, she thought again. What would a serious professional singer do? A serious professional singer would do the research necessary to play the part well, as the director wanted. A method actor, she reflected, would not have any reservations about throwing herself into the role. Jeannette and Catherine were right. It wasn't enough just to let Tony take her under his wing, she had to try and put herself in a situation where she could take command.

Well and good. But how could she get up the nerve?

Ahead of her a pub stood on the corner, all engraved glass and dark wood. It looked a smart, trendy place. Tess stood on the pavement for a moment, looking into the pub's dark depths. Then she muttered, 'Dutch courage,' and walked in.

'Gin and tonic, please,' she told the barman, and fished her purse out of her bag. She looked searchingly at herself in the mirror behind the bar, then lifted the drink to her lips at once and drained half of it.

Tess rarely drank, and the alcohol delivered an immediate buzz. She rocked a little and blinked. When she looked at herself in the mirror again her eyes were very bright and there was a line of red along her cheeks. She muttered, 'Looking better already,' and drank the rest of the gin.

There was a movement at her elbow. She glanced around and saw a man standing next to her, smiling at her. He looked like a businessman, something citified in a dark, expensive suit and a florid tie. He said, 'Hi. Are you waiting for someone?'

For a moment Tess looked wonderingly into his face. He was older than her, forty perhaps, with a strong bone structure beginning to sink back into his flesh and dark, curling hair. After a second he broke eye contact and his lids flickered like a lizard's as he glanced quickly down to her breasts and then up again. His eyes narrowed slightly and he smiled.

He fancies me, Tess thought. He was not amazingly attractive or exciting, but just being approached filled her with a rush of confidence that sent the gin soaring around her bloodstream. She smiled back and tossed her head. Her hair ruffled, then settled on her neck. 'Sorry,' she said. 'I've got an appointment.'

Without waiting for his response she turned and left the bar. Her parting smile lingered on her lips. She knew that she was walking differently, with a studied poise and body-consciousness that drew glances from men as they passed her on the street. Every look, every turned head straightened her spine with a new belief in her own attractiveness. She ran up the stairs to the rehearsal room and pushed open the door without hesitation.

'Tess!' Julian got up from behind the piano, smiling at her. His face changed a little. 'Are you going out somewhere afterwards?'

'Going out?' She raised her brows. 'No. Why?'

'You look – ' Julian faltered, as if he were afraid of saying the wrong thing. 'You, er, you look as though you might be going on somewhere special. You look . . .' His voice tailed off. Tess smiled at him encouragingly, but he turned away from her and went to sit down behind the piano. His eyes fastened on the score. 'Well,' he said in a businesslike way, stretching out his arms in front of him and cracking his knuckles. 'Well, what would you like to work on?'

A really confident woman, Tess thought, would say, *you*. But she hadn't got that far yet. She came over to the piano, fished her score out of her bag and leant on the glossy surface of the lid. Her folded arms framed the dark line of her cleavage. She said, looking at the music, 'The Habanera to start with, I think.' She didn't want to look up in case Julian wasn't noticing her, but in the end she made herself lift her eyes.

What she saw reassured her immensely. Julian was looking at her breasts, his lips a little parted and his china-blue eyes dark with the dilation of his pupils. He seemed not to hear her for a moment. Then he pushed back the floppy mop of his blond hair with one hand and said with a start of embarrassment, 'Right, right. Fine. Are you OK with the words?'

'Let's try,' Tess suggested. Julian nodded, looking intently at his music. Then he began to play.

Normally Tess would have stood up to sing. Now she leant on the piano like a jazz singer, watching Julian's long, elegant fingers moving over the keys. He was very aristocratic, very public school, fine-boned and delicate-looking, with slightly tanned skin that was as smooth a boy's. There were slight hollows below his cheekbones and the bridge of his nose was narrow and sharp. Tess ran her tongue around her lips as her eyes passed over

Julian's face. I am going to have you, she thought to herself. The deliberate, intense physicality of the thought shivered in her shoulders and she shifted a little from one foot to the other, feeling as she moved the wetness between her legs, warm and ready.

Julian glanced up at her to signal that it was time for her to begin and suddenly his eyes fixed on hers. Instantly Tess knew what James had meant that she should achieve in the first scene. Their gazes locked, yes, with an almost audible sound. She missed her entry entirely and Julian stopped playing. In fact he stopped breathing. Tess smiled a little, then said very softly, 'Oops.'

'Oh, good grief,' Julian said, pulling his eyes from hers. He shook his head angrily. 'Let's try it again.' He scowled at the score and played the introduction a second time, and this time he did not look up.

Tess knew this aria, the first big aria for Carmen, very well. The translation they were using was new to her, but she liked it and it was not hard to learn. Carmen sang to tease and torment all the men who watched her. Now Tess sang for Julian alone, willing him to look up again from the music and notice her.

> *'If you want me, I don't want you,*
> *but if you don't want me I'll take you there.*
> *And if I set my heart on you, sweetheart,*
> *if I love you, you'd best beware!'*

They played it all the way through, and all the way through Julian kept his eyes firmly fixed to the music and to the keys. When they had finished he frowned and said, still not looking at her, 'That was fine, Tess, just great. One or two places I felt you didn't hold the notes to quite the right length. Benedetto is fussy about that sort of thing – '

It didn't suit Tess that he should try to continue to work. Without the drink she would probably have acquiesced, but now she was feeling contentious. She spoke straight over Julian, making him look up in surprise. 'What lovely hands you've got. Musicians' hands are so businesslike.'

'What?' Julian looked as though he hadn't understood her.

'Lovely hands,' she repeated, reaching down to lift his right hand from the keys. He flinched, but did not withdraw. 'How long your fingers are,' she breathed, examining the strong, white palm and the neat, short nails. The warm, silky feeling of her arousal began to extend from her loins to her breasts, stiffening her nipples beneath the tight cups of the bra. 'Sensitive, I bet. Are they sensitive?'

She looked up into his eyes. He was frowning, and he licked his lips quickly, like a nervous dog. There was silence. Then he said unsteadily, 'Tess, don't tease.'

'Tease?' Tess was really surprised. 'What makes you think I'm teasing?'

Julian hesitated, then said uncomfortably, 'Because you went home with Tony last night.'

Tess dropped his hand, startled and annoyed. 'Good God!' she exclaimed. 'Does the whole company know about this? How the hell did you know that, Julian?'

'I – ' Julian stammered. He looked uncertain and very young. For a moment he looked down at his hand as if he could still feel her touch. Then he muttered almost beneath his breath, 'Emma was here this morning, and she told me.'

'Emma again!' Tess was really angry that Emma was spreading gossip about her. The anger added to her determination and gave her unsuspected courage. Without another word she leant forward and caught Julian by his thick blond hair and put her lips on his.

Julian made a little sound as she thrust her tongue into his mouth. Surprise, certainly, but pleasant surprise or shock and revulsion? She didn't know and she didn't care. She shut her eyes and kissed him as if nothing else in the world existed. For a few seconds he didn't respond. Then he moaned and opened his mouth wider beneath her searching lips and his tongue tentatively touched hers. He did not attempt to hold her. Tess opened her eyes for a moment and saw his hands hanging in mid air, knotted into tight fists, squeezing until the bony knuckles were white with pressure.

She sensed that he was about to try to pull away from her. This was not part of the plan. She put her right hand on his thigh, ran it upwards and let out a little gasp of delight as she found the outline of his cock, already thick and swollen. She pressed her fingers down on it and felt it pulse with answering life. Julian moaned again into her open mouth.

Tess drew back a little and looked into his face. He sat very still and stared at her, pale to his lips, trembling slightly. His light-blue eyes with their long fringe of golden lashes were dark with arousal. Tess's diaphragm flinched and shuddered with her uneven breathing. She had become absorbed in her character, and right now she wanted Julian desperately. She wanted to see that innocent, boy's face change as he felt himself penetrate her. His cock felt splendid, long and rigid with eagerness, and she wanted to feel it inside her.

His lips moved. In a moment he would say something. That wasn't part of the plan either, and Tess tossed back her hair and spoke before he could. 'Well, Julian, what about it?'

Julian's thick blond hair stirred as he shook his head very slightly. He didn't look frightened exactly, more disbelieving. His golden brows drew down into a knot and he whispered, 'What, here?'

'Here,' Tess confirmed, nodding her head. 'Now.'

'But – ' Julian's eyes slid to the door. It was shut. 'But anyone could walk in.'

Tess shrugged, but she stepped back from him, taking her hand from the bulge of his cock, and walked swiftly to the door. There was no key, but there was an old, rusty bolt at the bottom. She forced it into the socket, smiling at the phallic symbolism of the action. She smiled at Julian, who was still sitting motionless on the piano stool, staring at her like a rabbit in the headlights. She went to her bag, found one of the condoms and tucked it into the front of her bra. Then she straightened.

'Now,' she said, 'we won't be disturbed.' She took a step towards Julian, then stooped and unfastened the bottom button of her skirt. Another step, another button. By the time she was standing within his reach the buttons were undone more than half way up, and Tess was shaking from head to foot with excitement. Why not do what she had imagined? Why not? She let the skirt fall open, disclosing the tender white flesh of her inner thigh, and then unfastened it further to show her pubis, barely covered by the delicate black lace of the panties.

Julian was gazing, dry-mouthed and wide-eyed. He was taking long, deep breaths, his slender shoulders lifting and falling. Tess hesitated, her nerve faltering for a moment. Then she put her hand to her panties and pulled them aside, revealing the soft, dark-red fur and the beginning of the moist, pink lips. Julian breathed in quickly as if someone had slapped him. The tension between them was almost tangible. Tess couldn't bear the silence. She said softly, 'Julian, kiss me.'

He took her more literally than she expected. With a little cry, of relief or desire, she didn't know, Julian flung himself from the piano stool and fell to his knees before her. He wrapped his arms around her thighs. Her buttocks fitted snugly into the crook of his elbows and his hands spread across her back. Without a word he pressed his face between her legs and licked her, whimpering as he dragged his tongue lovingly over her trembling flesh.

'Oh God,' Tess exclaimed. The rush of pleasure was so complete that she staggered and almost fell. She caught at Julian's shoulders to steady herself and thrust her hips up towards his face, moaning with ecstasy, offering her sex to his caresses. His long, clever tongue wormed its way deeper through her folds, encircling her clitoris, teasing it, quivering against it. She cried out again and put her hands in his hair, jerking against his mouth almost as if he were a woman and she were a man. Her head fell back and she stared blindly at the ceiling as the wonderful sensations swelled and coiled and mounted within her, drawing her up, up towards the distant peak of climax. Julian held her tightly, supporting her, and as her movements became more urgent he responded, pressing directly against the stiff engorged bud and flickering his tongue against it like a snake's. Tess knotted her hands in his soft hair and arched her back and gave herself up completely to pleasure, crying out as she attained her peak.

As she recovered she held him there, his face buried against her mound. His breath stirred against her moist flesh and made her shiver with renewed desire. He was on his knees before her, like a prisoner or a slave before a powerful queen, and it thrilled her. When at last she let him go he sat back, looking up at her, his mouth and face slick with her juices, and said nothing.

'Now,' she said, her voice husky, 'Julian, I want you to fuck me.'

He frowned. 'I – I don't have a . . .'

A smile twitched at the corners of Tess's lips. '*Voilà*,' she said, drawing out the little packet from her cleavage. Julian gave a nervous, helpless laugh and got to his feet. He stood for a moment irresolutely, as if uncertain of what to do next, and with a delicious sense of command Tess came to him and reached up to draw down his lips to hers.

His mouth tasted of her sex. She murmured with satisfaction and licked his face, cleaning her slippery musk from his skin. As she washed him like a cat she unfastened his shirt and felt inside for the warm smoothness of his chest. His skin was pale biscuit-gold and soft as thistledown. A pulse was beating in his neck, strong and fast. He breathed quickly and shut his eyes and his big, long-fingered hands ran down her neck, inside the soft fabric of her top, down towards the swell of her breasts. She gasped and pushed herself against him, wanting to feel him touching her nipples. For a moment he tried to unfasten some of the buttons, but they were small and his hands were shaking. He gave a stifled curse of frustration and pushed the top from her shoulder, baring her white skin and the black strap of the bra. She thrust herself towards him and he kissed her neck, her collar bone, her cleavage, and then at last he put his big delicate hand on her breast and lifted it from the cup of the bra. His fingers brushed over the stiff, swollen nipple, stroked at it, squeezed it.

She wanted to feel him inside her. The warm clutching fists of orgasm were still clenching in her belly, making her impatient to be filled. As he caressed her breast she felt for the buttons on his chinos, deftly unfastened them. The zip whined and Julian jerked with shock as she thrust her hand inside.

Boxer shorts, crisp and crumpled. She didn't bother to feel for the fly, just shoved her hand inside the elastic. His body was warm, warm, like new bread, and instantly her fingers found and fastened upon his erect penis. It was long and thicker than she had expected and slightly, charmingly curved. Julian set his teeth and gasped as she wrapped her hand around the hot, smooth column of flesh and stroked downwards, felt between his legs, probed the taut updrawn skin of his balls, weighed them, then returned to his cock. It twitched and jolted beneath her fingers. She gently drew it out of its prison of cotton and looked down, smiling dry-mouthed as she saw its swollen, scarlet head, already dewed with eagerness. It would have been nice to suck it, but her body demanded satisfaction, instantly. She pulled the condom out of her bra and tore the wrapping with her teeth.

He was ready, trembling as he looked down into her face. She realised with a delightful shiver that he was waiting, waiting for her to tell him what to do. The floor? Standing up, against a wall? Neither appealed. She put her hand on the glossy surface of the Steinway and smiled. 'Julian,' she said, 'on the piano.'

'Oh, Christ almighty,' Julian breathed. But he put his hands quickly around her waist and boosted her up to sit on the shiny black lid, then hooked the piano stool with his foot and caught it towards him to kneel on. The strings of the piano echoed faintly as Tess's weight shifted. As Julian came towards her with his cock sticking out of his open fly she eased off her panties and then opened her legs to him, slowly, deliberately. Her top was tugged off, showing one breast, and her skirt was crumpled beneath her bare buttocks. She looked like a slut and felt like Cleopatra.

He knelt before her and lowered his head to worship her breast with his mouth. For a moment she permitted it. The ministrations of his tongue, circling her nipple, flickering over it, made her set her teeth and gasp with renewed pleasure. But it was not what she wanted. She spread her thighs wide and caught hold of Julian by the shoulders and the buttocks and pulled him towards her. When she felt the heat of his cock pressing against the lips of her sex she reached down and guided him into her.

He slid up inside her in one smooth motion. She grunted and wrapped her legs over his buttocks, pulling him close. Her naked breast pressed against the bare skin of his chest. She clung to his arms, holding him to her, and looked up into his rapt, astonished face. His testicles nestled warmly against the crease of her arse. He stood very still, shuddering, and whispered again, 'Oh Christ.'

'Julian,' she hissed, low and determined. 'Julian, come on. Do it.' She tilted her pelvis, drawing away from him so that he slipped almost entirely out of her. The movement of his long smooth cock through her flesh made

75

her snarl with pleasure. 'Come on,' she repeated. 'Julian, fuck me.'

He stared at her for a moment almost as if he were angry. His lips were parted and dry with his quick breathing and they drew slowly back, showing his teeth like a dog's. His chest lifted and fell, squeezing her breasts into fullness and then letting them sink again. His big hands slid down her back, fumbled under her skirt, found her naked buttocks and clutched them. He clenched his teeth and thrust.

'Oh yes,' Tess gasped as he forced his cock deep inside her, over and over again. 'Oh, that's so good. Oh yes, yes.' She seized him by the hair and kissed him, thrusting her tongue into his mouth as he thrust himself into her sex. They were both grunting, making low wordless sounds as he took her, as he gave her what she wanted, the simple animal pleasure of his rigid penis sliding deeply into her and withdrawing only to penetrate her again.

Tess jerked her hips towards him, wanting to take him as deeply within her as she could. The remorseless, driving rhythm built up in her loins and her brain. She arched her back, leaning away from him, lying back on the cold slippery surface of the piano and writhing as he shafted her with all his strength. 'Don't stop,' she moaned. She knew she was coming. Julian cried out and leant forward over her, his sweaty hands slipping as he held himself up, and his cock drove ever deeper into her. She tilted back her head and closed her eyes and put her hands on her breasts. She didn't care about him, she didn't give a damn, he was nothing but a moving, thrusting penis, a dildo with a brain, the necessary instrument of her selfish pleasure. She pinched her nipples hard and her climax rose up within her like a dolphin swimming out of the depths towards the bright sunlight, its whole body one great muscle, scything upwards through the chill water with strong beats of its pulsing flukes until suddenly it breaks the surface and

76

arches free of its prison, leaping for an infinite moment into the glittering, dancing air, surrounded by fountains of spray and shards of light.

Julian gave an anguished, ecstatic cry and twisted over her. Vaguely, through the sparkling aftermath of her climax, she felt his penis pulsing deep within her. She lay spread-eagled on the piano, her breasts heaving as her breathing slowed, her eyes closed, utterly pleasured and completely without shame.

Presently she sat up and pulled herself free of him. He gasped and sank down on the piano stool, fumbling at his crotch and hanging his head. He was still panting and the back of his shirt was damp with sweat. He rubbed one long hand over his face and looked up at her.

She shook back her hair. Beneath its heavy weight on the back of her neck her skin was slick and hot. She ruffled it with her fingers and then slipped down from the piano to the floor, smoothing her skirt and rebuttoning it. Her panties were some distance away. She went and picked them up, smiled ruefully at them and in the end stuffed them into her bag,

'Tess,' Julian said huskily. She turned to look at him. 'Tess, could we – would you – would you like to come out with me? Or come home?'

For a moment she didn't say anything. She was wondering what to say, how to refuse him. Then the answer came to her. She laughed and used Carmen's own words, singing them mockingly to Julian's anxious face. *'Maybe not at all, tomorrow maybe. But one thing's for sure – not today!'*

'But – ' Julian began.

She came over to him and kissed him quickly on the lips. 'You were wonderful,' she said, 'but that's it, Julian, darling. And if you breathe a word of it to anyone in the company, I'll shut your fingers in the piano lid.'

He flinched, drawing his hands protectively into his lap. He looked so distressed that Tess felt a twinge of remorse. She knew Carmen wouldn't, but she was still a long way from understanding her character. She touched Julian's face gently and asked, 'Isn't once better than never?'

He looked away. Tess straightened and stretched. 'God, I feel great,' she said. 'I could take on the world. Come on, Julian, we've got work to do. Let your fingers do the walking.'

Act Two, Scene Two

That afternoon

*A*s Tess climbed the stairs to her flat the door opened, revealing Catherine's eager face. 'Well?' she demanded.

Tess reached the top landing and punched the air in the classic victory gesture. 'Mission accomplished!'

'Tess, that's brilliant.' Catherine reached out and took her by the arm, drawing her inside the flat. 'You know, I could have guessed just by looking at you. You're all flushed and that lovely skirt is a wreck.'

'I haven't got any knickers on, either,' Tess giggled.

'What?' shrieked Catherine. 'And you've come all the way back on the tube like that?'

'I don't believe it myself,' Tess said, shaking her head and laughing at the same time. 'Hey, this is little me! The Northern line with no knickers!' She extended her arms and whirled joyfully around. 'This demands a celebration. Come on, let's have a drink.' She went through towards the kitchen, asking, 'Where's Jeannette?'

'Gone to get some stuff in for dinner. Your cupboards are bare. She should be back soon.'

'Three glasses, then.' Tess hurried into the kitchen and opened the fridge. At the back was the bottle of champagne that she had failed to open, weeks ago, when Dan had robbed her of her triumph. 'Look,' she said, 'here's some champagne. Shall we? There's no rehearsal tomorrow.'

'Champagne!' Catherine looked surprised. 'Do you always keep bubbly in your fridge?'

'It was going to be to celebrate getting the part,' said Tess, 'but Dan was a miserable bastard and he put me off. So I think we should drink it now. I'm as proud of what I did this afternoon as I am of playing Carmen, and that's the truth.'

'I'm always game for champagne.'

They found glasses and popped the cork with shrieks and giggles. Then they carried the glasses through to the living room. Tess kicked off her sandals and flung herself onto the sofa and Catherine sat beside her.

'Now then, Tess.' Catherine's face revealed avid curiosity. 'Tell me all about it. Don't miss anything.'

Tess took a deep draught of the champagne and frowned for a moment into her glass. Then she said, 'I nearly bottled out. Very nearly. If I hadn't gone into a pub and bought myself a gin I would have done. But when I actually tried it, it – it was easy.'

'He fell for it. For you.'

'Hook, line and sinker. Men are real animals, aren't they? I mean, even a nice young sensitive boy like Julian is just an animal under the surface. He got a hard on, I swear it, he got a hard on just looking at my breasts.'

'That's understandable,' said Catherine gently. 'They are pretty much on the counter in that bra, Tess.' She leant forward a little. 'But was he good?'

'Good? Oh . . .' Tess lay back against the cushions and drank again. 'Yes,' she said, in a far away voice. 'Yes, he was good. He used his mouth on me, and it made me come. He was kneeling in front of me, like an acolyte, and I was holding his head right against me and he licked and licked at me until I came. It was amazing. Wonderful.'

The bubbles of the champagne seemed to fizz and sparkle in her brain, gently eroding her inhibitions. She described what had happened in a disjointed, random way, a collection of images and sensations. Julian's long fingers squeezing her breast, clutching her buttocks. His cock penetrating her completely on that first unbelievable thrust. His face, transfigured with shock and ecstasy. Sweat beading on his forehead and falling from his narrow nose to land on her breasts. Her sense of power, of manipulation, and the overwhelming response it had triggered in her.

'It was like – like masturbating with a real person. Selfish. Fabulous.' She did not speak for some time, just lay with her head tilted onto the back of the sofa looking up at the ceiling. Sunlight lay across it, turning the white paint to primrose. At last she realised that Catherine had said nothing for some time. She lifted her head to look.

Catherine had put down her glass and was lying with her head resting on her left arm. Her dark eyes were fixed on Tess's face and her full lips were slack with pleasure. Her right hand was between her legs, beneath her skirt, moving. When she saw Tess look at her she smiled dreamily and said, 'Don't stop.'

'But, I'd finished,' Tess said. Her eyes travelled down to watch Catherine's moving hand. She was fascinated and horrified at the same time. Catherine's fingers moved again between her parted thighs and she sighed, a long breathy sigh, a sigh of pleasure. Tess knew the sound well. She made it herself when she masturbated, alone in bed at night, sending herself to sleep with her fingers and her fantasies. The sound itself was a powerful erotic stimulant.

Tess hesitated, irresolute. The anxiety that had made her refuse Jeannette all those years ago was still there, but working against it was the tingling elevation of the champagne and the warm delicious echoes of her earlier orgasms. Her body heard the sound of Catherine's pleasure and demanded further pleasure for itself. If it were on offer.

81

Tess said after a long moment, 'Catherine.'

Catherine's opulent hips were beginning to move in the slow, swelling wave that meant that she had penetrated herself with her fingers. Her tongue showed between her parted lips. She smiled at Tess very slowly and murmured, 'Tess. You turned me on so much.' Her hand moved again and she made another sound and closed her eyes and quickly licked her dry lips. Tess shivered with sudden, direct wanting. The urge to touch herself was almost irresistible.

Catherine's eyes opened again, dark and languid. She said very softly, 'Do you want to make love?'

There was a long pause. Tess's belly and breasts were tight with tension and a spasm of lust clenched in her sex. She didn't know what she wanted. After a moment, resorting to humour as she often did to try to extricate herself from awkward situations, she said jerkily, 'I don't think that was on James's suggestion list.'

Catherine drew her hand out from between her legs. Her lips curved in a warm sensual smile. 'Oh, it is,' she said softly. 'In fact Jeannette and I discussed it with him yesterday. He would be very happy for us to suggest that Carmen and Frasquita and Mercedes are more than just good friends.'

'Seriously?' Tess breathed, hardly daring to move.

'Truly.'

Tess swallowed. She was sure that she could smell the scent of Catherine's arousal. It knotted her stomach with desire and the urge to discover the unknown. What would it be like to love another woman? She looked at Catherine and saw her still smiling, not pressuring her. No seduction: her decision. She put down her glass of champagne beside Catherine's with a definitive clink.

'Yes,' she said. 'Catherine. Yes.'

'Oh, Tess.' Catherine reached out for her. Tess moved hesitantly into her arms, waiting for the shock of that first kiss. Their lips met and pressed together and within their open mouths their tongues touched, exploring first

82

gently, then deeply. Catherine's lips were full and incredibly soft, like satin, like the infinite feathery velvetiness of an erect cock. Her tongue was thick and short and mobile. As they kissed she put her fingers to the little buttons that fastened Tess's top and began to undo them, one after the other, quick and deft. Tess shivered with anticipation. She knew what she would have wanted if she had been Catherine and so she did it. She put her hand on Catherine's bare calf and ran it up under her dress, over the cool fullness of her smooth thighs to where her moist pubis bulged against the restraining cotton of her knickers. The fabric was already damp with need. Catherine whimpered as Tess touched her, but did not stop unfastening the blouse. Tess remembered the times that a man had put his hand inside her knickers, how sometimes they were rough and demanding and made her jump, and with infinite delicacy she insinuated herself and slid her fingers through the crisp curls of Catherine's luxurious pubic hair to the swollen wet lips of her sex.

'Ah,' Catherine moaned into her mouth. Tess explored gently, parting the soft moist labia, finding the open, grasping tunnel and slipping one finger deep into it. Catherine groaned and her soft body tautened. The sensation of giving her pleasure was incredible, so powerfully erotic that Tess thought she would come herself on the spot. She slid another finger in beside the first and with her thumb gently caressed the stiff stem of Catherine's clitoris.

'Oh God,' Catherine cried out. 'Tess.' Her hips began to undulate, lifting towards Tess's probing hand. Tess found the rhythm and began to move her fingers in and out, in and out, shutting her eyes tightly and listening with every ounce of her attention to Catherine's trembling cries. She could feel the orgasm hovering in Catherine's limbs as if it were her own. She knew instinctively what to do, where to touch, when to thrust deep, when to withdraw and tease the quivering, swollen bud of pleasure until Catherine's body stiffened and became rigid as her sex clamped and shook around Tess's plunging fingers.

She waited some time and then very, very gently withdrew her hand. Catherine shivered and moaned, then opened her eyes. 'Oh, Tess,' she said, 'you star. That was wonderful.'

Tess shifted uncomfortably. She wanted to feel Catherine's mouth on her, loving her, giving her pleasure, but she didn't know how to ask. Instead she finished unfastening the buttons on her top and pulled it off, then reached round behind her back to unfasten the bra.

'Oh, you have gorgeous tits,' Catherine breathed. She leant forward and kissed Tess's left nipple, first very gently, then harder and harder. She drew the stiff peak into her mouth and sucked on it until pleasure became pain, but such a sharp sweet pain that Tess did not want it to stop. She cried out sharply and Catherine drew back. Tess looked down and saw that her nipple was incredibly swollen, much larger than its usual size even when erect. She reached up hesitantly and touched it and flinched with the strength of sensation.

Catherine smiled at her and stripped off her clothes, revealing a firm, full body with opulent flanks and high breasts, like a Renoir nude. Then she turned her attention to Tess's other breast and as she suckled and lapped at the stiffening nipple her fingers continued to torment the left pap, flickering against the engorged point, keeping it unbearably stimulated. Tess moaned and writhed. When Catherine drew back and began to unfasten her skirt and take it off she flung up her arms in wanton abandon, longing for further pleasure.

'No knickers,' Catherine whispered smiling as she set her lips to the very gentle swell of Tess's belly. 'No knickers on the tube. Tess, you slut. You whore.'

Tess was not insulted. She arched upwards, parting her thighs and feeling the air cool on her slippery sex.

'Just getting into the part,' she said. 'Understanding my character. Catherine, Catherine, oh God.'

Catherine kissed her belly, her hipbone. She kneaded with her fingers at the tender skin of Tess's inner thighs and it fluttered in response. Tess let her head fall back and moaned with helpless longing as Catherine teased her, brushing her lips against the hollows of her loins, twisting her tongue playfully into the dark-red curls of her pubic hair and tugging at it, pursing her lips and blowing. It was torture, but blissful torture because Tess was certain that pleasure would follow it.

It did, as day follows night. Catherine drew back, waited an infinite moment and then leant forward and wrapped her mouth around the warm silken pouch of Tess's sex. Her lips and tongue were cool and firm. She thrust her tongue deep into the trembling hollow of Tess's vagina and quivered it like a butterfly's wing, titillating the outer lips until Tess's body heaved and she sighed with ecstasy. Then she began to lap gently, diligently, persistently at Tess's clitoris, teasing it into a swollen turgid peak and then tormenting it, soothing it, bathing it with her tongue and lips. Her hands left Tess's white flanks and crept up her body to find her breasts. As Catherine licked and licked at Tess's sex her fingers kneaded and squeezed her breasts, found the hard nipples and pulled at them.

Tess lay spread-eagled and open to her caresses, oblivious to everything except the wonderful sensations that were filling her. She felt an extraordinary sense of freedom. She knew she would come, she knew that Catherine was skilled and that as a woman she would understand and not settle for anything less than perfect pleasure. And then, and then, they could lie in each other's arms for a moment and then do it again, again, again, until they were exhausted and slick with sweat, drowned in sensual delight, their eyelids heavy with the weight of repeated orgasm.

And yet as she lay there, her clitoris flaming beneath

Catherine's tender caresses and her heaving breasts swollen with desire, the image that came to Tess's mind was of a man. A faceless man, a beautiful man, tall and muscular, coming to her in the night in the gloom and taking her. He came to her room and drew back the covers from her bed with one strong tug, leaving her on the sheets writhing as naked and helpless as a creature fresh from the womb. Before she could rise he flung himself on her and pinned her down, holding her wrists above her head and lowering his hard heavy body onto her. He forced his knee between her flinching thighs and drove them apart and she felt the hot glossy head of his cock between her legs, massive and smooth as marble. She tried to move beneath him and moaned in delirious assent and he laughed and rolled onto his side and pushed her head down, down to his crotch, and his strong hands were in her hair and he pulled back her head until her mouth opened and then thrust his cock into her mouth so hard that she thought she would choke. Then he used her mouth, coldly, violently, taking her with brutal force, grunting as he thrust the thick shaft between her lips so hard that he bruised them. His taut testicles brushed against her chin, cool hairy globes throbbing with the potential of his seed. He gasped and began to clench his fists in her hair and as Catherine drew her clitoris into her mouth and sucked at it and her orgasm rose spinning inside her Tess imagined this faceless man's massive cock spurting into her throat, jerking and surging with the power of his ejaculation, drowning her with his come.

She lay very still, shuddering, her eyes closed. White and red sparks danced behind her eyelids. A hand ran over her shoulders and onto her breasts. It stroked and weighed and fondled, then moved further down. A quick harsh voice said, 'Tess, I should be as jealous as hell.'

Tess's eyes flew open. Jeannette was kneeling on the sofa beside her, naked, legs spread wide, her long black limbs glistening. Her body was like an athlete's, slender and muscled, with breasts shallow as saucers tipped with long, cornelian nipples. The fur on her pubic mound was short and scanty and the pink sexual flesh between her legs glowed like a beacon. She had one hand on Tess's abdomen and the other in Catherine's hair. Tess stared upwards, speechless, and Jeannette smiled slowly. Her teeth were very white. 'Mind you,' she said, 'Catherine's good, isn't she? She had you so far away you didn't even hear me come in.'

Catherine smiled a creamy, cat-like smile of pride and satisfaction. She said, 'I don't think Tess knows that we had, er, become quite so close.'

'She knows now,' said Jeannette.

Tess was still half absorbed in her fantasy. Jeannette's sudden presence was surprising, but not threatening. She was too deep in erotic overload to feel fear now. She was filled with the urge to service, to subsume herself to someone else's pleasure. With a little whimper of submission she reached out and caught hold of Jeannette's tight buttocks and pulled at her. Jeannette quickly straddled her and pushed her hips towards her face and Tess obediently lowered her head and extended her tongue to lap. Jeannette's body perfume was intense, subtle and deep, and her sex was already wet and glistening with desire. Tess knew she would taste delicious, and she delicately and with relish slithered her tongue deep into the luxurious folds of flesh, remembering what Catherine had done to her and doing her best to do the same to Jeannette. At one stage she glanced up and saw that Catherine had got to her feet and was standing behind Jeannette with her hands beneath the slender black arms, cupping her shallow breasts, her long dark nipples tightly trapped between her fingers. Jeannette's head was turned towards Catherine and they were kissing, tongues twisting in their open mouths as Jeannette sighed and whimpered with the pleasure of what Tess was doing to her. The contrast of white and black flesh was startling and beautiful. Tess watched for a moment in rapture, then slowly closed her eyes and concentrated on the simple, delectable task of taking Jeannette to orgasm.

Jeannette climaxed with a desperate cry and subsided slowly onto the sofa between Catherine and Tess, her long limbs stretched out in delicious, abandoned weariness. She was breathing in deep, long gasps, her breasts rising and falling. 'Ah,' she said at last, 'That was wonderful, Tess.' She stroked her slender dark fingers down Tess's face, smiling with pleasure and affection. Then she turned her head. The muscles flowed on her neck as beautifully as a young boy's. To Catherine she said, 'I don't know what you did, Cath, but it must have been something right. I did my damnedest to get Tess into bed last time we met, and I didn't manage it.'

'Ah well,' said Catherine, 'perhaps she hadn't just successfully seduced a 22-year-old répétiteur.'

'That's true,' Jeannette admitted. She leant forward and poured herself a glass of champagne. 'And you've polished off half the bottle,' she commented, holding it up.

'What's for dinner?' Catherine asked, her eyes bright.

'All you think about is food. Lots of nice things. How about taking it to bed?' Jeannette suggested. 'Tess, what do you think?'

Tess stretched luxuriously. 'I'm not really hungry yet,' she said. Then she added shyly, 'But I don't mind going to bed, if – if you think we'd all fit.'

It was a slight squeeze, but they all fitted. They lay in a heap, Jeannette's dark limbs elegantly intertwined with Catherine and Tess's pale ones, and drank what was left of the champagne. It made them cheerful and giggly. Tess felt very strange. The combination of the relaxed friendliness of a girls' night out and the potential for almost infinite sensual discovery was a potent one, and it was new to her. In her experience sex hadn't really gone hand in hand with straightforward companionship, she had always been a sort of junior partner in the relationship. Jeannette questioned her about Julian and she told the story all over again, and when she had finished added cautiously, 'Jeannette, you said you wanted him when I had finished with him. You should – I mean – I mean, go ahead, if you want to.'

Jeannette smiled archly and shook her head so that the bright beads tipping her hair clashed together. 'What d'you think, Cath?' she asked languidly. 'Should we get him back to our place, just the two of us, and blow his tiny mind?'

Catherine shrugged. 'If you like. I like my men a bit more grown up.'

'Well,' said Jeannette, wrinkling her nose, 'let's face it, the chances of us managing to get him on our own in the flat are pretty small. That Emma's always hanging around like the spectre at the feast, looking disapproving whenever we have a good time.'

Tess frowned a little. 'Does she – ' she hesitated. 'Does she know? About you and Catherine?'

Catherine laughed. 'She'd have to be deaf and blind not to know,' she said. 'We've been sharing a bed for a week. Poor little maidenly Emma doesn't know where to put herself.'

'Doesn't know where to put herself? Don't make me laugh.' Jeannette put back her shoulders and stroked her fingers down over the long, taut tips of her breasts. 'She's outside our room every night with her ear to the keyhole listening. She's like all bloody prudes, absolutely fascinated by everything everybody else gets up to.'

'Is she really a prude?' asked Tess, absolutely fascinated herself.

'Certainly is.' Catherine reached over to Jeannette and began to caress her breasts. 'One hundred per cent, gilt-edged virgo intacta.'

'No wonder Leo's so taken with her,' Tess said, feeling a rather melancholy regret for the loss of her own innocence, though it was Leo himself who had taken it.

'You said,' commented Jeannette, sighing as she offered her long nipples to Catherine's enquiring fingers, 'you said he liked virgins. Well, I wish him luck with this one, but honestly I don't think he'll get anywhere. She's far too fond of her own self-image to let him tarnish it by taking her cherry.'

Tess drew down her brows, thinking. Catherine smiled and kissed Jeannette's shoulder, then said, 'James has really got himself a cast and a half, hasn't he? A tenor who thinks he's a reincarnation of Don Juan, a baritone who can't wait to deflower the soprano, a now-not-quite-so-innocent young répétiteur, a couple of second sopranos enjoying themselves amusing each other, and a mixed up mezzo just bouncing around between them all.'

'Oh,' said Jeannette, 'and don't forget the director's pretty assistant.'

'Oh, Adam,' simpered Catherine, pulling back her thick dark hair in mockery of Adam's ponytail. She mimicked his aristocratic voice. '"You'll all be expert by the time I've finished with you."'

'All be expert!' snorted Jeannette. 'All Adam knows about is how to take James's cock up his tight little arse.'

'Oh, Jeannette,' Tess exclaimed. She was trying to seem cool and sophisticated, but this was all too much. 'Do you really think so? I mean, do you think they actually *do* anything?'

'Think it? Tess, sweetie, I know it,' said Jeannette archly. 'Didn't you hear about the time I caught them at it?'

'Never mind her,' said Catherine with interest, 'I didn't hear about it, either. Come on, dish the dirt.' She sat up and snuggled closer to Jeannette, looking eagerly up into her eyes.

Jeannette smiled down at Catherine and Tess like a story-teller waiting to begin. 'Well, all right,' she said, 'here goes. It was a couple of years ago, when James was doing a sort of studio *Porgy and Bess* up at Opera North.

An all black production, apart from James and Adam of course. I was singing Clara, which means I sang "Summertime". The high spot of my career to date. Anyway, James was with Adam then, too, I think they'd not long met, and they took a place together out in the country, which is a bit shocking in Leeds! And I went out there one day to do some checking on something in the score, I can't remember exactly what now. It was a gorgeous day, the middle of July, and when I rang at the door of the house there was no reply.'

'A house?' Catherine sounded surprised. 'He was living it up, then.'

'Oh, I think it belonged to a friend of his. It wasn't a huge house, but it had a big garden and it was all on its own, no other houses nearby at all. Anyway, I rang the bell a few times and nobody came. I was a bit pissed off, because I'd borrowed a car and everything, so I thought I'd just poke about and see if there was someone in the garden. I went round the back and found it was like something out of a film, a fabulous garden, with a fountain and a little stream and drifts of flowers everywhere. The back door of the house was open and I went in and called a bit, but nobody answered.'

'And it's not as if they wouldn't hear you,' joked Catherine. 'With your hog-calling voice.'

'Gosh, Catherine, what I love about you is that you're so sweet and supportive,' said Jeannette, tugging Catherine's thick brown hair sharply. Catherine yelped and grinned. 'Do you want to hear this story or don't you?'

'Please go on,' Tess begged. She was really interested. 'Please.'

'Well, then, just for you, Tess,' said Jeannette. She turned her shoulder to Catherine in exaggerated annoyance and leant forward, setting her lips to Tess's left nipple. A quicksilver jolt of pleasure arrowed through Tess, making her shoulders tense and her heart thump. She closed her eyes and lifted her shoulders, offering her breasts to Jeannette's mouth. For a moment there was a

91

delicate silence. Then Jeannette drew away and lay back on the bed, stretching her lean arms above her head. 'I wandered around the house for a while,' she went on, 'but I couldn't find anyone. It was obvious they were living together, though. Only one of the beds was made up. Well, I went back out into the garden and began to look for them there.'

'Did you call out?' asked Tess.

'Not in the garden. It was such a lovely afternoon, I didn't want to shout the place down and spoil it. So I walked down the lawn and into a sort of shrubbery at the bottom, all big rhododendron bushes and wild roses and stuff. It was lovely. The stream ran down through it over little rocks, you can imagine the pretty sound it made. Then I heard them.'

Tess breathed faster and swallowed. 'What?' she asked, unable to conceal her eagerness. 'What were they saying? What was happening?'

'No words,' Jeannette said. Her voice had become soft and her eyes were unfocused as she plumbed her memory. Tess was pressed close to her on one side and Catherine on the other, both of them looking up into her face. 'There weren't exactly any words, not then. Just murmurs, you know, little lovey dovey noises. So I crept closer, hiding behind bushes.' A quick, wicked grin lit up her face. 'There's an advantage to being black, if you like. I fade into shadows a lot easier than a blonde would. It wasn't long before I saw them. They were lying in the sun on a little bit of soft grass next to the stream, snogging like a pair of kids, both of them absolutely starkers. Their clothes were all in a heap on the ground.'

'Wow,' said Catherine. 'What sort of a body has James got?'

'Pretty good for his age. Quite hard, really. And a big cock. And Adam, well, he's like a wet dream if you like them thin. All bones and muscles, and a stiffy like a milk bottle. If you ask me, gay guys are a lot more hung up about big cocks than women are. They live cock-centric lives.'

'How big is Adam's?' demanded Catherine. Tess shrank down into Jeannette's side, thrilled and shocked at the same time.

'Christ, do you think I had a ruler? It looked like a double handful, anyway. And really fat. Honestly, if he wanted to have me, I'd say yes. I've always wanted to feel a really big one, just to see if it does make any difference. But I didn't get to see it for that long, because I'd only been standing there for a minute when they sort of swung together and started doing a 69.'

Tess bit her lip. Her mind filled with the image of the two men together, their faces pressed between each other's legs, lips fastened around their erect cocks, sucking. She had never thought before about what two men might do and she found the thought unexpectedly and powerfully erotic. Two hard male bodies, two stiff swollen penises, unlimited abandoned virility, concentrating on itself alone.

'What then?' asked Catherine. 'Did they fuck? Who did it to whom?'

Jeannette shivered. Looking down, Tess saw that Catherine's hand was resting on the dark crisp curls of Jeannette's mound, and her fingers were gently, diligently fondling between Jeannette's slender thighs. It was as if Catherine were thanking her for this story. Tess was grateful too, and she lowered her head and drew one of Jeannette's long cornelian nipples into her mouth and flickered her tongue across it, probing delicately into the tiny crease at its tip. Jeannette's body shuddered and tensed. 'Yes,' Jeannette whispered, and it was hard to know whether she was asking for more or continuing her story. 'Yes, they fucked. Let me tell you what they did. It was amazing, I could have stood there all day. After a while – oh, Cath, that's wonderful, don't stop – after a while they split up and James knelt over Adam and sucked and sucked at his cock. He took it really

93

deep, I can't swallow that much of a man. I was impressed. And Adam just lay there like a young god and humped upwards towards James's mouth and you could see he was coming. He arched and the muscles in his stomach and his flanks fluttered and then James was swallowing. He looked as if he was enjoying a big ice cream cone. He loved it.'

'That's our director,' smiled Catherine. She slid her hand further between Jeannette's thighs and slipped one finger deep into her. Her other hand reached out for Tess. Tess jumped as she felt a touch on her hip, then she relaxed and let her legs part and sucked harder at Jeannette's swollen nipple as Catherine's hand brushed across her mound, wet itself with her juices, and began to stroke her swelling clitoris.

'Then,' Jeannette murmured between gasps, 'then James sat up and sort of rolled Adam over. Adam lay on his front and James kissed his back, between his shoulders and all the way down his spine to his bum. I tell you, girls, Adam's got a really gorgeous arse. I'd kiss it, too. And that's what James did, he pulled Adam's cheeks apart with the palms of his hands and then just buried his face between them and tongued his arse.'

'Eurgh,' said Tess, wrinkling her nose.

'Eurgh?' repeated Catherine. 'Tess, sweetie, just you wait. I'll roll you over in a little while and show you what it feels like. It's lovely.' And as if to illustrate her probing finger slipped backwards, teasing at the silky, sensitive membrane of Tess's anus.

'Don't,' said Tess. She remembered Tony putting one finger, two fingers inside her, and how it had made her writhe with a sort of horrified pleasure. 'Don't.'

'James liked it,' Jeannette said, 'and so did Adam. He was moaning and pushing his arse up towards James and James was eating him out, tongue-fucking him. They carried on doing that for a while, then James sat up and got a condom out of their clothes and rolled it on.

And Adam opened his legs and said, "Come on, James, darling, please." So James did.'

'He – ' Tess hardly knew how to express it. 'He put his cock in – in Adam's arse? Really?'

'Really,' said Jeannette, lifting her hips up towards Catherine's fingers. 'All the way in, Tess. Right in, up to the hilt. And then he fucked him, and I stood there behind a bush and watched.'

'Did it make you horny?' asked Catherine softly.

'God, it did. I'd have liked to join in, but those two really aren't interested in women at all.'

'Not like you and me, darling,' said Catherine, smiling.

A wicked thought crept into Tess's brain. She suppressed it for a moment, then suddenly laughed. Why should she hold back in front of Jeannette and Catherine, who were probably quite unshockable? They were both looking at her, a little surprised, and she grinned at them. 'Why don't we suggest to Leo that he tries that with Emma?' she said.

Catherine's face also lit with a wicked grin. 'What, having her up her arse?'

'She'd still be a virgin, wouldn't she?' said Tess.

'I heard that women used to do that years ago,' commented Jeannette, 'when it was important that you were a virgin when you married. You'd have a lover, but you'd only ever let him have you up the arse. Then who's to know?'

'I don't think Emma would like it, though,' said Catherine, still grinning wickedly. 'She'd think it was dirty, I bet. She'ε such a goody-two-shoes it hurts. No wonder she has so much energy left to run about being a bitch and spreading gossip.'

Suddenly the phone beside the bed rang, making all three of them jump. Jeannette said, 'Oh, Tess, let the machine take it.' But Tess had never been able to ignore a ringing phone. She lifted the receiver and said, 'Hello?'

'Tess,' said a voice at the other end. 'Hi, it's Tony. How are you?'

'Tony,' Tess breathed. She felt herself blushing, thinking of how she had spent the day. First seducing Julian, and now lying in bed with two women. 'I'm, ah, I'm fine,' she lied, and then she stifled a gasp, because Catherine's hand was back between her legs, fondling and probing. Tess swiped at her, trying to get her to move away. 'Just fine. How are you?'

'I wondered if you'd like to come over for dinner,' said Tony, 'to discuss the production, you understand.'

'Oh, I'd love to,' Tess said, 'but I'm a bit – tied up right now.' Jeannette giggled in her ear and began to fondle her breasts.

'I've got something in,' Tony said, sounding hurt. 'Don't say no.'

'Well –'

'Come straight over.' Tony's voice allowed for no disagreement. 'It shouldn't take you long, should it? I'll see you in an hour or so, yes?'

Tess wanted to say no, but wasn't quite sure how. 'I – ' she began, and then finished lamely, 'all right.'

'Great. See you then.' The phone clicked and purred into her ear.

Jeannette and Catherine were looking at her with disapproval in their faces. 'You didn't say yes, did you?' demanded Catherine.

'Well –'

'Don't go,' Jeannette told her. 'Stay here. You'll have a better time with us.'

Tess shook her head, feeling miserable. 'I ought to go. Really. He wants to discuss the production.'

'Tess,' said Catherine patiently, 'he doesn't want to discuss the production, he wants to fuck you. He's got you eating out of his hand. What's the matter with you?'

Tess scowled. Catherine's patronising tone brought her hackles up. 'I think it's up to me whether I go or not,' she said crossly. 'And if he wants to sleep with me, what's the problem with that? You two can stay here if you want. Have dinner. But I have to go.'

She got up from the bed and reached for her dressing gown. Jeannette and Catherine relaxed into each other's arms and watched her for a moment. Then Catherine said, 'Tess, be careful about what you tell Tony.'

'What? What do you mean?'

'About anything else you get up to,' Catherine explained. 'He's a real old-fashioned guy. I mean he's possessive. He thinks he owns his current woman. And he can be a real bastard, Tess. I know for a fact he hit the girl he was with the last time we worked together. Go carefully. Don't mention Julian.'

Tess looked at them, wondering if they were teasing. The black and the white faces looked back at her, sober and even a little anxious. It didn't look like teasing. She said after a moment, 'Yes. All right, I'll remember.'

Tony had bought dinner in from a caterer. He seemed almost proud of the fact that he could not cook and was domestically incompetent. Tess found herself in the kitchen, looking for plates and everything else required to serve the food. However, the meal looked delicious. It had probably been extremely expensive.

They did discuss the production, for approximately five minutes. Then Tony opened a bottle of wine and pushed a glass into Tess's hand. She said, 'I shouldn't, honestly, Tony,' but it was like trying to stop a flood. Before she knew where she was they were sitting in the living area on the huge sofa, sipping the wine, and she was listening to Tony talk. He was talking about opera. Occasionally Tess made a comment, but Tony didn't seem to need much stimulus to keep talking. When she agreed with him it was encouragement, and when she disagreed he either simply ignored her, or allowed her her opinion in a way that made it clear that he knew more than she did.

The trouble was that he *did* know more than she did. He was older, more experienced, he had sung in dozens of international productions, and in general his opinions were interesting and sensible, if not particularly original. So she sat and listened, interested almost despite herself, and entranced by the way that his handsome face showed every emotion. He lit up with enthusiasm, crackled with laughter, smouldered with anger, and Tess lay back on the sofa and ate him with her eyes.

When she had arrived Puccini had been playing – a *Bohème* this time, one of Tony's own recordings – but at some point Tony went over to the sound system and changed the CD. 'Here,' he said, 'here's the role I'd love to play.'

Tess recognised the music at once. 'Mozart,' she said, puzzled, '*Don Giovanni*? But the Don's a baritone, Tony. And the tenor's a wimp.'

Tony smiled ruefully. 'It's always the way, isn't it,' he said. 'Never enough tenors to go around, all the heroic parts written for tenors, and here's me, a tenor, and the one role I'd kill to play is Don Giovanni.'

Tess sympathised. There were many days on which she wished she had been born a soprano. She said, 'So what is it about the role that you like?'

'Oh,' said Tony, stretching out his arms, 'opera's always sexy. It's so physical, you see, the actual act of singing. You sing with your body. And Don Giovanni, that's the sexiest role in the whole of opera. The man no woman can resist! I was born to play it, and what happens? I'm a tenor.'

This was the first time Tess had heard Tony admit there was anything he couldn't do. She smiled. 'I know how you feel,' she said. 'Sometimes I – '

'Did you see the production at Covent Garden a few years ago?' Tony interrupted. 'With Thomas Allen?'

Tess shook her head. 'Not live. They televised it, and I caught a bit of it. I thought it was a bit dull, in fact – '

'Do you remember the way they did the Don's final scene? His last meal? They had this great heavy table right at the front of the stage, and there was a naked woman on it. A beautiful, naked woman, spread out on

98

the table like – like a floral decoration. And he ate his dinner off her.'

'I – I don't think I saw that scene,' Tess admitted.

'God, it was fabulous.' Tony's eyes and voice were burning with enthusiasm. 'That's the way to show Don Giovanni. What are women to him? He doesn't care about them. Get them into bed, fuck them, leave them, laugh at them. He doesn't care. He eats his dinner off them! And they're his slaves, so much his slaves that they let him do it. That's the part for me!'

'But – ' Tess began.

'Hey.' Tony's face was bright. An idea had struck him. 'Hey, Tess, how about you being that girl? Let me eat my dinner off you? What about it?'

Tess was so taken aback she hardly knew what to say. She did a double take, then shook her head. 'Ah, no thanks, Tony,' she managed. 'I really don't fancy it.'

'No, no, come on, let me.' He came across the room towards her and caught her hands, pulling her wine glass from her fingers and setting it down. 'You'll enjoy it. I promise. Listen, I can make sure you have a good time. We've got everything we need, look.' He extended one hand in a bold gesture towards the massive, heavy dining table, another piece of modern art in blond wood on sculptured metal legs. 'Table big enough for three women side by side. Delicious food. Beautiful woman' – he leant forward and kissed her – 'irresistible man. Come on, Tess, come on.'

'No,' Tess protested, trying to push him away. 'No, Tony, I don't want to.'

'You do,' he insisted. He pressed her into the sofa, resting his weight on her so that she would have had to struggle to release herself. His mouth fastened onto hers and he kissed her so deeply that she gasped. His strong hands felt for her breasts, found them, squeezed them. Tess wanted to resist him, but all day she had been in a state of intense arousal and the feel of his hard fingers tugging at her nipples threw her into a state of immediate erotic expectation. He was so eager, burning with eagerness, and his excitement communicated itself to her despite her reluctance. He unbuttoned her blouse and pushed it off, pulled her breasts from the cups of her bra and lowered his face to them, squeezing them together so that his tongue could flicker from one erect nipple to the other. Tess flung back her head and gasped and let him strip her naked, tugging her clothes from her limbs, revealing her pale skin. When he pulled off her skirt he reached down to her panties, could not at once free them, and with a snarl of impatience yanked at them so hard that the flimsy fabric tore. She tried to protest, but his eager lips gagged her.

'Come on,' Tony hissed. He caught her up in his arms and with his fingers snagged some of her clothes, the rags of her knickers, her stockings, the silk scarf she had draped around her neck. She let him carry her over to the table and lie her down on its cold, hard surface. 'Beautiful,' he hissed, 'Tess, you're my wet dream. God, you're beautiful.' He kissed her hard, his tongue exploring deeply, and she moaned. Between her legs she was wet and warm. Then she felt him spreading her wrists, holding them high above her head, and she opened her eyes and said anxiously, 'Tony, what are you doing?'

'Tying you up,' Tony said, suiting his actions to the words.

'No,' Tess said, trying to pull free. But one hand was already secured and his strong fingers were on her other wrist, wrapping one of her stockings round it, tying it quickly to the metal leg. 'No!' Tess cried, her legs thrashing as she tried to pull free. 'No, Tony, this isn't funny!'

'It's not supposed to be funny,' Tony said. He leant over her, his face over hers, and she fell still and stared up at him, her breath coming quickly. 'It's meant to be sexy. Hasn't anyone ever tied you up before? Give in to it, Tess. Trust me. You'll love it.'

You'll love it. Trust me. Leo had said exactly the same

thing to her a few moments before he took her virginity, and he had told the truth. She had loved it. And hadn't sex with Tony, the previous night and that same morning, been great? Tess stopped struggling and let Tony spread her legs and bind her ankles too. The bindings were loose, so that she could wriggle, but not so loose that she could escape.

Tony stood back and surveyed his handiwork. 'Gorgeous,' he said, in a voice that was almost a sigh of satisfaction. 'Simply gorgeous. And now for dinner.'

In a few moments he was at the table again, plates in hand. 'Here we are,' he said. 'Warm salad of duck breasts and green beans in a hazelnut oil dressing. Delicious. Now, where shall we put it.'

'Tony,' Tess whimpered, 'don't. You'll get me all sticky.'

'Sure I will. And remember how much fun we had in the shower?' Tony looked down at himself, then put down the plates on the table beside Tess's pinioned body and began to remove his clothes. He did not hurry. It seemed that Tess's flinching and whimpering, her ineffectual little protests, aroused him, because when he removed his shorts his cock sprang forward, so erect that it almost touched his flat belly, swollen and glistening and eager.

'Now then,' he said, and with one hand he reached into the plate of salad. He lifted out a sliver of duck breast and suspended it over Tess's lips. 'Try some,' he suggested.

Tess obediently reached up and ate the sliver of meat. It was, as Tony had said, delicious: rich and complex and satisfying. She swallowed eagerly and Tony smiled and fed her a little more of the salad, more duck, a few strands of the long crisp French beans, a couple of wild mushrooms, all bathed in the delicate, nutty dressing. 'Yum, yum,' he said, as she licked her lips. 'That's enough for you for the time being. Time for my dinner, table decoration.'

He picked up the dish and tilted it. Slivers of duck and a few beans and mushrooms fell from it and landed on Tess's breasts. She shrieked as she felt the warm, oily dressing trickling down her ribs, under her arms, around her areolae. 'Oh God, Tony,' she cried, 'oh God, that's awful, oh for God's sake.' She pulled at the bindings of her wrists and ankles, but she couldn't free herself.

'Be quiet,' Tony said, in a voice of monotone stillness that was so commanding that Tess closed her mouth and just stared at him. He leant over and reached with lips and teeth for a piece of meat, caught it, pulled it into his mouth and ate it. A piece of mushroom, a French bean, another piece of meat. One of the mushrooms had landed beside Tess's right nipple and as he drew it into his mouth he flickered his tongue across the coral tip of her breast. There was something so greedy, so salacious in his movements that Tess breathed quickly and arched her back in delight. It was erotic being tied there, helpless, unable to resist, used by him as if she were a piece of living furniture. She closed her eyes, giving herself up to the sensations as he ate every piece of the salad from her breasts and then began to lick off the dressing.

'More,' Tony said, putting another handful of salad on Tess's quivering body. She breathed more quickly as he reached with his lips for piece after piece. His body too was shaking, she could feel him trembling, and it aroused her to know how much he wanted her. Occasionally he fed her something and it was as if she was eating her own desire.

At last all the salad was gone. Tony looked down at her, breathing hard. The whole of her upper body glistened with oil. He took her breasts in his hands and began to squeeze and stroke them, teasing her nipples until she gasped. Then he said, 'Slippery and delicious. God, Tess, your breasts are fabulous.' And without another word he swung himself up onto the table and straddled her waist with his strong thighs, pushing her breasts together into a shining mound of inviting flesh. He thrust his hard cock between them and Tess whimpered as she felt the hot shaft slide to and fro. She opened her eyes and looked down and saw the head of his penis moving towards her, scarlet with aggressive lust, the little eye at its tip weeping with eagerness. Tony held her breasts between his hands and pinched and pulled her nipples as he moved forward and back. It was an extraordinary sensation, unexpected, sensual, and Tess gave herself up to it. She could not take her eyes from the swelling tip of Tony's pulsing cock.

He thrust faster and faster, beginning to pant as he shafted the silken cleft of her oiled breasts. He grunted wordlessly, like an animal, as his pleasure grew and his surging phallus thickened and twitched as it prepared for orgasm. Tess felt frightened for a moment, helpless, vulnerable, stunned by his sudden, selfish fierceness. But although she tugged at the bonds around her wrists, she could not escape, and half of her did not want to.

Suddenly Tony began to cry out, 'Oh God, yes, that's it, yes,' and he stopped moving and Tess felt his cock between her breasts throbbing and jumping as the semen surged up the shaft and spurted out. She closed her eyes instinctively and flinched as the warm drops fell on her face, on her cheeks and lips. Tentatively she reached out with her tongue and tasted the mild saltiness of Tony's cooling seed. Then she opened her eyes and looked up.

Tony's dark face was flushed with pleasure. He was not smiling, but he looked satisfied, like a lion after the kill. With his fingers he pinched Tess's nipples until she gasped, and only then did he smile. 'I knew this was a good idea,' he said.

Tess tugged at one wrist. 'Tony, let me go,' she said. 'I'm getting stiff.'

He grinned. 'I'll soon take your mind off that. Time for dessert.'

'No,' Tess protested. But she could do nothing. Tony climbed off her. His penis was slightly deflated, like warm Plasticine, but not really soft. It was clear that he was still fiercely aroused. He picked up the bowl of fresh strawberries and the jug of cream, still cold from the fridge, and grinned fiendishly. He lifted the jug and poured a trickle of icy liquid directly onto the warm, damp flesh between Tess's legs.

'Jesus,' Tess cried, heaving her hips upwards in a vain attempt to escape. 'Oh, God, that's cold.'

'Now,' said Tony. He picked a strawberry from the bowl and without a word pushed it between Tess's sex lips, deep inside her. She cried out and he smiled and knelt between her legs and with his tongue felt within her, licking the berry, catching it, withdrawing it slowly from her and tugging it into his mouth. Then he licked the mixture of her juices and the cold cream from her and she moaned with astonished pleasure.

Tony pushed berry after berry into Tess's body and removed them with his tongue. He let her eat one or two, sometimes dipped in cream, sometimes dipped in her own juice. Time after time he drew her to the point of orgasm, then trickled icy cream directly onto her trembling clitoris, making her cry out with misery and frustration as the incredible sensations faded. It seemed to please him to torment her. She writhed in her bonds, begging him to finish her off, to let her come. He would have gone on for ever, but at last he misjudged the strength of his caresses and a massive, pulsing orgasm wracked Tess's pinioned limbs, making her forget everything that had gone before in a shuddering, heaving clench of ecstasy.

She would have begged him then to untie her, but before she had got her breath back Tony had unfastened one wrist and quickly tied it again to the other table leg, so that her hands were pinned together above her head. Then, while she still gasped and whimpered, he freed her ankles and quickly flipped her over, making her kneel with her face pressed to the cold slimy surface of the table so that her bottom was thrust up into the air.

He felt in the salad bowl for remnants of the dressing and began to anoint the cleft of her arse, rubbing the oil into her skin, pushing the tip of one finger gently into her tight anus.

Tess knew what he was going to do. She could have protested, but it would have been hopeless. Her hands were tied, she could not prevent him, and if she struggled he could always tie her legs as well. And also – also, she wanted to feel him in her arse. Jeannette's description of James and Adam making love had aroused her ferociously, and she wanted to know what it was like.

'Relax,' Tony hissed, trying to push his finger deeper. Tess began to breathe deeply and let the delicious after-effects of her orgasm bathe her in libidinous bliss. 'That's it,' said Tony, as her resistance suddenly ceased and first one finger, then two, slid into her to their full length. 'That's it.' He withdrew his fingers and replaced them with the head of his cock, again stiff and proud and ready. It felt different, sticky: he must have put on a condom. Tess drew in cold air through her swollen lips and moaned as the hot smooth shaft began to penetrate her, entering her, taking the virginity of her anus. 'Oh,' she gasped, because it was wonderful. She moaned and pushed herself up towards Tony, welcoming his thrusts. Her clitoris ached and quivered and the nipples of her dangling breasts rubbed against the table. She longed to be touched, she knew that if he would touch her she would come again, but Tony had other things on his mind. He was holding onto the swell of her hips and plunging into her, shafting her as hard as he could, grunting as his balls slapped against her body with every surge of his cock deep inside her.

'Christ,' he gasped, 'that's so tight. Oh God, it's good.' His fingers dented her white flesh, holding her still against his ferocious thrusts. 'Slave,' he growled, 'my slave, tied up for me to fuck her. Say something, slave, slave.'

Tess's hands clasped and unclasped frantically. She felt like an animal, powerless, possessed. 'Please,' she moaned, 'don't, don't,' and she did not know whether she was really begging him to stop or only saying what she knew would give him pleasure.

'I will,' Tony snarled, 'I will!' and with a final, desperate thrust he forced his throbbing penis deep into Tess's anus and as his orgasm seized him he leant forward and caught her nape between his teeth like a beast and Tess cried out with shock and pain and fell forward onto the table, crushed beneath him, panting and slippery with oil and trembling with astonishment at the irresistible power of her own response.

After a few long moments Tony leant forward and slackened the bonds round her wrists, but he did not lift his weight from her. 'There,' he whispered in her ear, 'I told you so. You loved it.'

Tess did not deny it. She moved a little, actually enjoying the feeling of him lying on top of her, crushing her against the cold wood. She pillowed her head on her hands and said sleepily, 'Tony, I'm still hungry.'

Act Two, Scene Three

The rehearsal studio, one week later

Rehearsals went on, and James gradually stopped shouting and began to nod approvingly when Tess sang. She had mastered the first act now, in which Carmen first falls for Don José. It was easy. When she met Tony's eyes she would imagine the moment when Julian had looked from her breasts into her face, his expression burning with sudden lust, and everything that James wanted was there – the instant desire, the audible click. So things were improving. But no sooner had she managed one thing, than another reared up to challenge her.

Tess rested her chin between her fists, staring down at her score as if it could talk. She was sitting in a corner of the rehearsal room, using a few quiet moments to study the scene in which Carmen and her friends Frasquita and Mercedes play at fortune-telling, looking for their futures in the cards. Frasquita and Mercedes are half-joking, hoping for love, for riches, for an elderly million-aire to marry them and drop dead soon after. But to Carmen the cards tell a different story.

> *Let's see what the cards say to me.*
> *Diamonds – spades –* Another card turns – *death!*

It's all true – first for me – then for him –
For both of us, it's death!

'How are you doing?' said Jeannette's screech-owl voice, pitched at a careful whisper to avoid disturbing Tony and Emma, who were busily rehearsing, under James's watchful eye, the critical moment at which Micaela tells Don José that his mother is dying and he will have to leave Carmen. As always James was giving every second his attention and making the singers work with equal intensity, insisting that Tony and Emma repeat the scene over and over until it was exactly as he wanted it. Tess had almost forgotten that she was supposed to be on stage, and so had the rest of the cast, who were standing around the room relaxing. Catherine was in the corner, leaning on the piano and looking meaningfully down at Julian, who was trying to look as if he hadn't noticed and was simply concentrating on the score. Despite her expressed preference for men a little more grown up than Julian, Catherine seemed to have decided that the young pianist was a worthy prey, and she was leaning on the piano's glossy lid watching him rather like a female tiger considering a gazelle as a possible appetizer.

Tess shook her head and looked up with a sigh. Since their afternoon in bed together Catherine and Jeannette had become rather protective of her, like older sisters, and she was beginning to rely on their interest and concern. 'It's no use,' she said. 'I'm getting closer to the character James wants, I know it. But how can someone as – as strong as the person he wants be to be, someone that sassy, how can she believe in what a pack of cards tells her?'

Jeannette sat down on the floor beside Tess, spreading her slender denim-clad legs in an inelegant sprawl. 'Ever been to a Tarot reader?' she asked.

'No,' Tess laughed scornfully. 'Why should I? It's all mumbo-jumbo.'

Jeannette raised her dark, pencil-thin brows. 'If you feel that way, no wonder you can't understand what Carmen thinks.'

'Don't tell me you believe it,' Tess said.

'I wouldn't say that I did believe it or I didn't,' Jeannette said with a shrug. 'But I certainly wouldn't write it off. A friend of mine is interested in that sort of thing, casts horoscopes, reads the Tarot, and she's got her head screwed on. She did a reading for me once and I was really surprised by how accurate it was.'

'Anyone could do something like that for a friend,' said Tess. 'She knows you anyway, doesn't she? Of course she could say the right things.'

'It wasn't just about my past,' said Jeannette. 'She – ' but then she swore and jumped to her feet. 'Come on, you're on.'

Tess had missed her cue. James shook his head disapprovingly and Tony and Emma stood looking at them expectantly. Emma drew her small mouth together in a pout, then said, 'It's not very polite to keep us waiting. Is it, Tony?'

Emma didn't really need to say anything to make Tess feel uncomfortable about missing her cue. Also she didn't need to make up to Tony quite as obviously as she was doing now. When she spoke to Tony Emma's big blue eyes looked very innocent and trusting and she stood rather closer to him than was necessary. This was not lost on Leo, who was standing at the other side of the room chewing his lip in annoyance, and Tess could see that it wasn't lost on Tony either. He smiled down at Emma with a not entirely paternal look, his dark eyes twinkling at her, and Tess felt a sudden spurt of jealousy. Emma had Leo crawling to her feet and that wasn't enough for her, she had to go fluttering her golden eyelashes at Tony as well. Little tease. Tess would have liked to go and touch Tony or in some other way show her proprietorial interest, but that wasn't possible in rehearsal. She just said, 'Sorry. I beg your pardon, James,' and carried on. It wasn't as if she actually had anything to say at this point: she just had to look as if she didn't give a damn that Don José was leaving her.

Happy now? Tony sang, his golden voice heavy with bitterness. *I'm going. But I'll be back!* He took Emma's arm, ready to lead her off stage.

Tess tossed her head and turned away. She knew it wasn't right, and she wasn't a bit surprised when James stopped Julian playing and said, 'No, Tess, no.'

Tess turned back, taking a deep breath. 'I know, James. I ought to look as if I don't care.'

'You're bored with him,' James insisted. 'You've had enough. Escamillo's the one you fancy right now. You couldn't be happier that José is off. But at the moment you look just jealous!'

That's because I am jealous, Tess thought. It had bothered her much more than she expected to see Tony touching Emma. Aloud she said, 'Don't you think Carmen might be – might be jealous, to see José with another woman?'

Emma said sweetly, 'It would be understandable,' and moved a little closer to Tony, who grinned broadly down at her. Behind Tess Leo clenched his fists and Tess thinned her lips angrily.

'In my reading,' James said, 'Carmen doesn't give a damn about José at this point. She wouldn't care if he chucked Micaela down on the stage and raped her, which, if you remember, is exactly what all the dealers want to do the moment they see her. Carmen would actually enjoy that. The one thing she wouldn't be right now, Tess, is jealous.'

They worked the scene over and over again and at last Tess managed to produce a performance that satisfied James for the time being. They moved on to the end of the act and James announced that the rehearsal was over for the day.

At once Leo swooped upon Emma and bore her off into a corner. Tess heard him saying in tones of real distress, 'Look, Emma, darling, I really *wish* you wouldn't . . .'

Tony sloped over to Tess and lifted her hand to his lips. He was always very attentive to her at rehearsal, making it clear to everyone in the cast that she was his personal property. 'I'm sorry I can't see you tonight,' he said softly. 'Or tomorrow. It's one of those things. It was arranged ages ago.'

'I know,' said Tess. 'It's all right, Tony, honestly. I'll have a quiet night in.' For a moment she wanted to tell him that she would really prefer it if he didn't play up to Emma every time they were together on stage. But she didn't think she could muster the nerve, and it wouldn't be right to criticise him in public, either. She just reached up her lips for a kiss.

'Be good,' Tony whispered. For a moment his agile tongue slipped deep into her mouth, twisting until she gasped. Then he drew back and patted her bottom and went away.

Jeannette came and stood at Tess's elbow and watched her face as she gazed after Tony's retreating back. 'You look like a Walt Disney puppy,' she said. 'What's the matter? Not got a life when he's not around?'

Tess frowned angrily, but she couldn't deny it. Tony was very demanding, and it had been easy over the last week to allow her life gradually to become subsumed into his, waiting for his calls, living for seeing him, only half herself when he was somewhere else. She looked ruefully up at Jeannette and shrugged.

'Listen,' Jeannette said, coming closer, 'Catherine managed to persuade Julian to come over tonight. Leo's taking Emma out, we'll be all alone in the house. Come on over and join in. We're going to show him what he's been missing.'

For a moment Tess was tempted, but then she shook her head. 'No,' she said, trying to smile. 'No, I think I had better just go home.'

Around them the cast were chatting, splitting into

111

small groups and heading out for a meal or a drink. Catherine was still leaning on the piano, smiling down into Julian's pale incredulous face like a mermaid luring a mariner. Jeannette glanced over at the two of them and then back to Tess, shaking her head. 'Listen,' she said, 'don't let him take you over. You need to stay independent, Tess. How will you ever manage the part if you don't? Keep something back. He's so greedy. Don't let him own you.'

Tess looked up into Jeannette's face. She knew that what her friend said was true, but to admit it seemed weak and disloyal to Tony. It wasn't as if he had done anything wrong, after all. He might flirt with Emma, but nobody suggested that he had been unfaithful, and his appointments that night and the following day were the sort of thing that any famous singer has to put up with: meetings with his agent, with producers, with casting directors, with someone from Channel 4 and someone from *Hello!* magazine. He was possessive, but was that so very wrong?

'Look,' Jeannette said softly, 'I'm not telling you to drop him. I just think you should do some more research, that's all. On your own. You need time on your own.'

'On my own,' Tess said slowly, 'means not with you and Catherine. Or with Julian, come to that. I told him I wouldn't see him again.'

Jeannette raised her eyebrows. 'Fine,' she said. 'Like James says, go out and screw someone. Anyone, Tess, it doesn't matter who. Tony's away tomorrow as well, isn't he? Make the most of the opportunity.'

Tess shrugged. 'Maybe,' she said. 'Maybe.'

She returned home alone and lowered her bag slowly to the floor inside the door, sighing heavily. Although it was late, the June light was still bright outside the flat, and green leaves stirred at the tops of the trees, level with her windows.

'I'm tired,' Tess told the flat. And she was, very tired.

For a week she had worked hard at rehearsals, gone to movement and body workshops run by Adam, visited her teacher for technical coaching through the hardest parts of the score, worked with Julian at solos and ensembles so that she understood what the conductor wanted, and each night she had gone to Tony's flat and allowed herself to be drawn into his sexual world, which each night had become more and more strange, exotic and peculiarly satisfying. There were blue bruises on the white skin of her haunches where Tony's strong fingers had gripped her tightly and pulled her violently back onto his throbbing phallus, and her wrists and ankles were red and raw where he had tied her up. She knew that he behaved as if he owned her, but she could hardly decide whether he was in love with her and eager for her to experience the whole gamut of lust, or whether he hated her and simply wanted to degrade and humiliate her. Either way, he was opening her eyes to an entirely new sensual world. But sexual discovery was time and energy consuming. Tess had hardly been in her own flat all week, and now she was so exhausted that she could hardly see it.

She walked wearily into the kitchen, thinking with pleasant anticipation of a mug of hot chocolate, and opened the fridge. An unmistakeably cheesy smell told her that the milk had gone off. She said heavily, 'Bugger.'

There wasn't much point in thinking about hot chocolate without milk, and Tess simply didn't feel up to going back into Hampstead to find some. So she slammed the fridge door, picked up an apple from the fruit bowl and stalked through to the bathroom, moodily munching.

She looked at herself in the bathroom mirror. There were rings under her eyes and her skin looked pasty. 'Early night for you,' she said to her reflection. 'Nice hot bath and an early night.'

Moving slowly, she turned on the taps and then pulled off her clothes and dumped them into the laundry basket. It was almost full, because she hadn't even had a chance to do the washing for about a week. I'll run out of clean knickers soon, she thought, and then where will I be? And then she reflected that Tony would probably approve heartily of her going without knickers, and the thought made her laugh.

Presently she was naked and the bath was almost full. Tess poured a little body oil into the water and added a few drops of tea tree oil, because her voice felt furry and she wanted to inhale the sharp, soothing steam while she soaked. She got into the bath and lay back, looking up at the ceiling.

After a while the clean, antiseptic smell of the oil cleared her head and made her feel able to sing a little. She closed her eyes and began to murmur to herself, very soft and low:

> *There's somebody here who's waiting for me,*
> *I hope that he turns out to be*
> *Someone who'll watch over me . . .*

Then she stopped and lay still, breathing deeply and frowning to herself. Why sing that song? What did it mean?

Every man Tess had known had been, in the physical sense, someone to watch over her. Leo had taught her how her body could give her pleasure and how she could give pleasure to a man. Dan had used her, but his extraordinary beauty had made her actively desire him. And Tony – Tony was possessive, physically affectionate, kinky, masterful. Certainly someone to watch over her. So why sing that song now, and why sing it in that tone of soft, aching longing?

Carmen wouldn't have wanted someone to watch over her. Tess shifted a little in the bath, letting the warm, silky water play over her floating breasts and between her legs. She thought of Carmen, her character, as she would like to portray her. Strong, beautiful, callous, doomed. Doomed because she insisted upon her passionate independence, her freedom to love whom she chose, and a man's jealousy could not bear it.

Tess caught the chain with her toe and let a little of the water run out of the bath. Then, hardly knowing what she was doing, she picked up the shower head and turned on the shower. Hot water pulsed out onto her warm wet body. She let her head tilt back so that her hair floated around her and gently, slowly guided the spray between her legs.

She let out a long, blissful sigh as the tingling stream of water caressed her thighs, her labia, the entrance to her sex. The bobbing orbs of her breasts tensed and tautened with sudden arousal and her nipples erected, stiff symbols of desire. The beat of the water on her sensitive flesh was almost too much, and for a moment she drew the shower head away, letting the weight of the flow fall onto the furred mound of her pubis. But it wasn't enough, and after a moment she moved the spray infinitesimally, until one glittering thread of water sprang through the air and struck the swelling bud of her clitoris.

'Ah,' Tess breathed slowly. Her diaphragm rose and fell, drawing air deep into her lungs, and as she breathed her hips also lifted and fell, surging up towards the insistent touch of the spray.

She felt her body floating in the warm water as if she were the only living creature in the world, as if she were isolated and alone, seeking her solitary pleasure without compunction or shame. The ripples lapped across her breasts, stroking her tight nipples, and between her pale, parted thighs the shower beat down onto her quivering sex, pummelling the sensitive flesh with unbearable pleasure.

For a moment Tess thought of Tony, his smooth, olive skin and his dark eyes and hair, the way that when he prepared to take her his lips would curl with lustful anger as if he were the toreador and she the bull, run down, exhausted, helpless, waiting for him to plunge his spear into her shuddering body. But although she did not consciously know it, her body had had enough of being Tony's slave. She wanted variety, and of itself her brain provided the image that would accompany her pleasure.

A mermaid on a rock, silver-green tail coiled onto the slimy, cold stone. Her breasts are small and round and high and her body is white as a corpse's, starred with her coral lips and her rosy nipples like bright shells upon a beach of white sand. Her eyes are the colour of her tail, the colour of the sea, and her hair is dark red, like dried blood. It is long and thick and shining and she sits very calmly on the rock amid the foaming sea and combs her long tresses with a comb of pearl. She is beautiful, but with an unearthly beauty, a deadly beauty, and her eyes are cold as the waves and quite pitiless.

She lifts her head, never once interrupting the rhythm of her combing, like the rhythm of the waves that beat against her limpet-studded rock. In the distance she has seen a ship. It is a warriors' ship, brightly painted, and on its square sail is drawn the figure of a bull. She can see the men in it at their oars, naked for their labour, rowing with all their strength against the surging might of the contrary sea.

Men are her prey, she needs them as a beast needs meat to live. Her cold eyes brighten and she flickers her tail against the rock like a cat that sees the mouse. She combs and combs her heavy hair, and as she combs she opens her soft, red lips and begins to sing.

Her voice is like wine, like dark, soft fur, like a coil of smoke that seeps from the hearth fire to draw the man home from the hunt. She does not sing loudly, and yet that sweet dark voice carries over the crash and roar of the waves and flies straight to the ears of the young warriors rowing their ship. They hear it and stop their work, helpless, enchanted, dumbstruck and frozen by the promise of delight in the mermaid's song.

Still she sings, and now the young men tremble. Her

116

song is wordless, and each of them hears what he wishes, and each of them hears her singing of the zenith of sensual delight. Each one hears her telling him how she longs for him, how her small snowy breasts are taut with yearning, how her nipples are tight and hard as rose hips, how her soft white flesh aches for him to come to her and take her in his arms and possess her with his strong, male body, thrusting himself into her, making her cry out, her sweet voice crying out in pleasure for him alone. They see her beautiful whiteness, her breasts stirring as she combs her hair, and they forget that she is a sea creature, that where a woman has a sex she has nothing but a fish's tail, and they cannot tell that her song is no more than the web a spider spins to catch a fly. They drop their oars and begin to fight among themselves for the privilege of flinging themselves over the side into the heaving surf to swim to her.

The mermaid watches them and sings still, and now her song is more urgent. The young men fight furiously upon their shuddering ship, drawing blood, for they can hear her singing, *Draw me on to ecstasy! Make me yours! Take your pleasure in my body, spill your seed within me, ravish me, possess me!*

At last one of them flings another aside and leaps up onto the side of the ship, which is protected and bedecked with painted shields. For a moment he stands poised, splendidly naked, his beautiful body taut with eagerness, his face bright with anticipation as he hears the siren's song. He flings himself at last from the ship's gunwale and cleaves the foaming sea in a perfect dive, and the mermaid smiles and drops her pearly comb and slides from her rock to meet him in the tumbling waves.

Her song has ceased, and the other young men on the ship suddenly stop fighting and draw apart and look at each other with horror in their eyes. While she sang they were bewitched, and now they are freed they know their danger and run to their oars to try to save their foundering ship, unable to spare even a glance for their companion as he cuts through the surf towards the white body of the mermaid. But they are too late, they are doomed, the rocks are snapping their eager teeth at the ship's frail timbers and in moments they will be shivered into spars and flotsam.

In the sea the mermaid dives and swims once around the swimming youth. He is as strong and beautiful as her cold heart could wish. She swims up beside him and rubs her soft breasts against him. His body is muscular and warm and it pleases her to touch him, as it pleases a cat to rub itself against a stranger's hand. She laughs to see how his flesh reacts to her, his strange male sex stiffening despite the cold kiss of the fierce sea, and he laughs to see her laughing. She presses her chilly skin close to him and reaches up to kiss him with her mouth. Her tail locks around his thighs and her arms wrap around him, pinioning his hands to his sides, and with the tip of her tail she caresses that strange stiff rod of flesh, rubbing it, stroking the soft skin up and down until the young man groans into her open mouth and his body heaves against her and warm pearly liquid bursts from the end of his male organ and floats like froth on the surface of the waves.

He is limp in her arms, as if he has spurted his strength into the sea with his seed, and she smiles at him again and puts her lips over his. She pulls him down beneath the waves. He does not struggle, and as he drowns in her cold grasp she puts her tongue into his warm mouth and tastes his fleeing soul.

Tess arched in the warm water, her eyes tight shut, every muscle tense as the cascading liquid drew her into an orgasm that shuddered and rippled through her like the cold sea that was the mermaid's home. For an infinite second she hung there, not breathing, not thinking, a body of pure pleasure suspended in nothingness. Then she relaxed and lay back, her breath coming raggedly, her lips dry and aching.

As she made her way slowly to bed she thought about

that strange fantasy. It was new to her. Where had it come from? Why should it arouse her to think of dragging a beautiful young man to his doom? That it had aroused her was clear: her climax had been tremendous. For a moment she was afraid that Tony's dominance was making her strange. Then she realised the meaning of it. The mermaid was another personification of the character she was trying to become, of Carmen, a callous, cold, beautiful creature, binding men to her with the powerful spell of her lovely voice, sucking the strength from them and then abandoning them, limp, lifeless husks.

Tess slid down below the duvet and shivered. Such power, such control, and all springing from that extraordinary gift, her own voice. For a moment she was almost afraid. But then as sleep crept up on her the sense of fear began to fade, and when she slipped into dreams they too were dreams of strength and erotic power.

She woke very late. Fuzzy with sleep she rolled over in bed and caught hold of her alarm clock. It was quarter to eleven, and she blinked and swayed as she sat up and pushed her hands through her hair.

A day to herself. She had nothing planned, and it felt quite odd to have time to do nothing if she wanted. She got up slowly, made herself tea, sorted out a wash, showered and then put her dressing gown back on and went and sat on the sofa, still half dozing. Outside the weather was gloomy, with heavy clouds threatening rain. Tess considered the dark sky for a few moments, then went to find warm clothes and her Wellington boots.

By the time she was ready to go out the rain was coming down in sheets. She pulled the hood of her Goretex jacket securely up round her ears, galumphed down the stairs and out into the rain. Within a few minutes she was on the Heath. There was nobody else about, even the most diligent dog walkers were waiting for the weather to improve, and she splashed across the soft leaf-mould under the great oaks, breathing in the fresh, wet air. There was something about the quality of the air when it was raining that she found irresistible, healing and soothing both to her vocal chords and to her mind, and she stood in a little glade on a patch of new fresh grass and put back her hood and turned up her face to the pouring rain. The cold drops stung her eyelids and her forehead, her cheeks and chin, and she stretched out her hands and breathed deeply.

She would remember how it had felt to be the mermaid. She would remember that sense of power and strength, of sexual desire and sexual desirability combined with absolute callousness. She would infuse her portrayal of Carmen with that feeling.

Jeannette had been right, she had needed time on her own. It was so easy to allow herself just to become an adjunct of Tony, something that went along with whatever he wanted, acceding to all his demands. Not good enough.

As she turned for home another thought occurred to her. If research was what it took to play a part well, then perhaps she ought to do some research on the other point of Carmen's character that was giving her problems: her reliance on the cards.

Back at the flat Tess shed her soaking clothes and wrapped herself in a warm towel, then picked up the phone and dialled. She made a face when after three rings Emma's sweeter-than-honey voice said, 'Hello. You've reached the answering service of Emma Ridley, Catherine Gibbs and Jeannette Baldwin. Please leave a message after the beep. Thanks ever so much.' Awful woman, Tess thought. She even gushes at her answering machine.

'Jeannette,' she said after the beep, 'hi, it's Tess. It's Sunday morning and I – '

'Hi, Tess!' Jeannette's voice was breathless. Tess held

the receiver away from her ear. Talking to Jeannette on the phone was like talking to a sawmill. 'What's up?'

'How are you?' Tess asked. 'Did you have a good time last night?'

'Wow, did we! You were right about Julian, Tess. He's got a tongue like a corkscrew. Though I think the two of us must more or less have worn it out last night. And we stripped his thread, too.'

'He's not still there, is he?'

'Oh no, he went home in the small hours. He didn't want Emma to see him here this morning. Don't blame him, either. She sniffed around a bit before she went out, you could almost hear her thinking *I'm sure I smell a man*, like the witch in *Hansel and Gretel*. But Cath and I have kept mum, so Julian's secret is safe with us.'

'Listen,' Tess said hesitantly, 'I was thinking about what you said. About research. And I wondered if you would give me the number of your friend, the one who reads the Tarot? I'd like to call her.'

'Why, sure!' Jeannette sounded surprised and pleased. 'Hang on while I get my organiser. Here you go. Her name's Sarah, Sarah Carter.'

'Very ordinary name,' said Tess, surprised.

'She's just a friend of mine,' said Jeannette. 'We met at a party, years ago. She's not a singer or anything, she works in an office. But she's a good reader.' She read out the number. 'Lives in Bow. Give her a call, go and see her. Say I sent you.'

'Is she expensive?'

'She does it for fun. I doubt she'd charge you anything.'

Early in the afternoon Tess found herself at Bow station, looking at the map of the local area on the station wall and trying to find out where Sarah Carter lived.

She had sounded almost absurdly normal over the telephone. Maybe a little older than Tess, in her thirties perhaps, and quite straightforward and pragmatic. Tess had explained that she was only doing research for a role and she really just wanted to talk in principle and Sarah had said, 'Well, why not? Why not come and have tea? I've got nothing particular to do this afternoon. I'd love to meet you.'

Tess found the house quite easily and stood in the street outside, looking at it. It was a very ordinary Victorian terrace house, nicely kept. There were roses in the front garden, bowed down almost to the ground with the weight of raindrops in their tumbled flowers, and the door and the window frames were painted dark blue and white.

The door opened and a woman stood there, a nice-looking fair-haired woman. Yes, early thirties, tall and rather stately, with strong bones and deep-set grey eyes. She was smiling. 'You've found it,' she said. 'Come in. You must be Tess.'

Tess expected the house to be full of all sorts of arcane paraphernalia, but it wasn't. It was a perfectly normal house, tidy rather than not, comfortably furnished, with real fireplaces and what estate agents call 'original features'. Some of the pictures on the walls were rather odd, and the books in the drawing room bookcase revealed a very eclectic interest in all sorts of things – whale songs, folklore, herbalism, holistic remedies, aromatherapy, astrology and the occult – but there was nothing frightening about it.

Sarah brought a tray of tea and Digestive biscuits. The tea was Earl Grey, which Tess took as a good sign, and served in astrological mugs, dark blue with little golden star signs on them. It was excellent tea. Sarah smiled over her mug at Tess and said, 'So from what you told me, you're a sceptic and you want enough information to be convincing as Carmen.' Her voice was very reassuring, soft and pleasantly modulated.

'Well – ' Tess began to protest, but then she shrugged. 'No, you're right. That is right.'

'I would have thought', said Sarah, 'that the best way

to proceed is for me to do a reading for you. Then you can see the style, and even if you aren't convinced you'll understand how it comes over.'

Tess shook her head. 'No,' she said, 'I don't think that would be a good idea.' She was filled with apprehension.

'Why not?' Sarah didn't seem offended, just interested.

'Because – ' because it might be true. Tess realised that she must be looking as if she was frightened, and she was angry with herself. If it was all rubbish, why be afraid of it? 'Well,' she said, trying to look casual, 'well, what the hell? Why not?'

Sarah looked quietly at her as if she were not the least convinced by this bravado. She said simply, 'I'll get the cards.'

When Tess left the house in Bow more than two hours later she was shaken. She had expected to hear nothing but platitudes, obvious statements which anyone with any sense of the dramatic could have concocted from what they already knew about her. But Sarah, in her calm, serious voice, had laid one pattern of cards, another, and from them drawn so much that she could not possibly have known.

She had said that Tess had worked hard to achieve her current position. Well, anyone who knew anything about singing could have said that. That she was now facing a challenge: fair guess. That in order to achieve what she now sought she would need to change herself, or at least to appear to others that she had changed herself.

By this stage Tess had felt uncomfortable. She had asked Sarah about her love life, making light of it, as if it were some sort of a joke, but Sarah had seemed equally serious on this question. She laid another pattern of cards and frowned, then said, 'You haven't had a great many lovers. Two or three, perhaps. And they have dominated you. The current man especially is jealous.' She looked up into Tess's eyes, perhaps seeking confirmation, but Tess looked hunted and unconvinced. Sarah could have learnt this from Jeannette. After a little pause Sarah laid an extra card and frowned again. 'Men dominate your work life as well as love. That's not surprising, men are in such a strong position. I suppose the person you are working for at present is male and you have to seek to please him. But the pattern is very strong for love, too. You allow your man to dominate you.' She looked concerned, and after a while she said, 'In the future perhaps – perhaps you will free yourself from this dominating influence and find your own way. If you are going to develop as much as you can, if you are going to achieve everything you want, then you have to do it. You have to free yourself. You can't go on relying on your lovers as you do. But, you should be careful.'

'Careful? Why?'

'I don't quite understand this,' said Sarah. 'It's as if – as if you are two people at present. And for both of them there may be – danger, conflict, but for one it is real, for the other – potential, or imaginary, I can't tell. But if you are to progress, if you are to succeed, you will have to face the conflict and brave the danger.'

Despite herself Tess was caught up. She leant forward, studying the cards Sarah held: the Chariot, the Swords. 'Will I succeed?' she asked in a low voice. 'In – in love, I mean?'

'Are you talking about love, or sex?' Sarah asked calmly.

'Sex,' said Tess, though she meant love.

Sarah turned another card. It was a Star. She said very slowly, 'If you come through the conflict, then there is great potential. But you must take control.' She looked up. 'I can't say yes or no. It depends on you.'

This was the sort of prevarication that Tess had expected. She refrained from curling her lip and asked in a cynical voice, 'Tell me, Sarah, can you ever see death in the cards? Can you tell if someone is going to die?'

Sarah's voice was very level. 'Sometimes, yes. But I would never tell them.'

Tess didn't want to go back to the flat with all of this rocketing around inside her head. At Tottenham Court Road she got off the Central line, intending to change to the Northern, and then on impulse left the station instead and walked down Charing Cross Road towards Trafalgar Square. Her head was buzzing with possibilities. It wasn't so much what she had been told as the way Sarah had spoken. It was clear not only that she believed what she said, but that in the past her observations and predictions had been confirmed as true. And Sarah seemed like an ordinary, sensible person, not a charlatan. She hadn't charged Tess anything, she didn't make her living from it, it was just something she did.

It's as if you are two people at present . . . Yes, two people. Herself, Tess Challoner, and Carmen, her character, the character she was trying to make her own. And unless she freed herself from the dominance of the men in her life, she would fail. It was horribly persuasive. Certainly she no longer had trouble in understanding why Carmen might believe what she saw in her own cards.

A savoury, delicious smell came to Tess's nose. She lifted her head, realising suddenly that she was starving. She hadn't eaten since the morning, and now it was nearly seven o'clock. She thought of her empty fridge and the smelly milk and turned without a second thought towards Soho and a bowl of pasta cooked by someone else.

Sunday evening, and the pasta bar she settled on was fairly quiet. A waiter showed her to a table in a corner and put a menu in front of her. She looked through it absent-mindedly, still thinking hard about what Sarah had told her. If this meant that she should not continue her affair with Tony, what would she do? And what would Tony do? It was true that he was jealous and possessive. How would he react if she ended it? Could this be the danger, the conflict that Sarah had foreseen?

What should she do? With Tony in charge she never had to think for herself, never had to worry. He took

125

care of everything, deciding where they should go out to eat, when they should stay in, where they should make love, exactly how he intended that Tess would achieve orgasm that night. It wasn't always exactly the way she might have chosen if she had been left to herself, but it happened. What was she supposed to do without him? Take Julian home to Hampstead and keep him as a pet?

'Hi, good evening,' said a male voice. 'I'm Dean. Can I take your order, or are you waiting for someone?'

Tess looked up, her mouth open to speak. But she said nothing. The young man standing in front of her met her eyes, then slowly raised his brows and smiled at her.

There it was again, that audible click of sexual attraction that James had asked her for. It was even stronger now, when she was faced with a man she didn't even know, had never seen before. It was there, undeniable. She looked at the waiter for a long moment, committing the feeling to memory.

He was very handsome in a male model sort of way, fairly tall and broad shouldered, with very clean-cut features, bright blue eyes and light brown, thick hair which should have hung on his shoulders but was tied back for his work. Like all the staff he wore black trousers, a white, open-neck shirt and a long, white apron. His face was mischievous, with a deep dimple on one cheek. He looked into Tess's eyes and smiled slightly. The dimple deepened. His smile said, *You think I'm a hunk, and by God, you're right.*

Cocky sod, Tess thought. He was a hunk, but that wasn't the point. She shook back her hair and said coolly, 'I'm not waiting for anyone, and yes, you may take my order.'

At that his expression changed. Now his eyes told her that he had enjoyed her little spark of temper and that he thought that she was very attractive too. He drew his order pad from the pocket of his apron and held his pen poised over it, looking attentive. 'What can I bring you?'

he asked. He had a deep voice tinged with East End, the voice of a bit of rough.

For one delicious moment Tess imagined herself saying, *Your cock on a plate, with a salad garnish.* She bit her lip and smiled to herself, then said, 'Spaghetti al pesto, please. And a bottle of sparkling mineral water.' She allowed herself to smile at him. *Yes,* her smile said, *I think you're a hunk.*

'Right away,' Dean said. He smiled back at her and then folded his pad and turned to go off to the kitchen. Tess watched him go. He had a really lovely bottom, high and taut, and it was framed by the ties of his white apron in a way that might have been designed to call attention to its pertness. Tess leant her chin on her folded hands and watched appreciatively as that athletic arse moved away from her, carried her order through the door and vanished into the kitchen.

A very good-looking young waiter indeed. And what, just what, did she propose to do about it?

Her mind shied away from the obvious suggestion. It made for a pleasant fantasy, but she couldn't make it reality. She moved her finger on the marble top of the small table, musing.

Somebody changed the background music from jazz to classical, the CD of the Three Tenors concert. The ringing voice of Pavarotti filled the restaurant, singing the most famous aria of all, the World Cup anthem from *Turandot. I shall conquer,* he sang, *I shall conquer.*

A movement by the table made Tess jump. She looked up and saw Dean looking down at her, smiling, a bottle of mineral water in his hand. He poured it into her glass and set down what was left on the table, then said, 'The pasta in just a few minutes.'

'Thank you,' Tess said. Their eyes met again. She thought, *He really is very good-looking indeed,* and she saw her attraction mirrored in his blue eyes. How old was he? 26, 27? He had an uncomplicated face and a splendid strong body under his waiter's uniform. She let her eyes follow him as he left the table, and before he went through into the kitchen he glanced over his shoulder at her.

She couldn't. She didn't dare. But as she sipped the cool water she imagined what she might do. She could lay her hand on top of his as he set her plate on the table or filled her glass. She could put her fingers on his thigh, on the back of his thigh where the apron did not cover him, where the skin was tender and sensitive below the fabric of his trousers. Any movement, one touch on her part would be enough. He would know what she meant – that she wanted him.

And then what? Ask him when he finished work, meet him outside, go for a drink, go back to his place or ask him back to hers? Oh come on, Tess, she thought. You're in a relationship, you don't want to start another. Why can't it just be a simple question of sexual satisfaction? You fancy him, he fancies you, you do something about it, you scratch the itch, no more to be said.

Because life's not like that, she told herself. She took a deep draught of her water and shook her head. Then she saw him coming towards her, her plate of spaghetti in his hand.

'Spaghetti al pesto,' he said, putting it in front of her. 'Enjoy it. Would you like some extra parmesan?' She shook her head mutely. 'Black pepper?'

'Yes please,' said Tess. Dean smiled and fetched the pepper mill, which was as long, thick and phallic as all its kind. He held it up and raised his eyebrows at her. 'All over?' he enquired archly.

'Please,' Tess managed to say, though she wanted to laugh.

'There you go,' said Dean, obliging. 'A couple of good screws is enough for most people.'

Tess couldn't resist it. 'Really? Only two?'

They had been joking, but suddenly he met her eyes and there was something more there, something hot and earnest. The pepper mill dangled unnoticed from his

128

hand. For a moment they didn't move, didn't speak, just looked into each other's eyes and breathed shallowly. Then Dean shook himself and said, 'Excuse me. *Buon appetito*,' and turned to leave the table.

Tess slowly addressed herself to the plate of pasta. It was delicious, but she barely tasted it. Her heart was beating fast and between her legs her sex was clenching in the way that always signified a sudden swelling of desire.

She wasn't just imagining things. She really did want to taste Dean's body. She didn't care what sort of a man he was, she just thought that he was handsome and she lusted after him. Her hand covered her mouth as if she were afraid that the other people in the restaurant would be able to read her thoughts.

Research. Take control. *I want you to be amoral*, James had told her. *Self-centred. Just going after kicks.*

Why not?

She ate a little more of the pasta, but her appetite was gone. Presently she set down her fork and leant back in her chair, turning her head to look for Dean.

There he was. She caught his eye. Her face was serious, and he came at once over to the table. 'Is something wrong?' he asked her.

'No.'

'Have you finished?' he asked, gesturing at her half-eaten pasta.

Tess took a deep breath. She was excited and nervous, but her singing training allowed her to speak without a shake in her voice. 'Dean,' she said softly and clearly, 'where can we go?'

Dean's face changed at once. His attentive, well trained waiter's expression changed, fading into a look of half suspicion, half shocked belief. 'Where can we go?' he repeated, speaking very quietly. He didn't have her control, and his voice was trembling.

Quickly Tess moistened her lips with her tongue and swallowed. 'Where can we go to make love?' she said. It wasn't as hard as she had feared. Startled lust flared in his eyes and she added quickly, 'Right now, Dean. Right now.'

His lips were parted and his chest rose and fell with his quick breathing. For a moment he didn't speak. Then he said, 'Are you joking?'

Tess shook her head. 'I'm serious. Try me.'

He was silent again. Then he said in a rush, 'The manager's office. At the bottom of the stairs, next to the Ladies loo. It's open. You go first. I'll be there in a minute.'

Tess nodded quickly and got to her feet. He stepped back to let her go past him and as she did so she let her hand trail across the front of his apron, directly over his crotch. He drew in his breath quickly and pulled away from her. She smiled to herself and went to the stairs.

As she descended she felt her heart pounding, thumping as if it would leap from her chest. Her nerves, her caution, her sense of propriety said, *Go into the Ladies, hide in there, don't do it, you're an idiot, what will Tony think of you?*

But inside her mind the character of Carmen said, *I want him. Tony doesn't need to know. I want him, and for once, tonight, I am going to have what I want. I am going to tell him what I want, and he's going to do it to me.*

Tess put her hand on the door of the manager's office and pushed it open. Inside it was dark. She didn't turn on the light, just closed the door and stood in the darkness, waiting.

Footsteps on the stairs. She tensed, but the footsteps turned aside and went into one of the toilets. She began to breathe faster and faster, her desire fighting her better judgement. More footsteps, and then the door opened.

It was Dean, eyes wide and dark in the faint light. He saw her standing just inside the room and his eyebrows drew down tight over his blue eyes. Tess realised with a shock that he was afraid too, afraid of her. The knowledge filled her with eagerness. She glanced around the room, saw a light on the desk and switched it on.

Dean closed the door and turned the key in the lock, then stood by it with his hands opening and closing by his sides. 'I can't stay long,' he said, his voice no more than a clotted whisper. 'I just asked for – for ten minutes.'

Tess wanted to say that that would be long enough, but she couldn't make herself speak. She drew in a long, deep breath and took a single step towards him.

It was enough. In two strides he crossed the room to her, stood in front of her, staring down into her face. There was a second of silent tension, and then at the same moment she reached her arms up to him and he took her face in his hands and his mouth was on hers.

His lips were softer than Tony's and his kisses were not so demanding. It seemed as natural that Tess should put her tongue into his mouth as that he should taste hers. They stood for long seconds, gasping as they kissed. Then Tess reached behind him for the ties of his apron and unfastened them.

'Christ,' he hissed into her lips, and then his arms were around her, catching her under her haunches and lifting her. He pushed her back and up until her bottom was resting on the edge of the manager's desk and he was pressing against her, pushing her legs apart, reaching up under her skirt. She gave an urgent gasp of lust and heaved her hips up towards him, inviting him to touch her. His hand was shaking and his fingers fumbled before he got hold of her panties and pulled them aside, feeling inside them. Tess knew she was wet, but even so it was a delicious shock to feel his strong thick fingers sink without hesitation into her, penetrating her so firmly that her sex clenched around them as if to keep him there.

'God, you're wet,' Dean hissed. He felt with his other hand for his fly, unbuttoned it and unfastened the zip, and in one swift motion pulled his erect penis from his underpants and advanced upon her.

'No,' Tess said, pushing against him. He looked up into her face, scowling with anger and frustration. He looked as if he thought that she was about to change her mind. She gritted her teeth and said, 'No, not yet. I want you to make me come first. Then – then you can fuck me.'

'What?' said Dean, as if she hadn't spoken English.

Tess's hand was on his arm, holding him away from her. 'Make me come,' she said. She remembered Julian falling to his knees before her. Yes, that would be good. That was what she wanted. 'Use your mouth on me,' she said. She saw refusal beginning in his eyes and went on quickly, 'You'll get what you want, won't you? You get to have me. Well, I want to be sure I get my share. Use your mouth on me, Dean. Make me come.'

Still for a second it looked as if he would refuse. His face was set in lines of reluctance. Tess held his eyes and lay back a little on the table, spreading her thighs, waiting expectantly for him to obey her.

'Selfish bitch,' Dean said through his teeth.

Her expression didn't change. She said, 'Dean.' It was odd and powerful that she knew his name and he didn't know hers. 'Dean. Make me come.'

He stood still for a moment, then hissed, 'Shit.' But it was the protest of acquiescence. Even as he spoke he was dropping to his knees, moving up between her parted thighs, ready to serve her.

Tess let her head fall back and closed her eyes. She waited, every nerve tingling, for his first touch. She expected him to be rough, to devour her and try to drag her to sudden pleasure, but she was wrong. For long moments nothing happened. Then she felt his breath on her. His mouth was hovering over her open sex and he was breathing, warm steady breaths that quivered against her trembling flesh. She gasped in response and whimpered, and only then did he touch her.

He was very tentative, very hesitant, flickering the point of his tongue along her labia, first one side, then

132

the other, gently poking it into her vagina, seeming to ignore her engorged clitoris completely. My God, Tess thought, does he know what he's doing? Has he ever done this before? He touched her everywhere but there, teasing, drawing up her expectation to the limit. And then, just as she was about to cry out *Lick me there, for God's sake, lick me there*, his warm, wet mouth clamped down over her warm, wet sex and he began to suck, burrowing into her as if he were extracting the flesh from a juicy orange, using his teeth and his lips as well as his tongue, stimulating her so unbearably that she bit her arm to prevent herself from screaming aloud. He drew the whole of her sex into his mouth and thrust his tongue deep inside her and then withdrew and tormented her quivering clitoris, lapping at it with firm deliberate strokes, lifting her to a higher and higher plateau of pleasure. His hands gripped tightly at the soft flesh of her inner thighs, pulling them wider apart, opening her to him. Tess arched her back and strained up towards him, overcome with joy and amazement that it was really happening. Her climax began in the soles of her feet and climbed slowly, rippling through her loins, cold as ice in her spine and hot as fire in the pit of her belly, building and building until it soared to her brain and exploded there and she cried out and tensed against Dean's mouth as he thrust his tongue deep inside her and she gripped frantically at it as she gave herself up to spasms of delirious pleasure.

Then he let her go, quite roughly, and stood up. He wiped his hand hard across his glistening mouth. 'Good enough for you?' he demanded fiercely, leaning over her.

Tess almost laughed. She pushed herself up from the desk and shook her head. He was holding a condom, fumbling with it as he tried to tear it open. She said, 'Let me,' and took it from him. Her deft fingers quickly opened the packet and she leant forward to where his scarlet, swollen cock stood up from his trousers. She opened her mouth and quickly drew the smooth, shining head between her lips, flicked her tongue over it and heard him gasp. Then she rolled the condom down the straining shaft and ran her hands gently over his tight updrawn balls, feeling them heavy and turgid with the weight of his seed.

'All right,' she whispered, looking up into his face. 'All right, Dean. Now.'

He moved towards her and she lifted her thighs and hooked them over his hips, opening herself to him. He did not guide his thrusting penis but prodded blindly between her legs until he found the moist notch and then groaned as he pushed himself into her, all the way up her wet, hungry vagina in one strong stroke.

'God,' Tess moaned, locking her ankles in the small of his back and lifting her hips. She wanted to feel him even more deeply inside her, filling her, penetrating her. 'Oh God, that's it. That's it.'

But Dean didn't move. He held onto her tightly, clutching at her haunches, and pressed his body closely against her. Looking down into her face, he hissed, 'I'm going to fuck you so hard.'

'Yes,' Tess moaned. She tried to move against him and a pulse of urgent pleasure radiated from her throbbing clitoris and made her sex clench around him, gripping him so tightly that he gasped. 'Yes, do it.'

'I'm going to fuck you – now – ' And Dean withdrew his whole stiff length from her and plunged it back into her with all his strength, his hips meeting her open thighs with a sharp slap. The impact made Tess groan with pleasure. Dean snarled and pounded into her again and again, harder than she thought possible, grasping her hips tightly to hold her open to his determined, ravaging thrusts. Within a dozen strokes Tess was at the point of climax again and as he continued to shaft her she knotted her fingers in his hair and clamped her mouth against his to keep in her shuddering cries. There was no end to her response, it was as if every stroke drew her up to another level of sensation. Dean's tongue lashed against hers and his hands were slippery with sweat and he grunted as he took her. Not sex, not making love, fucking. Pure animal pleasure, direct and unadorned. He didn't even know her name. Gradually he built up speed until he was pumping into her like a great engine, until the blows of his hips bruised the tender skin inside her thighs and her whole body was juddering with the power of his thrusts and she was biting his lips in the intensity of her pleasure. With what was left of her mind she thought that he couldn't do it any harder, it wasn't possible, but even as she thought it he snarled against her devouring mouth and began to move even faster, working his iron-hard penis brutally to and fro with such savage strength that pleasure and pain merged into one and sparks burst behind her eyes. And then he groaned and pulled his mouth free of hers and flung back his head, baring his teeth as his whole body shuddered with the desperate ferocity of his climax.

Tess shut her eyes and revelled in the pure physical pleasure of feeling his cock buried deep inside her and throbbing urgently as he came. She wanted to remember this feeling, the sense of uncomplicated, amoral, remorseless lust. She pulled back a little and Dean staggered and put his hands on the desk to support himself. He withdrew from her with a jerk and turned away, covering his face.

For a moment Tess stayed where she was, eyes closed, regaining control. Then she slipped down off the desk and straightened her skirt. 'Thanks,' she said. 'I needed that.' And without another word she went to the door of the office and out into the lobby.

She left a ten pound note on the table and walked straight out of the restaurant before Dean reappeared. She didn't care about him now, she had had what she wanted. Her thighs and sex ached as if she had been beaten, but her whole body was quivering with the echoes of pleasure and she felt elevated, excited by what she had done and not the least ashamed.

Well, she thought, two weeks into rehearsal and what have I achieved? I've got Tony Varguez as my lover, I've slept with two women, seduced a 22-year-old and screwed a total stranger on a restaurant desk. Carmen is certainly making some changes to my character.

Then she thought again about what Sarah had said. Other things faced her now, both in her own character and in Carmen's. Conflict, challenge. Danger. Was the danger to her, Tess, or to Carmen?

And what more could she do than she had already done?

INTERVAL

Act Three Scene One

Green Park, two weeks later

*T*ony's dark eyes were glittering with anger. 'Come on,' he said through his teeth, catching Tess by the arm. 'We're going back to my place. I want to talk to you.'

'No,' Tess protested. Her stomach coiled with the knowledge that once he was angry Tony was hard to deal with and that she couldn't control him. 'Look, Tony, they're just building the set, I need to take the time to wander about on the stage a bit.'

'Listen to me,' Tony said in a hissing undertone, leaning forward until his face was close to hers. His lips drew back from his white teeth as if he would bite her. As always when he was excited his Spanish accent became stronger, emphasising his foreignness. 'When I say I want to talk to you, you come with me. Understand?'

Tess bit her lip. The rest of the cast had already noticed Tony's annoyance and she couldn't face the idea of having an argument with him in public. She said quickly, 'All right, all right, you don't have to drag me.'

For a moment he still held her arm. She glared at him and at last he angrily released her. 'Come on.'

She followed him across the park, in between

deckchairs and the figures of office workers sprawling on the grass to catch some sun in their lunch hour, eating sandwiches, sitting with their noses buried in books or just watching the world go by. He was walking quickly. Occasionally he glanced behind him to reassure himself that she was following. Tess hurried at his heels, feeling like a dog in disgrace. She knew why he was angry, and she knew there was nothing to be done about it.

When they reached Piccadilly Tony hailed a taxi by the simple expedient of stepping in front of somebody else waiting for one on the kerb. Tess tried to step back and let the offended businessman take the cab, but Tony exclaimed in exasperation and crammed her into it. He snapped his address at the driver and slammed the door.

'Now, Tess,' he said at once, 'listen to me. I've had just about enough of you behaving like a – '

'Tony, don't.' Like many English people Tess hated public rows. She couldn't bear Tony's Mediterranean propensity to say whatever he thought, no matter who might be listening. 'Please.'

'Listen to me, woman,' Tony snapped. 'You know what I'm talking about. Don't try to change the subject. What do you think you're doing? Every time you're on stage with a man you behave as if you slept with him last night!'

The taxi driver cocked an interested eye over his shoulder and Tess winced with embarrassment. In a low undertone she said, 'Tony, for God's sake. You're being jealous over nothing. There's no need. You know it's acting. It's not real, it's what James wants me to do. He wants me to look as if I've slept with every one of the smugglers, not just you – not just José.' Her voice rose a little. 'It's not as if it's easy for me,' she protested. 'But James – '

'James, James, James!' Tony caught her wrist and glared at her. 'I don't agree with James. Carmen's in love with José right up to the end, she only takes Escamillo because José has to go away. It's just her pride that makes her refuse him when he comes back. You understand?'

'Where's the flat, guv?' asked the driver, and Tony angrily released Tess for long enough to give instructions. He bundled her out of the cab, flung a five pound note at the startled and amused driver, and pushed her into the lift.

'I don't want you playing the whore on stage,' he said. 'People will think it's real. They'll laugh at me.'

Tess was afraid of Tony when he was angry, but this was too much. 'Don't you dare call me a whore,' she said fiercely.

At once Tony turned on her, catching her hands by the wrists and slamming her hard against the wall of the lift. 'I'll call you what I like,' he snarled into her face. 'I don't take orders from you.'

The metal wall of the lift was cold against Tess's back. She looked into Tony's eyes, which glowed with his anger, and shivered. Tony's jealousy was frightening and vicious, but it spurred him to passion. In two weeks Tess had tried three or four times to say the words that would end their affair, but she had never done it. It was as if she secretly liked his possessiveness, his dominance, his openly stated ownership of her, body and soul. He was a bastard, but still . . .

The lift door slid open. Tony held her by the wrists and dragged her across the landing, forced the key into the lock and tossed her through into the flat. She staggered backwards, watching him as he advanced on her. The outline of his erect penis showed through his tight jeans and she chewed her lip in a mixture of desire and fear.

'You pretend not to listen to me in rehearsal,' Tony said slowly. 'You know you drive me mad when you – make up to all those others. You do it to make me jealous.'

It wasn't true, but she didn't deny it. It was pointless to deny it. Once his jealousy was aroused Tony wasn't rational. 'You tease,' he hissed, 'you bitch. I'll make you know who's master.'

Tess continued to back away, her hands held up in denial. 'No,' she moaned, 'Tony, please, no.' They had played this violent game before, and Tess did not know whether her protests and struggles were real or imaginary. Perhaps they were half real and half simulated, half expressing genuine fear and revulsion and half intended to drive Tony to more ferocious heights of passion. It was like playing with fire, she never knew what he would do to her. It was dangerous and thrilling.

'Bitch,' Tony whispered, and he dived across the room and caught her. She struggled and fought and he subdued her, pushing her hands behind her back and holding them there so that her body was pressed against his. His erection throbbed against her. He forced her into the bedroom and hurled her from him to land face down on the bed. She twisted around to defy him and he stood over her, staring down. 'Strip,' he said.

'No.'

'Strip, or I'll tear the clothes off you.'

He had done that before, too. Tess didn't want an entire wardrobe composed of designer rags, so she stopped protesting and pulled her T-shirt over her head and began to unfasten her jeans. Tony stood still, his chest heaving with his panting breath, and watched her remove her clothes. At last she was kneeling on the bed entirely naked, looking up at him with a mixture of submission and defiance. What would he do? She hoped that he wouldn't whip her. Only a few days ago, when he first started to feel jealous of the other men in the cast, he had tied her down across the bed and lashed her with his belt until her backside was red, then flung himself on top of her and taken her in her arse. Although it had aroused her ferociously, it had been quite painful and she didn't really want it to happen again. But it was no use saying so. If she expressed an opinion he would do the opposite, just to spite her and put her in her place.

Tony looked at her kneeling naked before him and nodded slowly. He tossed back his glossy black hair from his eyes and smiled with harsh satisfaction. With one hand he unbuttoned his flies and pulled out his cock, a smooth thick column of olive flesh. He slowly drew back the foreskin, revealing the glossy, scarlet head of the glans, and then began to masturbate, ringing the thick shaft with finger and thumb and rubbing steadily to and fro. 'Touch your breasts, whore,' he said to her. 'I want to see your nipples harden.'

For a moment Tess thought of refusing, but she was already aroused and she wanted pleasure. She raised her hands obediently to her breasts and cupped them, lifting them towards Tony as if she offered them to him. He took a deep breath, staring. Tess rubbed her thumbs gently over her nipples and the little buds of flesh began to stiffen and swell. Her breath tingled with the sensation.

'Good,' said Tony, still rubbing at his cock. 'Good. Pinch them. Pinch them hard.'

Tess obeyed and closed her eyes with the sharpness of pleasure-pain. When she opened them again she saw Tony shrugging off his shirt and pushing his trousers down. He stepped out of them and stood before her naked, still tugging at his rampant cock. She gazed at him avidly. She hadn't tired of the splendour of his smooth, dark body, the close, oily texture of his skin, the glistening blue-black nest of curls at his groin. She would have liked to feel him pushing her back on the bed, lowering himself onto her, penetrating her with his thick penis. But she said nothing.

'All right,' Tony said softly. 'All right, slave. Prepare yourself.'

He walked to the bedside table, opened it, pulled out a couple of long silk scarves. Tess said, 'No,' and tried to retreat across the king-size bed, but he leapt after her and caught her and wrestled her into submission. He was very strong, and it aroused her to see the muscles moving on his chest and shoulders and belly as he held her down and tied her wrists to the iron bedstead. He tied both hands together, quite loosely. Tess swallowed hard, brimming with the erotic closeness of fear and eagerness. She struggled and writhed and Tony put both hands on her body, restraining her. His fingers were warm and hard on her cool skin. She heaved up towards him and he smiled, showing his white teeth. He ran his hands down to her thighs and pulled them apart. She squealed and moaned in protest.

'Let's have a look,' Tony muttered. He released one thigh and with his fingers probed between her legs. What he found seemed to please him, because his face lit with dark gratification. 'Good,' he said through his teeth. 'I like a nice, wet hole. Shows that you want me.' He pushed two fingers deep into her, making her arch her back and cry out. He drew slipperiness from her and spread it around her labia, flickered his fingers over her clitoris, oiled her crack with her own secretions. Please, she thought to herself as she strained against her bonds, please take me now, Tony, please push your thick cock up me and make me come, please, please. But if she asked him he would refuse, just to torment her. She bit her lip and tried to pull away from his exploring hand, hoping that her struggles would arouse him to take her.

He grinned. 'Not yet,' he said. 'Not quite yet. First a little something for me.'

His strong thighs straddled her body and he came towards her face. Tess thought that he meant to plunge his stiff penis into her mouth and she gave a little moan of consent and parted her lips. But to her surprise Tony turned around and presented her with his taut smooth arse, lowering it towards her. 'Lick me,' he ordered her sternly.

This was new, and for a moment Tess felt a stir of revulsion. She flinched, trying to turn away. But her hands were fastened and Tony's thighs were on either side of her head, she could not escape him. Uncertain of what to do, she reached up a little to kiss one of the muscular cheeks of his bottom. He said thickly, 'Don't kiss it. Lick it. Lick me.'

Tess let out a little moan of protest and arousal, and very slowly extended her tongue. She touched the tip of it to the top of his crease, tasting the salt of his skin. Small, dark hairs tickled her lips. Tony drew in a whispering breath and slowly she moved the tip of her tongue, trailing it down the crease of his arse, waiting, ready to be disgusted.

It was not disgusting. It was sensual. He was clean and sweet and when she found the puckered ring of his anus the delicate skin around it was as soft as a flower, as soft as the silken covering of his cock. She hesitantly licked him and he moaned with pleasure. Delicately Tess circled the little hole with her tongue, pressed her lips to his cheeks, lapped at him almost as if she were licking a woman's sex, and above her Tony writhed in ecstasy.

He was so sensitive, so responsive. She remembered Jeannette describing how James and Adam had made love in their garden and how James had pushed his tongue deep into Adam's arse. Emboldened, she pressed the tip of her tongue directly against the tight, soft ring and thrust. Tony cried out and the taut sphincter tensed almost as if she had hurt him. She pressed her lips closer to his soft skin and tried again, keeping up a gentle, constant pressure, and at last he opened to her and the tip of her tongue slipped inside his delicate anus. Tess felt a surging rush of pleasure as she tasted the faint nuttiness of Tony's secret passage. Although she was tied and pinned down by his weight, she was using her tongue to give him pleasure, rimming the tender ring of his arse, actually penetrating him as if she were a man. Tony was a homophobe, disgusted by even the suggestion of homosexual activity, but now he was moaning and whimpering as Tess slipped her tongue deeper and deeper into the hidden channel of his body. She thrust at him eagerly, digging deep into his quivering anus, and from somewhere a rhythm emerged, steady, remorseless, building as the tempo of copulation builds to its inevitable climactic conclusion. The hairy sac of Tony's balls was taut and shivering with readiness and she thought for a moment that he would actually come, reach orgasm just with the sensation of her fucking him with her tongue. She wanted to make him come. But before he reached the point of no return he pulled away with a desperate cry and moved away from her, his breath shuddering.

'Let me go on,' she whispered. She knew the moment she had spoken that she should have kept silent. He never let her do anything that she asked for, and she wasn't surprised when he shook his head.

'No.' Tony grabbed a couple of pillows and pulled them towards her. 'No, I want your arse.'

'Not again,' Tess protested. Recently Tony seemed to have developed a fixation on anal sex, preferring it to everything else, and while Tess enjoyed it she reasoned that she was designed to receive pleasure from both orifices, not just one. She wriggled angrily as Tony caught her by the hips and turned her over, but even as she struggled she knew it was hopeless. He dumped her on top of the pillows so that her round backside was thrust up in the air, lasciviously presented to him, ready for his use. 'Please, Tony,' she begged, trying to turn back over, 'please fuck me properly.'

'Listen, slave,' Tony hissed, his mouth so close to her ear that his warm breath stirred her hair. 'I do what I want to you. And today I want your pretty little crack.' He withdrew a little and took a deep breath. 'But don't say I ignore your pleasure,' he said, and he reached again into the bedside table. He caught Tess's head by the hair and jerked it around so that she could see what he was holding.

A massive phallus made of gleaming black plastic, like something on sale in the lowest of Soho sex shops. Tess stared at it, at the same time appalled and shiveringly excited. 'My God,' she whispered, 'it must be nine inches long. Tony, don't – '

'And that's not all,' Tony said. He pressed something and the plastic phallus began to vibrate, making a noise like a food mixer. Tess cried out in protest and began to struggle in earnest, tugging at the scarf that held her wrists, shuffling her bottom and thighs off the pillows, trying to get away. But Tony just laughed and caught hold of her thigh and jerked her back into position.

'No,' Tess cried, flinging her head to and fro in protest. Tony laughed more loudly and pressed the cold slippery plastic against her thigh and then pushed it up between her legs and touched the engorged bead of her clitoris with the vibrating head.

'Christ.' Tess's hips jerked and arched with a sudden agony of sensation. 'Oh Christ in Heaven.' Tony circled her pleasure bud with the throbbing tip, parting her labia, lodging the massive head between the lips of her sex for a fraction of a second and then withdrawing it to buzz again against her peak, against the place where she was so sensitive that the brutal stimulation of the vibrator was almost unbearable.

Almost, but not quite. After a second Tess gave herself up to the feeling, writhing desperately on the pillows and lifting her bottom to allow the thick length of the dildo to rub against her quivering sex. Tony leant over her and whispered in her ear, 'I'm going to shove it up inside you and just leave it there while I do what I want. But first – ' he drew the vibrator away from her, making her moan with loss, and then very gently placed the tip against her clitoris and began to move it in tiny, delicate circles, stimulating every infinitesimal area of flesh to such a degree that Tess screamed and began to beat her head on the pillows, jerking from head to foot as orgasm flared from her tormented clitoris and rushed through her body like consuming flames.

'Enough,' Tony growled, and without another word he placed the massive slippery head of the vibrator between the lips of her sex and pushed. Tess screamed again as the giant rod penetrated her, throbbing right through her loins, filling her sex and her bowels with shuddering sensation so strong that it was not pleasure, making her thighs quiver with irresistible response. She tried to squirm on the pillows but Tony was on her, lying on her, nestling his hot, erect cock between the cheeks of her arse and rubbing it to and fro with eager, jerky movements that betrayed the heat of his lust. In what seemed like seconds he shouted with pleasure and convulsed over her and his warm seed spurted into the small of her back.

He lay on top of Tess like a dead thing. The vibrator hummed and shuddered within her vagina and she moaned in feeble protest. It was too much, too thick, too strong, more than she could bear. Her orgasm had been violent, but it had gone as quickly as it had appeared, leaving no afterglow to protect her from the fierce throbbing of the plastic phallus within her. She squeezed hard with the muscles of her sex, trying to eject the invading presence. 'Please,' she moaned, 'no more.'

Tony's hand moved between her thighs and pushed the vibrator a little deeper within her. 'Who is master?' he whispered in her ear.

'You are,' she whimpered, and indeed she felt entirely conquered, subdued to his will.

He nodded slowly. 'Good. Remember it.' With one swift motion he withdrew the vibrator and switched it off, and Tess's head slumped with relief. Tony reached up above her head to unfasten the scarf and release her bound wrists. He rolled away from her and lay asprawl, a cat-like expression of satisfaction on his aquiline features. Tess lay still for a moment, then reached over to the bedside table for a handful of tissues to wipe his seed from her skin.

'Well,' Tony said after a long pause in which the only sound was their panting breath, 'I'm glad that's agreed.

Now then, Tess, what are you going to make us for dinner?'

It was barely six o'clock. Tess lifted her head in exhaustion and amazement and said, 'I think I'd rather go out, actually.'

Tony didn't open his eyes, just shook his head. 'No, I fancy some real food. Make me something English. Someone at rehearsal was talking about a most peculiar thing, what did they call it? Toad in the hole. It sounds rude. Make me that.'

'Tony,' Tess said very steadily, 'I'm not your servant.'

He rolled over suddenly and caught her hands, pinning her down and grinning into her face. 'But you are my slave, aren't you? So cook me my dinner.'

Suddenly Tess felt weary and disgusted. She pushed at him and scowled and he released her, surprised. She swung her legs off the bed and got up. 'A slave in bed is one thing,' she said. 'In the kitchen it's another.' She wiped herself again and then began to dress, biting her lip nervously. Tony lay back on the bed and folded his hands behind his head and watched her with an expression of steady, cold disapproval.

When Tess was dressed she drew herself up, trying not to show that she was trembling a little. 'I want to go out for dinner,' she said, 'and if you don't want to come, I'll go on my own.'

'Rebellion!' Tony exclaimed, raising one lazy, dark eyebrow. 'Well, fine. Go ahead. I'll see you tomorrow, anyway.'

He sounded as if he didn't care, as if her pathetic attempt at independence was no more than a child's tantrum. Tess opened her mouth to argue with him, but suddenly she felt that if she once began the argument it would have to end in a break between them. She shied away from the prospect. All she said was, 'Bye.'

'Enjoy your dinner,' Tony said mockingly.

In the lift Tess closed her eyes and struck her clenched fists against the metal wall in anger and frustration. He

147

only treated her seriously in bed, and then only as his 'slave'. Sometimes she couldn't bear it.

And yet wouldn't a lot of women be perfectly happy with Tony as a lover? He might be unreasonable, masterful, demanding, but he was handsome and virile and there was one major fault that he did not have. Nobody ever intimated that he was unfaithful. Even Emma, who seized instantly on the smallest piece of relationship-related bad news and broadcast it enthusiastically to whoever would listen, even Emma had not been able to detect the slightest tendency in Tony to stray from Tess's bed. He might flirt, but he did nothing else.

You couldn't say the same for me, could you? Tess thought. Her sexual research of the early weeks of rehearsal seemed a long time ago now, but even so she had been unfaithful and Tony hadn't. This made her feel guilty, and her guilt made her put up with him even when he was at his most unreasonable.

But even so, the research had been a challenge. And an enjoyable one. As she left the lift and walked out into the hot London streets Tess wished briefly that she could undertake some more research to deal with the latest problem that James had presented her with. Carmen was one of the band of smugglers – cocaine dealers in this production – and in several of the scenes she sang with half a dozen of them. James kept insisting, 'Listen, darling, you've slept with all of them. All of them separately and maybe sometimes a few of them together. You've done it all. So when you look at each of them there's something you remember about them, right? This one's got a big cock, this one's a fellatio freak, this one likes to come between your tits – '

'Christ, James, for God's sake, give it a rest,' she had said. But of course he hadn't. He never gave it a rest.

Now she was alone in Covent Garden, entitled, if she wished, to take herself off for dinner on her own. It didn't appeal. She wandered along to the Donmar Warehouse and amused herself for a little while poking about the boutiques, then succumbed to loneliness and sought out a phone box.

She dialled Jeannette's number, hoping her friend was in. They hadn't seen very much of each other outside rehearsals for the last couple of weeks, because Jeannette and Catherine openly disapproved of Tony and said he wasn't improving Tess's performance. Now, in a state of annoyance with Tony, she was eager to talk to them both.

The phone rang a couple of times, then Catherine's pleasant husky voice said, 'Hello?'

'Catherine, hi, it's Tess.'

'Tess? This is a surprise. To what do we owe the honour?'

'Oh – ' Tess hesitated, uncertain of what to say. 'Oh, Catherine, I just had a spat with Tony and I don't want to spend the evening on my own.' The words came out in a rush and suddenly Tess felt on the point of tears.

There was a silence. For a moment Tess was afraid that Catherine had put the phone down. Then she said slowly, 'Well, Tess, the thing is, Jeannette and I had some company coming round here already.'

Tess felt dashed. 'Oh. I'm sorry. Don't worry about it.'

'Well – ' there was another pause. 'Look, Tess, we've asked Bob and Stefan round for the evening. Emma's out with Leo again.'

'Bob and Stefan?' Tess searched her brain, then remembered the names. They were two of the stage hands who were involved in building the sets.

'Yes. Remember them? Bob's a hunk, don't you think? Anyway, look, you can come round if you like, we could always ask another one for you.'

Tess shook her head, then remembered that she was on the phone. 'No, honestly, Catherine, I couldn't – '

'Why do you always say no to everything?' Catherine demanded in irritation.

For a moment Tess didn't reply. She was thinking of what Sarah had said to her. *You have to free yourself from dominance and find your own way.* She needed to undertake some further research, didn't she? And what she had done before had been fun. And she knew that she would have to break with Tony in the end. She said at last, 'All right. I'll come.'

'Hey, brilliant! The boys won't know what's hit them. Come straight over, Tess, we'll be waiting.'

Catherine was waiting at the door of the flat to let Tess in. The three girls were lucky in their accommodation. A Friend of Opera in the Park had offered a business flat to the company for the duration of the production, and Catherine, Jeannette and Emma were living in comparative splendour in a big mansion block not far from Piccadilly. The rest of the cast called it the Cat Flat, because Emma lived in it.

'Hi!' exclaimed Catherine. Her heavy dark hair was piled up on her head and she was wearing a thin shift dress, made of white, embroidered cotton, that barely contained her full, heavy breasts. The dark shadow of her pubic hair was just discernible through the delicate fabric. She seemed very excited, and Tess thought that she might have had a drink already. 'Hi, Tess, come in. Come and see what we've thought of.' She caught Tess by the hand and pulled her through to the big main reception room. It was furnished in a very big-business way with damask-covered sofas and polished wood occasional furniture, but right now it was hardly recognisable. The sofas and chairs were draped with rugs and throws, some of brightly patterned Indian fabric, some of heavy, crunchy cotton, some of fur, real and fake. The curtains were drawn, shutting out the bright evening sunlight, and candles glowed on every flat surface. A big wine cooler stood on a low table and sensual music was playing softly in the background. Tess recognised Debussy's *Pelleas et Melisande*.

'Wow,' said Tess. 'Well, Cath, nobody would guess what you had in mind. Where's Jeannette?'

150

'Right here,' said Jeannette, emerging from the master bedroom. A blue and gold sarong was wrapped tightly around her long, slender body, and the beads that tipped her myriad tiny plaits were cobalt-blue flecked with gold. Big gold discs gleamed in her ears and her huge, liquid eyes were outlined with blue kohl. She looked like an Ethiopian queen. 'What d'you think?' She raised her arms and turned on her heel, showing herself off.

'I feel underdressed,' Tess said uncomfortably, looking down at her jeans.

'Hey, no problem.' Catherine caught her by the arm and towed her into the bedroom. 'Let's find you something. I think there's a silk slip somewhere. Jeannette, bring the wine in, will you?'

As they turned over heaps of clothes Catherine and Jeannette explained the plan. 'Last night,' said Jeannette, 'we brought Bob home with us. You know Bob, the big muscly one with long hair. I can't remember whose idea it was – '

'It was his,' put in Catherine. 'Cheeky sod, he said to me that someone had told him Jeannette and I were gay and he thought it was a waste. So I told him to come back and find out for himself. And he did.'

'All night,' Jeannette added. 'He's quite an athlete. So we suggested an action replay tonight and that he bring someone else along. He thought of Stefan.'

'Isn't Stefan the one with red hair and freckles?' Tess said, sounding confused.

'That's right. Looks like a teenager, but Bob says – well, he said he was hung like a donkey, to be honest. And you know I've always wanted to try a really big one.'

Tess smiled nervously. Catherine gave a little triumphant cry and held up the petticoat. 'Here we are,' she said, 'perfect.' It was oyster-coloured satin, with spaghetti straps and a delicately flared skirt. 'Come on, Tess, put it on.'

'So they're coming just to – ' Tess said uneasily.

'We're going to have a competition,' crowed Jeannette. 'Look.' She held up a handful of A4 cards with numbers on them from one to six. 'See? Like figure skating, marks for artistic impression and technical difficulty.'

'And I'm on the jury, am I?'

'Sweetheart,' said Catherine, 'you're one of the competitors. We've asked Charlie for you.'

'Which one's Charlie?' Tess asked awkwardly. She had been so taken up with Tony in recent days that she hadn't really noticed the stage hands. She tried to imagine herself making love before an interested audience, in public, if you please. Her mind recoiled from the prospect.

'The Asian one,' said Jeannette. 'Looks like a young Omar Sharif. Gorgeous.'

Tess couldn't remember Charlie at all. She slowly took off her T-shirt and jeans, letting out a nervous sigh. Jeannette hesitated, then said, 'I was a bit surprised that you agreed to come over, Tess, honestly.'

'Well,' Tess explained, 'I was mad with Tony. And I thought – I thought it might help with what James has been saying to me recently, about how he wants me to look as if I know something about each of the men in the gang.'

'Hey, good idea!' said Catherine with a grin. 'Tell you what. Tomorrow morning we'll ask you what especially you remember about each of these three guys. Good memory test.'

Tess slipped on the satin petticoat. The cool, slippery fabric caressed her skin. She took a deep draught of wine and felt the alcohol begin to work on her, eroding her inhibitions, empowering her. 'When are they coming?' she asked.

'Any minute. We have to finish early. Leo and Emma are going to the theatre and then out for dinner, but they'll be back some time after midnight.' Jeannette picked up a rather dog-eared book from the floor of the room and held it out towards Tess. 'Here,' she said. 'I thought we could use this for a few ideas.'

It was a modern version of the *Kama Sutra*, attractively presented with photographs of appealing, sexy young models. Tess flicked through the pages, raising her eyebrows. 'Some of these are impossible,' she said.

'Oh, I don't know,' said Catherine. 'Jeannette's pretty limber. Me, I'm going to stick to nice simple ones.'

'How do we decide who gets whom?' Tess asked, still looking at the pictures. The sensuality of the images began to work on her. The whole situation seemed so unlikely that she couldn't even feel afraid, because she didn't really believe that it was happening. Jeannette and Catherine did this sort of thing, but not little Tess Challoner.

'Random selection,' said Jeannette. She showed Tess slips of paper with their names written on them. 'And why not.'

'I thought you wanted the really big cock,' said Catherine.

'Well, if I don't get him first time, he'll just have to get it up again,' said Jeannette, and she laughed like a kookaburra.

The doorbell rang. Tess jumped and Jeannette and Catherine both giggled at her. Catherine ran out of the bedroom and the other two followed her more slowly as she went through and opened the door. 'Hello,' she said, gesturing welcomingly. 'Bob, Stefan, Charlie, hi. Come on in.'

'We brought a bottle,' said Bob, leading the way. He was a big man, thirty perhaps, heavily built and long-haired. The open neck of his denim shirt showed fur curling across his chest. He put a bottle of wine into Catherine's hands, leant forward and kissed her without preamble.

'It's not the wine we're interested in,' said Jeannette from the doorway. Bob looked up at her and grinned, then continued to kiss Catherine with lustful diligence.

Behind him Stefan and Charlie hesitated in the doorway. Stefan was quite small, thin and pale-skinned, with a shock of carrot-coloured hair and very bright blue eyes. Freckles marched across his narrow nose. Charlie was gorgeous indeed, with smooth coffee-coloured skin shaded blue with stubble around his fine jaw and soft black hair hanging in curls to his shoulders. He wore jeans ripped at the knees and a dilapidated T-shirt. Both Stefan and Charlie looked rather like boys who have found an unattended sweet shop and can't believe their luck.

'Come in,' said Jeannette. She walked smiling across to Stefan and stroked his face with her hand as she shut the door behind them. He looked down at her for a moment in complete astonishment, then very hesitantly lifted one hand to touch the swell of her breast under the thin cotton of her sarong. She arched against his hand and with a gasp of surprised lust he caught her into his arms and kissed her hard.

Tess found herself standing alone in the hall, looking at Charlie. He looked back at her. After a moment his lips curved in a smile and he raised his eyebrows. 'Well,' he said, 'fancy meeting you here. Do you come here often?'

Thank God, a man with a sense of humour. 'Well,' Tess said, 'not that often, no. How about you?'

'I'm as surprised as you are,' Charlie said. He came close to Tess and stood looking down at her. His smile vanished. Very softly he said, 'I – I've seen you on stage, of course. I think you're marvellous. You're the sexiest Carmen I've ever seen. Do you know that all the men in the crew would like to give you one?'

Suddenly the dry tension of desire filled Tess's throat. She swallowed hard. Beyond Charlie she could just see Stefan fumbling with the knot of Jeannette's sarong, trying to free it, and Bob pulling up Catherine's dress by the hem. They had wasted no time. Jeannette was

154

laughing breathlessly as Stefan tried to undress her and her long black fingers were deftly undoing his fly.

Charlie glanced over his shoulder, following the direction of Tess's gaze. 'Wow,' he said softly, 'no kidding, then.' He looked back at her and licked his lips. They stared into each other's eyes, each of them wondering who would make the first move. At last Charlie very gingerly put his hand on the fine strap of the silk petticoat as if he would pull it down. He didn't move it, just looked into Tess's eyes. 'Shall I?' he asked softly.

The breath was cold between Tess's lips. Her nipples tautened and stood out beneath the satin. She glanced again at her friends and frowned, then said, 'I thought – I thought Jeannette had something special in mind.'

Jeannette heard her name and pulled away from Stefan's searching mouth. Her hand was inside his trousers and she was wearing an expression of manic glee. 'You're right,' she said, 'absolutely right. Everyone into the lounge, and I'll explain. And bags me and Stefan go first.'

'Got what you want again, Jeannette?' Catherine asked with a smile as she guided Bob through into the candlelit drawing room. He noticed the small, ceramic bowls which had been filled with a variety of condoms and placed strategically around the room. Tess poured wine for everyone, sensing rather than seeing Charlie standing close behind her, so close that she could almost feel the heat of his body through the thin satin slip.

Jeannette took a gulp of wine, then said, 'OK, guys, it's like this. We take turns and the others watch, and then they can give us marks. Look, here are the score cards. Just like skating, yeah? Stefan, come on.' She turned and caught hold of Stefan's fiery hair and kissed him and as she kissed him she began to unfasten the buttons on his shirt. For a moment Tess thought that Stefan would protest or pull away, but after standing frozen for a few seconds he acceded and returned Jeannette's kisses. They were the same height to within an inch. Stefan's hands returned to the knot of Jeannette's sarong and at last he managed to open it. The bright fabric slipped down her back, crumpled above her taut high buttocks, and then fell to the floor.

'Jesus,' Charlie whispered. He picked up a pair of the score cards and glanced at Tess. 'Ah, shall we sit down?' he suggested.

Catherine and Bob were already seated on one of the big sofas, half watching Jeannette and Stefan, half engaged in pulling off each other's clothes. Tess breathed fast. Arousal was stirring strongly in her. 'All right,' she said.

She sat on one of the fur rugs. The downy soft fur caressed her thighs. Charlie sat down beside her and stared at the space in the middle of the room where Jeannette and Stefan were still kissing. Jeannette had Stefan's shirt off now and was working on his trousers, and he was devouring her and squeezing the firm orbs of her buttocks. His skin was very white, and the contrast of his clutching fingers with Jeannette's ebony rear was very pleasing.

'Oh God,' Jeannette whispered as she pushed down Stefan's trousers and underpants. 'Oh God, look at it.'

Stefan was thin and wiry, but his penis was huge. It stood up from the flaming red curls of his groin like a young tree, stiff as a piece of wood and as long and thick as the vibrator that Tony had used on Tess that afternoon. Jeannette's dark fingers wrapped around the ivory stem and she whimpered with delight as she felt its length and hardness. 'God,' she whispered again, 'oh God, I want to feel it.' She began to sink to her knees, drawing Stefan down with her, never for a second releasing the splendid pillar of his rampant cock.

'So much for artistic impression,' Charlie whispered in Tess's ear. 'I thought you couldn't hurry art.' His hand brushed against her shoulder. She turned to him in surprise and he smiled at her and trailed his long fingers across her breasts. With a startled gasp of pleasure she reached out for him and caught hold of his head by the hair and drew down his face to kiss her.

For a moment she was immersed in the sensation of his soft lips on hers. He kissed very gently and his breath tasted sweet and spicy, and his tongue was long and slender, strong and sinuous. His hand caressed the outer curve of her breast, making her whimper. Then he said, 'We don't want to miss the main attraction.'

They turned back to see Jeanette kneeling before Stefan, her lean dark thighs spread wide. She slowly leant back, back and back like a limbo dancer until her hips were arched up towards him and her garnet nipples pointed towards the ceiling. Stefan frowned in concentration and moved up between her widespread legs. For a moment his white fingers disappeared into Jeannette's sex. Then he paused to slide a condom over his massive cock, lodged it between her labia and began to push it into her.

'God almighty,' Jeannette moaned. 'Oh, oh, oh.' Her flexible spine twisted in an agony of pleasure as Stefan penetrated her, sliding his long, thick penis deep into her slender body. 'Oh, it's stretching me. Oh yes, Stefan, please.'

'My God,' Charlie whispered, and Tess gasped with soundless wonder. Watching Stefan's glistening penis appearing and disappearing from the dark cushion of Jeannette's mound was like seeing the new moon racing between banks of midnight clouds. It was beautiful. Almost without realising it Tess and Charlie moved closer together, hands searching, exploring, seeking the other's sex. Tess opened Charlie's jeans and felt for his penis. It was smooth and hot and eager. As she touched it she felt his fingers on her, slithering between her labia, settling on her clitoris and beginning to rub at it with a persistent delicacy that made her whimper.

Jeannette was crying out with eagerness. Such was her need to feel Stefan's huge member deep inside her that she changed her position, lifting her slender thighs to wrap them around his waist, clutching at his shoulders with her long fingers. Her dark red nails dug into his spine and he yelped and began to move faster, ramming into her with merciless determination. He reached under her and caught her buttocks in his hands, lifting them to open her to him even more, and she screamed. The enthralled audience watched Stefan's long, rubber-clad shaft, gleaming with Jeannette's moisture as it slid in and out of her dark juicy flesh.

'Now,' Jeannette yelled, 'now, now!' and her heels drummed against Stefan's back as he lunged into her with desperate ferocity, once, twice, three times, and on the third thrust she wailed and arched tightly against him and the scarlet softness of her sex convulsed around his plunging prick and he snarled and shuddered as his climax shook him.

There was a long silence. Stefan slumped down onto Jeanette's heaving body. Black and white limbs were glistening with sweat. Charlie took a sharp breath and his erect penis twitched in Tess's hand. He looked at her and said in a whisper, 'Who's next?'

Tess licked her lips and glanced at the other sofa. Then despite her tension she smiled. 'I think we've been forestalled,' she said.

And they had, because on the other sofa Bob and Catherine were already engaged. Catherine was bent over the arm of the sofa, her dress forced down off her shoulders and thrown up around her waist in a ruined mess of crumpled cotton. Her lush full buttocks were thrust upwards and her heavy breasts dangled, and she was moaning as Bob shafted her vigorously from behind, his thickset hips slapping hard against her with every lunge. She lifted her head as Tess spoke. Her hair was hanging around her face, swinging to and fro with the rhythm of Bob's urgent ramming, and her cheeks and lips were flushed with pleasure. She grunted as a lurch of Bob's heavy buttocks drove him even deeper into her. With one hand she reached back between her thighs and winced with pleasure as her fingers touched her swollen clitoris. 'Bob,' she gasped, 'you bastard, do it harder.'

And Bob obliged, grabbing at Catherine's full white hips with his big hands and holding her still while he screwed his cock into her with such brutal energy that she gasped as if she were being beaten. Her hand moved between her legs, faster and faster, and the dangling tips of her breasts scraped against the rough cotton of the throw. Her dark eyes widened and her lips parted in a soft triangle of delight. 'Oh,' she whispered, 'I'm coming, I'm coming,' and then a series of juddering spasms ran through her soft flesh from buttock to shoulder. Her spread thighs shook with ecstasy and she fell forward onto her face, twitching helplessly as Bob drove himself to a savage orgasm within her soft, clutching sex.

After a little pause, Jeannette said from the floor, 'Tess, your turn.' Her raw voice was husky and smothered with satisfaction.

Tess swallowed hard and turned to Charlie. He smiled at her. If he had been nervous intially, his anxiety seemed to have gone now. He said, 'Don't worry, leave it to me,' and put his dark hands to the straps of the silk slip. He coaxed them gently down over Tess's shoulders to reveal her naked breasts.

His hands touched her. Tess closed her eyes. Behind the shield of her eyelids she could forget that there were other people in the room, that every move, every turn of her head was observed. She breathed deeply and concentrated on the sensation of Charlie's gentle hands touching her, exploring her.

'You're ready for me,' he whispered, dipping one finger deep inside her and coaxing the sweet juice from her. 'You're ready.'

Tess moaned, a moan of acquiescence. Charlie drew back from her and for a moment she sat up, opening her eyes. She saw him tugging a sheepskin rug from the sofa and laying it on the floor and she closed her eyes again quickly before she saw Bob and Stefan and her friends, greedily watching.

'Come on,' said Charlie's voice in her ear, and then his strong hands were slipping under her shoulders, under her thighs, lifting her. She hung limply in his arms, the air cool on her exposed throat. He kissed her just under the line of her jaw and she shivered and turned her head helplessly. Then he swung her through the air and laid her down on the sheepskin, soft as clouds. His hands pulled down the shift to expose her breasts and pushed it up around her hips. She tightened her closed eyes and lay quivering, knowing that everyone could see the glistening flesh of her sex between her softly parted thighs.

There was movement above her and she felt Charlie lowering his body onto her. His mouth met hers and he kissed her deeply, sliding his tongue hard into her mouth. His hot, erect cock stirred against her belly and she silently spread her legs wider, accepting him.

'No,' he whispered against her lips. 'Artistic, remember?' He pulled back and knelt between her open thighs, then leant towards her. He drew one of her legs under his arm and laid the other on his chest so that her calf rested on his shoulder. Tess lay very still, breathing in quick shallow gasps. She felt helpless, exposed, possessed. Charlie's hands slid up her body, up her ribs, onto her breasts, and as he squeezed the heavy orbs his penis nudged between her labia and began to enter her.

He seemed to go on for ever. Something about the position meant that her hips were tilted up to him and he penetrated her completely, to the neck of her womb, filling her deliciously. Tess sighed with pleasure and opened her eyes, looking up into his face. His dark eyes glowed at her and he began to move, leaning gently forward, rocking back. Every move seemed to spread her wider and his hands cradled the weight of her breasts as if they were the treasures of the world. She gripped at him with the muscles of her sex, wanting to give him pleasure too, and he gasped and smiled and thrust again, slow and deep and gentle.

The soft sheepskin caressed Tess's back, her neck and shoulders. Charlie pushed until his body was pressed hard against her and then he stopped moving and rested his weight on her. He teased at her breasts, stroking and kneading, and very gently his body leant against her and fractionally withdrew, leant and withdrew. His stiff penis barely stirred within her quivering tunnel, but the whole weight of his torso rubbed against her vulva with a firm inevitability that made her shudder with pleasure. She gasped and flung her head from side to side, not knowing whether she wanted him to move faster or not, and he continued the same steady, slow, pulsing pressure and his dark fingers ceaselessly fondled her swollen nipples.

Watching the others coupling had aroused Tess more than she could have imagined, and now the gentle insidious touch of Charlie's body against hers was driving her into a fever of ecstasy. She moaned and heaved, but he did not increase the speed of his movements. Very slowly, very steadily, he drew her up and up onto a plateau of pleasure and held her there, and then as her sex began to tense and clench around his deep-thrust penis he squeezed her breasts hard and began to move, lunging forward and back within her as she cried out and convulsed in the throes of a violent, consuming orgasm. She felt him shuddering inside her, himself overtaken by pleasure, and the sensation drew her back to the peak and filled her with sweetness like a cup overflowing with wine.

Tess lay beneath Charlie with blood rushing in her ears, feeling his heartbeat pulsing in his buried cock. She felt sated and yet ready for more. She arched her back lasciviously, pushing her breasts up towards Charlie's face. She was glad, yes, glad that she had done it, glad that she had offered herself. For the first time in weeks she felt free of Tony's selfish dominance.

What did Carmen say to José at the end of the opera? *I was born free, and I will die free*. Yes, that was the feeling. She tried to commit it to memory. How long would it last, after tonight? Would it survive another night in Tony's bed?

On the floor near her Jeannette stretched like a cat and grinned. 'Sod the score cards,' she said lazily, reaching out to stroke Catherine's limp hand. 'Let's just enjoy ourselves.'

Act Three, Scene Two

The Cat Flat

Just after midnight Tess and Jeannette and Catherine finished clearing up the flat. The stage hands were gone and the wine glasses were washed up, and now Catherine was crawling on hands and knees around the drawing room, scanning the patterned Persian carpet for abandoned condoms while Tess and Jeannette folded up the rugs and throws.

'Well?' said Jeannette, staggering a little. 'What d'you reckon, Tess? Remember them all?'

Tess shook her head, somewhat at a loss for a reply. After that first fabulous orgasm in Charlie's arms everything seemed to have blurred. She remembered a number of things with a remarkable combination of vividness and confusion. There was Charlie lying between her thighs and stabbing up into her with his long strong tongue while Bob pushed his sturdy prick between her lips. Charlie's tongue was exquisite, firm and sensitive, now quivering against her clitoris, now coiling deep inside her. He was gasping as he licked her, but she couldn't recall who had been pleasuring him, offering a soft mouth or a moist sex for the satisfaction of his rampant cock.

There were Catherine and Jeannette moaning in each

other's arms, fingers probing eagerly between their wide spread thighs as they watched while all three men occupied themselves with Tess's body. Bob was still in her mouth, thrusting his fat penis avidly between her soft lips and grunting as his hairy balls frotted against her chin. Charlie gasped as he rubbed his cock between her breasts, and she moaned as she felt him tugging at her taut nipples, pinching and pulling with the rhythm of his body's urgent movement. And then she cried out past the gag of Bob's stifling cock because she felt Stefan thrusting feverishly into her spasming vagina with his huge phallus, stretching her until she thought she would never again need to feel another man inside her, shafting her with joyful energy. Three men enjoying themselves with her, three stiff swollen penises burying themselves in her body, and an orgasm so powerful that she had actually blacked out for a minute.

And more: Jeannette whimpering with anticipation as Charlie prepared to push his taut shaft into her anus; Tess and Catherine staring in aroused amazement as big, thickset Bob knelt down in front of Stefan and moaned like a child to feel that huge, powerful cock sliding deep between his lips.

But what order it had happened in, or how, she couldn't imagine. 'Well,' she said, 'I remember Stefan's cock, of course, and Charlie's tongue, and Bob – well, Bob was so heavy, and sort of solid.'

Catherine got to her feet, grinning. 'Sounds good enough to me,' she said. 'Think of that next time you're on stage and you'll be there.'

Jeannette lowered the last rug into a heap and stretched. 'I'm cream crackered,' she said. 'Bedtime for me. You going to stop over, Tess? The little bed's made up in the boxroom.'

'Yes,' said Tess, gratefully. 'Thank you.' She knew if she went back to her flat she would start having second thoughts.

Within half an hour she was tucked up on the little

bed in the narrow boxroom beside the drawing room, gently stretching muscle after muscle, testing herself. She ached between her legs. Stefan wielded his massive penis more like a blunt instrument than anything else. But altogether she felt good. Satisfied, that was the word.

The hall door creaked open and footsteps entered the drawing room. Tess cocked her head to listen. She heard Emma's voice giggling and Leo murmuring softly, then the breathing silence of two people kissing. A pause, then a grunt of effort from Leo and a few moments later the sound of bodies landing on one of the sofas.

He's going for it tonight, Tess thought. She was tired, but the thought that she might overhear Leo taking Emma's virginity made her shiver with excitement. Stifling guilt, she got to her feet and padded silently across the room to open the door a fraction and press her ear to the crack.

'Oh,' whimpered Emma's voice. 'Oh, Leo, that's so nice. Oh, touch me there. Oh yes, yes.' Then her words stopped. Leo must have stopped them with his mouth. Tess knelt by the door, stiff with tension, listening as Emma's little whimpering cries became more urgent. At last Emma took several quick regular breaths, as if she was going to sneeze, and then let out a long, ecstatic sigh of relief and pleasure.

'Emma,' said Leo's deep voice. 'God, Emma, let me – '

'No!' Emma's little-girl voice was suddenly sharp and stern. 'No, Leo, no.'

'Please,' whispered Leo. 'I have to. I'll explode, Emma. At least touch me. Kiss it, stroke it – something – anything, Emma.'

'No,' said Emma, and you could hear the pout. 'I'm going to bed. Thank you for a lovely evening, Leo.'

And to Tess's amazement she did just that. She switched on the light, making Leo wince and Tess flinch back from the doorway in case she was seen, and flounced out of the drawing room and down the long corridor towards her bedroom, where her battered teddy bear awaited her.

Leo sat on the sofa, staring after her. When the door at the end of the corridor closed he buried his head in his hands, the picture of despair.

Tess was very fond of Leo. She hated to see him so distressed. She quickly pulled on the dressing gown that Catherine had lent her and opened the boxroom door. 'Leo,' she whispered.

Leo's head jerked up. His face was pale, with a hectic flush on his cheeks. He gazed at Tess in astonishment, then got angrily to his feet. 'Christ,' he said, pushing one hand hard through his tousled fair hair.

'Oh, Leo, I overhead,' Tess said, coming closer. 'I'm sorry. She's such a little tease.'

'No,' said Leo, shaking his head. 'I don't think she means to tease, she just – can't help it.'

Tess watched him uncomfortably adjusting his trousers, trying to take the pressure off his swollen penis. After a moment she said with a solemn look, 'Why don't you get her drunk? It worked on me.'

That made Leo smile despite himself. 'I didn't get you drunk,' he said. 'What an accusation! You got yourself drunk. I just spotted the opportunity.' Then his smile disappeared. 'Anyway,' he said, 'she won't drink. Not even a glass of wine. Mineral water, fruit juice and Aqua Libra. I used to think you were abstemious, Tess, but she takes the cake.'

He looked so unhappy that Tess came forward and stroked his face with her hand. He turned away, embarrassed at her sympathy. 'Poor Leo,' she said. 'You really want her, don't you.'

'My God,' said Leo, 'I do.' He turned back, suddenly earnest. In a very low voice he said, 'She's not putting it on, Tess, you know. She lets me – touch her. I know she's a virgin, I've felt it. Twenty-six years old and a virgin! She says she's saving herself for the right man,

166

but I know, I know she'd love it. She likes it when I kiss her hard. She just needs someone to – to master her.'

'Sounds like she would suit Tony,' Tess muttered. Leo looked puzzled and she shook her head. She wanted to do Leo a kindness, to offer him a return for the way he had led her gently by the hand into the world of sexual reality. She frowned after a moment, wondering whether an offer of some sort of physical consolation might be appropriate. But things were over between Leo and her, had been over for years, and although she was very fond of him she no longer found him as attractive as she once had. Cuddly and lovable, yes: sexy, no. She said at last, 'Look, Leo, maybe I could – we could help. Me and Jeannette and Catherine, I mean.'

'Help?' asked Leo blankly. 'How?'

Tess shook her head again. 'I'm not sure. Not sure, but I know Jeannette will have a few ideas. She always has ideas. Why don't we talk to you about it tomorrow, at rehearsal? Make plans then?'

Leo frowned at her for a moment, then laughed. 'Whatever you say,' he said. 'I need help, don't I? Good grief, look at me. I fancied myself as a seducer, and here I am, bent double while she stomps off to bed.'

'We'll talk about it tomorrow,' Tess promised, and she kissed Leo's cheek before he left.

The following day at rehearsal Tony was on stage with Emma when Tess arrived. They were deeply embroiled in the Act One duet, but she knew that he could see her lurking in the wings. He ignored her, not even turning around to acknowledge her when some technical hitch stopped Emma in mid-note for a few moments. This was unlike him, and Tess felt a stir first of guilt, then of discontent and rebellion.

Eventually Emma left the stage, looking coyly over her shoulder at Tony. It couldn't be hard, Tess thought sourly, for Emma to play Micaela. So sweet and innocent, saccharine even, the perfect little virgin, mother's choice.

She was born to play the part. Tess had to admit that Emma also had a lovely voice, strong and sweet and sustained on the crippling high notes of Micaela's arias, but that was almost incidental. Tess folded her lips as Emma came past her in the wings, fluttering her eye-lashes at the stage manager. She wondered briefly if she disliked Emma because she was jealous of her. Was she jealous of Emma's looks, or her voice, or the fact that she was still a virgin? Was it wicked to plot that she should cease to become one?

The chorus milled past Tess onto the stage and she poised herself for her entry. Tony appeared beside her: in this scene Don José led Carmen on, under arrest. She glanced at him but he refused to look at her. 'Did you have a good meal?' he said, staring straight ahead.

Any remnants of guilt that Tess had felt about her behaviour the previous night evaporated. 'I had an extremely pleasant evening, thank you,' she said coldly, and then it was time to go on stage.

Her anger carried through into her performance. James was delighted. 'That's it!' he yelled from the middle of the area where the seats would be. 'That's it, Tess. Insolence! Impudence! You don't give a stuff! That's it!'

The scene continued. Carmen, left alone with Don José, seduces him despite the fact that he has just promised himself that he will marry Micaela. As Tess sang her aria she knew that for the first time she was reaching the core of her character, the strength, the callousness that sees what it wants in a man's body and reaches out and plucks it like a flower, only to toss it away the moment its first bloom fades.

Something was working on Tony, too. Earlier he had been angry and cold, but now he looked hungry, jealous, desperate for her. She met his eyes and saw them dark and hot with passion, and his voice when he sang had a tinge of fevered rawness that was quite new. It gave Tess great satisfaction to see Tony wanting her, and she began to think that perhaps, perhaps after all she might be able to free herself from him. It would be good if she were the one that ended it. Leave him begging for it, the way he had so often made her beg him.

The act finished to applause from chorus and stage hands. James came towards them, exclaiming enthusiastically, and Tony turned to Tess and said, 'Come round this evening. Straight after rehearsal.'

Now or never, Tess. 'Sorry,' Tess said, more evenly that she felt. 'I can't.'

'Come round!' Tony caught at her arms, holding them so tight that he hurt her. 'Tess, what's going on? I want you to come round tonight!'

She pulled away. 'I promised Jeannette and Catherine.' *And Leo*, she thought. 'Sorry, Tony. It'll have to be tomorrow.'

Then James was with them and their chance for private conversation was over. Tess managed to free herself for five minutes and found Leo standing in the wings, watching Emma discussing her costume with the designer. His pale-blue eyes were very wide and yearning and his chin was propped on his hand in an attitude of the purest melancholy.

'Cheer up, chicken,' Tess said in his ear, making him jump. He spun on his heel and looked at her in surprise. 'Got it sussed,' she said. 'Simple but effective. Bring dinner round to the Cat Flat tonight. Catherine and Jeannette and I are going out.' Emma turned towards them and Tess finished in a hasty undertone, 'I'll brief you later.'

'Why, Tess,' said Emma, coming up to Leo and taking hold of his arm with possessive speed, 'you were wonderful. Whatever made you change your performance that way? It was great. Anyone would think you had been up to something.'

'Oh,' Tess said with a bland smile, 'just thinking about it.' Did Emma suspect something about Tess's research activities? How could she know? Could one of the stage hands have blown the whistle? If she found out she would run off and tell tales to Tony before you could sing two bars.

'Well, it was marvellous,' said Emma. 'You really do make a most convincing tart. I'm sure I couldn't do it.' And she looked up into Leo's face and smiled with infinite sweetness.

If Tess had had any misapprehensions about what she and the others had planned for Emma, that little remark removed them. That evening she and Jeannette and Catherine gathered giggling in the kitchen of the Cat Flat and proceeded to empty about a quarter of all the bottles of orange juice, Appletise and Emma's favourite Aqua Libra down the sink. Then they filled up the vacant space with the strongest Polish vodka the off licence could sell.

'Does it taste?' asked Catherine anxiously as Jeannette sniffed at a small glass of extremely alcoholic Aqua Libra.

'Nope.' Jeannette's plaits bobbed as she shook her head. 'No, I'm sure it doesn't. And if she never ever drinks, it should have one hell of an effect.'

'Stuff them in the fridge,' said Tess urgently. 'They'll be here any minute.'

They were ready to go out by the time that the door opened to admit Emma and Leo and a number of bags smelling of Thai food. In the doorway Jeannette called back, 'Have a nice time. Don't do anything I wouldn't do!'

'Will it work?' asked Tess in the lift.

'Up to your friend Leo now,' said Catherine. 'From what Jeannette tells me he knows what he's about. And did you pass on our suggestions?'

'Certainly did.' Tess gnawed at her lower lip. 'Gosh, I hope it works.'

They crept back into the flat at one in the morning, ostentatiously hushing each other. The drawing room was empty. Catherine pushed at Tess and said, 'You go and look in her room.'

'Forget it!' Tess hissed. 'We'd wake – '

'Them? Her?' whispered Jeannette. 'If you don't look, we'll never know.'

'You look,' protested Tess.

'He's your friend. You look.'

And Tess put her hands over her mouth and made a face and then crept down the corridor to the far end of the flat and Emma's room.

The door was shut, but the catch was not quite engaged. Tess winced, then stretched out one finger and pushed the door. It swung open a little way, silent on its well greased hinges. The light from the hall fell into the room and Tess pulled back quickly into the wall, but there was no sound from inside. She leant forward, very, very slowly, and looked into the room.

There were two bodies in the bed. Leo's big bulk was curled protectively around the little, frail figure of Emma and his hand was resting on the pillow on top of the golden-brown strands of her hair. Tess stared, then reached in to catch hold of the door and slowly pull it closed. She tiptoed down the corridor and whispered to Jeannette and Catherine's tense faces, 'Yesss!'

They congratulated each other in undertones and then went into the kitchen to destroy the evidence in the fridge.

The following morning Tess woke in the boxroom bed quite early. She got up at once and pulled on last night's clothes. Jeannette and Catherine had offered her their bed to share for the night, but she hadn't wanted to miss the sight of Emma facing the world the morning after the night before. She went into the kitchen and put the kettle on to boil.

The tea was made and half the pot drunk before she heard a sound from the bedroom at the far end of the corridor. At first it was a low murmuring of voices. Then Emma's voice, loud and clear, shouting, 'You bastard!'

'Emma.' Leo, trying to defend himself. 'Emma, listen – '

'You bastard!' And the door burst open. Leo backed out of it, half-dressed and holding up his hands to protect himself from the tiny figure of Emma, who was wrapped in her dressing gown and battering him wherever she could reach with her fists.

'Emma,' he said between blows, 'I thought you enjoyed it!'

'*Oh!*' Emma exclaimed, as if words failed her. She stood for a second simmering like a pot that is about to boil over, and then she jerked up her knee and caught Leo amidships. She just missed his crotch, but her kneecap sank deep into his stomach and he let out a whistling cry and bent over.

'Emma!' Tess cried, running forward to intervene. But before she could reach them Emma had linked her little hands into a fist and hit Leo in the throat as hard as she could. He gave a strangled cry and fell forward onto his knees, gasping for breath.

'Emma, for Christ's sake!' Tess shouted, getting between Emma and her helpless prey. But Emma jerked up her head and looked down at Leo for a moment with stern disdain, then turned on her heel and stalked back into her bedroom and slammed the door. A moment later it opened again and the rest of Leo's clothes were hurled through it to land in a heap on the floor of the corridor.

'Leo,' said Tess urgently. She bent to help him up as the other bedroom door opened and Jeannette and Catherine emerged, tousled and sleepy. 'Leo, are you all right?'

'Shit,' Leo whispered. His hand was on his throat, rubbing. He looked panic-stricken. 'Shit, she got me right in the vocal cords. Shit, shit – '

'Don't talk,' Tess told him hastily. 'Don't say anything.

172

You'll strain it. We'll get you to casualty, come on. Come on, get your clothes on.'

A taxi whirled them to the South Bank and a hospital in no time, but then they sat among a queue of the usual denizens of the casualty department: cuts, sprains, breaks, bruises and children with saucepans stuck on their heads. Leo was obviously not an urgent case, and the waiting dragged on and on and on.

'Shit,' Leo said for the umpteenth time. He was sitting in a corner on an uncomfortable plastic chair, his head tilted back against the wall. A dark bruise was spreading across his throat. 'Shit. Fuck. Bugger.' His voice was hoarse and rough, not at all like his usual dark, velvety tones.

'Leo, please don't talk,' Tess said anxiously. 'You'll make it worse.'

He shook his head. 'I can't make it worse. It's no good, Tess, I can feel it already, the voice-box is bruised. I won't be able to sing for weeks.' He opened his mouth and made a short, strangled sound, quickly cut off. 'No. No way. The bitch, the bitch, she knew exactly what she was doing.'

There was a long pause. Then Tess said, 'No need to ask you if it worked.'

Leo laughed at that, a rueful laugh. 'Listen,' he said, getting to his feet, 'there's no point in waiting around here. Casualty is the grimmest place in the world. I'll go and see my own doctor at home. Come on, let's go along to the South Bank and have a drink and I'll tell you what happened. Then we'd better go and break the news to James that he's going to need another Escamillo with ten days before the first performance. God, what a bummer.'

It was a beautiful day, and they walked along past the Royal Festival Hall and the National Theatre to the little clutch of boutiques and restaurants in the Gabriel's Wharf development. Several of the cafés had tables outside, and Tess and Leo sat at one of them and ordered long cool drinks. 'Plenty of ice,' Leo said huskily.

173

'Leo,' Tess said, 'I'm so sorry. I feel responsible.'

Leo shook his head and smiled at her. 'Listen,' he said, 'to be honest, in a few weeks' time I'll probably say it was worth it. Right now my voice hurts and I'll have lost most of my fee for this show and my agent will be furious with me, but believe me, Tess, I wouldn't have done anything differently.'

The drinks came. 'Tell me about it,' Tess said, leaning forward and looking eagerly into Leo's face.

When the door closed Emma tossed her head and said, 'That Jeannette, honestly. *Don't do anything I wouldn't do.* Doesn't rule out an awful lot, then.'

'What d'you mean?' Leo asked, indecently curious.

'She'd do anything, that woman. And Catherine is just as bad. They're leading poor little Tess astray between them. I'm sure they've,' Emma's voice dropped to a prurient hiss, '*slept* together. All three of them. I mean, eww! I thought Tess was quite nice when I met her.'

'I think she's quite nice now,' Leo said reasonably.

Emma pursed her rosebud lips. 'Oh, well, she's an old friend of yours, isn't she.'

They set out the Thai food on the table and Emma sat down with an expression of satisfaction. For a very small person she had a remarkably large appetite. 'Yum,' she said happily. 'I love Thai. Where are the satays?'

'Here.' Leo passed the appropriate carton. 'I'll just get a drink. What would you like?'

'Aqua Libra, please,' said Emma. Leo raised his sandy eyebrows and went into the kitchen, found a bottle, sniffed at it, nodded appreciatively and poured a long glass of pale liquid over several ice cubes.

When he returned with the drinks Emma had unpacked the satays and was holding one gingerly by its wooden stick, dipping it into peanut sauce. 'Mmm,' she said as she lifted it to her lips, 'peanut sauce, my favourite.' The sauce dripped and she caught the drip on her tongue and licked the satay clean.

Leo stood watching her, shuddering. Her mouth was small and red and her teeth were small and white and her little tongue flickered across the satay like a cat's. He imagined that little neat tongue quivering between Emma's parted lips as he drove his cock deep inside her, imagined it moving delicately across the throbbing head of his penis as she whimpered with expectation and arousal.

'Here you are,' he said, passing her the spiked drink.

'Thanks,' said Emma. 'Gosh, that's a spicy sauce.' She gulped down half the drink in one. Leo watched her swallow, tense with apprehension. Would she notice? But she just said, 'Ah, that's better,' and dipped the satay again.

Leo sat down heavily at the table. He had meant to play it cool, but obviously the message had not reached his genitals. He could feel that beneath his trousers his cock was beginning to swell. To distract himself he opened a few more cartons and tried to concentrate on the food, but it was hard.

Tonight, it would be tonight. He would deflower her tonight. For Leo, nothing matched that moment, that first moment, when he thrust himself up inside a virgin and watched her face change, overtaken with amazement and pleasure to feel that throbbing presence moving within her, filling her, clutched between her silken walls like a sceptre in a velvet case. He knew that he was skilled, that he had never been a disappointment. Once or twice, just once or twice, he'd given a girl her first orgasm, too. Now that really was amazing. It wouldn't happen with Emma, who had shuddered her way to ecstasy practically every night they had been together, moaning in his arms as his deft fingers felt between her slender thighs. He'd had to be careful, though, since she would never let him penetrate her with his fingers, only caress her clitoris and the lips of her sex until she was running with honeyed juice and her mouth was slack with pleasure. But she had always come, trembling as she reached her climax and letting out sweet little cries of joy that made him long to show her that there was more, so much more for her to relish in the garden of earthly delight.

'Pass me the rice, would you?' asked Emma. 'And the chili beef?'

'You need another drink,' Leo said evenly. He got up from his chair and took Emma's glass out to the kitchen and refilled it with the booby-trapped Aqua Libra. What a comedown, he thought. Reduced to alcohol to get my wicked way. Oh well: candy is dandy, but liquor is quicker. He poured a beer for himself, intending to go easy on the booze in case it affected his prowess.

'Gosh,' Emma said as he returned, 'this food is great. Honestly, I don't think I've ever tasted better. Where did you get it?'

'Little place in Soho I know.' Leo looked closely at Emma and was reassured by what he saw. A hot pink flush was creeping up her porcelain cheeks and her eyes were suspiciously bright. 'If you'd come and stay with me after the production, Emma, when we have more time, I could take you round more of London than we've had time for.'

'Gosh, I'm thirsty.' Emma drained half the glass, swallowing at least three measures of vodka in the process. 'Spicy food does that to you, doesn't it.' She hiccuped unexpectedly and put her hand to her mouth, giggling. 'Oops! Leo, you're not eating.'

I'm too excited to eat, Leo thought. My prick has other things on its mind. 'Just not terribly hungry,' he said with a smile. 'Anyway, you can eat for two. I'll just put some music on.'

'It's a really weird selection,' Emma warned him as he went over to the CD player. 'Catherine listens to jazz mostly and Jeannette likes all this multi-cultural music. And pop music. Yuk.'

Leo looked at the CD on the top of the stack. It was

called *Music To Make Love To*. He smiled and shook his head and opened the CD box.

A little while later Emma said, 'Oh wow, I don't know what's wrong with me. I feel really odd.'

'Are you all right?' Leo asked with well simulated anxiety. He got to his feet and hurried round the table to catch Emma in his arms as she swayed in her chair.

'I feel giddy,' she whimpered.

'You've been working hard,' said Leo. 'You need to put your feet up.' He stooped and caught her up, holding her tightly. She was so light it was easy. She protested faintly, but he said, 'Hush,' and she closed her eyes and put her arms around his neck.

'I feel so odd,' Emma said again as Leo carried her to the sofa. 'What's the matter with me?'

Three double vodkas. Leo sat down beside her. A sudden pulse of desire beat through him from head to toes and he shuddered. She was so pretty, so delicate, like a china doll. She was no chocolate-box innocent, he knew that, but she was a virgin. A real virgin, for perhaps another half an hour. He touched her face with his fingers. His hand was trembling. 'Emma,' he said softly, 'you're so beautiful.'

She purred a little, like a young kitten, as his fingers moved gently over the downy skin of her cheek. 'You're very sweet, Leo,' she murmured.

Without another word Leo leant forward and set his lips to hers. She made a little surprised sound, then turned to him and opened her mouth. He kissed her hard, searchingly, long-drawn kisses that made his chest tighten and his loins tense with desire for her. She responded, turning her face up to his and moaning softly as his lips travelled from her mouth to her jaw, to her delicate swan-like neck, to her little pretty ears. 'Emma,' he murmured against her pale skin. 'Emma, Emma, Emma.'

'Oh,' she whispered, 'that's so nice.'

His hands found the buttons on her white blouse and

began to unfasten them. This would be a good sign of whether he stood a chance. She had let him touch her breasts before, but only through or beneath her clothes. He had never seen them bare. Now, though, she made a little noise of protest but did not pull away. He unfastened the last button and pushed the blouse open.

She was tiny, slender, and under the blouse she wore a little lacy bra, there for looks, since her small upturned breasts needed no support. Leo drew in a hissing breath through his teeth and put his hand on her collar bone and very slowly moved it down until he could catch hold of the stretchy fabric of the bra and push it aside.

Her breasts were like shallow snow-covered hills and her nipples were perfect, small and round, coral-pink, tipped with hardness like the stem of a succulent fruit. She said, 'Oh Leo, don't,' but she did not try to stop him as he whispered in delight and put his hand on one soft mound, squeezing it gently.

'Ah,' Emma breathed. Leo put his mouth over hers and kissed her and as he did so he caressed her breast. His hands were big, he could cup the whole tender swell in one palm, and as he softly squeezed the delicate flesh he felt the small, tight nipple stiffening beneath his hand. Emma gasped and began to breathe unsteadily and Leo thrust his tongue deep into her mouth and took her taut nipple between his fingers, lengthening it, pinching it until she moaned.

There was something deliciously wanton about a woman with her clothing open. Emma lay on the sofa with her head tilted back, exposing her white throat, and the fronts of her blouse were pushed back to show her tender breasts naked above the lacy scrap of her bra. For a moment Leo thought of holding her down and just doing it to her, parting her thighs with a jerk of his knee and then sheathing himself within her to the root in a single thrust. But that was not what pleased him. It was the gentle urging of seduction that made him feel powerful. Instead he lowered his head to her breasts and began

178

to suck and lap against her nipples until the coral flesh engorged, even the areolae stood out proudly from the white skin of the breasts. One of his hands was free, and with it he began to lift Emma's skirt.

'Leo,' she whimpered, 'don't,' and for a moment her hands fastened on his upper arms and pushed as if she would push him away from her. But he sucked harder at one proud nipple and Emma's protests died away into a groan of pleasure.

As always, she was wearing hold-ups and panties that were no more than a scrap of flimsy lace. As Leo's hand moved up over her slender thighs she sighed and her legs moved apart almost of themselves. The crotch of her panties was already warm and damp with readiness. Leo stroked his finger over the taut fabric and she shivered and moaned with pleasure.

With the ease of long practice Leo slid one finger below the lace panties and at once found the tiny stiff pearl of Emma's clitoris, already engorged and begging his attention. He stroked at it and sucked harder at her nipple and she began to cry out and move her hips regularly.

How many orgasms would he give her before he took her? How many times would he make her cry out before he parted those soft, damp lips and pushed his way between them? She seemed already to be nearly there, shuddering and whimpering as he caressed her secret flesh with gentle, deliberate precision. Leo traced his finger along the soft moist folds of her labia, probed for an instant at the entrance to her tight, virgin tunnel, then returned to the little proud bead of flesh at the front of her sex and stroked and stroked it until Emma arched and tensed against his hand, crying out with little sweet sounds as her first climax took her.

Leo lifted his head from her breast. She opened her big blue eyes and looked up at him, astonished and breathing fast. 'Good?' he asked softly.

'Oh, Leo, I – '

'I've got a special treat for you tonight,' Leo said. 'I'm going to make you come another way.'

'How?' asked Emma, opening her eyes even wider.

'Here,' Leo said, pushing her skirt up around her hips, 'down with the panties.'

'No,' Emma said, fighting against the alcohol that coursed through her blood, 'no, Leo, I won't let you.'

'Don't worry!' he reassured her. 'I'm going to use my mouth on you.'

Emma was suddenly very still, breathing quickly as she looked at him. She was tempted. Her little pink tongue ran quickly around her lips, moistening them. 'Your mouth,' she said softly.

'You'll love it.' Leo took hold of the edges of her panties and rolled them down her thighs to her ankles. 'Put your ankles over my shoulders,' he suggested, kneeling at her feet. 'Then I can get at you.'

'Oh,' Emma whispered, 'that's so dirty. Oh, I don't believe it.' But she lifted her thighs and rested them on his shoulders as he had asked.

The whole of her tight, tender sex was exposed to him, beautiful, delicious, gleaming with honey-smelling juice. The curls of fine fur were pale brown and the hole was small, delicately made, asking for him to caress it. Her labia and clitoris were swollen from her earlier orgasm and when he leant forward and touched his tongue to the little pink pearl Emma shivered from head to foot and let out a wavering cry. 'Oh God, oh that's amazing, oh, Leo, Leo.'

Very gently, very diligently, Leo lapped at her. His tongue was strong and skilled and he flickered the tip against her, then flashed the whole blade across her quivering flesh until she moaned aloud. Emma writhed on the cushions of the sofa, entirely overtaken by pleasure, and Leo continued to serve her with his mouth until she was pushing her slender hips up towards his face, desperate for him to lick her harder, to take her to the heights of pleasure with his tongue and lips. He obeyed her, aroused to fever pitch by her delicious responsiveness and by the knowledge that in only a few minutes he would be the first man ever to plunge his penis into that fragrant, trembling flesh.

'Leo,' Emma wailed, 'oh, Leo, I'm coming. Please, please don't stop.' And her slight body bucked and shuddered against him as her orgasm possessed her utterly.

Leo knelt between her thighs, not moving, hardly breathing. For long moments Emma was still, and then she let out a long, long sigh and relaxed. Leo reached down and opened his trousers, releasing his massively engorged cock from its prison of cotton. He thought she might detect the rustle of the packet as he opened a condom, but he moved his tongue gently against her and she moaned with resurgence of pleasure.

He was ready. All that remained now was to make sure that she could not resist him. In his pocket was one of Tess's long silk scarves, ready tied into a loop. He reached up behind his head, felt for Emma's slender ankles, and fastened the loop of silk tightly around them.

'Leo?' Emma said in a voice that was suddenly puzzled and anxious. Leo smiled to himself and lifted himself over her. Her tied ankles were hooked around his neck, opening her to him so wantonly, so helplessly, that he shook with arousal. Her eyes were open too, startled pools of blue. 'Leo!' she said, trying to struggle.

'Emma,' Leo said softly. 'I've given you an orgasm with my fingers, and I've given you one with my mouth, and now I'm going to give you one with my cock.' He felt huge, smooth and strong and powerful, bigger than he had been in his life and ripe with seed. He lodged the swollen, shining head of his cock between the lips of Emma's wet sex and leant towards her.

'No,' Emma moaned. Her little hands were flat on his chest, trying to push him away from her. 'Leo, no.'

'Yes,' Leo whispered. This was not the time for mercy, and the very mercilessness of it aroused him so strongly that he shuddered. He thrust a little and felt resistance. Her maidenhead, her virginity, waiting for him, and his thick stiff cock was there, ready to take it.

'Please, please,' Emma moaned. She writhed beneath him, trying to escape, but her tender body was fixed beneath him like a nail prepared for the blow of the hammer. 'Leo, Leo, oh God.'

'Oh, Emma,' Leo gasped, and he clenched his buttocks and thrust and thrust, slow and strong, until at last her maidenhead gave way and his penis entered her, penetrating her completely, sliding up and up into her tight, sweet sex until it was all hidden.

Emma's blue eyes opened very wide and she stared up into Leo's face. 'Oh, my God,' she whispered, stunned with disbelief and pleasure, 'oh, my God.'

'Feel me,' Leo whispered. 'Feel me inside you, Emma. My cock's right up inside you, buried inside you. Feel it.' He withdrew a little and thrust again and Emma gasped as if she could not breathe. 'Feel how deep it is, Emma.'

'Oh,' Emma moaned again, 'Leo, I can't . . .'

Leo withdrew almost entirely and then let his weight bear him down on top of Emma's small slender body, driving him within her until he was embedded to the neck of her womb. Emma cried out and twisted her head on the cushions. Leo ran his hands down her body and took her small, firm buttocks in his hands, lifting them, opening her to him even wider, and she cried out again.

'Emma,' he hissed, and he thrust again, a long, slow, juicy thrust. Emma groaned. He put his mouth on hers and kissed her and as he kissed her he slid his thick shaft out and in again and felt her lips flinch and her tongue shudder as he penetrated her utterly.

He took her relentlessly, without his usual gentleness, lunging into her with frantic energy until his body slapped against hers and her cries became shrill and trembling. He was determined that she would come, and his hands were everywhere, tugging at her taut nipples,

182

caressing her white shoulders, pulling apart the cheeks of her bottom and even stimulating the delicate ring of her anus until at last her body responded and she began to cry out in rhythm with his urgent thrusting.

'That's it,' he gasped, shafting her with delirious strength. 'That's it. Come, Emma, come now, come now,' and as if obeying his order Emma's body twisted beneath him and her eyes rolled back and her lips parted. Her tight sex spasmed about his plunging cock, gripping feverishly at the thick glistening rod that ravished her, and Leo roared aloud and flung back his head as his balls tightened and twitched with the spurting of his eager seed.

Tess rested her chin in her hand and shook her head disbelievingly. 'What then?'

Leo grinned. His bruised voice was hoarse, but he wanted to tell her everything. 'I picked her up with my cock still in her and carried her to the bedroom. When you've wanted a woman as long as I've wanted her you can get it up as often as a thirteen-year-old. By that stage I think she'd forgotten everything except pleasure. She even used her mouth on me, and she's always sworn she would never, ever do that. And I remember she knelt on the bed with her face on the sheets and her lovely bottom stuck in the air and I took her from behind. I lasted for ever that time, by the time I came she was slumped forward and I was beating myself into her like – like a battering ram. And when I'd finished she sort of subsided, like a pricked balloon. It looked so incredibly voluptuous, Tess, I can't tell you, I just wanted to do it to her again and again. And she liked it when I was rough. I know I'm not imagining things. At one point I – I put my finger in her arse while I was doing it to her, right up inside her arse, and she came screaming. She liked it, I know she did.'

'But she was sorry in the morning,' Tess said ruefully.

'You win some, you lose some.' Leo looked up at the

blue sky with a far away expression. 'Christ, though, it was worth it. To see that little doll's face change when she felt my prick sliding up inside her. It was worth it.'

There was a long silence. Then Tess said in a very small voice, 'Did you like doing it to her more than you did with me?'

Leo frowned, apparently surprised. Then a very tender smile lifted the corners of his mouth. 'Tess,' he said, 'what can I tell you? I'll never sleep with Emma again, she made that clear this morning, and to be honest, I don't care. I wanted to take her cherry, not have an affair with her. With you – well, we stayed together for months. It wasn't the same at all. We were in love for a while, weren't we?'

'I suppose we were,' Tess said, feeling a pang of nostalgic regret.

'Do you love Tony?' Leo asked, suddenly sounding stiff and awkward.

Tess looked into his face for some time before replying. At last she said, 'No. No, I don't love him. Sometimes I don't even particularly like him.'

'He's such a sexist bastard,' Leo said angrily. 'Why does he get away with it?'

'And Emma's such a little prick teaser,' Tess answered. 'Why does she get away with it?'

'She didn't last night,' Leo grinned. Then he shook his head. 'And the wages of sin is death: at least as far as this production is concerned. Come on, Tess: time we went to give James the bad news.'

Act Four, Scene One

The theatre, Green Park

'OK,' called the voice of the stage manager, 'places for the bar scene. We've just got time for the Act Two opening, folks. Places, everyone.'

'So,' said Tony in a low voice, 'we're on for tonight?'

Say no, Tess thought. *Say no, Tony, I don't want to go back to your flat again. Why don't you come over to my place, just for once? Just for once? And I don't want to be your sex slave, I've had enough. Just say it.* But Tess looked up into Tony's hot dark eyes and heard her own voice saying, 'All right, Tony, sure. Straight after rehearsal.'

'Good. You know I'm not around for a couple of days. I'd miss you if I had to go without for three nights.'

Tess heard her cue and pulled free from Tony's possessive hand. 'I'm on,' she said quickly. He let her go and she ran onto the stage for the gypsy dance that opened the act.

The costumes were nearly ready and Tess was wearing her second best outfit to get used to the way she needed to move in it. She liked it a lot. All the girls liked their costumes, except Emma, who seemed to be displeased by everything at the moment. She was not at rehearsal today, since Micaela wasn't in the acts on the schedule, and Tess was frankly relieved. Since breaking up with

Leo, Emma had been spending even more of her time flirting with Tony, playing up to him in a simpering little-girl kind of way which set Tess's teeth on edge and made her want to scream.

The costume designer had been very careful to take the physical shape of the singers into account when putting the clothes together. So Jeannette, who was as slender as a wand, wore tight, tight Capri pants that clung to every inch of her taut buttocks and a short Lycra top that showed off her athletic frame and her high pointed breasts. Catherine had a sort of flounced gypsy outfit that exaggerated her already generous curves. And Tess wore a skintight skirt split to the thigh on one side, scarlet heels, and a tight, low-cut, uplifting bustier that set out her splendid bosom as if on a shop counter. The first time she had appeared in it the stage hands had greeted it with cheers and a chorus of wolf whistles. As a costume it restricted her movements somewhat, reducing her gypsy dance to a sort of circum-scribed gyration on the spot, but it was without doubt the sexiest thing that she had ever been asked to wear on stage. At the beginning of rehearsals she would have felt uncomfortable in it, but not now.

> *The dance's rhythm draws them on,* she sang,
> *Burning, crazy, mad with passion,*
> *They are drunk with joy, wild with passion,*
> *Sweetly ravished by the gypsy's song!*

The dancers joined her and Jeannette and Catherine on stage and whirled around her as she stood with her hands thrust skyward and her hips swivelling to the rhythm of the dance, closing her eyes as she tried to capture a sense of power, the sense of power that had filled her when she dreamed of the mermaid. But she could not find it. All she could think of was how Tony had demanded what he wanted of her, and she had submitted to him.

The dance crashed to its end. For a moment there was

a tense silence where the applause should have been. Then from the auditorium Adam's aristocratic voice said, 'Hold everything, darlings. There's someone arrived you have to meet.'

'The new Escamillo,' Jeannette whispered in Tess's ear. They stood side by side, wondering what would appear. It had been hard for James to find a replacement. He had picked some young unknown, a Canadian baritone whose only appearance in England to date had been in a televised singing competition, which he hadn't won. They knew his name, Richard Shaeffer, but they didn't know any more.

'Ladies and gentlemen,' said James's voice off stage, 'let me introduce you to our new Escamillo, Richard. He's been studying the production for three days and he joins rehearsals tomorrow. I know you'll all be pleased to see how well the costume fits him.'

Cast and stage hands laughed as James came onto the brightly lit stage, his arm on the elbow of a lean, dark young man dressed already as Escamillo, the TV star, Carmen's last and fatal love.

Tess sensed Jeannette's jaw dropping, but she couldn't take her eyes from the new arrival. He was wearing Leo's costume, which was made mostly of black and silver Lycra and concealed nothing about him, but there was no similarity between him and Leo. Chalk and cheese. The new Escamillo was a little taller than Leo, which made him just over six foot, and where Leo had been growing distinctly soft edged he had the build of an athlete. His strong shoulders were wide and a fine chest tapered beautifully to a narrow waist and hips with the pencilled muscles of a runner.

'Hi, everyone,' said the new arrival in a voice which sounded charmingly modest. 'Good to see you. Richard Shaeffer.'

He had a really attractive voice, warm and caressing with a rough edge to it like plush. Tess tore her eyes from his body and looked at his face. Handsome, with soft dark hair in rough curls like a lion's mane, a narrow nose, fine-cut, flaring nostrils, a mouth that was far too sensual to belong to a man, and wide-set, bright eyes that were an intriguing mix of green and brown and starred with long, dark lashes.

'Richard,' said James, 'meet our Carmen, Tess Challoner.'

'Hi,' said Richard again, holding out his hand. It was warm and dry and his grip was surprisingly strong. 'I'm really pleased to meet you, Tess. Wow, you sounded fabulous on stage just then. That's real power you've got in your voice.'

'Thank you,' said Tess, spellbound by his handsomeness and his simple, direct, modest manner.

He smiled at her. 'You look great too, of course, but hey, get these costumes, aren't they something? I feel like a character out of *Blade Runner*.'

'You look good too,' Tess heard herself saying. She was looking into his eyes, and she knew that her eyes were telling him that she thought he was beautiful and that instantly, viscerally, she had liked him.

'Thanks. Won't matter if I can't sing a note though, will it?' he said with a smile. His eyes looked straight into hers, making her midriff melt. 'I'm really looking forward to working with you,' he said. 'I've been working hard to learn the moves, but I'll have to rely on you a lot, with only a few days before the performance. I'm shit scared, believe me.'

His honesty disarmed her completely. 'Anything I can do,' she said, 'just ask.'

'Jeannette Baldwin, Catherine Gibbs.' James was continuing with the introductions. 'And Tony Varguez is lurking here somewhere. Ah there you are, Tony. Meet our new Escamillo, Richard Shaeffer.'

'It's an honour to meet you,' said Richard, and his face matched his words. 'I've got so many of your recordings.'

'Good to meet you too, Dick,' said Tony, with a smile that looked more like a snarl.

'Richard,' Richard said, wincing slightly.

'Well,' said James, 'that's enough for tonight. Richard, I'm glad you could make it this evening. You're coming back with Adam and me, we'll go over more of the production details with you. Everyone else, you know Tony can't be with us tomorrow, so we'll concentrate on the openings to Acts Two and Four. Usual time, see you then.'

'Tess,' Richard said, turning quickly to meet her eyes, 'it really was good to meet you. I'm looking forward to tomorrow.' Then James's hand was on his arm, steering him away. He looked over his shoulder at Tess as he went and smiled and waved at her.

'Wow,' said Jeannette in a smothered voice, but before Tess could respond Tony was there beside her, reaching out to catch hold of her elbow with one strong hand. 'Home,' he grated through his teeth. 'Now.'

What did he think she was, some little wifey? Tess swung to face him, bristling with anger and ready for a fight. But the sheer fury that she saw in Tony's eyes struck her dumb. He kept hold of her arm and towed her through the staring cast, out from the bounds of the temporary theatre and into the park.

She had got control of her shock by the time they reached Piccadilly. 'Christ,' she exclaimed, 'Tony, for God's sake, I'm still wearing my costume – '

'One word,' Tony said, swinging on her with venom, 'and I'll rip your costume off you here and now.'

His face showed that he meant it. Tess flinched unconsciously away from him, afraid of his vehemence and the sheer physical threat in the way he loomed over her. He flagged down a taxi and pulled Tess into it after him.

The taxi drove along Piccadilly and from Piccadilly Circus up Shaftesbury Avenue towards Seven Dials. Tony sat absolutely silent, his jaw set hard. A muscle twisted beside his mouth, over and over again. The

189

traffic was bad and the journey took a long time. Tess cleared her throat, took a deep breath, made all the preparations for speaking, but in the end she was afraid. She remembered what Catherine had said, that Tony had once hit the woman who was his lover. He looked now as if he might hit her. He looked sullen and dangerous and she did not dare to speak to him.

They drew up outside the flat. Without a word Tony got out, paid the driver, held the door for Tess and escorted her into the lift. His courtesy was exaggerated and served only to make her even more uncomfortable. As the lift slid silently up to the penthouse he began to breathe deeply, as if he was preparing himself.

The moment they were inside the flat he turned on her. 'So,' he said thinly, 'what do you think of our new baritone?'

Tess shook her head before she answered. His jealousy was obvious and stupid and it made her angry, but he had right on his side, too. She had thought Richard attractive instantly and she must have showed it. That was improper, when Tony was openly her lover. He had reason to be jealous. In a voice which shook, although she fought to keep it calm, she said, 'Tony, listen. You don't need to – '

'I asked you a question,' Tony snapped. 'I asked you what you thought of him. Answer me!'

'I thought he was – ' Tess extended her hands, help-less. How could she say the right thing in such a situation? 'Very – nice,' she finished lamely.

'*Nice?*' Tony repeated, with infinite scorn. 'Nice? You bloody English are all the same! What does *nice* mean now? It means you want to fuck him!'

'How dare you!' Tess shouted, jumping forward, really incensed. She raised her hand as if she was going to slap Tony's cheek, but he caught hold of her wrist and held it tightly, glaring at her. 'Let go of me, you bastard,' she shouted. 'You bastard! How dare you?'

'How dare I?' Tony's lips drew back from his teeth in

a snarl of rage. 'Because you're my woman, that's why, you bitch! Did you really think I'd let you go drooling over some new man the moment he shows his face on the stage?'

'You don't own me!' Tess cried, trying to pull free. 'You don't own me! Let go of me!'

For a moment they stood poised, balanced against each other, staring into each other's eyes. Tony's face was tight with passion, his black hair disordered and falling over his high brow, his nostrils flaring, his black eyes glittering with rage and jealousy. His cruel lips twitched as if he would speak, but for long moments he said nothing.

Then, quite suddenly, his face changed. It was still taut with jealousy, but the anger was gone, replaced by vivid, ferocious lust. 'Christ,' he hissed, 'you're beautiful, Tess.'

'Don't,' Tess said, still pulling against his grasp.

'You don't want some other man,' Tony said, more quietly now. 'I know it. You just do it to drive me mad, don't you? You just love making me jealous. Little witch, little witch, it works every time.' And he pulled her towards him and caught her face in his hand and dropped his mouth onto hers with such strength that she could not resist him, just stood passive and whimpering beneath his fervent kisses. She was angry and afraid, but she could not restrain her instinctive, physical response. Her breath came faster and her body tautened, seeking the pressure of his strong limbs against her.

When at last he lifted his mouth from hers she tried to pull away. She was still angry, she couldn't bear being treated like a possession. In a smothered, urgent voice she said, 'Tony, don't behave like this. I didn't do anything on purpose. I don't like it when you're jealous. I –'

'You didn't?' He had his hand on her face, holding her still so that he could look down at her with his snapping black eyes. 'You didn't do it on purpose? You mean you really – wanted him?'

'No,' Tess protested hopelessly.

But Tony's hand tightened on her chin, gripping so hard that it hurt. 'Listen to me,' he said, and now his voice was thick with cold anger. It made Tess shiver. 'Listen to me, Tess. Keep your hands off him. If you go near him, you'll wish you had never been born.'

'Tony – '

'I can make you a success, Tess,' Tony hissed, 'or I can wreck you. Understand me? Nobody wants a young singer without looks these days, do they?'

'What?' Tess gasped, hardly believing what she heard.

'In here,' Tony said, dragging her after him into the bedroom. He flung her across the bed so hard that she fell sprawling. While she recovered herself he opened the drawer of the bedside table and drew out a small object. As Tess came upright, floundering and opening her mouth to protest, he held it out towards her and suddenly, before her eyes, a bright, steel blade sprang out, glistening with sharpness.

'You know what this is, don't you,' Tony said. 'It's a flick knife, isn't it. Just like the fakes we use for the duel, huh? But there's a difference, Tess.' He took a step towards her and Tess scrabbled across the bed away from him, gasping, her eyes fixed on the gleaming blade. 'This one's real, ' Tony said. 'Real and sharp. Wouldn't it be a shame if I got the real one and the fake mixed up? Wouldn't it be a shame if I – injured you? An industrial accident, if you like?'

He looked angry enough, crazy enough to do it. Tess slipped down from the far side of the bed and retreated until her back was against the wall and still he came on. She swallowed hard and said, 'Tony, don't be a fool. You can't do this. You can't behave like this.'

He was standing before her, the knife held at the length of his arm. It didn't look remotely like the fake. The blade was blue at the edges and faintly oily, horribly businesslike. 'Promise,' he said, 'that you won't go near Richard Shaeffer, except on stage.'

'Tony – '

'Promise!'

This isn't happening, Tess thought. I'm standing in a flat in Covent Garden and a Mediterranean maniac is threatening me with a knife. It's not happening.

But it was happening, and she was afraid. Sarah had been right to see danger in the cards. At last she said, 'All right! All right, I promise!' and covered her face with her hands, because as well as fear she felt horribly ashamed of having given in.

Tony straightened and folded the blade back into the flick knife. It vanished as if it had not existed and Tess took a long breath of relief. 'Good,' he said. 'That's good. Now, Tess, I'm going to remind you just why it is you don't want any man other than me.'

'You're not going to touch me,' Tess said quickly, full of anger now that her cause for fear had gone. She moved quickly to push past Tony and make her escape, but he reached out almost lazily and caught hold of her arm.

'Come here,' he said, pulling her to him.

She fought him, trying to scratch him, to hit him, anything to get him to take his hands off her. But he ignored her blows and at last got hold of both her wrists in one strong hand and wrestled her to the bed. 'Fight me,' he hissed, leaning over her and staring down into her furious eyes. 'That's it, fight me. Fight, Tess. It makes you look so gorgeous. Fight me before I fuck you.'

'You're not going to fuck me,' Tess protested, doing her best to knee him where it hurt. But her tight skirt prevented her and Tony laughed and lowered his body onto her with an abruptness that made her gasp with shock and sudden consciousness of his strength and the hard eagerness of his muscled body. 'No,' she said again, 'I won't – '

One of Tony's strong hands thrust inside her bustier,

catching hold of her breast and squeezing so hard that she cried out. Pain, but pleasure too. And his body was thrusting against her, so heavy and powerful, holding her down. No, she thought furiously, I won't let him do this to me, I won't.

But his hand squeezed her breast again, forcing the nipple into stiff readiness and then bruising it with the ferociousness of his caresses, and as she struggled and arched her body against him, trying to resist, he gave a cry and pressed his mouth to hers in a kiss that seemed to suck out her soul.

Tess could not tell when her desperate resistance changed, sliding seamlessly into equally desperate compliance. Suddenly the tense spring of her spine was pushing against him not to try to throw him off but to encourage him to press against her harder, her mouth was searching his not to bite him but to draw his kisses to her ever deeper, her hands were knotted in his glossy black hair not to hurt him but to hold his lips more firmly on hers. His furious assault did not change, no tenderness crept into it, and her response matched it, equally vehement, avid and lustful, wanting to feel him beating her into submission with the blows of his strong penis.

He did not trust her. One hand still held her wrists, pinioning them above her head. With the other Tony dragged up her tight skirt, rucking it around her waist. He caught hold of her panties and ripped them off with a curse, then thrust his knee between her thighs and jerked them apart. His glans nestled between the lips of her sex, hot and smooth, ready. She could sense the power of his cock behind it, swollen-shafted, hard as a piece of bone.

There was a silence. They stared into each other's eyes, tense with hatred and anger and desire. Then Tony snarled and drove himself into Tess as if he was splitting a tree with a wedge, and her white throat twisted and she screamed with bitter pleasure. Her nails raked his

194

back and she lifted her head and set her teeth into his bare throat and he roared and took her harder still, beating his body against hers as if he could conquer her and possess her with the simple power of his thrusts. She pulled at his hair and writhed under him and cried out, 'Bastard, bastard, bastard!' and he laughed and spread her wrists wide and held her still as he rammed his thick strong cock deeper and deeper into her with every stroke.

'Bastard,' Tess wailed again, heaving her hips up to meet him, offering the soft mound of her sex to his impassioned lunges, grunting like a beast as he sheathed himself to the hilt inside her with every jolt of his fevered body. She had not expected pleasure, and it took her by surprise. 'Oh Christ,' she cried, jerking up towards him in amazement and delicious agony, 'oh Christ, I'm coming, I'm coming ...' And then her eyes rolled back and her whole body was twisting and flopping beneath him like a landed fish, helpless, spasmodic movements that convulsed her from head to foot, her breasts juddering as he snarled and let go of her wrists to clutch her buttocks tightly in his fists and hold her still to receive his final desperate thrusts. When she felt his cock pulse and twitch inside her she dug her fingers deep into his scalp as if she would hold him there for ever, as if she wanted nothing more than to be the eternal receptacle of his vivid, furious lust.

He fell forward onto her and lay still for a moment, his weight smothering her. She lay very still, feeling the shuddering echoes of her orgasm pulsing through her, gradually fading. As her thoughts cleared she realised that although he had given her pleasure her feelings to him had changed. She detested the way he behaved to her. She felt as though she stood on a great cliff. With only a tiny push she would fall forward and spiral down through the clouds and cry out as she fell that she hated Antonio Varguez.

Say something awful, she thought. Make it easy for me.

But Tony rubbed his cheek against the skin of her breast like a big satisfied cat. 'Beautiful Tess,' he whispered, kissing her. 'Gorgeous Tess.' And she couldn't summon the energy to be angry with him when he was kind and attentive.

'Come on,' Tony said. 'Let's get into the bed, hmm? Kiss and make up?'

He helped her undress and smooth out her crumpled costume, then slipped with her beneath the sheets and drew her into his arms. Suddenly Tess remembered how on their first night together he had held her in his embrace all night, and she had felt so warm and safe. Was she being ungrateful, absurd?

Tony's breath stirred against her ear as he laughed. 'Don't know why I'm worrying,' he said softly. 'Dick's gone home with James and Adam, hasn't he? He's probably just another bum-boy. The woods are full of them.'

The following day Tess arrived a little late for rehearsal. Tony had found her again in the kitchen and as always the sight of her being domestic had acted as a direct stimulant to his sexual nerve endings. He had pressed her up against the wall of the kitchen and taken her there, roughly, brutally, without preliminaries, muttering Spanish obscenities beneath his breath. Then he had said, 'Remember, Tess. I'm back on Monday. And if I think you've done anything with Richard Shaeffer that I wouldn't approve of, you'll be sorry.'

And so Tess arrived subdued and unhappy, feeling bullied and manipulated. She wished she had told Tony to fuck off and die. But it wasn't that easy.

They were rehearsing Act Two from where they had left off the previous night. Tess looked around when she arrived, rather dispiritedly, in case Richard should be there, but he was not to be seen. The day was clammy and hot, threatening thunder. Yellow clouds veiled the sun. Tess shifted from foot to foot, flapping her shirt to try to encourage some cool air to move inside it.

'He's changing,' said a voice in her ear, making her jump.

'Catherine!' Tess turned, clutching her pounding heart. 'Who's changing?'

'Richard Shaeffer, of course. You were looking for him, weren't you?' Catherine grinned. 'Like every other woman in the cast.'

'No,' Tess's denial didn't sound convincing.

'Right,' called Adam's voice from the auditorium, 'number thirteen, entrance of Escamillo. On stage, everyone! Places!'

Tess took up her spot with Jeannette and Catherine, right at the front of the stage by the proscenium arch. She was intrigued. What sort of a performer would the young Canadian turn out to be? She had met singers before who were personally charming, and had been disappointed to find them insipid on stage.

Insipid. Dan had said she was insipid in bed. Was she still? Tony didn't think so. He thought she was gorgeous, he wanted her every time. Was that why she could not bear to leave him? Because, for all his faults, he made her feel eminently desirable, everything Dan had told her she was not?

Julian crashed the opening chords on the piano and the chorus burst into song. Carmen and her friends were supposed to look curious and excited, and all three of them were.

The piano launched into the introduction to Escamillo's aria and the scenery and crowd parted to reveal Richard, wearing his amazing black and silver costume with a helmet not unlike a Roman centurion's and high, black boots. Tess almost recoiled. He looked relaxed despite the cloying heat, and he moved forward like a panther, like a leopard on a leash, conveying in his movements a sense of controlled ferocity that made her spine tingle. Yesterday his hazel eyes had been warm and cheerful, but when he turned and looked at her for the first time in the character of Escamillo a shock went through her from her nape to her ankles. He looked powerful, virile, dangerous – and yet, behind the sense of physical strength, there was a warmness in his eyes, in his voice, that suggested a vast capacity to love and be loved, a selflessness that was utterly lacking in Tony's macho egotism.

He was looking at her as if he thought she was beautiful. Of course he is, Tess told herself desperately, that's what James has told him to do. It doesn't mean anything, he's acting. And yet as her eyes met his she felt her blood leaping with a surge of response so strong, so gut-wrenching, that she almost staggered. She wanted him more than anything she had ever seen, more than Dan, more than Tony, more than Julian, more than her success.

Richard was a professional to his fingertips. He delivered the aria very competently and the rehearsal ran straight on. Escamillo advanced across the stage towards Carmen, his eyes fixed on hers.

Sweetheart, he said, *I'd like to know your name. Next time I appear, I want to mention you.*

Me? Carmen responded. Tess's excitement, her pleasure were only half acting. *It's Carmen. Carmencita. You choose which you like.*

And suppose I said that I loved you?

You'd be wasting your time, said Carmen, looking deep into vivid sparkling eyes. *I'm not free right now.*

Not very promising, said Escamillo, *but I can wait and hope.*

Anyone can wait . . . and hope is sweet.

The act ran on, but for Tess it was as if a light had been switched off when Richard made his exit. She was glad that Tony wasn't there. She didn't feel that she could have put any emotion at all into Carmen's eager reunion with Don José.

When Adam called, 'OK, principals, thank you, that's all for today. Chorus on stage please for technical,' Tess stood in the wings not knowing what to do. Go home, said a little voice in her brain. Just go home and walk on the Heath until you're tired, then go to bed.

'Tess,' said Jeannette beside her, 'are you all right?'

'Fine,' Tess said, looking up with an artificial smile.

'Want to come home with us?' Jeannette asked encouragingly. 'Emma's out with some friends, Bob and Stefan are coming round this evening, I know Charlie would come too if you liked.'

Tess shook her head. 'No thanks.'

She stood for a while in the auditorium, alone, watching the lights going up and down and the stage hands crawling about the gantries to ensure that everything was just so. The chorus stood on the stage like sheep under the hot lights, fanning themselves and chatting to each other. Tess noticed in the front row the two she had seen making love at first rehearsal, Tom and Gina. They both saw this production as their big break. Lying half-naked on stage, simulating sex for an audience of prurient middle-aged opera-goers! Christ, Tess thought, there's no business like show business.

'Do you always watch technical rehearsal?' asked a warm transatlantic voice behind her. 'Or don't you have any paint to watch drying right now?'

Tess spun round and found herself looking into Richard Shaeffer's changing hazel eyes. He had changed out of his tight sweaty costume and now wore loose, soft stone-coloured chinos and a fine-gauge T-shirt that showed off the shape of his broad, elegantly muscled shoulders. Tess swallowed, feeling tongue-tied, like a fourteen-year-old. 'I – ' she faltered. 'Nothing better to do, I suppose.'

'If you've got nothing better to do,' Richard said with a smile, 'how about showing a poor hapless stranger how London fits together?' He gestured towards the edge of the park. 'They've got me a room at the Ritz.

Great, huh? But so far I've gone there and walked here and ventured up and down Piccadilly a bit. I got as far as Fortnum & Mason last night, daring stuff! But I don't know where to start.'

'Haven't you been here before?' Tess asked, genuinely surprised.

He shook his head. His soft, dark, curly hair fell into his eyes and he pushed it back with a graceful, unconscious gesture. 'No, not to stay. I came through when I was in England before, but just in a taxi. If you're not busy, could you?'

How could she refuse? Tess smiled and shrugged. 'I'd be glad to. What d'you want to see? Art? Architecture?'

'Listen,' said Richard, smiling more widely, 'you're talking to a boy from Saskatchewan. I have a family who live in the middle of nowhere. You know what I really want to do? I want to go somewhere cool and have something to eat and buy my sister a present.'

'Really?'

'Really. Where should we go, Harrods?'

Tess pursed her lips, considering. She was considering whether she should go at all as well as where they should go. But after all, he was a stranger, and she was a native of London, and it was no more than one singer should do for another under the circumstances. It didn't have to mean anything, did it?

'Well,' she said, 'we could go to Covent Garden, or the Kings Road, but they'd be bloody hot in this weather. How about walking across the park to Harvey Nichols?'

'To Harvey whom?'

'Harvey Nicks. It's a great shop, and the café has a balcony and it's seriously trendy.'

'Lead the way!'

They walked together across Green Park to the corner of Piccadilly and then through the network of tunnels at Hyde Park Corner into Hyde Park itself. Tess led them by devious routes, taking in the Serpentine, the statue of

Peter Pan, anything to allow her to saunter along beside Richard, talking to him.

Talking with him. It was so unlike talking to – being talked at *by* Tony. Richard seemed to be well educated and well read and he was certainly intelligent, but he seemed just as interested in what Tess had to say as what he was saying. They talked mainly about the production, about James's ideas and the designer's conceptions, about working with the conductor, Benedetto Corial, a flamboyant young Venetian who was also making his London debut with this production. They talked about music in general too, and found that their opinions and attitudes were sufficiently different to provoke stimulating debate, but not so far apart that they would annoy each other.

At last they arrived at Harvey Nichols and fought their way through the crowded ground floor and up through the increasingly rarefied air of three floors of expensive fashion to the exalted heights of the living area and further beyond to the food hall and café.

'Well,' said Richard slowly, looking from side to side, 'this is a bit different from Fortnum & Mason.'

'See here,' said Tess, 'here's the cook book of the most trendy restaurant in London right now. Italian cooking, basically. And look here, a whole rack of nothing but oils and vinegars. The best bred salad dressings start here.'

'How does this compare to Harrods?'

'Oh, we'll go there in a minute. They're completely different, Harrods is all solid and reliable and this is, ah, self-consciously chic. Have you seen *Absolutely Fabulous?*'

Richard shook his head, looking blank. 'Heard of it. Isn't it a TV show?'

'I couldn't possibly explain,' Tess said with a smile. She stretched to see over a small woman in an extraordinary hat. 'Hey look, no queue for the café. Come on, let's go.'

They were fortunate enough to get a table by the door

to the balcony, where the fresh air wafted pleasantly past them. A dappy young waiter brought the menu, which they studied in silence.

Presently, Richard said, 'What's aïoli? Isn't it garlic mayonnaise?' Tess nodded and he asked rather plaintively, 'So why serve it with chips? Wouldn't ketchup do?'

'And balsamic vinegar with everything,' Tess said. 'But it's nice food, Richard, honestly.'

All through their light, perfectly presented, rather expensive meal they continued to talk and Tess found herself unable to concentrate on the seriously trendy people coming and going. Richard watched the people, and she watched Richard.

This is infatuation, she told herself. You only want him because he's forbidden. You can't possibly feel like this about someone you've only known for a day.

But every time she opened her mouth she felt that she was at risk of saying something out of place, something about how attractive she found him, how much she enjoyed his company, how much she would like to – to make love to him . . .

Richard leant forward and lowered his voice. 'Table beside us,' he whispered. 'Check it out.'

Tess turned her head as if she were looking through the window and let her eyes rest on a couple. The man was a good looking 45 or so, with a Caribbean tan and very expensive, very casual clothes. The woman might have been thirty, but it was hard to tell under the make-up. Her hair was the shade of platinum blonde that comes from an expensive hairdresser. Her long legs were clad in glossy dark mink tights and her very short skirt and the jacket that skimmed her slender, perfectly proportioned body were black and edged with white trimming with tiny diamanté chips that glittered. She wore high strappy sandals that would have crippled Tess in five minutes and while her companion was munching his way through the most substantial dish on the menu, complete with chips and aïoli, she was toying with a small green salad and a mineral water.

'Trophy wife?' Richard mouthed at Tess. She looked at the woman's left hand and raised her eyebrows at the huge, square diamond she saw there above a plain, white gold band. She shrugged.

'They haven't exchanged a word in twenty minutes,' Richard said beneath his breath, shaking his head. 'I don't get it. What do they see in each other if they've got nothing to talk about?'

Tess looked at him, amazed. She almost said that Tony would love to have that sort of woman, then closed her lips tightly and shook her head, feeling wretched. She liked Richard as much as any man she could remember, felt she had a huge amount in common with him, thought him exceptionally attractive and would be pleased to share his bed. But if she did ... If she did, she could imagine Tony's anger. And, possibly, his revenge.

'Tess?' Richard asked. 'Are you OK?'

'Sure. Fine.' Tess managed a smile which she knew would look artificial. 'Shall we, er, go and find your sister's present?'

Like many foreigners Richard wanted to send his sister something typically English, and although both of them agreed it was dull, they settled on a pretty ribbed cashmere sweater. 'Very suitable for Canadian winters,' Richard said. Tess was impressed by the fact that he not only knew his sister's size, but also what colour would suit her.

They walked out onto the street and recoiled from the intense, sweltering heat. 'Jesus,' Richard said, 'I thought England was supposed to be cold. Is there any water around here?'

'There's boats on the Serpentine,' Tess said, and then before she could control herself she had run on, 'but it's the place that does it, being in the centre of London, I mean. If we went out to where I live, out to Hampstead, on the Heath it wouldn't be half so hot.'

'What's Hampstead?' Richard asked.

'It's, a suburb, I suppose. It's quite expensive and smart,' Tess explained. And then felt constrained to add, 'My flat used to belong to my grandmother.'

'Wow!' said Richard, obviously impressed by this evidence of English history. 'That's pretty cool. I'd love to see it. Hampstead, I mean,' he added hastily, as if trying to change the subject.

Tess looked into his brilliant eyes. A slight flush coloured his high cheekbones. Perhaps it was embarrassment at a near miss, perhaps it was just the heat. She wanted him so much that her abdomen ached with the heavy weight of desire. How could she have got herself into this situation?

But it couldn't hurt just to go and look, could it? 'If you can stand the tube,' she heard herself saying, 'we could be there in half an hour.'

The tube was purgatory, like the seventh circle of Hell, hot and noisy and crowded with rush hour travellers. Tess and Richard were pushed apart and she almost lost him at King's Cross where they changed to the Northern line. They barely exchanged a word until they were out of the lift at Hampstead, drawing in great breaths of warm, sticky air.

All through the journey Tess had been arguing with herself, trying to suppress her growing attraction for Richard. She wanted him, but she was afraid of Tony. It wasn't until she felt her feet on her own home ground that some of Carmen's strength and stubbornness rushed into her and made her say, 'Would you like to come back to my flat and have a drink before we go and look round the Heath?'

They stood in the street, commuters whirling round them, and Richard looked into her eyes. She watched his expressions, surprise, shock, delight, anxiety. 'I'd love to,' he said at last, began to say something else and hesitated. At last it made itself heard. 'Tess, excuse me if I'm talking out of turn. But Emma Ridley told me that you were, er, in a relationship with Antonio Varguez: with Tony. I don't want to put a spanner in the works, cause problems, you know what I mean?'

Now's your chance, said Tess's cowardice. Back off. But she thought of Sarah's words: *you have to take control.* And she thought of Carmen saying to Don José, *I don't love you any more: it's over.* Aloud she said, 'I have been seeing him. But, but it's over. It's over now.' Richard still looked uncertain. His bright eyes narrowed as if he wanted to see through her, to look to the bottom of her soul. 'Will you come back to my flat?' she asked, and she knew she was asking him to her bed.

His expression showed that he understood her. 'Yes,' he said simply.

They walked side by side along the sweltering streets, not hurrying, both of them looking straight ahead. Tess's pulse beat hard in her temples and her throat was taut with excitement. All the research she had done should have been a good grounding for this deliberate admission of lust, but it was not. It was no help, because this time her heart was involved.

She sneaked a sidelong glance at Richard and found that he was looking at her. She stopped moving, startled and embarrassed, as if she had been caught doing something wicked. For a long moment they looked into each other's eyes. Richard's tender, sensuous lips were parted and over the noise of the traffic she could hear his breath whispering between them. She was riveted by the beauty of his face, the warmth of his breathing lips. Very slowly she lifted one hand as if she would touch his mouth. It felt as though she were pushing her fingers through thick treacle. At last her fingertips just brushed his cheek, and as she touched him he gasped her name and closed his eyes as he reached for her, pulling her to him as blindly as a drowning swimmer seeking safety. Her other hand caught at his hair, felt its softness, and then his lips were on hers and they were locked together, devouring each other, smothering under the weight of their desire.

Every nerve, every muscle of Tess's body strained to draw him closer to her, to squeeze him within her until her bones were his bones and his flesh was her flesh. His tongue quivered in her mouth. When at last he lifted his lips from hers she whispered, 'Richard, I want you so much,' and she was not afraid of his reaction. She knew he felt the same way.

'Christ,' he hissed, 'come on, Tess, come on, take us home, or we'll have to do it in the street and shock all these respectable people.'

Tess laughed and caught his hand and they ran together along the street towards the small, tree-lined avenue where Tess's house was. The key leapt from her bag to her fingers, the door was open and they were racing up the stairs and through the inner door into the cool, airy lightness of the flat.

Richard didn't even seem to see it. He stopped inside the door and stood still, panting. Tess slammed the door and caught again at his hand and drew him after her through the drawing room to the bedroom. She went to the window and flung it wide open, then drew the curtains. For a moment she rested her forehead against the heavy fabric. Then she turned and looked into Richard's eyes.

'Tess,' he said softly, 'I want you too.' And he put his hands to his T-shirt and with one quick movement stripped it off.

His torso was as beautiful as she had known it would be, pale, golden skin, smooth and fresh. His muscles were well developed, but not too prominent. He looked like a healthy young man who earns his living in the open air, natural, not created. There was a long white scar on one shoulder, old and faded, a teenager's scar. His flat belly lifted and fell, his singer's diaphragm working hard to suck in air, to control his breathing. He

206

stood very still with the T-shirt held in both hands, looking into Tess's eyes.

Slowly she unbuttoned her shirt and let it fall behind her. She walked across the room to him and reached up her lips to kiss him again, and as their tongues met and caressed her hands went to the button of his chinos and he reached for her skirt. Tess pushed down the waist-band of his trousers and then caught her breath in rapture as she felt how soft and warm his skin was, faintly beaded with sweat from the heat, slick beneath her exploring fingers. She could smell the scent of his body, complex and musky and intoxicating. For a moment they wriggled in ungainly eagerness, like a pair of snakes trying to mate and shed their skins at the same time. Then the last garment was discarded and they were naked, their bodies pressing together, closely as twining creepers. His penis shuddered against her belly, hot and dry and hard as wood. She moaned with a sudden upsurge of lust and pulled herself free and dropped to her knees before him, reaching up to take hold of him and draw down the glistening head of his splendid shaft to within reach of her wet lips.

'Jesus,' Richard groaned as Tess extended her tongue and flickered the tip of it against the taut shining dome that crested his rigid phallus. 'Oh Jesus, God, Tess.' And as if taking pity on him she opened her lips and let first the tip, then the head, then the thick pillar of his flesh enter her mouth. She wanted to take all of him and moaned in disappointment when she could harbour only a few inches of that proud, splendid rod in her throat. With her hands she caressed the tight orbs of his beauti-ful buttocks, squeezing them, digging her nails into the tender skin, and she let her wet lips slide slowly, lasciviously up and down his quivering penis.

'Tess,' Richard whispered, and his strong long-fingered hands suddenly caught at the thick mass of her tumbled dark-red hair. He pulled her up and back, drawing her into his arms. 'Tess, Tess, not just me, not just me.'

Clutching each other, shaking with desire, they swayed together to the bed and fell onto it. The warm breeze through the window made their skin glisten with perspiration and their limbs alternately stuck and slithered across each other, slippery with need.

Tess had not had her fill of his wonderful cock. She wanted to taste it again, to feel it moving within her mouth, swelling and tightening with the waiting seed. She began to slide down his damp body, kissing the hollow of his shoulder, sucking one of his flat male nipples until it stood up just as hers would have done, rubbing her cheek against the delicious hardness marking the edge of his rib cage. But he murmured in protest, reaching out for her. 'Let me,' he breathed. 'Let me do something for you too.'

She knew what he meant. Briefly, like the last flare of a sunset, she remembered how it had felt to be shy, to be afraid of showing herself to her lover. She had not dared, with Dan, to do this same thing, to offer her sex to his mouth as she caressed his penis with her lips. But the memory only added piquancy to the eager desire she now felt. With a smothered cry she turned her body over him and pressed her face between his thighs, kissing and licking the hot, swollen shaft of his cock, loving it. Her legs were parted, her knees planted on either side of his face, and she rejoiced to feel his eyes resting like a touch on her secret centre, opening her, knowing her.

She drew the head of his cock into her mouth, moaning with the joy of feeling him stirring in her throat. He groaned: beneath her his taut body vibrated with the deep sound of his pleasure. Then he reached up and his hands took hold of her white buttocks, pulling them down towards his mouth, spreading her. Tess's closed eyes tightened, waiting to feel his tongue and lips there, there where she burned with need for him.

First she felt his hair, soft against her thighs, and then

at last his lips upon her. His mouth embraced her sex, warm and yielding, and she gasped with expectation. Her mouth moved faster on his throbbing cock. But he did not use his tongue, and after a moment she hesitated, suddenly anxious.

Then, without warning, Richard drew in a long breath and let it out in a deep, vibrating hum. The sound startled Tess, and then she pulled her lips away from his penis because she was crying out with sudden, shocked pleasure. His whole mouth, his warm, wet mouth, was quivering against her sex, a deep elemental vibration that made her shudder with delight. The sensation was so intense, so unexpected, that she could not keep her balance. She fell to one side and Richard moved with her, his lips pressed between her open legs, playing out his expert breath in long, shivering whispers of music that thrilled through her body as if he had tapped her spinal cord. He moved a little to bring his cock within reach of her mouth and she opened her lips blindly to admit him, but she could not concentrate on sucking him. She lay on her side, moaning with helpless ecstasy as his humming lips impelled her towards orgasm, and he thrust his taut penis gently in and out of her unresisting mouth.

The moving shaft of his flesh gagged her, holding in her sounds of pleasure. Richard continued to hum, and now as he did so he began very gently to touch her with his tongue, moving it with infinite delicacy against the engorged, quivering bud of her clitoris. Tess cried out past the gag of his thrusting cock and arched her body helplessly and Richard held on tightly to her soft haunches and began to lick her harder and harder, sweeping strokes of his strong tongue that lifted her to the height of bliss in seconds. Her hips jerked against his mouth and her lips slackened, allowing his rigid penis to slide deep into her throat as she hung in momentary eternity, burnt and frozen by orgasm.

Then he was moving, turning, until he was lying

209

beside her and looking into her face. She opened her heavy eyelids and whispered, 'Richard.'

'Tess, Tess.' He pressed close to her, raising one hand to weigh her breast, stroking the nipple so that she sighed with resurgence of joy. He had not come yet, and his cock was thick and strong, feverishly swollen, his balls drawn snugly up beneath his body, heavy with lust. He gently caught hold of her knee with one hand and lifted her leg over his thigh and then moved between them and positioned the head of his penis at her entrance.

Then he waited. He met her eyes again and smiled a little. Tess let out a long breath of yearning and murmured, 'Yes, Richard, yes. Now.'

And at her words he thrust and the whole of his long, thick cock slid up within her, penetrating her with gentle deliberacy, remorseless as the root of a tree which can split the rock. When he was sheathed inside her he paused, waiting, looking into her eyes. She gave a little eager gasp and tugged at his tight buttocks, wanting him to take her, and he began to move.

So slow, so deep, like the currents of the deepest ocean stirring inside her. For a while she watched his face, watched the sensations changing his expression as he drove his body deeply into her, his eyes narrowing and his nostrils flaring and his lips drawing away from his teeth almost as if he were in pain. But then the pleasure was too much, and she closed her eyes and tightened her hands on his haunches and felt his fingers closing on hers in answer and immersed herself in the rapture of his possession, letting her hips sway towards his thrusting penis like the waves of the sea. She imagined herself as a chest of treasure cast up on a sandy beach, its timbers weakened by the roaring ocean. The winds rise and soon the chest is pounded by waves, great arching waves of enormous power that toss it from side to side and beat it down upon the unforgiving sand, curling up above it higher and higher, falling upon it with merciless

210

force until at last it shudders and yields and bursts asunder and everything it holds is thrown up and spilt into the foaming sea, starring the wilderness of white with gems and gold, littering the sand with tumbled pearls.

Through the red mists of her second orgasm she sensed him crying out, holding her, shuddering as he spent himself within her. His hands on her flanks held as tight as claws. After a long moment of stillness the tension broke and they relaxed, holding each other, looking into each other's eyes with faces of wonder and disbelief.

The curtains stirred and flapped, driven away from the window by a sudden fierce gust. Tess and Richard moved a little apart and sat up, holding each other, looking out at the blackening sky.

'It's going to thunder,' Richard said, and as if in answer a low rumble shuddered across the roofs. 'I love thunderstorms.'

Tess felt light-headed with bliss. She wasn't ready to sleep. 'So do I,' she said, trying to shake her heavy hair off the nape of her neck. 'What do you say, do you want to go for a walk in it?'

Richard stared at her, shook his head disbelievingly, then grinned. 'You're off your head,' he said. 'Why the hell not?'

She lent him an old baggy sweatshirt, because the wind was suddenly cold, and they tumbled down the stairs of the flat and ran hand in hand towards the Heath. They were like lovers, laughing, kissing, pointing up at the sky when quick lightning flared in one part or another.

'This is amazing!' Richard exclaimed as Tess led him to her favourite dell. 'It's like the country, not like a park. It's wonderful.'

'I love it,' Tess said. 'Especially now, in the rain, when there's nobody here.'

'Nobody except us,' he said, and kissed her.

Above them lightning split the sky and suddenly the rain was falling, huge drops like steel-headed nails, falling so thickly they drew vertical lines across the landscape. Richard and Tess gasped and retreated automatically beneath the thick canopy of an oak tree.

'It's dangerous to stand under trees in a lightning storm,' Tess said suddenly, looking around from side to side. 'We could be hit by lightning.'

The sky lit again with brilliance and the thunder roared. Momentarily blinded, Tess closed her eyes. When she opened them again she was looking into Richard's face. What she saw there took her breath away.

'I've already been hit by lightning,' Richard whispered. He looked desperate, driven, like a lost soul. 'I'm scorched,' he said softly. 'Scorched and still burning.'

His lips fell upon hers as if her mouth was the cool stream that would quench his scalding thirst. He pressed her back against the rough bark of the oak tree and kissed her with feverish eagerness, trembling as he touched her. His hands thrust inside her shirt and found her breasts and began to stroke them with such fervent gentleness that Tess moaned aloud and spread her hands flat upon the tree's broad trunk, her fingers digging into the twisted grooves of the bark. Richard jerked up her shirt and sweater and bared her naked breasts and the cold rain fell upon them, startling her nipples into stiff points of hardness and trickling in transparent rivulets down the silky white crease. He bent his head and kissed her breasts, sucking the points until they swelled and blossomed and she whimpered and closed her eyes. Then he pushed up her skirt and pressed close to her and she felt his penis naked against the naked skin of her belly, hard and burning, and without a thought, without a sound she parted her thighs and opened herself to him and he penetrated her.

This time it was not gentle, but furious, filling her with pleasure as brilliant as the lightning that flashed above them, as piercing as the cold rain that stung their bare skin and soaked their clothes, as deep as the thunder that shook them where they stood. The harsh bark of the tree scraped against her naked buttocks and her head snapped to and fro as he thrust himself into her so fiercely that the sound of flesh meeting flesh was clear over the steady hiss of the rain. He held her breasts tightly in his hands, closing his fingers on her tormented nipples, and as he took her he looked down to see his golden body entering her white one, the thick rod of his flesh sliding up inside her until it was sheathed to the root and then withdrawing, gleaming with her juices, only to lunge again.

The rain ran down her face and his. When their lips met they tasted the rain, fresh with thunder. He beat his body against her with astonishing power, all the lean strength of his muscles intent on that one movement, and as he thrust she felt the claws of climax beginning to grip her, shaking her until she would have fallen but that she was impaled on the strong shaft that worked to and fro within her clasping sex. 'Richard,' she gasped, 'Richard,' and above them a huge fork of lightning speared the sky and the thunder grasped them and shook them until they fell together to the wet earth, shuddering bodies joined in ecstasy, twitching still with the aftershocks of orgasm as if the lightning animated their lifeless limbs.

Act Four, Scene Two

The Hampstead flat

*B*irdsong and traffic noise competed to wake Tess up. She lay still for a moment, stretching, looking at the bar of sunlight laid like a ruler across the white ceiling and savouring the delicious ache of her limbs.

After returning to the flat they had made love again, and again, all evening, wrapped in a sensual ecstasy as deep as winter, as glorious as spring. Richard was tirelessly and endlessly inventive, finding one new way after another to bring Tess to orgasm, and when sheer exhaustion denied her another climax he laughed at her and pushed her to the floor and held her there as he took her for his own pleasure, the simple direct masculine pleasure of possession, thrusting into her with feverish energy until he twisted and shuddered in the grip of his urgent release and she moaned beneath him with the delirious bliss of total, rapturous submission.

The memory alone made Tess ready for more. She yawned and licked her lips and lifted herself on one elbow, looking down at Richard asleep beside her.

He did not have Dan's classical perfection or Tony's dark Mediterranean glamour, but his sleeping face revealed everything about him that she delighted in, in his character as well as his body. Lips so finely cut, so sensual, that just to see them was to imagine them kissing, licking and caressing. Sharp, narrow nose and cheekbones, making him look lean and fierce as a prowling wolf, and soft tumbling dark curls which her fingers longed to disarray even further. And those wide-set eyes, shielded now by his heavy, long-lashed eyelids, which only had to open to bathe her in glittering warmth like sunlight reflecting from a forest pool.

He turned in his sleep, flinging one arm up above his head and taking a deep, slow breath. Tess gently caught hold of the single crumpled sheet that had covered them and drew it away, revealing his nakedness. His body was lean and strong as a predator's, muscled and taut, ready even in his sleep to leap up and seize its prey. Blue veins were etched finely onto the lightly tanned skin of his forearms and throat, moving faintly with the hidden power of his pulsing heart.

Once upon a time, Tess thought, I didn't dare to wake my lover. But that was before Carmen. She leant slowly towards him and let her lips hover above his mouth. She knew he would wake, and he did, stirring very slightly before his eyelids flickered and opened.

She smiled into his face. 'The problem with going to bed with a handsome prince,' she said, 'is the risk that when you kiss him in the morning he will turn into a beautiful frog.'

Very gently she set her lips on his, tasting him, savouring him. He closed his eyes and lay very still, allowing her to control the kiss. Then, when she lifted her mouth from his, he croaked softly, 'Ribbit,' and smiled at her.

Then he reached up and drew her down to him, pressing her body beneath his so that their naked flesh clung from breast to ankle. They kissed as if they wanted to become one creature, fusing together gradually, first skin, then muscle, then bone, finally the soft pulsing organs of their bodies, lungs and brains and thumping hearts melting one into another, mingling and welding

215

in a conjunction of oneness until their souls, too, were united.

'Richard,' Tess whispered into his breathing mouth. 'Richard.' And he groaned and strained her closer to him and his hot, stiff cock moved between her parted thighs, prodding with its blind eye as if seeking its way. She opened her legs wider, offering herself to him, yearning for him to sheathe himself within the aching cleft of her sex. The smooth, dry head of his penis pressed against her, soft as sueded silk, hard as bronze, and then it entered her, filling the empty hollowness within her, sealing their union, completing her.

The soft walls of her vagina and the delicate flesh of her labia were tender and bruised from the last night's endless love-making, and a spurt of exquisite pain filled her as his loins nestled closely against hers. The sharp bones of his lean hips fitted into the hollows of her thighs as exactly as an egg in the cup. At the same moment their hands sought each other's haunches, drawing themselves yet closer together, striving for the ultimate contact.

'Oh,' she moaned in delicious agony and blissful fear, feeling him so deep within her that another hair's-breadth of penetration would impale her very essence. 'Oh God, Richard, be gentle.'

'I have to be cruel to be kind,' he whispered, and he held her still to receive the first surging blow of his body. She cried out in desperation, writhing like an animal dying on the spear as he took her with a slow deliberate power that reduced her to nothingness, to a moaning wreck, a helpless captive of his remorseless phallus.

There was pain. Every soft tissue of her sex was swollen and sensitive, complaining shrilly as it felt itself again invaded, stretched, wrenched open and possessed. For a few moments the pain obliterated the pleasure, like the dark disc of the moon covering the sun at the point of total eclipse. But even at that point of pain the glow of ecstasy surrounded her like the sun's corona, visible only then, only then when its white heart was shielded, arching from the surface of her pleasure into the dark unfamiliar reaches of space, leaping sprays of liquid flame that curved from her sex to her limbs, from her limbs to her brain. And then Richard held her more firmly and slid his thick, rigid penis faster and faster in and out of her quivering flesh, and as he took her, thrusting his hard cock with feverish urgency into the yielding centre of her body, the obscuring shadow of her pain moved aside like the moon to reveal the blazing core of bliss, dismissing the aurorae with its brilliance, blinding her with the molten conflagration of climax.

She clung to him, listening to his slowly pounding heart. Its steady, strong double thump measured words that filled her brain but which she was not yet ready to utter. *I love you. Love you. Love you.*

His cheek rested on her hair and his eyelashes fluttered against her skin. 'Tess. Did I hurt you?' He touched the inside of her thigh, very gently. 'You're bruised. I'm so sorry. Are you all right?'

'Yes. No. It doesn't matter, it's all right. Oh, Richard – ' and she lifted her face to his, wanting still to feel his lips on hers.

The telephone rang. Tess stiffened and tried to ignore it, but she couldn't. As the answering machine clicked she reached over and seized the receiver and said huskily, 'Hello?'

'Hello Tess?' said a honey-sweet voice. Tess screwed up her face in distaste as she recognised the dulcet tones of Emma Ridley. 'Sorry to bother you, but James called me. He's looking for Richard, apparently he didn't go back to the hotel last night and James is worried.'

'What time is it?' Tess asked blankly.

'It's nearly half past eleven,' said Emma. 'You don't know where Richard has gone, do you? Gina told me that she saw him going off with you after rehearsal yesterday.'

Tess held the receiver at a little distance from her ear,

thinking fast. That little bitch! James wasn't pursuing Richard, he wouldn't, it was the weekend. Richard knew his schedule, and besides, he needed time to recover from travelling. Emma was just indulging her own prurient curiosity. But she was chummy with Tony, too. If she had guessed what had happened, she would as usual broadcast it far and wide, and she would certainly tell Tony. It would at least mean that Tess didn't need to break the news to Tony herself.

'Tess?' said Emma's voice. 'Tess?'

'Yes,' Tess said quickly. 'Sorry, Emma. Yes, Richard's here, actually.' Beside her Richard straightened up in bed, looking shocked, and Tess shushed him. 'Yes, I showed him around London yesterday for a bit and then we went up to Hampstead and then it was rather late for him to be going home, so he stopped here. Shall I get him to ring James?' That'll call your bluff, she thought.

'Oh,' said Emma quickly, 'no, no, no need, I'll just let him know that everything's OK, I think he was just checking up.'

I think you were just checking up, Tess thought sourly. 'Right then. 'Bye.'

She put down the telephone. 'That was our little bush telegraph,' she said to Richard. 'Emma Ridley on line. Everyone in the cast will know about this first thing Monday morning, Richard. I hope you're ready for it.'

'Why,' Richard asked innocently, 'is it a problem?' His brows drew down over his eyes, making them glitter. 'Tess, will you be in trouble? Is Tony –'

'Don't worry,' Tess said with more confidence than she felt. 'I'll handle Tony.'

Richard smiled at her, leant forward and kissed her. 'If you say so,' he said, 'I'll believe you.' He stroked his hand gently through her hair and looked into her face, then touched his fingers to her lips. 'Stay here,' he said, 'keep yourself comfortable. I'll bring you breakfast in bed.'

Tess lay sprawled on the crumpled sheets, her limbs

blissfully relaxed, looking up at the sunlight crawling across the ceiling and listening to the little comforting domestic sounds emerging from the kitchen. The clink of crockery, water running, then Richard's footsteps in the living room. His face at the bedroom door, grinning. 'Hey,' he said, 'there's one thing you Brits have sorted out, and that's making tea. Just tell me, why don't we have electric kettles on the other side of the Atlantic?'

'Search me,' Tess said, with a smile and a shrug.

'Mind you,' Richard added, 'you seem to be a bit short of food. I'll see what I can do, though. Earl Grey all right for you, or would you prefer,' he adopted an accent vaguely reminiscent of John Gielgud, 'English Breakfast?'

'Earl Grey,' said Tess, with a sigh of simple pleasure. 'Please.'

He was actually making tea for her. A man was making her tea in the morning! Even Leo, who was not proud, had been far too dozy on first waking up to stagger out to the kitchen and switch on the kettle, and as for Dan and Tony . . .

After a little while the warmth of the room and the warm slick sensation of her love-juices trickling gently between her thighs lulled her into a doze. At once she began to dream, an odd, confused, disturbing sequence of images that were both erotic and frightening. She was a slave, stripped naked for sale, and the man who dragged back her shoulders to show off her breasts and forced her thighs apart to show her moist secret flesh to the silent sweating purchasers was Richard. Then she was waiting for her flight in the airport departure lounge, plastic bags of duty free goodies clustering around her feet, and suddenly James and Adam were standing before her, hand in hand, and Adam said, 'Right, now everyone watch this demonstration,' and as all the travellers got to their feet and clustered around Tess felt her clothes evaporate like smoke and she was naked and ashamed and Adam opened his fly and took out his cock, huge, gnarled, like the stump of a tree, as big as Jeannette had said, and he said to her, 'Turn round, bend over,' and she tried to protest but there was nothing she could do. Adam's fingers were diving between her legs to anoint her arse with her juices and then he spat in her crease and it was cold and it tickled –

'Tess,' whispered Richard's voice in her ear. 'Hey, wake up. It's nearly noon. Wake up.'

She opened her eyes. He was sitting beside her on the bed, holding a mug of tea towards her. His naked body glowed pale gold in the sunlight and his eyes glittered as he smiled at her. She whimpered gratefully and took the mug and buried her face in it, inhaling the fragrant steam.

'Now,' said Richard, 'breakfast, that was tricky. So I thought I'd just do something simple, you know, something delicious . . .'

He brought out his other hand from behind his back. In it he was holding a large tub of Häagen Dazs ice cream and a spoon.

'Ice cream?' Tess asked, astonished. 'For breakfast?'

'Not just ice cream,' Richard smiled. '*Real* ice cream. Sexy ice cream. Didn't they run an advertising campaign here that suggested the best thing you could do to this stuff was find interesting ways to melt it?'

Tess finished the tea, set down her mug and regarded the tub of ice cream soberly. 'Fudge ripple,' she said softly, 'my favourite.'

'Yeah? Well, I should hope so, in your icebox.' Richard said, holding the tub towards her. 'Here you go. Eat it straight out of the carton if you like, or maybe, ah,' he put it into her hands and stretched out on the bed along one of the bars of sunlight, 'maybe you could think of a more unusual receptacle?'

Tess bit her lip, then laughed. 'Receptacle?' she repeated, looking admiringly at the flat, lean planes of

Richard's prone body. 'Richard, just tell me one place I can put it, apart from your navel.'

'How about here?' Richard suggested, pointing to the delicate hollow of his throat. 'Or here?' The curve of his shoulder. 'Hey, use your imagination.'

'I could imagine a banana split,' Tess said, sliding one hand down the smooth warm skin of Richard's body towards his flat stomach. He smiled at her and between his legs the soft curl of his resting penis stirred and began almost imperceptibly to thicken. He leant back into the pillows and closed his bright eyes.

For a moment Tess knelt beside him, considering. Then she dipped the spoon into the ice cream and lifted it to her mouth. The delicious, sweet taste spread slowly across her tongue. A drop fell from the spoon onto her naked breast and she jumped at the sudden cold. 'Won't the, ah, the temperature put you off?' she asked hesitantly. 'I thought men had an optimum operating temperature, you know, they need to be warm.'

Richard's lazy eyelids opened and he raised his eyebrows at her. 'Maybe, maybe not. You never know till you try.'

'Well,' said Tess, 'OK. Here goes.' And she let a small spoonful of ice cream fall delicately into the hollow of Richard's smooth, muscular shoulder.

'Ah,' Richard breathed. His whole body tensed, then relaxed. Between his legs his cock continued to grow. Now it was almost at its full splendid length, although it was still soft as dough. Tess leant slowly forward and extended her tongue and licked the cold melting ice cream from Richard's tanned skin.

She hadn't expected to be able to taste him, but she could, a subtle, salty counterpoint to the sweet main theme of the vanilla and fudge ice cream. A pale thread of melted cream slipped down towards his nipple and she smiled and caught it up on her tongue and Richard's breath hissed through his teeth.

Another spoonful, this time in the centre of his chest,

just on the flat, bony plate of his sternum. It was so delicious and his reactions were so arousing that Tess began to become artistic. With her tongue she swirled the ice cream out to surround his nipples, smiling as they tautened just as hers would have done. Her own breasts ached with an echo of Richard's pleasure. She dug the spoon in again and let the soft, cold substance fall onto his stomach, just below his navel.

'Christ,' Richard breathed. His cock was fully hard now, lying tautly along his abdomen, a glistening pillar of flesh. Tess licked all around it, but didn't touch it. He moaned with faint protest and the shining head of his cock lifted towards her lips all by itself, as if it were desperate to seek the soft haven of her mouth.

'Banana split,' Tess whispered, and dropped the next spoonful directly onto the head of Richard's cock. He cried out and his back arched in protest: then his cry was stifled as Tess leant further forward and gently, deliberately drew him into her mouth, swirling her tongue around the hot shaft to clean it of dribbles of cream.

'Oh,' she said, surfacing, 'that's delicious. Oh, God, I can taste your come, and me, and you, and it's gorgeous.'

The next spoonful fell onto his taut updrawn balls. Tess laughed as she burrowed to retrieve it, pushing her face in between his legs, getting ice cream on her nose, in her eyebrows, in her hair. Sweet trickles ran down the insides of his thighs and between the cheeks of his taut arse. 'Open your legs,' Tess mumbled.

'Oh, Jesus,' Richard moaned, but he obeyed her. She thrust her tongue closely between his spread thighs, caressing the delicate skin behind his balls, just beginning to probe at his crack, and he whimpered and shivered. For a moment she thought of licking him there, forcing her tongue into him, but she didn't want to startle him. So she moved back up his body and with delight and relief opened her lips to accept his taut, straining cock into her mouth.

She would gladly have sucked him until he came, but

Richard had different ideas. 'Hold on,' he said through his teeth, lifting himself from the pillows to catch hold of her tousled hair and lift her gently away from him. 'Hold on, Tess. Your turn.'

He positioned her on her knees, leaning backwards, her weight supported on her arms. Thus arranged her breasts thrust forward, lustful and eager. She let her head fall back and closed her eyes, waiting with a shiver of delight for what she knew was coming, the delicious coldness of the ice cream caressing her taut, aching nipples. Her breasts felt tender and swollen, desperate for his soft mouth upon them to soothe them and torment them further.

Richard dug the spoon into the tub of ice cream and without a word dropped a small mound of it onto Tess's left breast, then at once plunged his mouth down and sucked and sucked until she writhed and spread her knees wide apart as if she wanted him to take her now, at once, slide his hot, thick cock right up inside her as his warm mouth worshipped her straining nipple. He laughed at her wantonness, but he did not take her, only anointed her other breast and sucked at it until it too was swollen and engorged with fevered lust that the cold liquid could not soothe, only increase.

Then he made her lie face down on the bed, her head pillowed in her arms, her face hidden. She wriggled where she lay, anxiously anticipating the chill kiss of the ice cream. Where would it fall? Shoulders, neck, spine, buttocks?

He took her entirely by surprise, dropping a little liquid gob into the hollow of one knee. She squeaked with shock, then the sound changed to a moan of incredulous ecstasy as she felt his warm, soft tongue there, caressing the delicate skin, moving up a little to stroke the inside of her thigh. He parted her legs and gradually moved upwards, trickling the slowly melting ice cream further and further up her thighs until she thought she would scream with pleasure and frustration.

223

Her whole body shivered and her tight, hard nipples rubbed against the sheet, sending quick barbs of bliss through her.

Then he let one spoonful fall directly into the crease of her buttocks. She cried out in surprise and anticipation of ecstasy. She had done it to Tony, but despite Jeannette's promise it had never been done to her and she wanted –

'Oh God,' she moaned as she felt his tongue there, probing between her cheeks, slithering delicately along the length of her crease. It found the puckered ring of her anus, touched it, circled it and moved on. Tess heaved with disappointment and whimpered helplessly, then cried out again as another spoonful of chilly ice cream landed on the spot.

'Jesus,' hissed Richard's eager voice, 'Jeez, Tess, you have a beautiful ass. Christ, it's gorgeous. It's edible.' And she felt his face there again, pressing between her cheeks, and this time there was no hesitation. His warm, wet, strong tongue collected the chilly melting liquid, conveyed it to the tight flower of her anus and gently, gradually thrust its way inside. Tess shut her eyes tightly and lifted her buttocks towards him, eager, wanting more. His hands were on her thighs, on the insides of her thighs, moving up, moving closer, almost touching her, and as his tongue penetrated her delicate forbidden passage his hands found her sex and began to stimulate her, touching her clitoris, stroking her labia, sliding inside her. First one finger, then two, moved slowly and strongly in and out, in and out of her wet sex.

'Richard,' Tess moaned, 'Richard, Richard, oh God that's amazing,' and as the warm point of his tongue tenderly rimmed the satin flesh of her anus and his fingers drove into her sex she began to shudder and tense as the strong claws of climax gripped her and shook her and left her gasping. He did not wait, but laid his body directly on top of hers, so that his skin pressed against her all down her, and he spread her thighs wide

224

apart and without a word he pressed the searing tip of his cock against her sex and entered her. She cried out with shock and delight, because in this position he seemed to penetrate her incredibly deeply and the strange angle of his stiff cock sliding deep within her bruised, tender vagina was almost unbearably stimulating. At once he began to move, quick urgent thrusts that made her white flesh shake as his body struck hers, and after only a few minutes he started to groan and shudder and he took hold of her hips and pulled them up towards him so that he could shaft her even harder, fill her even more, drive himself into her like a nail into an oaken beam.

'Oh Christ,' he cried out. His breath was hot on her neck and his warm skin slid over hers on a glistening sheen of sweat and cream. 'Christ, Tess, I'm coming, I'm coming, oh God your ass is so beautiful – ' and then he was there, snarling with the urgent power of his release within her.

He was hers for what was left of Saturday. They slowly staggered to their feet, committed the wrecked sheets to the washing machine and then crawled to soak their sticky, weary limbs in a hot and entirely necessary bath. Bathing gave them the opportunity for further leisurely sensual exploration of each other's bodies, after which they went out to walk on the Heath.

Every leaf and blade of grass was glittering with raindrops and the paths steamed as the bright warm sun sucked last night's storm back into the sky. They walked hand in hand, hardly talking, and Tess let her fingers gradually familiarise themselves with the shape of his hand, the big square palm, long fingers, wide flat nails, until she would have known that hand among a million others.

Then back in the afternoon to the flat and out onto the secluded roof terrace, where Richard covered Tess's naked body with his own to protect her from the hot sunlight that might otherwise scald her white skin.

On Sunday Richard had to work. He went to the theatre to meet the fight director and commit all the stage fights to memory and Tess went too to watch. She took keen pleasure in seeing Richard learning his moves, his strong agile body flexing and twisting like an athlete's. The main fight was between Richard's character Escamillo and Don José. Although Escamillo is the better fighter he slips on the garbage-strewn streets and loses his weapon, leaving him at José's mercy and enabling Carmen to intervene to save him. It was a spectacular piece of theatre, quick and vicious as a real knife fight must be. Richard learnt the moves fast and then went through the whole thing with the fight director standing in for Tony as Don José. Although Tess had seen the action built up piece by piece and she knew that at no time was Richard in any danger, he acted so well that when at the end he lost his knife and stood helpless she felt her heart pounding with fear for him.

Monday's rehearsal was a full run through, but without the conductor. The singers would just mutter their notes, saving their voices for the dress rehearsals and first night later in the week. Tess arrived alone, since Richard had gone back to the hotel that morning to sort out some business, and she realised that she was afraid of what Tony might do when he knew that she had broken her promise. She was late on purpose and her luck was in, Tony was already on stage. She stood in the wings waiting for her entry and watching his face. He looked and moved as if he were containing tremendous rage, and it was no surprise to Tess when Emma brushed past her as she made her exit and whispered archly, 'Think you're in for a bit of a storm today, Tess darling.'

She had to admit that Tony was a professional. When they were on stage together he acted his part perfectly, and in the face of his concentration Tess found it surprisingly easy to become Carmen, falling in lust with Don

José at first sight. At the end of Act One she fled the stage, hoping to avoid Tony entirely, and took refuge in the dressing room she shared with Emma, one of a number of well-appointed Portakabins.

She had hardly caught her breath when in her mirror she saw movement behind her. She looked up quickly, sure that it would be Tony, but it was Richard, leaning against the doorframe and smiling his warm, slightly lopsided smile.

'Hi,' he said. 'I was out front. You were great. This is a hell of a production.'

'Thanks,' Tess said, turning and walking straight into his open arms. 'Thanks, Richard. If it had been for real I thought I might have cracked my top note, I was so nervous.'

'Nervous? Why?' He held her more tightly. 'You don't need – '

'Act Two is about to start,' said a silky, tautly controlled voice with a Spanish accent. 'Don't you think you should be on stage, *signora la diva?*'

Tess pulled away from Richard, cold with apprehension, and looked up into Tony's bleak, furious face. His cruel mouth was twisted with anger. She bit her lip and took a quick breath, but before she could speak he had turned his back on her and stalked away.

'What's bugging him?' Richard asked, raising his eyebrows. 'I thought you said you two were finished.'

'We are,' Tess said, with a guilty sense that she had not been entirely honest. Well, they were certainly finished now. She thought that Tony's expression and behaviour had made that abundantly clear.

Act Two went well, without a hitch. At the end of the act Carmen and Don José embraced before they left the stage. Tess was ready for a half-hearted stage clinch, but Tony surprised her. He caught her into his arms as if they had been in the bedroom, knotted his strong fingers into her mane of tousled hair and dragged back her head with such violence that she gasped. Then he pressed his mouth onto hers with feverish urgency and despite herself she felt her body responding, jerked into arousal by the darting thrust of Tony's hot, eager tongue. The curtain fell and she tried to pull free, but Tony would not release her. She groaned with a potent mixture of fear and shame and sheer excitement as he kissed her so forcefully that her breath lurched and fluttered and the soft flesh between her legs tautened involuntarily.

At last she tore herself away. 'No,' she protested in a fierce hiss, 'Tony, don't.'

'You bitch,' Tony whispered into her face. 'You lying bitch, Tess. You'll be crawling on your knees to me for forgiveness.'

Was he going to play the irrational jealous lover till the end? Couldn't he see that it was over? She couldn't see any point in arguing, and so she pushed her hands through her hair and stalked away across the stage without looking back.

They ran on straight into the next act. Tess moved as if sleepwalking through the ensemble that opened the act and then stood off stage, watching in the wings as the action flowed on towards the duel between Escamillo and Don José. She could not speak to Richard, he was on the other side of the stage waiting for his entrance. Though she could see him, his face revealed that he was concentrating totally on the action and she did not want to interrupt him. She felt an extraordinary sense of dislocation, total confusion. The sensual paradise of her weekend with Richard had begun to be obscured in her mind by the ferocious erotic passion of Tony's kiss. She knew that between her legs she was wet. Why was her body so treacherous? She was sure that she was in love with Richard, so why was there anything left in her to respond to Tony's possessive, macho posturing?

Perhaps, said her intellect, this is the price you pay for understanding Carmen. She desires two men at once, she wants Escamillo while she is still in love with José. Why should you be any different? Why shouldn't you want Tony and be in love with Richard at the same time? You can't deny that Tony was exciting in bed.

She couldn't deny it. She thought of the incredible things he had done to her, tying her up, almost choking her with his thick penis, dining off her naked breasts, using her anus for his pleasure with almost greater frequency than her sex, treating her as if every orifice of her body were provided purely for his convenience, for his use. And in the process, giving her orgasms of a violence and ferocity that she never before experienced.

And yet the weekend with Richard had been, not just different, but better. There were a lot of similarities between the way each man made love and the way he conversed. But Tony had to be in control, he always had to have things his way, while Richard had the confidence to accept her ideas, to allow her to lead on occasion as well as follow.

Once, she remembered, on Sunday, when she was sucking Richard's cock, greedily laving its proud, glossy head with her tongue and lips, she had parted his legs and pushed her hand between them and felt between the cheeks of his bottom, letting her spittle trickle down the shaft of his cock to provide lubrication, and gently, firmly pushed the tip of her index finger into his quivering arsehole. He cried out and the tight rim of his sphincter contracted so fiercely that her finger was almost expelled, but she persisted, pushing further, deeper into him until her whole finger was buried in her secret crevice and he was moaning desperately with pleasure and shock and disbelief. Tony would never have allowed it. He always wanted to be in control and he had even stopped her from using her tongue on him when the pleasure became too extreme, but Richard trusted her with his body. He had pleasured her thus, and he would let her pleasure him. And as she sucked and sucked at his throbbing penis, she slowly, deliberately thrust her finger in and out, fucking his anus, shuddering with arousal at the thought of what she was

229

doing to him, and after only half a dozen thrusts he writhed and yelled and his cock exploded damply within her mouth, flooding her eager throat with his slippery seed.

And when he had recovered and his phallus was erect again she had turned her back on him and looked archly at him over her shoulder and with her hands opened her backside to him, offering him that tight puckered hole, wanting to feel him opening her, stretching her. Tony had always demanded this route to pleasure from her according to his whim, ignoring her preferences, and it gave her piercing satisfaction to be able to offer it to her lover. Richard had been startled, she remembered his expression, but he had not refused her, just fallen on her and lodged the staring tip of his cock in her crease and thrust and thrust until he penetrated her and groaned aloud with the sensation of her secret passage gripping his ravenous cock like a velvet gauntlet.

Give and take, mutual bliss, offering pleasure as well as having it thrust upon her. Tess shivered and wrapped her arms tightly across her chest, lost in erotic daydreams.

'Wow,' said a voice behind her, 'he moves well, doesn't he?'

Tess jumped and turned to look into Jeannette's huge, liquid eyes, then glanced onto the stage. The duel was just beginning: Tony and Richard, knives in their hands, were stalking around each other like a pair of dogs before a fight. She nodded and Jeannette grinned. 'You didn't waste any time,' she said softly. 'Straight into his knickers. What was he like, Tess? Any good? Was he as kinky as Tony?'

'Yes. And no,' Tess replied unhelpfully. She didn't feel in the mood to indulge Jeannette's curiosity.

'I think you had us all fooled,' Jeannette went on. 'Pretending to be Miss Innocent. First you fuck Tony ragged and now you jump straight into bed with Richard. I can't keep up with you.'

'I don't believe that for a minute,' Tess murmured. She was watching the knives and frowning. Tony's knife looked different from Richard's: longer, wider bladed, a slightly different colour.

'Hey, guess what,' said Jeannette. 'Julian came back home with us last night. Emma was out, she didn't say where, I think she'd gone round to find Tony and tell him all about you and Richard. Anyway, it was just us and Julian, and . . .'

She continued to talk, but in Tess's ears her voice faded and became no more than a sound. Tess stood perfectly still, hardly breathing, as she realised what was different about Tony's knife.

It was real.

She could not be wrong. That blue, oily, wavering gleam of sharpness reflecting from the blade was unmistakeable. Tony was lashing out at Richard with vicious, rapid thrusts, almost reaching him, almost slashing his face.

Oh my God, she whispered to herself over and over again, *oh my God, the real knife. He's gone mad, he's going to kill him, he . . .*

Richard stumbled on cue and dropped his stage fake and Tony pounced, kicking the fallen weapon halfway across the stage out of his opponent's reach. Richard drew back, bravely upright, unaware that the blade he faced was real and deadly.

Whether or not it had been in the script Tess would have done what she now did, which was to launch herself onto the stage and grab Tony by the arm, fighting with all her strength against his iron wrist until he cursed and dropped the knife and stared at her gaping with surprise.

With a superhuman effort Tess remembered her line. *Hey, José, stop! have you gone crazy?* And she stooped and picked up the flick knife and tried to make the blade retract. It slipped in her hand and she gasped with pain

231

and looked at a little cut in the ball of her thumb, slowly welling a bead of blood.

Tony swore in Spanish and snatched the knife from her hand. His eyes were dark pools of fury outlined in staring white. For a moment he was very still. Then, without warning, he hit her in the face.

It wasn't a particularly hard blow, but it was so unexpected that Tess staggered. In the auditorium James jumped to his feet with a cry of surprise and Richard saw at once the difference between a stage slap and the real thing. He leapt forward to catch Tess by the shoulders and hold her up, whispering anxiously in her ear. Then he lifted his head and stared at Tony, bristling with rage, and shouted, 'Son of a *bitch!*'

Julian stopped playing and everything ground to a halt, cast and crew and director all staring at the tableau on stage. Tony raised himself on his toes as if he would jump at Richard and without hesitation Tess shook herself free of Richard's grasp and stepped between them, her hands extended to keep them apart. They stared at each other, as tense and ready as beasts waiting to pounce, and Tess kept her position, hands outstretched, daring them to pass her, daring them to fight. At last Richard snarled and took a step back and the tension slackened slightly. Tess lowered her hands. For a few seconds she was still so angry that she couldn't speak. Then she said very slowly, 'That's it, Tony. That is it.' He tried to interrupt her, to shout her down, but she continued to speak with an icy determination that in the end silenced him. 'It's over. From now on I speak to you only on stage.'

'Tess – ' Tony said furiously.

'You've got no choice,' Tess said in a cold deadly undertone which reached Tony's ears alone. 'You've got no choice, unless you want me to tell everybody what you're hiding.' She looked pointedly at the pocket of Tony's jeans, where the flick knife made a barely discernible bulge.

'You bitch,' Tony whispered.

Tess shook her head, stalked to the front of the stage and called out to James in the auditorium, 'James, I want to go straight on to the next scene.'

'What the hell is going on?' James demanded, hands braced angrily on the front of the scaffolding that supported the stage.

'It doesn't matter,' Tess said coldly. 'It doesn't have to concern you. Let's go straight on.'

James stared up at her, frowning. He looked beyond her to where Tony stood, simmering with hate and jealousy, glowering first at Tess, then at Richard. At last the director raised his eyebrows and said with a shrug, 'All right, Tess. As you wish.'

Tess was as good as her word. On stage she was coolly professional, but offstage she refused to speak to Tony or even to acknowledge his presence. The rest of the cast were confused, but she never revealed the danger Richard had been in, not even to Richard himself. After a while people saw that she had finished with Tony and was now with Richard and they assumed that the whole thing had been a sordid lovers' quarrel enacted on the open stage, a typical manifestation of artistic temperament.

At first Tony pursued her whenever Richard was not with her, trying to assault her verbally if not physically, but she was immovable. Eventually Tony seemed to be in a state of such incoherent jealousy that he could not even express himself to her any more, and to her relief he left her alone. She was afraid that he might follow her away from the theatre, make her life a misery outside rehearsals as well as within them, but he did not do so. Perhaps he was ashamed to. Tess didn't know and she didn't care.

For a little while she worried about Tony's anger. Sarah had predicted danger, and she had been right. But hadn't the danger been to Richard, not to Tess? Did that mean that something else would happen, that Tony had not yet worked out all of his jealous rage?

But quite soon she forgot her fear and forgot even to think about Tony and what he might do. Outside rehearsals other things were on her mind.

Richard was on her mind. Every night he returned with her to the Hampstead flat and they made love. He was tireless, sensual, inventive, a delight. Nothing was beyond their joint imagination. They enjoyed each other in bed, in the bath, on the living room floor, on the roof terrace under a dome of neon glow crowned by hanging stars like little lanterns.

They even scandalised the ghosts of the nursery by making love on Tess's beloved rocking-horse. Richard sat on the saddle and Tess straddled him and lowered herself slowly until she was impaled on his throbbing penis and they could wrap their arms around each other, enfolded, breast to breast, mouth to mouth. Then Richard tensed his back and made a gentle thrusting motion and Tess moaned with pleasure as his penis stirred deep inside her and the horse began to rock, creaking gently, its deliberate movement like the waves of the sea, increasing the delicious sensations that filled them both. Richard's iron-hard penis stayed quite still within Tess's hungry silken sex, but as the horse rocked to and fro, to and fro, it felt to Tess as if he were penetrating her over and over again, filling her, and the constant pressure of her engorged, shivering clitoris against his hard, lean body drew her into such a height of ecstasy that she leant back in his embrace, eyes closed, lips parted, her vulnerable white throat helplessly offered to his predatory mouth. She moaned in desperate bliss, slack and shuddering as her climax blossomed inside her and went on and on and on until she hung in his arms, limp and sated, dimly sensing the pulsing surge of his cock embedded deep, deep in her tender flesh.

She loved him. She loved him more than she had ever loved a man. Her affection for Leo and her passionate crush on Dan seemed in retrospect no more than a teenager's flights of fancy. She thought, she believed that he felt the same, but she couldn't be certain, because neither of them spoke of it.

Neither of them dared. He was Canadian, she was English. Both of them were just beginning careers that could take them all over the world, Munich one day, Rome the next, Paris, London, Milan: never in the same place at the same time. And wouldn't he want to try to make his living on the other side of the Atlantic, in New York and San Francisco and Montreal, while she would prefer to work in Europe? The logistics of the situation defeated Tess every time she thought of them. So she did not dare to admit to Richard that she loved him, because she was afraid of the pain that she would feel when they were separated. Deep down she knew that whether she spoke or not the pain would still be there, but something irrational, something superstitious, prevented her still from admitting that she was in love.

The day before the first dress rehearsal the orchestra gathered in the theatre to practise the music where it would be heard. There was no production rehearsal that day, but Tess went anyway and stood on the stage, listening to the sound of the orchestra in the dense gloom behind the lowered curtain. She was worried that the different sound quality of the orchestra would prevent her from singing in tune and she stood with her head lowered and her middle fingers resting below her ears, listening intently.

The weather was still warm, and Tess was wearing a light button-through cotton dress, flat sandals and no bra. A temporary theatre, created out of scaffolding and planks like a Meccano model, does not benefit from luxuries like air conditioning, and while the auditorium was open at the sides and caught the breeze, backstage it was hot.

The orchestra played through the overture twice and

then launched into some of the main production numbers. They were good, very good. Now they were playing Escamillo's theme, his showpiece aria. Tess closed her eyes and immersed herself in the music, imagining Richard's rich, baritone voice singing the words, imagining his taut muscular body drawing in deep breaths and playing them slowly out with the line of the song. She could not conceive anything more beautiful than his body when it made that fabulous sound, an instrument perfectly under control and yet expressing such passion, such emotion, that Tess thought she would rise from her grave to listen to it.

Thinking about Richard made her think of sex. She couldn't help it. Whenever he was near her she wanted him, and she knew that he felt the same. She remembered seeing Tom and Gina making love at that first rehearsal, Gina pressed against the wall and moaning rapturously as Tom slid his erect penis deep within her. She hadn't been able to understand how anyone could couple in a public place. But she had changed since then. She knew that if Richard was with her now she would clasp him close and pull him down on top of her and open her thighs and gasp as he entered her with his wonderful, thick cock. They would do it there, on the stage, rolling to and fro entranced by the sensations that their bodies were sharing, and they would press their lips together in fervent kisses to smother their moans as he thrust himself ever deeper into her wet, willing flesh.

Suddenly she heard a footstep behind her on the stage. Richard! She turned, smiling in welcome, and froze as she saw that it was not Richard at all, but Tony.

After a second she turned to run off the stage, but Tony sprang after her and caught her by the arm. She whirled to face him, fighting against his grip, but he was strong. After a moment she stopped struggling, trying to seem calm. 'Let me go,' she said softly. 'Tony, let me go.'

The orchestra launched into one of the entr'actes, a fast exciting Spanish dance. Tony held on to Tess's arm, squeezing it so hard that he hurt her, and for a moment did not reply. His black eyes were narrowed into mere glittering slits and his thin cruel lips were slightly parted, showing his white teeth. He looked dangerous.

'Let me go,' Tess said again. She was afraid. Her heart was pounding and the breath shook in her lungs. Tony held her eyes, then slowly, deliberately, ran his gaze down her body from head to foot. It felt to Tess as if he had stripped her of her clothes and was touching her, running his cold hand over her naked flesh. She turned her head away and murmured protestingly, 'Tony – '

'You two-timing bitch,' he whispered at last. 'Just waiting for me to turn my back so you could jump into bed with Mr Canadian Perfect.' She swung around and glared at him, furious, and he laughed softly into her face. 'Is he a nice boy in bed, Tess? Squeaky clean? I bet he doesn't realise what a dirty girl you are under that cool English exterior. I bet he hasn't done what I did to you. Wouldn't be nice, would it? Does he stick to straightforward fucking? Him on top? Or maybe he'll go as far as letting you sit on his cock? What's his cock like, Tess? Clean cut as the rest of him?'

'Shut up,' Tess hissed, tugging again to free her arm. 'Shut up, Tony. I don't belong to you. It's none of your business. Fuck off and leave me alone.'

'Don't tell me to fuck off,' Tony snarled, and he jerked her towards him and caught hold of her other arm. 'Don't you dare, you bitch. I'll show you – '

'There's a whole fucking *orchestra* out there,' Tess said furiously into Tony's face. 'All I have to do is raise my voice – '

'Oh, no, you won't,' Tony breathed, and he dropped her arms and caught hold of her by the hair and drove his mouth down onto hers and kissed her, silencing her with his lips. She moaned in protest and struggled, tearing at his black glossy hair with her hands, bracing her body against his, but she could not free herself. Tony's strong tongue twisted within her mouth, forcing the breath from her, and his lips bruised her with their fierce demand.

She tried again to free herself, but he was strong, stronger than she was. His big body was hot and hard and she sensed rather than felt the quivering readiness of his cock, trapped erect and gleaming inside his jeans. She knew that if she couldn't get away from him he would have her then and there, on the stage.

Her body remembered the delicious power of Tony's penis and softened with eagerness, but her mind rebelled. She did not belong to him, he had no right. Her heart was given to Richard. She wanted to be faithful, and she fought against Tony's strong hands and against her own desire, forcing her body to struggle and writhe, trying to break free from his remorseless grip, attempting to subdue the hot lust that burned in her limbs. Tony grasped a handful of her hair so tightly that she flinched and kept his mouth pressed on hers, locking in her moans of protest. He hooked one ankle around her calf and jerked, pulling her off balance, and they fell together to the dirty grey vinyl that covered the stage.

Within seconds he was on top of her, resting the whole weight of his body on her, expelling the breath from her so that even if his mouth had lifted from hers she would not have been able to scream. His knee drove between her legs, parting them with a vicious jerk. He caught her flailing wrists and held them above her head with one hand as with the other he began to unfasten the buttons of her dress, revealing her white body.

Tess moaned and writhed, but she was helpless. She hoped that someone in the orchestra might hear the sounds of their struggle, but the music was growing louder and louder, beating in her ears, and she knew it was hopeless. She had played games of force with Tony often enough to realise that now there was no chance for her to escape. He meant to have her, and he would take her at his pleasure.

Her dress was open. Tony hissed with delight as his

238

strong hand explored her naked breasts. He lifted his mouth from hers for a moment, watching her carefully in case she drew breath to scream, and his black eyes were glinting with dark amusement as well as with arousal. 'No bra, Tess?' he whispered. 'I might almost think you were expecting me.'

'You bastard,' Tess replied through her teeth. 'I hate you.'

'Shut up,' Tony said, and gagged her once more with his lips.

With one hand he unfastened his jeans and pushed them open. Tess felt his cock against her inner thigh, hard and scalding as red-hot iron. The delicate flesh between her legs was wet, melting with readiness. Even though she hated him, her sex wanted to feel him inside her.

There was nothing she could do, and she knew it. He's a jealous idiot, she thought, and I hate him, but I might as well enjoy this. He's going to do it to me whether I enjoy it or not. She strained up against him, eyes tightly shut, waiting.

And it was there, the glossy head and thick shaft of his cock pressing against the damp willing lips of her sex, parting them, penetrating her. His mouth lifted from hers as he gasped with the sudden desperate pleasure of possessing her and Tess bared her teeth and hissed, 'Oh *fuck*,' and then reached up and pressed her mouth to Tony's neck, biting his olive skin, worrying at his flesh as if she wanted to eat him alive.

'Bitch,' Tony whispered as she bit him harder still. His hands were on her wrists, pinioning her beneath him, and his hot breath ruffled her hair. His body smelt of sharp sweat and sexual excitement and his buried shaft throbbed inside her. 'Bitch,' he whispered again. 'Sharp teeth, you bitch.'

He pulled away from her, dragging his strong throat out of reach of her teeth. Tess writhed in protest, trying to reach up to him, but he held her down. Their bodies were joined, linked by the thick bolt of his penis driven into the socket of her sex, and they stared at each other with lust and hatred. 'Fuck me,' Tess hissed over the growing roar of the orchestra. 'You bastard, fuck me.'

'Don't worry,' he told her, but he did not move. He stared down at her, his eyes glowing under the black bars of his brows. 'Christ, look at you. You slut. You're gasping for it. What a whore.'

'You – ' Tess protested, struggling with rage.

'A whore, yes, a whore. You couldn't be faithful to me and now you aren't going to be faithful to him. I wish him joy of you.'

Rage made Tess shudder. She hated Tony for doing this to her, for making her unfaithful to Richard, and she hated him even more because it was giving her pleasure. She wanted to hurt him, to make him suffer for what he had done to her, and she thought she knew how she could do it. The muscles of her sex clenched and spasmed around Tony's invading penis and he gasped.

'You don't know anything,' she said. 'Do you think it was just him? Listen, listen to me. While you were seeing me I had other men. Lots of them.' How many? She frowned in concentration, thinking back. Julian. Dean. Charlie and Bob and Stefan, one after another and all together. Tony was staring at her as if he didn't believe what he had heard and she smiled ferociously as she saw the success of her stratagem. 'Three of them all at the same time, once,' she told him with bitter satisfaction.

'You're lying!' Tony's body jerked with unconscious reaction, driving the thick stem of his cock into her even more deeply, so that she gasped.

'No,' she said, when her breathing had steadied.

Tony's face contracted in a sudden spasm of jealous rage and he snarled something in Spanish and forced his mouth down onto Tess's as if he would gag her, prevent her from saying more. He released her wrists and his hands grasped at her breasts, clutching them tightly. She moaned with reaction and he began to move inside her, fierce direct thrusts that shook her whole body. His tongue darted within her mouth and his hips beat against her as he shafted her. He was shuddering with excitement and Tess too felt herself possessed by manic arousal. The sound of the orchestra surged in their ears like the sea and unconsciously the rhythm of their fucking matched it, pounding on and on towards the final crashing chords that announced the death of Carmen and the end of the opera. The music drowned out their animal cries of pleasure. As she approached her orgasm Tess thought that the curtain separating them from the musicians began to rise, revealing her to an auditorium suddenly full of people, hundreds of people sitting in intense silence watching as she and Tony rutted like animals on the bare stage. Her naked body was pinned beneath him, her legs wrapped around his waist so that the whole of the audience could see the thick rod of his cock driving into her, sliding again and again into the soft heart of her sex until she could bear no more and the wall of avid eyes witnessed her writhing and crying out in the throes of her delirious climax.

The orchestra was silent, the curtain was in place. Tess returned to herself, shuddering. Deep inside her Tony's cock was still twitching with lascivious remnants of pleasure. She heard the voice of Benedetto Corial, the conductor. 'Very good, not bad at all. But at the climax there I want even more passion. Give it everything you've got. Too much is never enough.'

Tony was looking down into her face. Drops of sweat coursed down his high cheekbones and his dark throat. 'You lied,' he hissed softly. 'Tell me you lied.'

She pulled away from him, wincing as his softened cock slid out of her, and staggered slightly as she got to her feet. Slowly she began to fasten the buttons on her dress. When she was restored to decency she shook back her hair then lifted her head and looked coolly at Tony and said, 'No, I wasn't lying. It was all true.' She thought

241

back to the early days of rehearsals and remembered her afternoons of libidinous luxury with Jeannette and Catherine and smiled slightly, a secretive smile. 'In some ways, you could say I haven't told you the half of it.'

'I don't believe it,' Tony whispered. 'While you were seeing me?'

His anger left her quite unmoved. Her body was sated and her heart untouched. This is how it feels to be Carmen, she thought to herself. I have had my pleasure, and now I don't give a damn about him. I'm ready to go back to the man I love. And I'll tell him what happened today, I'll tell him everything.

Tony pursued her to the edge of the stage. 'Listen!' he called after her. 'Listen, do you think only women can play that game? I fucked Emma Ridley on Sunday, I've fucked her every night this week, what do you think of that?'

Tess turned and looked at him. 'Good luck to you. What's she like?'

For a moment Tony did not reply, as if Tess's calmness had surprised him. Then he said lewdly, 'A dirty little bitch,' as if he thought it might make Tess jealous.

'You seem to like turning your women into dirty little bitches,' Tess remarked. 'I wouldn't usually approve, but in Emma's case I think you're probably made for each other. Enjoy her, Tony.'

Tony frowned angrily then tried again. His voice was increasingly desperate. 'How about if I tell your precious Richard what happened just now? What if I tell him that you let me fuck you? That I made you come? I'm a better lover than him, aren't I? You know I am!'

'No,' Tess said simply, 'you're not. And don't think you'll break us up by telling him about this: I'll tell him myself. Not all men are jealous maniacs like you, Tony.' She straightened her shoulders and said firmly, 'Goodbye,' and as the orchestra launched again into the final number she turned her back and walked away.

Finale

The opening night

They sent a car to pick Tess up from the flat and take her to the theatre. In some ways this did not seem sensible, since it was a Friday evening and the traffic was appalling, but at least it meant that Tess would arrive rested and calm, without exposure to the rigours of the Northern line at rush hour.

At least, that was the theory. But as Tess sat in the back of the car, her head tilted up to stare blankly at the ceiling, she wished fervently that she were travelling on the tube, surrounded by its sound and fury and by infinite numbers of strangers. She could have watched their faces and tried to pretend to herself that some of them were as unhappy as she was.

She had told Richard at once what had happened between her and Tony, explained how she had felt and asked for his forgiveness. He hadn't been angry with her, but he had been distressed. After a long silence he had taken a deep breath, then said, very gently, 'Tess, everything is happening too fast, isn't it? I'm under quite a lot of pressure already, you know, having to step into this role at short notice, and I think that things are getting a bit heavy, a bit complicated right now. So why don't we just, ah, ease off for the moment? For the rest of the rehearsals?'

'But I want to see you,' she had protested. 'I don't want anything to change. I – ' She had been going to tell him that she loved him, but he was slowly shaking his head and her voice faltered.

'I'm not saying this is permanent,' Richard said, still very gently. 'I just think I need to concentrate during the remainder of rehearsals. I can't cope with you, and the production, and on top of everything Tony Varguez hovering around like Otello in the background. Let's just take a break, Tess. I can't cope with all of this.'

And since then she had seen him only at rehearsal, and he had been very proper, as if they had never made love, as if she had never seen him groan in the clutch of ecstasy or stir and wake in the morning, as if he had never pressed her up against the trunk of a tree and forced himself inside her while rain drenched their shivering skin and thunder and lightning shook their very souls. He was quiet and studious and when they were on stage he had kissed her as if they were strangers, in the approved drama school method that looked passionate and in fact was utterly impersonal. And Emma, eager as ever to report someone else's misfortune, had told everyone that Tess and Richard had broken up and that now Tess was on her own because she, Emma, was now firmly attached to the wonderful Tony Varguez.

So after all her work, after her striving to understand Carmen and learning to cope with Tony's sexist dominance, she had lost the man she really cared about. Was this the conflict, the challenge, the danger that Sarah had seen in the cards? Was this what happened when a woman tried to take control of her own life? If so, Tess thought, she wished she had never taken the part, let alone tried to master the character of the wilful gypsy.

The car dropped her at the entrance to the park nearest to the theatre and she made her way slowly across the parched, dusty grass. A trio of mallards whirred in front of her, heading towards the pond in St James's park. She watched them fly into the distance and sighed.

At the entrance to the enclosure which was acting as back stage she saw Leo waiting, looking around for her. He was holding an enormous bunch of orange and yellow lilies. His face brightened as she approached and he hurried towards her, holding out one hand. 'Hi,' he said. 'I knew you weren't here yet. I wanted to wish you luck.'

'Thanks, Leo,' Tess said, really touched.

She took the flowers from him and was bending to sniff them when he said warningly, 'Watch out, lily pollen stains. You don't want to go on with a yellow streak on your face.'

'Then I'll kiss you instead,' Tess said, lifting her lips expectantly. Leo smiled and gave her a soft, gentle kiss. When he drew back she said, 'How are you, Leo? How's the voice?'

'It'll be fine in a week or two. I had a lesson yesterday,' Leo assured her. 'How about you? You look pale. Are you all right? Are you scared?'

Tess considered the question, then laughed ruefully. 'To tell you the truth, Leo, no,' she said. 'No, not scared. I've got other things on my mind.'

'It's not that bastard Varguez, is it?' demanded Leo. 'Jesus, Tess, you should have dropped him by now. He was never any good for you. He – '

'No,' Tess lied, shaking her head. 'Look, Leo, I ought to go and get ready. Do you want to come backstage?'

'No, no, I won't bother you. I'm going to go and get a bite to eat and then come back to watch the performance. I'll sit behind the *Sunday Times* critic and talk loudly about how brilliant it is. And then I'll cheer. You'll hear me, Tess. I promise.'

Tess reached up again to kiss him on the cheek, then went through the little gate that pretended to be the stage door with the lilies in her arm. Other members of the cast and crew were hurrying purposefully about, and they all spoke to her as she passed them, wishing her luck.

She walked slowly up to the Portakabin that acted as dressing room for her and Emma. The door was shut. Outside someone had propped a big bucket of water, and it was full of bunch after bunch of flowers. This was usual before a show began, but Tess bent down to look at them in case any were for her. There were several bunches for Emma – no surprises there – and a massive garland of hot house blooms for Tess from her agent, Michael. He always sent her half of Kew Gardens on the first night.

And there, at the bottom, almost crushed by the other flowers, was a single white rose in a curl of cellophane. Tess lifted it and saw that the card was addressed to her. She frowned and opened it.

Good luck, Tess, said the tiny card. *Let's start again. R.*

Tess put one hand to her throat. Her heart beat strong and fast beneath her palm. For a long time she stood looking at the note, reading its six short words over and over again. Huge relief, huge happiness began to well up inside her. Then suddenly she thought that it was a joke, that someone was playing a cruel trick on her: Emma and Tony, perhaps.

But it was Richard's writing, she was sure of it. She clutched the flower closely to her, scenting its perfume, and tears of joy began to squeeze from beneath her closed eyelids. She wouldn't be able to talk to Richard until after the performance, but now she had nothing to fear. She kissed the rose and held it against her breast as she put her hand to the door of the dressing room and entered.

And stopped in her tracks. In the middle of the floor stood Antonio Varguez, panting with pleasure, and before him knelt Emma Ridley as if in worship, her rosy lips fastened tightly around the dark pillar of his erect penis. As Tess came in Emma rolled her eyes and squeaked with protest and tried to pull away, but Tony's hands were buried in her curling dark-blonde hair and he held her head still and thrust his swollen cock harder into her mouth as if her attempts to escape only aroused him more.

'Jesus,' Tess said, and she turned to flee. But before she could get out of the door Tony was there, pulling her into the dressing room, slamming the door and turning the key in the lock.

'Get out of here, Tony,' Tess panted. She was shivering with shock and anger. 'Get out. I have to get ready. Just get out.'

Tony shook his head and slipped the key into his pocket. 'I think not,' he said. 'I haven't finished yet. If you remember, Tess darling, it's Emma who's on first, not you. So if she's got time to suck me off, I'm sure that you've got time to watch.' He turned back to Emma, who was still kneeling on the floor looking up at him like a spaniel at its master. Her big blue eyes were very wide open and her lips looked swollen and tender. The skin of her delicate throat was flushed. 'Right, Emma,' Tony said, taking his cock in his hand and lifting it again towards her mouth. 'Open up. More.'

Emma's eyes flashed up to Tess. 'I can't,' she whispered. 'Not with her – with her watching.'

Tony leant unhurriedly forward and spoke very quietly into Emma's face. 'Emma, are you being *disobedient?*'

'Oh no,' Emma said hastily, 'no, no, Tony, no.' And although her eyes glanced anxiously again at Tess she made no more demur, but stretched up her soft lips and opened them and drew the broad shelving tip of Tony's penis into her mouth.

'Ah,' Tony breathed, thrusting gently with his hips until nearly the whole of his shaft was buried between Emma's trembling lips. 'Ah, that's good. Good girl, Emma. Now lick it, lick it, just beneath the tip, you know where I like it,' and Emma moaned in acquiescence and her cheeks hollowed as she obediently went to work with her tongue.

Tess felt behind her for the door handle and shook at it, but it was securely fastened. She didn't want to watch, but she found her eyes drawn inexorably back to the scene before her, little virginal Emma Ridley whimpering as Tony slowly shoved his thick rigid cock in and out of her willing, compliant mouth. What would Leo say if he could see this? He had guessed, he had known what Emma was like beneath the surface. He had said to Tess, *She just needs someone to master her.* How right he had been.

'See this, Tess?' Tony said softly. His breath was hissing as Emma worked on him. 'See what you're missing? And I hear you haven't been getting any satisfaction from Mr Canadian Perfect, either. Gone off you, has he, since our little escapade on stage?'

Tess tightened her lips and said nothing. The thornless stem of Richard's rose pressed against her fingers, calming her. Richard had forgiven her, he wanted to begin again, and it wasn't within Tony's power to hurt her any more.

But it was within his power to arouse her. As she watched him taking Emma's mouth she felt her bowels churning with need, readying her against her will for sex. She leant back against the door, breathing quickly. Tony's penis moved faster and faster in and out of Emma's mouth. Its thick stem was shining with her saliva and dark veins pulsed on its silken surface. Tony was panting now and his fingers were clutching hard at Emma's hair. He was within moments of orgasm. Tess expected him to thrust deeper between Emma's lips and force her to swallow his come. But Tony suddenly with a jerk freed himself from the velvet grip of Emma's mouth and groaned as at the same moment his cock twitched and spasmed and began to spurt in thick, milky jets. His semen fell onto Emma's face, onto her eyelids and cheek, and trickled down towards her gasping mouth. Tess thought she would flinch or protest, but she did not, just extended her little, pink, pointed tongue to catch the creamy trickle as it crept down towards her jaw.

Tony still held Emma by the hair. He pulled back her head and gestured at her face. 'See?' he told Tess fiercely. 'I said she was a dirty girl, didn't I. Aren't you a dirty girl, Emma?'

'Yes,' Emma moaned, catching up another drop of semen and running her tongue around her lips in lascivious delight. 'Oh, yes, Tony.'

'What happens to dirty girls?' Tony hissed. He spoke to Emma, but he was holding Tess's eyes, staring at her with an expression of cold deliberate challenge.

'They're punished, Tony,' Emma whimpered, rubbing herself against Tony's legs like a cat. 'Punished.'

'Get up,' Tony commanded, and Emma got to her feet. For a moment she stood still, her head bowed as if in shame and her hair hanging around her face. Then she looked up at Tess and their eyes met. Emma's face was rapt, transfigured, as if she were already on the point of orgasm, and Tess frowned in mystified horror.

'Open your blouse,' Tony said, and without a murmur Emma obeyed him. The white cotton parted to reveal her little, high breasts, the small, tight nipples already swollen with desire. 'Now touch your nipples,' Tony said, and Emma closed her eyes and sighed and lifted her hands. Her fingers caressed the points of her breasts, flickering gently over the taut peaks until the areolae swelled as if someone had sucked them.

'Good,' Tony said. 'Now lift your skirt. Show Tess your pretty little pussy.'

Emma's huge eyes opened, wide and glittering. She looked as if she was about to cry. 'I don't want to,' she whispered.

'You don't want to?' Tony repeated disbelievingly.

He jumped forward and caught hold of Emma's skirt and wrenched it up. Beneath it she was naked, and Tess gasped with shock and put her hand to her mouth. Emma's pubic mound was shaven, smooth and hairless as the tender flesh of her pale thigh. Emma moaned and lay back in Tony's arm, shivering with delicious shame as he pulled her legs apart and showed Tess the naked moist folds of her sex, damp and pink as the tumbled petals of a rain-soaked peony.

'Look,' Tony said. 'See what she's done? Taken all the hairs off her little honey pot just to please her master. Doesn't that look pretty?'

Tess wasn't sure whether it looked pretty or peculiar, but it certainly looked arousing. Tony dragged Emma's slender thighs wider apart and put his hand on the pale flesh of her hip. His dark olive skin made a pleasing contrast with her ivory whiteness. 'Let's see if she's ready,' he said to Tess, smiling cruelly.

His hand moved slowly across to Emma's naked mound and down it to where the cleft of her sex began, to where the delicate bud of her clitoris just showed between the labia that were swelling and flushing with desire. Emma sighed as his finger brushed across the epicentre of her pleasure and her legs parted even further, inviting his invasion. Tony smiled again and without a word thrust two fingers deep into Emma's sex, withdrew them gleaming with her juice, sniffed and licked at them approvingly, then replaced his fingers and began to move them in and out.

My God, Tess thought, gazing at Emma as if hypnotised. My God, she's actually going to come. And indeed Emma's body was heaving and tensing in rapture. Her little hands were opening and closing helplessly and her nipples were swollen and erect. Tony plunged another finger into her and flickered his thumb over her engorged tender clitoris and Emma's body shimmered like a reflection in broken water and she let out a high, wavering cry of ecstasy as she succumbed to orgasm.

'Isn't she a dirty girl?' Tony hissed as he supported the still twitching body of Emma on one strong arm.

250

'Fancy that, Tess, letting me masturbate her right in front of you. Making her come with somebody else watching, just imagine. Could you do that? I bet you couldn't. What a dirty little girl. So now she has to be punished.' He licked his glistening fingers and then took hold of Emma's rapturous face. 'Bend over,' he told her.

Obediently Emma bent, her hair hanging around her face, her breasts dangling. Tony heaved up her skirt around her slender rounded haunches and presented her bare buttocks to Tess's eyes. Between the white moons of her arse Emma's sex was pink and soft and gleaming with desire. Looking at her Tess suddenly realised how a man must feel when in the grip of dominating lust. She would have loved to have taken something long and thick and hard and driven it deep into Emma's moist willingness and made her cry out with shock and pleasure.

'Now,' Tony breathed, and with one strong hand he slapped Emma's bare behind, a sharp slap that left the imprint of his hand red on her white flesh. Emma moaned and trembled and Tony slapped her again and again, paying attention to each perfect buttock, spanking with a regular motion until Emma's round white arse was glowing pink and she was wriggling in his grasp.

Tony's cock was hard again, thrusting forward eagerly from the open fly of his trousers. He rubbed at it, checking its readiness, then without a word, slipped a condom over his length and positioned the glossy head between the lips of Emma's sex, caught hold of her white hips and pulled her violently back onto him. His thick penis slid quickly up into her wet vagina, burying itself entirely, and Tess gasped and bit her lip. She remembered vividly how it had felt when Tony had done that to her, how he had bruised the tender flesh of her haunches with his ferocious grip.

He was looking at her now over Emma's bowed body, watching her reactions as he drove himself time after time into the hot centre of Emma's naked sex. 'Don't you wish,' he gasped between thrusts, 'don't you wish I was doing this to you, Tess? Don't you? Don't you?'

Tess swallowed hard and shook her head. Richard's rose was held tightly between her tingling fingers, like a talisman. Tony snarled as he saw her denial and thrust harder, making Emma grunt and gasp as he shafted her.

'Tony,' Emma whimpered. Her hanging hair swung to and fro as Tony beat his body against her with the ferocity of his attack. 'Oh, Tony please, oh yes, my lord, please, please. Harder, harder. Oh God, God.' She staggered and would have fallen, but Tony's strong grasp held her up. Limp as a doll she hung from his hands and her body began to shudder in the grip of another orgasm. As she quaked and moaned Tony withdrew his prick from her sex and lodged it against her tight puckered rear hole and forced his way into her arse, invading her and stretching her until she cried out and writhed in his grip. One strong thrust, two, three, and suddenly Tony was gasping and his hands on Emma's haunches were like claws as he climaxed inside her.

After only a few seconds he withdrew and let Emma fall to a quivering heap on the floor. He turned and faced Tess, smiling slightly. 'Feeling jealous, Tess?' he asked.

'You must be joking,' Tess said. She was proud of the fact that her voice was steady. As she lifted her head with a jerk of scorn she caught sight of herself in the mirror on her dressing table and her eyes narrowed in amazement, because her face showed nothing but smouldering anger and fervent lust. It was the expression that she had tried to adopt, all those weeks ago when she stood before the mirror in her bedroom with Dan asleep in the bed behind her, and which had eluded her.

Tony frowned. He seemed for the first time to see the rose in her hands and without warning he stepped forward and snatched it from her. She cried out in protest and grabbed it back, but not before he had scanned the note attached to it. He turned to look at Tess with anger and disbelief, and she slapped his face.

'Get out of here,' she said, 'or I'll shout for help, Tony, I swear.'

The shape of her hand flared on his cheek like the mark of Cain. Tony's cruel lips drew back from his teeth. He was shaking, shuddering with emotion: fury, rage, jealousy, lust, all of them together. He looked more than half mad. 'You,' he said very softly, 'have made me look a fool, Tess. You'll be sorry, I swear. You'll be sorry you ever set eyes on me.'

Suddenly a chill of fear gripped Tess. To be forced to watch Tony screwing the guts out of Emma had been pleasantly arousing and mildly absurd, but now the expression on his face terrified her. She drew away from him instinctively, clutching the rose protectively to her breast. He gave her one long, cold stare, drew the key from his pocket and unlocked the door.

It opened to reveal the assistant stage manager, looking harassed. Tony brushed past him without a glance and stalked away.

'Ten minutes to curtain up,' the ASM said. 'Emma, are you ready?'

'Oh, God,' Emma exclaimed, jumping up from the floor and reaching out for her costume.

That performance was the most extraordinary experience of Tess's life. From the moment she walked onto the stage she felt as if something had bound the audience with a silken thread and placed the end in her hand. She had total control of them: they were enraptured, spellbound. They loved Carmen, they wanted her, just as José did, just as Escamillo did.

In the first act, when she was on stage with Tony, her hatred for him emerged as an electric current of lust that flowed almost visibly between them. She knew that he was desiring her even as he sang, that his fingers itched to touch her, that his lips burned to kiss her, that even on stage his cock was hard for her. She tormented him, teased him, played him as an angler plays a fish, as a cat plays with a mouse. How could little submissive Micaela compete with her, with Carmen, who possessed the stage and every man upon it with her blazing certainty, with the knowledge that she was desirable?

'You're red hot tonight,' Jeannette whispered in her ear before they went on for Act Two. 'What's got into you? They're eating out of your hand.'

Tess said nothing, just smiled. It was true. She had never in her life felt more powerful. It was as if everyone who looked at her was her captive, as if hers was truly the voice of the mermaid, the siren's song that held all who heard it in chains of adamant.

She did not see Richard until he entered as Escamillo, and then according to the production as planned he did not see her until nearly the end of his aria. When he looked at her his eyes were burning with love and desire and she knew that her response showed in her face. Their glances blazed across the stage, searing the air with passion. Tess wondered if he could tell that the rose he had given her was next to her skin, pressed within her bustier, its silken petals lying against the silken flesh of her breast.

At the interval the audience clapped and stamped. Behind the scenes the cast and crew milled about, excited, but superstitiously avoiding any comments about how well the show was going. Tess hurried to Richard's dressing room, hoping to see him alone, but it was full of people, other members of the cast changing, Richard's agent, two journalists from music magazines and one from Radio 3, and she turned away with a frustrated sigh.

Julian was standing before her, his pale face glowing with excitement. 'Tess,' he said, 'I've been down with the orchestra, I've been watching. It's marvellous, it's amazing, I can't believe how well it's going. You're fabulous.'

His blue eyes were fixed on her face. She smiled at him, remembering how she had seduced him, how she had opened the buttons on her skirt and shown him the naked skin of her white thighs. His expression showed that he knew that she was remembering and that he remembered too, that he was still enslaved to her. She reached out and touched his cheek, just touched it, and then walked past him.

She had no time after changing her costume to do anything other than run back to her position for Act Three. The ensemble passed fleetingly, like a dream, and then Emma was onstage singing Micaela's stunning second aria, so beautifully and with such grace and power that the audience's sighs of delight were audible in the wings. Then Tony and Richard were onstage, singing the duet that led up to their fight, and Tess stood staring onto the stage clenching her fists in fear in case Tony should choose again to take matters into his own hands.

But he did not. The fight passed off exactly as planned, and the gnawing apprehension in the pit of Tess's stomach began to fade. She fell effortlessly into Carmen's character, and when Tony as José seized her shoulders and exclaimed desperately, *I'll keep you, damn you, damn you, you are mine, I'll force you if I have to! I'll never let you go, I'll never leave you, never!* she lifted her head and stared into his eyes and laughed a mocking, silent laugh that revealed the depth of the scorn she felt for him.

At the beginning of Act Four Tess stood in the wings beside Richard, looking up at him. Neither of them spoke, they did not need to. Their love showed in their eyes, in their radiant faces. Tess was half aware of Tony standing behind her, waiting for his entrance later in the act, watching her with dark brooding anger naked in his eyes, and knowing he was there made her feelings for Richard all the sweeter. Then they walked on to the stage together, Carmen and Escamillo arriving at the studio to a rapturous ticker-tape welcome. Tess reached up and caught Richard's face between her hands and drew it down towards hers and they kissed, a passionate, unrehearsed kiss that made the watching audience shudder with voyeuristic delight and shook them both with the depths of desire that it stirred in them. Richard put one hand to Tess's breast and squeezed it as they kissed and she arched her body against him, racked with desire for him. If he had wanted it she would have submitted to him now, now on the stage, before the eyes of the world. She would have opened the heart of her body to him and received him within her with rapture. He did not require of her that she submit herself, but still her lust filled her and overran with longing. And she could sense Tony's hot, dark eyes watching her from the shadows of the wings, and she smiled bitterly to think of the pain she was causing him.

Now Escamillo was gone and Carmen was alone onstage, waiting for her final, fated rendezvous with Don José. Tony entered slowly, his eyes fixed on Tess's face, and as they began to sing it seemed to Tess that the separate threads of her real life and the life of Carmen twisted and knotted inextricably together, so that suddenly she *was* Carmen and everything that was happening on stage was real.

I know that this is the end, Carmen told José. *I know you mean to kill me. But whether I live or die, no, no, no, I will not give myself to you!*

That man in there, José demanded, *he's your new lover! You won't go to him, Carmen, you'll come with me, I swear!*

Let me go, Don José, I'll never go with you!

Do you love him? Tony's face was black with jealous rage. He drew out the flick knife from his pocket and touched the clasp. The blade sprang free, glittering in the lights of the stage. He held it towards her, and his hand was shaking. *Do you love him? Tell me!*

The blade gleamed blue and oily. Tess suddenly shuddered. Was it, could it be the real knife? Did he mean to kill her? Had Sarah seen death in her cards, but kept it a secret?

For a second she wanted to scream and flee. But how could she? She was Carmen, and she feared nothing. *Yes,* she sang, flinging back her head proudly and staring into Tony's maddened, white-ringed eyes. *Yes, and if it kills me I'll say again, I love him!*

The knife shivered in Tony's hand. Reflections leaped from the blade. *For the last time,* hissed José, *you bitch, will you come with me?*

It was her last chance. She was afraid, terrified, certain that in a moment he would leap on her and she would feel a real knife tearing at her flesh. But she shook her head violently and pressed her hand to her bustier, where the white rose lay next to her skin. *No. No!*

Die then, you bitch! José screamed, and flung himself on her. Tess flung open her arms as if receiving her lover, waiting for the blow. It came: but it was only the slight thump of the stage fake, the blade retracting the instant it touched her body. She fell to the ground and writhed and jerked as James had shown her, but as she 'died' she fought sternly against the urge to laugh. Tony had not dared to do it. She was the winner now, in every way. She had nothing more to fear from Antonio Varguez.

At last she lay still. Twelve bars to go, and then the curtain would fall. Tony dropped to his knees beside her, wracked with staged remorse, and then it was over and the audience burst into a storm of cheers even as the orchestra blared out the final chords.

Then everything seemed to happen in slow motion. The curtain calls went on for ever. A wall of faces, a wall of sound as the audience stamped and clapped and roared their approval and flung flowers onto the stage and called for her again and again. Tony's claque of female fans were there in force, but their rapturous cries were drowned by the cheers that the rest of the audience raised for Tess. She saw Leo standing up in the auditorium, clapping and yelling, risking his barely healed voice with his shouts. She caught his eye and he grinned broadly and pointed at the man sitting in front of him and mouthed, '*Sunday Times!*'

When at last she was allowed offstage her agent Michael was waiting for her in the wings and with him was a man Tess recognised with a shock as the director of Opera Shop, a small company famous for its innovative, commercially successful and sometimes scandalous productions, which were as popular with Channel 4 and BBC 2 as with the theatres.

'Tess,' Michael said, 'I don't have to tell you how amazing you were. Look who's here to meet you: Jeremy Tate.'

'Hi,' said the director, smiling libidinously at Tess. His casting methods were infamous. 'I was seriously impressed, Tess. We have a lot to talk about. Can we do lunch soon?'

'Sounds great, Jeremy,' said Michael. 'And there's lots of other things Tess and I need to talk about, right now. Tess, if you can, the sooner the better. Can you – '

'Michael,' Tess said huskily, 'I need to change, I need to – ' and she broke away and ran through the cool evening air towards her dressing room. Emma was probably in there, but she didn't care. She had to get away from all these people and hurry through the time that would pass until she could see Richard again. People called out to her with congratulations and praise, but she hardly heard them. Jeannette and Catherine were there, pressing forward to take her hands and kiss her on the cheek, but she couldn't make herself talk to them. She pulled herself away and pressed on.

She passed Emma standing in the open air, chatting and laughing cheerfully to a group of colleagues. Her part had gone well too, and it never does a singer harm to be involved in a truly successful production. She caught Tess's eye and grinned broadly and blew her a kiss. 'Great show, Tess!' she called out. 'Imagine what the rest of the run will be like!'

Tess smiled feebly back at Emma, then looked around for Richard, but he was nowhere to be seen. Nor was

Tony. She ran the few paces to her dressing room and pulled the door open and leapt inside.

It was dark within the little, boxy room. Tess closed the door and turned the key, then reached up to the light switch.

A strong hand closed over hers and pulled her fingers from the switch. She stifled a scream, certain that it was Tony lurking there in the gloom to wreak his final revenge on her. She tore herself away and fumbled for the key, but before she could open the door the hand closed on her shoulder and a soft, warm voice said reassuringly, 'Tess, darling, it's me.'

'Richard!' She turned to him as swiftly as breathing and flung herself into his arms. His lean, hard body pressed against hers and he enfolded her in his embrace, holding her so tightly that the air sighed from her lungs. Without a thought their lips found each other and they stood enraptured, kissing with fervent eagerness.

'Richard,' Tess said when she could speak, 'I love you.'

'Christ, Tess,' Richard whispered. His low voice caressed her ear. 'I've been going mad without you. I can't stand not having you. You looked so amazing tonight, I wanted you all night. Jesus, I thought the whole audience would see my hard on in these pants. I've got to have you. Now, Tess.'

'Yes,' she whispered. The unquestioning admiration of hundreds of people had left her already sensitised. She was wet and ready, and his passionate words inflamed her. Her hands went to his haunches, pushing down the tight Lycra of his costume. His cock sprang free, quivering with excitement. His hands fumbled with her skirt, trying to push it up around her waist. Its tightness defeated him and he struggled with the zip and grunted with success as it whined open. Soon the skirt was off and the bustier followed it and the corpse of the rose fell to the floor.

'You wore it,' Richard breathed.

'Next to my heart,' Tess murmured, and she reached

out for him. There were no preliminaries, she needed none. She lay back on the cold floor and pulled him down on top of her and parted her legs and he lay on top of her, crushing her with his wonderful male weight, and with one strong thrust he sheathed himself within her to the hilt and she gasped with the hot, dark pleasure of being penetrated.

'Tess,' Richard moaned, 'Tess, Tess, I love you.' He was shaking with need. He clutched her, his fingers twined in her hair. They lay together, mouth to mouth, and the silken fist of her sex grasped strongly at his thick cock as it slid deep within her. She held him tightly, her fingers exploring the strong muscles of his arms, his shoulders, his lean, flexible spine. His head twisted from side to side with bliss and she reached up to bite and suck at his vulnerable throat. He groaned with pleasure and rolled over, pulling her on top of him.

Tess let out a long cry and leant back, thrusting forward her taut swollen breasts. In an instant his hands were on them, fondling, squeezing, tugging at the hard pink tips until shivering flames of pleasure ran through her body like brilliant fish through murky water. She rose and fell on his throbbing cock, moaning with joy as she impaled herself over and over again. She grasped his strong thighs with her hands and arched her body to accept him within her, deeper and deeper, and as his powerful penis surged to and fro in the velvet tunnel of her sex she thought of a statue she had once seen of a female saint in ecstasy, glistening white marble that breathed as if the stone were flesh. The saint's hand was on her breast, squeezing it through her clothes, and her lips were soft and parted and you could almost see her eyelids fluttering as she was possessed and overcome by heavenly rapture. The cause of her ecstasy was a spear which a stern angel drove into her side. Tess pictured the angel with Richard's face, that perfect beauty imbued with heavenly rigour, and the angel's sharp spear was his thrusting, fervid penis. And as she imagined and felt

260

that remorseless spear penetrating her, violating the temple of her flesh with its bitter-sweet sharpness, the saint's ecstasy began to rise within her own body. She jerked and cried out and began to writhe with the desperate buffeting of her orgasm, and as she collapsed in the throes of climax Richard rolled her onto her side and then onto her back and began to thrust wildly into her, ravishing her, taking her with such fervent power that her orgasm seemed to be infinitely prolonged, infinitely consuming. When at last he cried out and his cock spasmed inside her she lay beneath his shaking body quite still, utterly vanquished, his and only his.

'Tess,' Richard whispered into her ear, 'I love you.'

Someone tried the door, then knocked on it. 'Tess!' It was Michael's voice. 'Tess, are you OK? Are you coming?'

Tess began to laugh. She laughed Richard right out of her body and held him tightly against her as she chuckled. 'I certainly am, Michael,' she called back. 'I'll be right out. Shan't be long.'

They clung together in the gloom, breathing each other's breath. She was naked and hot and his hand passed slowly over her shimmering skin, reacquainting itself with the complex curves of her body.

'Guess what,' Richard said softly.

'What?'

'I've got an offer,' he said. 'ENO want me as a company principal. English National Opera, Jesus! My agent's going to work on it. It would mean, ah, staying in England for quite a while, a year maybe, maybe more.'

'That's marvellous, Richard,' Tess said emphatically. 'It's wonderful. What do they want you to play?'

Richard smiled nervously, suddenly overcome by modesty. 'Don Giovanni. Can you believe it?'

'Don Giovanni?' Tess thought of how Tony would feel when he discovered that his hated rival had landed the part he most desired. 'Richard, that's amazing. I'm so pleased for you.'

'My agent has to do some negotiating, and I have to think about it, but you're right, as an offer it's pretty amazing. I had a lucky day when James chose me to sub for Leo.' His eyebrows contracted suddenly and his eyes glittered. 'I don't mean just for my career, either.'

There was a short silence. Then Tess asked quietly, 'Will you accept?' Her whole world hung on the answer.

He kissed her lips. 'If you love me,' he said, 'I'll accept.'

She held him more tightly and laid her head on his shoulder. 'I love you,' she said softly.

'Then I'll accept.' He kissed her again. Then he said slowly, 'I love you, Tess. I've never met a woman like you. You're strong, you're independent, and you're so goddam sexy I could go crazy just looking at you.' His arms tightened around her and the lashes of his closed eyes brushed her cheek. His lean, strong body pressed against her. 'I love you,' he whispered again.

For long moments they lay together, touching, kissing, exchanging love. Tess closed her eyes, savouring the joy that filled her whole body. Her future lay before her as bright as the dawn, and Richard glowed in the heavens like her morning star.

Then Richard lifted his head and against the faint light through the windows of the dressing room Tess saw him look at the door.

'Well, Tess,' he said, 'the overture's finished and the audience is waiting. Time to go on stage.'

They got up, preparing to face the world together. Tess hesitated and murmured with a frown, 'I wonder what the critics will say?'

He smiled down at her. 'Hey, who cares? Come on, Tess. Let's go.'

And, hand in hand, they went.

What the critics said:

'Exhilarating ... thrilling singing and a riveting production ... electric performances from new English star Tess Challoner and Canadian unknown Richard Shaeffer ...' *Financial Times*

'I felt Tess Challoner's definitive Carmen had taken the measure of every man she encountered ...' *The Daily Telegraph*

'Opera as you've never seen it!' *Daily Mail*

'The man behind me certainly seemed to be enjoying it ...' *The Sunday Times*

'Live sex on stage!' *Today*

THE END

VIRTUOSO – Katrina Vincenzi
ISBN 0 352 32907 6

MOON OF DESIRE – Sophie Danson
ISBN 0 352 32911 4

FIONA'S FATE – Fredrica Alleyn
ISBN 0 352 32913 0

HANDMAIDEN OF PALMYRA – Fleur Reynolds
ISBN 0 352 32919 X

OUTLAW FANTASY – Saskia Hope
ISBN 0 352 32920 3

THE SILKEN CAGE – Sophie Danson
ISBN 0 352 32928 9

RIVER OF SECRETS – Saskia Hope & Georgia Angelis
ISBN 0 352 32925 4

VELVET CLAWS – Cleo Cordell
ISBN 0 352 32926 2

THE GIFT OF SHAME – Sarah Hope-Walker
ISBN 0 352 32935 1

SUMMER OF ENLIGHTENMENT – Cheryl Mildenhall
ISBN 0 352 32937 8

A BOUQUET OF BLACK ORCHIDS – Roxanne Carr
ISBN 0 352 32939 4

JULIET RISING – Cleo Cordell
ISBN 0 352 32938 6

DEBORAH'S DISCOVERY – Fredrica Alleyn
ISBN 0 352 32945 9

THE TUTOR – Portia Da Costa
ISBN 0 352 32946 7

THE HOUSE IN NEW ORLEANS – Fleur Reynolds
ISBN 0 352 32951 3

ELENA'S CONQUEST – Lisette Allen
ISBN 0 352 32950 5

CASSANDRA'S CHATEAU – Fredrica Alleyn
ISBN 0 352 32955 6

WICKED WORK – Pamela Kyle
ISBN 0 352 32958 0

DREAM LOVER – Katrina Vincenzi
ISBN 0 352 32956 4

PATH OF THE TIGER – Cleo Cordell
ISBN 0 352 32959 9

BELLA'S BLADE – Georgia Angelis
ISBN 0 352 32965 3

THE DEVIL AND THE DEEP BLUE SEA – Cheryl
Mildenhall
ISBN 0 352 32966 1

WESTERN STAR – Roxanne Carr
ISBN 0 352 32969 6

A PRIVATE COLLECTION – Sarah Fisher
ISBN 0 352 32970 X

NICOLE'S REVENGE – Lisette Allen
ISBN 0 352 32984 X

UNFINISHED BUSINESS – Sarah Hope-Walker
ISBN 0 352 32983 1

CRIMSON BUCCANEER – Cleo Cordell
ISBN 0 352 32987 4

RUDE AWAKENING – Pamela Kyle
ISBN 0 352 33036 8

GOLD FEVER – Louisa Francis
ISBN 0 352 33043 0

EYE OF THE STORM – Georgina Brown
ISBN 0 352 330044 9

Published in January

WHITE ROSE ENSNARED
Juliet Hastings

When the elderly Lionel, Lord de Verney, is killed in battle, his beautiful widow Rosamund finds herself at the mercy of Sir Ralph Aycliffe, a dark knight, who will stop at nothing to humiliate her and seize her property. Set against the Wars of the Roses, only the young squire Geoffrey Lymington will risk all he owns to save the woman he has loved for a single night. Who will prevail in the struggle for her body?

ISBN 0 352 33052 X

A SENSE OF ENTITLEMENT
Cheryl Mildenhall

When 24-year-old Angelique is summoned to the reading of her late father's will, there are a few surprises in store for her. Not only was her late father not her real father, but he's left her a large sum of money and a half share in a Buckinghamshire hotel. The trouble is, Angelique is going to have to learn to share the running of this particularly strange hotel with the enigmatic Jordan; a man who knew her as a child and now wants to know her as a woman.

ISBN 0 352 33053 8

Published in February

ARIA APPASSIONATA
Juliet Hastings

Tess Challoner had landed the part of Carmen in a production of the opera which promises to be as raunchy as it is intelligent. But to play Carmen convincingly, she needs to learn a lot more about passion and erotic expression. Tony Varguez, the handsome but jealous tenor, takes on the role of her education. The scene is set for some sizzling performances and life begins to imitate art with dramatic consequences.

ISBN 0 352 33056 2

THE MISTRESS
Vivienne LaFay

It's the beginning of the twentieth century and Emma Longmore is making the most of her role as mistress to the dashing Daniel Forbes. Having returned from the Grand Tour and taken up residence in Daniel's Bloomsbury abode, she is now educating the daughters of forward-thinking people in the art of love. No stranger to fleshly pleasure herself, Emma's fancy soon turns to a young painter whom she is keen to give some very private tuition. Will Daniel accept her wanton behaviour or does he have his own agenda?

ISBN 0 352 33057 0

To be published in March

ACE OF HEARTS
Lisette Allen

Fencing, card-sharping and seduction are the favoured pastimes of Marisa Brooke, a young lady who lives by her wits amongst the wealthy hedonistic elite of Regency England. But love and fortune are more easily lost than won, and Marisa will have to use all her skill and cunning if she wants to hold on to her winnings and her lovers.

ISBN 0 352 33059 7

DREAMERS IN TIME
Sarah Copeland

Four millenia from now, two thousand people remain suspended in endless slumber, while others toil beneath a hostile sun for the means to wake them. Physical pleasure and desire are long forgotten, until Ehlana, a historian and time traveller, discovers that her own primal memories are the key which unlocks the door to another world – and her own sexual awakening.

ISBN 0 352 33064 3

If you would like a complete list of plot summaries of Black Lace titles, please fill out the questionnaire overleaf or send a stamped addressed envelope to:-

Black Lace
332 Ladbroke Grove
London W10 5AH

WE NEED YOUR HELP . . .
to plan the future of women's erotic fiction –

– and no stamp required!

Yours are the only opinions that matter.

Black Lace is the first series of books devoted to erotic fiction by women for women.

We intend to keep providing the best-written, sexiest books you can buy. And we'd appreciate your help and valued opinion of the books so far. Tell us what you want to read.

THE BLACK LACE QUESTIONNAIRE

SECTION ONE: ABOUT YOU

1.1 Sex (*we presume you are female, but so as not to discriminate*)
Are you?

Male ☐
Female ☐

1.2 Age

under 21 ☐   21–30 ☐
31–40 ☐   41–50 ☐
51–60 ☐   over 60 ☐

1.3 At what age did you leave full-time education?

still in education ☐   16 or younger ☐
17–19 ☐   20 or older ☐

1.4 Occupation _____

1.5 Annual household income
      under £10,000 ☐   £10–£20,000 ☐
      £20–£30,000 ☐   £30–£40,000 ☐
      over £40,000 ☐

1.6 We are perfectly happy for you to remain anonymous;
but if you would like to receive information on other
publications available, please insert your name and
address

_____

_____

_____

_____

SECTION TWO: ABOUT BUYING BLACK LACE BOOKS

2.1 How did you acquire this copy of *Aria Appassionata*?
     I bought it myself ☐   My partner bought it ☐
     I borrowed/found it ☐

2.2 How did you find out about Black Lace books?
     I saw them in a shop ☐
     I saw them advertised in a magazine ☐
     I saw the London Underground posters ☐
     I read about them in _____
     Other _____

2.3 Please tick the following statements you agree with:
     I would be less embarrassed about buying Black
     Lace books if the cover pictures were less explicit ☐
     I think that in general the pictures on Black
     Lace books are about right ☐
     I think Black Lace cover pictures should be as
     explicit as possible ☐

2.4 Would you read a Black Lace book in a public place – on
a train for instance?
     Yes ☐   No ☐

SECTION THREE: ABOUT THIS BLACK LACE BOOK

3.1   Do you think the sex content in this book is:
          Too much   □   About right   □
          Not enough   □

3.2   Do you think the writing style in this book is:
          Too unreal/escapist   □   About right   □
          Too down to earth   □

3.3   Do you think the story in this book is:
          Too complicated   □   About right   □
          Too boring/simple   □

3.4   Do you think the cover of this book is:
          Too explicit   □   About right   □
          Not explicit enough   □

Here's a space for any other comments:

SECTION FOUR: ABOUT OTHER BLACK LACE BOOKS

4.1   How many Black Lace books have you read?   □

4.2   If more than one, which one did you prefer?

4.3   Why?

SECTION FIVE: ABOUT YOUR IDEAL EROTIC NOVEL

We want to publish the books you want to read – so this is your chance to tell us exactly what your ideal erotic novel would be like.

5.1 Using a scale of 1 to 5 (1 = no interest at all, 5 = your ideal), please rate the following possible settings for an erotic novel:

Medieval/barbarian/sword 'n' sorcery ☐
Renaissance/Elizabethan/Restoration ☐
Victorian/Edwardian ☐
1920s & 1930s – the Jazz Age ☐
Present day ☐
Future/Science Fiction ☐

5.2 Using the same scale of 1 to 5, please rate the following themes you may find in an erotic novel:

Submissive male/dominant female ☐
Submissive female/dominant male ☐
Lesbianism ☐
Bondage/fetishism ☐
Romantic love ☐
Experimental sex e.g. anal/watersports/sex toys ☐
Gay male sex ☐
Group sex ☐

Using the same scale of 1 to 5, please rate the following styles in which an erotic novel could be written:

Realistic, down to earth, set in real life ☐
Escapist fantasy, but just about believable ☐
Completely unreal, impressionistic, dreamlike ☐

5.3 Would you prefer your ideal erotic novel to be written from the viewpoint of the main male characters or the main female characters?

Male ☐   **Female** ☐
Both ☐

5.4 What would your ideal Black Lace heroine be like? Tick as many as you like:

Dominant	☐	Glamorous	☐
Extroverted	☐	Contemporary	☐
Independent	☐	Bisexual	☐
Adventurous	☐	Naive	☐
Intellectual	☐	Introverted	☐
Professional	☐	Kinky	☐
Submissive	☐	Anything else?	☐
Ordinary	☐	_____	

5.5 What would your ideal male lead character be like? Again, tick as many as you like:

Rugged	☐		
Athletic	☐	Caring	☐
Sophisticated	☐	Cruel	☐
Retiring	☐	Debonair	☐
Outdoor-type	☐	Naive	☐
Executive-type	☐	Intellectual	☐
Ordinary	☐	Professional	☐
Kinky	☐	Romantic	☐
Hunky	☐		
Sexually dominant	☐	Anything else?	☐
Sexually submissive	☐	_____	

5.6 Is there one particular setting or subject matter that your ideal erotic novel would contain?

_____

SECTION SIX: LAST WORDS

6.1 What do you like best about Black Lace books?

_____

6.2 What do you most dislike about Black Lace books?

_____

6.3 In what way, if any, would you like to change Black Lace covers?

_____

6.4 Here's a space for any other comments:

_____

_____

_____

_____

Thank you for completing this questionnaire. Now tear it out of the book – carefully! – put it in an envelope and send it to:

Black Lace
FREEPOST
London
W10 5BR

No stamp is required if you are resident in the U.K.